# ATLANTIS BETRAYED

# ATLANTIS REDEEMED

*continued . . .*

# ATLANTIS UNMASKED

"Action packed and hot and spicy."                —*TwoLips Reviews*

"Day utilizes a nice blend of action, character building, and sexy sensuality in all her books. A terrific escape from reality."
                —*Romantic Times*

"As always, I loved this book. Each time I settle down to read about one of the warriors, I know I'm going to want more."
                —*Naughty Edition Reviews*

"I have been patiently awaiting Alexios's story, and let me tell you, it was well worth the wait. Ms. Day just has a way with these sexy warriors that leaves me breathless."
                —*The Romance Readers Connection*

"There were tears, there was laughter, there were moments my heart soared, and there were moments my heart feared for what was to come . . . I know what I will be doing on the next release day of a Warriors of Poseidon novel!" —*Leontine's Book Realm*

# ATLANTIS UNLEASHED

"This character-driven tale will grab the reader's imagination from page one . . . An epic thrill ride that should not be missed."
                —*Romance Reviews Today*

"A terrific romantic fantasy thriller."        —*Midwest Book Review*

"Day is back and better than ever . . . She doesn't skimp on the action, but this story also delves into the psychological, giving the characters real depth. Power and passion unleashed make for outstanding reading!"                —*Romantic Times*

"Action-packed adventure filled with magic and romance . . . Superb job of world building that will leave you stunned with the richness of detail. The characters of Atlantis are sexy, intelligent, and fascinating. I absolutely loved it and cannot wait for more!"
                —*Romance Junkies*

# ATLANTIS AWAKENING

"Fascinating, thrilling, and deeply romantic."
> —Jayne Castle, *New York Times* bestselling author

"Alyssa Day's Atlantis is flat-out amazing—her sexy and heroic characters make me want to beg for more! I love the complex world she's created!"
> —Alexis Morgan, national bestselling author

"Superb writing, fascinating characters, and edge-of-your-seat story bring the legend of Atlantis to life."
> —Colby Hodge, award-winning author

# ATLANTIS RISING

"*Atlantis Rising* is romantic, sexy, and utterly compelling. I loved it!"
> —Christine Feehan, #1 *New York Times* bestselling author

"The Poseidon Warriors are HOT!! Can I have one?"
> —Kerrelyn Sparks, *New York Times* bestselling author

"Alyssa Day's characters grab you and take you on a whirlwind adventure. I haven't been so captivated by characters or story in a long time. Enjoy the ride!"
> —Susan Squires, *New York Times* bestselling author

"Alyssa Day has penned a white-hot winner!"
> —Gena Showalter, *New York Times* bestselling author

"Wow! Alyssa Day writes a marvelous paranormal romance set on earth."
> —Susan Kearney, *USA Today* bestselling author

"Wow! What a spectacular series opener . . . The love scenes are sizzling hot."
> —*Once Upon A Romance*

"The world building is superb . . . The Warriors of Poseidon are a sexy, chivalrous, and dangerous team [who] create an atmosphere of testosterone so thick you can cut it with a knife."
> —*ParaNormal Romance*

## THE WARRIORS OF POSEIDON SERIES
### BY ALYSSA DAY

*Atlantis Rising*
High Prince Conlan's Story

*Atlantis Awakening*
Lord Vengeance's Story

"Wild Hearts in Atlantis" from *Wild Thing*
Bastien's Story

"Shifter's Lady" from *Shifter*
Ethan's Story

*Atlantis Unleashed*
Lord Justice's Story

*Atlantis Unmasked*
Alexios's Story

*Atlantis Redeemed*
Brennan's Story

*Atlantis Betrayed*
Christophe's Story

*Vampire in Atlantis*
Daniel's Story

Don't miss
*Heart of Atlantis*
High Priest Alaric's story
Coming soon from Berkley Sensation!

# VAMPIRE IN ATLANTIS

## A Warriors of Poseidon Novel

## ALYSSA DAY

**BERKLEY SENSATION, NEW YORK**

**THE BERKLEY PUBLISHING GROUP**
**Published by the Penguin Group**
**Penguin Group (USA) Inc.**
**375 Hudson Street, New York, New York 10014, USA**
Penguin Group (Canada), 90 Eglinton Avenue East, Suite 700, Toronto, Ontario M4P 2Y3, Canada
(a division of Pearson Penguin Canada Inc.)
Penguin Books Ltd., 80 Strand, London WC2R 0RL, England
Penguin Group Ireland, 25 St. Stephen's Green, Dublin 2, Ireland (a division of Penguin Books Ltd.)
Penguin Group (Australia), 250 Camberwell Road, Camberwell, Victoria 3124, Australia
(a division of Pearson Australia Group Pty. Ltd.)
Penguin Books India Pvt. Ltd., 11 Community Centre, Panchsheel Park, New Delhi—110 017, India
Penguin Group (NZ), 67 Apollo Drive, Rosedale, Auckland 0632, New Zealand
(a division of Pearson New Zealand Ltd.)
Penguin Books (South Africa) (Pty.) Ltd., 24 Sturdee Avenue, Rosebank, Johannesburg 2196,
South Africa

Penguin Books Ltd., Registered Offices: 80 Strand, London WC2R 0RL, England

This is a work of fiction. Names, characters, places, and incidents either are the product of the author's imagination or are used fictitiously, and any resemblance to actual persons, living or dead, business establishments, events, or locales is entirely coincidental. The publisher does not have any control over and does not assume any responsibility for author or third-party websites or their content.

VAMPIRE IN ATLANTIS

A Berkley Sensation Book / published by arrangement with the author

PRINTING HISTORY
Berkley Sensation mass-market edition / June 2011

ISBN: 978-0-425-24179-0

BERKLEY® SENSATION
Berkley Sensation Books are published by The Berkley Publishing Group,
a division of Penguin Group (USA) Inc.,
375 Hudson Street, New York, New York 10014.
BERKLEY® SENSATION and the "B" design are trademarks of Penguin Group (USA) Inc.

PRINTED IN THE UNITED STATES OF AMERICA

10  9  8  7  6  5  4  3  2  1

*This one is for my readers
who have been with me every step of the way
and for my new readers who are just
discovering Atlantis with me for the very first time.
Thank you from the bottom of my heart.*

# Acknowledgments

So I decided to move to Japan in the middle of this book. Well, Navy Guy had a lot to do with it, and sooner than you could say sushi, here I am, halfway across the world. Thanks to everyone who kept me sane along the way:

Cindy Hwang, always; my friends in the werearmadillos, at least we're crazy together; and Hedy Sberna, who is currently the proud owner of seventeen boxes of cleaning supplies she didn't need, plus a salad spinner.

And to Scott Sberna, for insights into the very real issues facing people with prosthetic limbs.

*Arigato gozaimasu* to you all.

Dear Readers,

We took a wonderful research trip to Sedona, Arizona, for this book, and I wish I could have taken you all with me. The red rocks of Sedona and the canyons and caves and vortex sites of the surrounding area are a spectacular part of our U.S. heritage. Of course, being me, I couldn't resist throwing in a little of my own twisted slant on history by adding a vampire apocalypse to the very real historical fact of the disappearance of the ancient Sinagua Indians.

Please visit the places Daniel and Serai see if you get a chance at all—it will be one of the best adventures of your lifetime, I promise. As to visiting Atlantis, well, I live in hope that one day I'll get to be the first to step foot on the lost continent. Won't *that* be a story to tell . . .

Hugs,
Alyssa

## The Warrior's Creed

We will wait. And watch. And protect.
And serve as first warning on the eve of humanity's
  destruction.
Then, and only then, Atlantis will rise.
For we are the Warriors of Poseidon, and the mark
  of the Trident we bear serves as witness to our
  sacred duty to safeguard mankind.

# Chapter 1

Daniel looked out at the sea of red eyes glaring back at him in the vast oak-and-marble chamber of the Primus and wondered, not for the first time, why the hell he'd ever wanted to be the ruler of the North American vampires. Also, how long it would be until the vampire goddess Anubisa discovered his ongoing betrayal and tortured him slowly to death.

The goddess of Chaos and Night was really, really good at torture. It was her specialty, in fact.

"So, shall we call you Daniel, then?" the vampire from South Carolina called out from behind the false safety of the rich mahogany semicircular desk. His voice was a bizarre hissing drawl: Deep South meets bloodsucker. "Or Drakos? Maybe Devon? You have so many identities; we wouldn't want to use the wrong one."

"You may call me Primator, Ruler of the Primus, the third house of the United States Congress. Or sir. Or even master, if you adhere to the old ways," Daniel said, smiling. It wasn't a nice smile. He made sure to show some fang.

"Or you can call me the one who delivers you to the true

and final death, if you continue to be an obstacle to these negotiations," he continued. Still polite. No longer smiling. "If we cannot work amicably and peacefully with the humans, we will find ourselves back to the days of angry mobs with wooden stakes and flaming torches. Except this time, the mobs will have missiles instead of pitchforks."

The South Carolinian sat down abruptly and clamped his mouth shut, with not even a hint of fang showing. Daniel's sense of victory was as fleeting as it was futile. They'd never agree. Humans were sheep to them, especially to the oldest ones. Predators couldn't become politicians, and he had no wish to continue in the role of trying to lead them. It was, as his Atlantean friend Ven would say, like herding seahorses: a task that would always fail and usually leave the herder with a severe case of nutjob. Daniel's sanity was precarious enough already.

A flash of memory tugged at him: Quinn's face when he'd forced the blood bond on her to save her life.

Another: Deirdre's face as she lay dying in his arms.

It was the only thing he was really good at—failing to protect the women he cared about. He'd started that tradition more than eleven thousand years ago, after all.

*Serai.*

Daniel's assistant shuffled some papers on his desk and glanced up at him. "Shall we adjourn then, Primator?"

Daniel snapped out of his dark thoughts and looked out at the members of the Primus. Still glaring at him, for the most part. Undoubtedly planning a coup or some other evil manipulation, except with them, unlike with the rest of the members of Congress, *actual* bloodshed would be involved. After all, they *were* vampires.

He recognized the irony.

"Adjourned." He struck the gavel once on its sound block, but they were already up and streaming out the vaulted double doors. Not a single one stopped to speak to him or even looked back. Plotting, always plotting.

After eleven thousand years, he was tired of all of it. Tired of the loneliness, the constant despair. The futility of hope. He'd had enough. He'd *done* enough. It was time for one last glimpse of the sun, before it incinerated him.

He stood in a single fluid motion and tossed the gavel on his assistant's desk. "Adjourned and done. I'm resigning the title and job of primator and getting out of Washington, D.C. Good luck with my successor."

Before the poor man could form a single word, Daniel leapt into the air and flew through the room and out the doors—right into the waiting ambush. Four ready to hurt him. None ready to help.

The pundits were right. D.C. *was* a dangerous town.

"Are you ready to die, *master*?"

It was South Carolina again. Daniel didn't recognize the trio of flunkies with him. Hired muscle, maybe, or members of South Carolina's blood pride. Didn't matter.

They wouldn't be around long.

"Actually, I am ready to die," Daniel said, enjoying the look of shock that widened the other vampire's eyes. "But not at your hand."

He hit the first two flunkies with a flying kick so powerful it crushed the first one's head and left the other unconscious on the ground. The third he dispatched with a blow from his dagger that removed its head from its body, both of which began to disintegrate into the characteristic acidic slime of decomposing vampire.

Then Daniel turned to South Carolina, who was backing away from him.

"I'm sorry. They made me do it," he cried out, trembling and whimpering like the coward he was.

"Then die with them," Daniel replied, realizing he didn't care enough to even ask who "they" were. He caught South Carolina's head between his hands and, with one powerful twist of his arms, wrenched it off the vampire's neck. The body fell to the ground, already decaying before Daniel realized he still held the head. He flung it away in disgust and scrubbed his hands against his pants.

The voice from behind him was uncharacteristically serious. "You didn't get anything on your hands."

Daniel whirled around. "Ven? What are you doing here? Or, more to the point, why didn't you help?"

The tall Atlantean prince rolled his eyes and shrugged while flashing a grin. "Seriously? Against only four of them? Are you a girl, now?"

"Better not let Quinn hear you say that," Daniel said, before the pain of her name caught up to him. She'd been his friend. Until the forced blood bond. Now she was—if not an enemy, still no longer a friend. Wary. Not afraid, not Quinn, but she'd never trust him again. He knew, because he could still feel her inside him. Whispers of her emotional resonance touched his mind at times. The blood bond.

He'd saved her life and killed her trust. He'd thought it a fair trade, at the time.

"Quinn's not a girl. She's a rebel leader. Now are we going for a beer or what?" Ven demanded, gesturing toward Daniel's hands. "Also, quit going all Lady Macbeth and wiping your hands on your pants. You don't need to 'out, damned spot,' when you didn't get slime on them."

"Quoting Shakespeare? I expected something from *The Rocky Horror Picture Show*." Daniel tried to smile but couldn't sustain the effort. "Lady Macbeth. Interesting you say that. I feel like I've gotten slime on my hands every day since I took this job." Daniel forced himself to quit rubbing his hands on his pants and took a deep breath. "I'm not a politician."

Ven threw back his head and laughed. "Nobody sane is. You're a warrior, my friend, like me. Now, let's go get that beer and talk about how we're going to keep you bloodsuckers from taking over the world. No offense."

"Not tonight. I'm not a politician anymore anyway. I just resigned." Daniel looked up at the stone front of the Primus entrance, built only a few years ago but designed to look like it had existed for millennia. The vampire aristocracy was big on pretense. Like the idea that they *were* aristocracy. Daniel's own mother had been a peasant who owned a single mule.

Ven whistled long and low. "Conlan is not going to be happy to hear that."

"With all due respect to your brother, whether or not the high prince of Atlantis is happy with my career choices is not big on my list of concerns. Good-bye."

Ven's hand grasped Daniel's arm with almost vampire-like speed. Damn Atlanteans anyway.

"Remove your hand, or I'll do it for you," Daniel snarled. "You presume too much."

"I've been told that before," Ven said, but he released Daniel's arm. "You saved my life. I'm not going to stand idly by while you sacrifice your own."

"How did you—"

"You said good-bye. You never say good-bye. Ever. It doesn't take a genius to guess that a vampire who has lived for thousands of years might get tired of putting up with life every once in a while. Especially when every day brings a new battle."

Daniel looked into his friend's eyes and lied to his face. "I'm not there yet."

Ven stared back at him, hard, but finally nodded. "Fine. Take a rain check on that beer?"

"Another night," Daniel agreed. He watched as the prince of Atlantis, one of the few men Daniel had ever called friend, leapt into the air and dissolved into a sparkling cloud of iridescent mist. The Atlantean powers over water were both beautiful and deadly. Daniel had seen both.

He waited until the last droplet of mist had long since vanished from his sight before he spoke, repeating the words that had given away his intent. "Good-bye, my friend."

And then he went to face the dawn.

# Chapter 2

## The Maidens' Chamber, Atlantis, deep beneath the Mediterranean Sea

"They might die. They might all die."

The frantic words sliced through the fog that kept Serai's mind in a near-permanent state of peaceful rest. The speaker's urgency was such that she cast around in her memory for his name, but she couldn't find it. One of the many, many attendants who had come and gone, lived and died, while she and her sisters waited out the millennia until they were freed. After the first thousand years, she hadn't bothered to try to learn their names. They almost never spoke to her, after all. Only around her. About her.

"*So beautiful,*" they'd say. Or, more often, "*What a waste.*"

The fact that she agreed with the second assessment didn't make it sting less.

"The companion stone is no longer sufficient," another one said, breaking into the painful memories. "If we can't find the Emperor, the maidens are all going to die."

Die. She and her sisters were going to die? No. *No.* Serai jolted awake with the same painful wrench in her chest that accompanied each year's brief period of consciousness. But something was wrong this time. Her internal clock, finely tuned after more than eleven thousand years of existing in the prison of stasis, told her that it hadn't been an entire year since her last brief period of semi-wakefulness. It hadn't even been half that. The pattern that had ruled her life for so long had changed, and she didn't know why.

From the sounds of the controlled chaos in the room, she wasn't the only one who didn't know what was going on. Normally tranquil attendants, the current high priest's acolytes, scurried around like rodents caught in a marble-walled trap. Voices that were always kept at hushed, serene, tones were raised in agitation, loud enough to drown out the ever-present gentle music. They were all panicking, and their fear transmitted itself to Serai—primal instincts that had long been buried shot into instant awareness.

*Danger. Daniel.*

Why did the two go so naturally together? Why, even after all this time, did her mind instinctively turn to the only man she'd ever wanted to rescue her? The only one she'd believed she could count on. She'd been wrong, though. So very wrong. Her heart, however, seemed not to have given up its lonely, helpless, hope.

*Daniel.*

Daniel. She used to pray she'd forget him, but she gave that up as futile after the first half a thousand years or so. How long must she be tortured with memories of the man who'd abandoned her? She had no time to think of long-lost love or the searing guilt that had followed her fateful choice on that long-ago day. This time, she had to rescue herself.

Serai opened her eyes and—it took nearly a full moment—the realization of the miraculous nature of that action flooded through her with the power of a lightning strike on storm-tossed waves.

*She'd opened her eyes.*

For the first time in millennia, she'd opened her eyes, and she had no intention of closing them again. In the spirit of the moment, she tried yet another impossible task and raised her arm from the pale cream- and rose-colored cushions of the silken pallet upon which she'd lain, encased in crystal and powerful magic, for so long. Action followed thought and she watched, wondering, exultant, as her hand touched the crystal covering of her prison.

A shudder of relief wracked her body—her limbs were obeying her commands—and a cry escaped her throat. Hoarse, rusty, and almost unrecognizable, but it was still her voice making that sound. *Her* voice. The stasis had done its job, then, as promised by a long-dead high priest, and kept her safe and whole throughout the turning of the world.

Kept *them* safe. She and her sisters-in-captivity. There were so few of them left now.

Pain stabbed at her, biting into her insides, and she instinctively hunched over to curl into the cramping ache. Unfortunately, the crystal case had been designed for sleeping maidens, not those having contortions, so she smacked her head into the gently curved cover and cried out again.

Pain. Sensation. Feelings she'd lacked for so long she couldn't remember them. The shock of tactile sensation strangled the words she'd been about to speak, and before she could even remember what they'd been—What *does* one say after eleven thousand years of silence? Shouldn't it be weighty and profound?—the first crack appeared in the surface of her crystal cage.

As she watched, her eyes still open—maybe it was a dream, yet another dream where she believed she'd woken up; no it couldn't be a dream, she'd never felt pain in one of those dreams—the small crack widened and lengthened into a rapidly growing spiderweb.

Her confusion turned to terror and her mind started screaming at her, a mindless howl of fear that turned to rage. *LET ME OUT, LET ME OUT, LET ME OUT!*

Almost before she had time to realize she might be in danger, a wave of power built up in the crystal case until the cover shattered, exploding outward as if she'd shoved it with a giant smithy's hammer. She couldn't breathe, couldn't think, couldn't process the shocking truth.

She was free.

*Free*.

And her magic had grown exponentially since she'd last attempted to use it, thanks to the influence of the Emperor's power.

Ignoring everything outside her immediate actions, she took a deep breath and then the next step—the *first* step. Carefully, oh so carefully, she lifted one leg, bare under the long tunic she wore, and stepped out onto the marble floor, easily avoiding the glass shards that had blown several paces away from her small pod. She stood, gazing around herself in wild-eyed wonder, for nearly the space of a single thought, and then her legs gave way beneath her and she collapsed onto the cool, hard surface.

Magic and stasis had kept her body in perfect working order, but neither could overcome the dueling emotions warring inside her. Ecstasy fought terror and her mind was the battleground—the shock of finally, *finally* attaining the freedom she'd dreamed of for so very long threatened to shake her rational mind free of its foundation. She huddled on the floor for a moment, then lifted her head and forced her voice to work. "I'm free. Oh, thank Poseidon, I am free."

Perhaps not words profound to anyone else but her, but that was enough. She scanned the room, still lying on the marble floor she'd last touched when Atlantis rode the surface of the waves, finally thinking to wonder why the attendants hadn't come to her aid. The answer was instantly apparent. The burst of power that had shattered her crystal cage must have smashed the three of them against the walls of the chamber, and they lay unconscious on the floor.

She *hoped* they were only unconscious. She summoned long-unused senses, tentatively reaching out to them. Yes, unconscious. Relief poured through her. Three hearts beating strongly. She hadn't woken into the new millennium as a murderer, even an accidental one. She pulled herself up to stand, moving cautiously, not trusting that the magic had really kept her limbs in working order. But both legs worked and her muscles felt as firm and flexible as if she'd walked across the palace courtyard just hours before, instead of countless years ago.

A high priest's magic, fueled by a god's power, had held her safe and whole for so long. But what, then, was happening now? Still moving slowly, she made her way to the other glass cases, one by one, around the room, to all five that still held occupants. Five more women, all so young when they'd been encased in crystal. The youngest, Delia, had been only twenty-five years old, the same age as Serai, when they'd trapped her. Just barely old enough to wed, by Atlantean standards—ten or more years past that by the conventions of the rest of the world at that time. But Atlanteans lived a very long life span, and a quarter century was barely old enough to risk the soul-meld—hundreds of years bound to the same person.

She shook her head, impatient with her wandering thoughts. Perhaps the stasis that hadn't weakened her body had weakened her mind. Shouts in the distance alerted her to the very real possibility that the priests of Poseidon's temple had sensed the disturbance here.

"If they catch me, they'll try to trap me," she said, either apologizing or making excuses to Merlina, the woman sleeping in the pod nearest to her. "I can't take the chance. I can't be caged again—not ever. I have to run." Desperation shuddered through her, but she forced her trembling body to move. One step, then another, until she came to the first attendant lying so still against the marble wall. A painting, of, oddly enough, peacocks wandering in the palace gardens, had fallen and crashed onto the floor near the man, luckily missing his head. Or maybe it had fallen first, then he. She didn't know, and she didn't need to know.

She needed to run.

No weapons anywhere in sight, not that she wanted to use them, but if she had to defend herself, she would. Daniel had taught her basic sword fighting during the hours she'd escaped her guards and met him at his forge.

Daniel, again. Always hiding in her mind, a ghost haunting both her dreams and her waking mind. The memory of his bare, muscled arms gleaming in the reflected light of the fire as he worked on one of his commissions caused her breath to hitch a little. The blacksmith and the lady. So impossible.

No time for memories. The shouting voices were coming closer. She'd always been fast. She would run so far they'd never find her. To the portal and even beyond. She slipped through the doorway that she remembered entering on that last, horrible day, saw the sunlight from windows down the hall, and nearly fell down to her knees from pure joy. But it was too late to run, the door at the end of the hall was opening, so she ducked behind a column and called on Poseidon to hide her from her enemies. And, even more important, to hide her from anyone who wanted to be her *friend*.

Or—worse—her *husband*.

High Prince Conlan made it to the Maidens' Chamber close on the heels of the priest running flat out in front of him, because he flew there in mist form and didn't bother with walking until he hit the doorway.

"Tell me," he demanded, knowing the priest, too, had felt the massive power surge, unlike anything Conlan had ever experienced in Atlantis.

"You know the gem from Poseidon's trident, the Emperor, controls the stasis pods," the man told him, stumbling over the words. "It has been erratic lately. Causing some sort of magical stuttering in the connection to the maidens."

Conlan managed not to slice skin off the man's hide with a blistering reply, but he had little patience these days for people wasting his time by repeating what he already knew.

"What I *know* is that you have five seconds to explain what just happened, or find someone else who can." Conlan strode past the man and into the main chamber, pausing at the threshold at the sight of shards of crystal littering the floor and fallen attendants lying scattered, like discarded dolls flung by a careless child.

"Poseidon's balls. What in the nine hells happened here?" He didn't stop for the priest's reply, but crouched down by the first fallen attendant, checking for a pulse. The man turned his face and opened his eyes, blinking in confusion.

"What happened?" His eyes widened and he tried to push himself upright. "Your Highness."

Conlan recognized Horace, the chief attendant. "Rest a minute, but tell me what happened while I check on these others."

Horace nodded but then shook his head and scrambled to his feet to follow Conlan. "Yes, sire. I mean, no, I have to check on the maidens."

Both of the other attendants, two women Conlan recognized by face only, were already stirring, so he turned to the priest who was still standing in the doorway, wringing his hands. Conlan narrowed his eyes. He needed to talk to Alaric about his choice of acolytes. This one was useless.

"You," he snapped. "Get the healers over here. Now."

The priest bobbed his head and then, backing out and doing a bizarre sort of dancing bow, turned and ran for help. Conlan shook his head in disgust. Damn Alaric anyway. The high priest should be here to help him with this, not off in North America somewhere pining over Quinn.

Horace was bent over one of the crystal stasis cases, his hands splayed on the surface, his eyes closed, perfectly still, but Conlan could feel the power humming from whatever the chief attendant was doing.

"She's fine," Horace said, opening his eyes and sighing. "I'll check the others."

Conlan nodded and headed for the case that clearly wasn't fine. The case he'd stared into with mixed portions of anticipation and dismay on many occasions throughout his life. The case that had held the incredibly beautiful woman who once was to have been his wife and the future queen of Atlantis.

Except it was empty. *Shattered.* Clearly the explosion of crystal had originated here.

He spoke out loud the words he couldn't quite believe. "She's gone. Serai is missing."

~~~~~~

Serai, still crouching down in hiding, heard the voice she'd once anticipated with such fear and longing. It was him. The high prince. The one who'd been destined to marry her. The one who'd abandoned her for the charms of a human woman, according to the attendants and their gossip.

She hated him. Not that she'd ever wanted to marry a man she didn't know and could never love. No, she despised High Prince Pretty Boy Conlan because he wasn't Daniel, and because he'd been her chance for freedom and he'd left her to rot.

Enough woolgathering. Conlan had called for healers. More people would be coming. And Poseidon only knew where High Priest Alaric was—if he appeared, her brief moment of freedom would be over. The high priest terrified her.

It was time to run, and she knew exactly where to go. The portal and then the surface. The Emperor's unique magic had fed knowledge of the outside world and of Atlantis to her and the other maidens for all these years. She could hide there; she would be inconspicuous and fit in—just another human woman, not a discarded Atlantean queen-to-be. She knew the languages. She could speak modern slang, even.

"Groovy," she whispered. "That's a bitchin' idea."

And then she picked up the hem of her skirt and ran.

# Chapter 3

### Reflecting Pool, Washington Monument, Washington, D.C.

Daniel walked into the water in the cool pearly light of impending dawn. It had been water that separated him from Serai, after all, and it only seemed fitting that water stand guard and witness over him at the time of the true death. The few people he could see were jogging, that peculiar human preoccupation with spending hundreds of dollars on shoes and clothing to drive their cars for an hour, so they could run for five minutes.

Human logic. It would have destroyed them all thousands of years ago, their stubborn, foolish excuse for logic, but the humans had one crucial quality that neither the vampires, the Fae, or even the shape-shifters could ever possess: they bred like rabbits. The sheer overwhelming numbers of them far outweighed any concentrated threat by any of the supernatural factions.

But unlike rabbits, humans had forgotten how to run—*really* run—most of them. Daniel bared his teeth in what passed for a smile with him these days, not even caring for once if his fangs were showing. He could show them again what it was to run. Run for their lives.

Run from the *monster*.

He'd done it before. He'd even enjoyed it. Ripping throats open with his teeth. Bathing in fountains of blood. Brutal, violent, glorious death. Back in the dark days. The lost days. After he'd died the first death and risen, cold and alone and without the only woman he'd ever loved. He'd become a monster and a killer, and he'd reveled in it.

But no more.

Now it was time to die.

He thought briefly of last words as dawn edged its way into the world, turning the edges of the obelisk from silver to a rosy glow as the sun rose, proudly silhouetted against the morning sky. What would be fitting to close the chapter of a single lonely vampire who'd lived for so very very long? Memory was nothing more than a collection of clutter, polished and positioned to shine in the light of untrustworthy wishful thinking and hindsight. Death took its final inventory, and nothing survived it except deeds recorded in history books by the victorious.

So he didn't try for the momentous, instead speaking only the truth of his heart.

"Good-bye, Serai. I have always loved you. If there truly is a land beyond this one, may I find you again."

Then he raised his face to the horizon and watched the sun rise for the first time in thousands of years. The shimmering first rays swam toward him on the surface of the water, changing the deep rose of dawn to burnished gold. Closer, ever closer, until the first questing ray of light from something like his four millionth day on the earth reached his legs.

No pain—not yet—just a sense of wonder at the glory of it. How could he ever have resigned himself to eternal night? Especially alone in the darkest reaches of his own heart. Always alone.

Closer. Rising to his waist. Still no burning—no uncovered skin yet touched by the deadly glow.

He took a breath, drew it deep into lungs that hadn't breathed daylight air in so long. Closed his eyes, then opened them again. He'd face this final test with the same defiance with which he'd lived his entire life.

Heat now. Burning. Fire sizzled across the skin of his throat at his open shirt collar. He raised his chin. Only one final moment of life—but no regrets. It was too late for that. Agony seared through him as the sun struck his face, full-on, and he clenched his teeth against the scream.

A final blast of heat and pain crushed his courage under the sun's indifferent power, and he fell forward into the pool, silently screaming or cursing or praying, and the vortex of light and sound sucked him in, sucked him under, pulled him through, whirling and twisting, over and over, around and around, until a shove from a mighty force smashed him face-first into a solid surface.

He was dead, finally, finally dead. And he was lying on . . . *grass?*

The afterlife was paved in grass? He'd not expected that. Not for one such as him. Maybe oceans of burning lava or canyons filled with blazing fire. The deepest levels of the nine hells were surely reserved for vampires. However, not only was he lying on grass, which smelled like a particularly ripe and blooming spring, but he was lying in the sunlight. He was lying in some verdant field of the afterlife in sunshine . . . and he *wasn't burning*.

Defiance gave way to joy, and he murmured thanks to any gods who would listen. All save one. The vampire goddess Anubisa deserved no thanks from him, and may she rot in whatever dark corner to which she'd escaped. Maybe not an appropriate thought for heaven, though.

He rested there for a long minute, with his face pressed into the grass, every bone in his body aching with the force of the collision, and considered whether or not to lift his head and look around. Before he could make that crucial decision, the unmistakable point of a spear jabbed him in the side of his neck, and a voice that had haunted him since his first death spoke.

"Who are you and whence did you come, Nightwalker?"

Daniel moved his head just enough to look up into the

bright sunshine, and the sharp point of the spear bit into the flesh of his neck—just as his fangs had done to so many thousands of humans during his life. Irony, again. Perhaps this was yet to turn out to be one of the levels of hell and he'd be tortured not with fire but with a million tiny cuts, until his own blood ran free and dark into eternity.

The slender, curving silhouette of a woman wearing a long gown stood beside him. She held the non-pointy end of the spear. He could see nothing of her features at first, and then he saw her face, shining more brightly than a thousand afterlife-created suns.

*Serai's* face.

She was to be his personal tour guide to heaven, then. Or his personal escort to hell. But her gasp spoke of disbelief, even shock.

Her next words were nothing that he could have expected, though. "I am Serai of Atlantis, a princess of Poseidon. Remember you me, Nightwalker? Be warned that you are now my prisoner."

Memories long unused returned to him and allowed him to understand her. Her words were musical, the cadence liquid and lyrical. Ancient Atlantean. He answered her with the rusty pronunciation that was all he could manage. Shock and thousands of years of non-use had robbed him of fluency.

"Serai? I have waited more than eleven thousand years to hear your voice again." He jumped to his feet and moved to take her in his arms, but was stopped again at spear point.

"No," she said, the strain evident in her face, turning her perfect skin even paler than he remembered. "I'm leaving here. Now. Come with me or stay, but don't even try to stop me."

For the first time, he took the time to look around at his surroundings and saw the two fallen guards lying unconscious on the ground, but when he looked up to ask her about it, the sight in front of him stunned him to speechlessness for several seconds.

"What?" she snapped. "I didn't kill them, if that's what

you're thinking, although now that you're a nightwalker, can't you hear their heartbeats to confirm my claim?"

He pointed, still unable to form words. At the dome. The freaking *glass dome* that surrounded them as far as he could see—and the deep, dark blue currents of the ocean beyond it. A dark form swam past, and a single giant eye blinked at him.

"Is that . . . is that a *whale*?" He stared, feeling like his eyes would bug out of his head at any minute as it finally hit him. "Are we . . . are we in *Atlantis*?"

She rolled her eyes, apparently a timeless gesture. "Where else would we be? Now, move."

She raised her arms and began to sing. Sing. The woman he'd loved and lost eleven thousand years ago—loved all of that time, if he wanted to be honest, although he didn't—was *singing*. In *Atlantis*.

Or else, and he sighed as he came to the obvious realization: he really was dead. Somehow he'd ended up in the good grace of the gods instead of in the nine hells. He was here with Serai and she was singing and . . .

She'd stabbed him. With a spear.

"Nope. Probably not any form of heaven," he muttered.

A shimmering oval of pure light appeared in front of Serai, and the smile that crossed her face in response blinded Daniel more than the light. She was so beautiful. Every bit as beautiful as he remembered, and more. Her silken dark hair was so black it had blue highlights in it, and longer than he remembered, swinging past her perfect, curving hips. Her eyes matched the ocean waves, just as blue. Just as deep.

And her lips—oh, her lips. He reacted just as strongly to their sensual curve now as he had when he was a young apprentice, showing off a little with his metal-working skills and his muscles for the most beautiful woman he'd ever seen.

She still was.

The oval grew larger and wider, and he knew what it was. He'd seen Atlanteans use its magic before.

"The portal. You're singing to the portal? I've never seen the warriors sing."

She cast an amused glance at him. "They are barbarians. The portal only gives fully of its magic to those who understand and appreciate it."

"Ven did mention how capricious it could be. Dumps them in the middle of the ocean sometimes."

She laughed and then looked as startled as he felt, before she touched her fingertips to her lips. "I haven't laughed in so very long," she whispered, but then she took a deep breath. "Portal, take me where I need to be, I ask and beseech you."

A wave of golden light shimmered over the silvery surface of the portal's oval form and Serai smiled. She took a step forward, then hesitated before turning back to Daniel.

"Come with me?"

She held out her hand, and the ocean itself took a deep breath. She held out her *hand*. To *him*. He reached for her, and then paused, as a horrible thought struck him.

"To where? It was full daybreak where I came from, and if the sunlight strikes me, I'll die in flames. I would risk that for you without hesitation, but I would not have you in danger from the fire."

"We have no time for this. Conlan and his guards will be after me, or these guards will wake up . . ." She broke off mid-sentence and smiled at him, and he realized he would follow her smile into the fires of all nine of the hells, without question. "Trust me?"

He took her hand and they stepped forward into the portal, but as the light surrounded them, she cried out and doubled over. He caught her in his arms and held tight to the beautiful woman, who was his past and his future, as the world fractured around them in a vortex of spinning light, and he prayed to any god who would listen. He couldn't lose her again.

Never again.

Serai fought against the pain ripping through her insides as the vortex swallowed her and Daniel. It was the Emperor. Someone had it and was trying to work its magic. Someone not Atlantean—someone who didn't know what he or she was doing. That must be why she'd awoken now, off schedule, and had been able to escape.

The fluctuation in the gem's energy seared through her and doubled her over. She thought instantly of her fellow maidens, still trapped in stasis, and wondered how this would affect them. If they would survive it. Another burst of pain wrenched through her, and she wondered if *she* would survive it. What a great joke the universe would be playing if she survived millennia in stasis only to die in the first short hour of freedom.

The portal's light warmed around her in a magical caress, as if it felt her pain and wanted to comfort her. At the same moment, Daniel's strong arms wrapped around her. She rested her head against the hard muscles of his chest and sent a mental thank-you to the portal, just as it opened again and deposited them in the torch-lit darkness of what looked like a smallish cavern. Stumbling a little as her bare feet touched the cold stone of the floor, though she was still safely ensconced in Daniel's embrace, she had a mere second or two to register the small cluster of humans surrounding them before the tiger attacked.

# Chapter 4

Serai screamed and Daniel pushed her behind him, putting his body between her and the tiger and yelling at it.

"Jack, no!"

*Jack?* He knew the tiger's name?

The tiger ignored Daniel and charged, leaping through the air in full feline fury, its mouth opened in an earth-shattering roar. If she hadn't been so terrified, Serai might have admired its feral beauty. Daniel leapt up to counter the tiger's attack, and the two of them met in midair with a crash that resounded like thunder.

The tiger caught Daniel in its deadly embrace and swiped at him with paws the size of dinner plates, each tipped with long, sharp claws. Daniel's nightwalker strength was a match for the tiger, though, and he shoved the beast's forearm away from his face and then hurled it across the cavern, where it smashed into the wall.

A woman yelled at Daniel, by name, and Serai's eyes narrowed as she examined the human female. Scruffy, small, and tough, with a waiflike exterior that covered a steel core, if the look in the woman's dark eyes told true.

"Daniel, leave Jack alone. How dare you blast in here and hurt him?" the woman shouted in one of the landwalker languages. English. Serai knew it, of course. The Emperor had taught her all languages.

"Quinn, he attacked me, in case you didn't notice," Daniel replied, with what Serai believed to be admirable calm, under the circumstances.

"What do you expect, you idiot?" Quinn snapped, hands on hips, as the tiger shook its massive head and staggered to its feet.

Serai's fear vanished and anger took its place. Lovely, warming anger, which stiffened her spine and reminded her she was a princess of Atlantis. She stepped forward until she was standing next to Daniel and gave Quinn her haughtiest glare.

"Stand back, female, or face my wrath," Serai declared in English, holding her hands out to her side in the ready position.

Quinn's mouth fell open, and the impudent woman began to laugh. At Serai. Anger heated up, became rage.

"Seriously? 'Face my wrath'?" Quinn shook her head. "Daniel, where did you get her? Melodrama R Us?"

Serai's face flushed. It had sounded a little over the top even as she said it, but she wasn't exactly experienced at facing down humans in combat. The tiger paced forward, snarling at Daniel, until it stood next to Quinn.

"I'm out of practice at issuing warnings, human," Serai snapped. "But how is this for something you can understand? Keep your pet kitten away from Daniel, or I will be forced to harm it."

The tiger paused, mid-snarl, tilted its head to the side, and stared at her, its tongue hanging out of the side of its mouth. It almost looked like he, too, was laughing at her.

Quinn laughed. "Right. Daniel, tell your girlfriend there that we don't have time for all this posturing and to stay away from Jack or she'll get hurt. Now we need to talk about what you're doing here—"

The tiger's snarl interrupted the human just before it signaled its intent to attack by bunching its powerful muscles and tensing for the leap. Daniel growled deep in his throat, almost as wild as the tiger, but Serai was suddenly fed up with all of them. She called to the pure magic of Atlantis, the magic she had once wielded with little skill but that now rushed to her call. Jack leapt into the air again, but this time Serai knocked Daniel out of the way, and *she* sprang up to meet the tiger.

On its own terms.

~~~

Daniel fell backward, knocked out of the way by more than a quarter ton of tiger. He landed on his ass, and bounced back up immediately, wincing as the tigers crashed into each other. Serai had transformed in an instant's shimmer of magic into an enormous tiger—bigger even than Jack, nearly as big as a horse. She roared, and Daniel almost fell over.

She wasn't just a tiger. She was a saber-toothed tiger.

"Daniel!" Quinn screamed, just as he leapt toward the two tigers. "Do something! She's going to kill him!"

The few other humans in the room that he'd ignored up to that point suddenly had weapons in their hands, and Daniel didn't know what to do first to protect Serai. As it turned out, he didn't have to do anything at all. Jack, who was probably even more shocked than Daniel, did it for him. The big cat rolled onto his back and presented his snowy white belly to Serai in a blatant display of surrender and submissiveness. Daniel, who'd seen Jack fight in both his tiger and human forms, was amazed. No way would the Jack he knew have backed down from a fight.

The shimmer of shape-shifter magic curled around Jack's form even as Serai lightly clamped her massive jaws around his neck, so gently that the enormous curved sabers of her teeth didn't break the skin of Jack's human neck when he returned to human form.

His naked, human form.

It was Daniel's turn to growl. "Get dressed, shifter."

Quinn made some kind of signaling gesture and the rest of them immediately put their weapons down. Daniel nodded to himself. When the leader of all North American human rebels gave her troops a command, she could expect instant obedience. She'd certainly earned their respect.

She'd always had his.

"Maybe you could ask your girlfriend to let me up?" Jack said, smiling a little but carefully not moving at all. Serai released him and backed away, then stalked over to Quinn and snarled at her.

Quinn held her hands up in front of her, the universal signal for "you win, don't bite me," and Daniel could have sworn Serai, still in tiger form, smirked. She padded over to him and curved around his body for a moment, then shifted from extinct tiger to haughty Atlantean princess in seconds. She, unlike Jack, was fully clothed.

Jack laughed and quickly dressed in clothes someone tossed him. His shifter magic was so powerful he generally shifted into human form with his clothing intact, but he either had been shocked out of his routine by the saber-toothed tiger suddenly appearing from nowhere, or the display of nakedness was simply to poke at Daniel.

If the latter, it had worked. Daniel started after Jack again, but Serai caught his arm.

"I think we've had enough of this," she said quietly, and he whipped his head around to look at her, *really* look at her, and realized she was on the brink of collapse. "I'm very tired, Daniel. It has been a long . . . time."

Her eyes rolled back in her head and he caught her, swinging her into his arms just before she fell to the stone floor of the cave. Pain and remorse stabbed at him. Yet again, after all these years, even when given a miraculous second chance, he was failing her.

"Quinn, I need your help," he said, ignoring Jack. "She's weak and needs to rest."

Quinn swept her gaze over Serai's unconscious form, still dressed in the silken gown, and then she nodded. "Of course. We can get you a place to sleep and warmer clothes for her. We're camping out here, but you probably knew that, or why would you be here?"

He grimly shook his head. "Trust me, I had no idea. I don't even know where 'here' is."

Jack walked closer, ignoring Daniel's scowl, and inhaled deeply, as if scenting Serai. "I wasn't about to hurt her, and you know it, vampire," the cat shifter said. "She's beautiful, Daniel. She's not a shifter, though, and she smells like . . . Atlantean? How did she do that? And a saber-tooth? They've been extinct so long—"

"Probably around ten or eleven thousand years," Daniel interrupted dryly. "I'll explain later, if you're done trying to kill me."

Jack scowled at him. "If I'd been trying to kill you, you'd be dead."

"Think again, little kitten," Daniel advised flatly. "Remember who hit the wall."

"Children," Quinn interrupted. "Enough. Let's get her some rest, and then you have some explaining to do, Daniel."

Daniel's temper flared, and for the first time in the years he'd known her, he let it loose at Quinn. "I am vampire. Senior mage of the Nightwalker Guild, and formerly primator of all vampires in this infant of a country. Tread softly before you think to issue orders to me, human."

He felt her shock through the blood bond he'd once had to force on her to save her life. Jack started to say something, but Quinn cut him off with a raised hand. The uncomfortable truth was, the blood bond ran both ways. She could probably sense Daniel's emotions, too. She was certainly looking at him with more than a little sympathy in her dark eyes.

"Daniel deserves our trust, Jack." She issued a few quiet requests, and one of the humans motioned to Daniel to follow him down a dark corridor.

Quinn's slightly raised voice stopped him. "We're near Sedona, Arizona, Daniel. And we're in big trouble."

He almost smiled. "With you, what else is new?"

~~~

Serai woke as Daniel put her down on a pallet in what looked like another room in the same cavern. Same dark stone walls. Same dank stone-and-dirt-cavern smell. A small fire glowed in a corner of the room, giving off a bit of heat and light, but not enough to really help. She was shivering bone deep and felt like she might never be warm again.

Daniel sat on the edge of the narrow bed as he pulled rough blankets around her, but his hands stilled as he realized she was awake and looking at him.

"How are you feeling?"

She lifted one shoulder. "I've been better, but I'm alive. I'm free. There's much to be said for that."

An awkward silence fell, and she watched him as he looked at the blankets, around the room, anywhere but at her. Maybe he didn't want to be around her. Maybe he'd forgotten about her long ago, and she was an unwelcome reminder of a painful past. Maybe—

His hands shot up and grabbed her shoulders, and he finally stared directly at her—into her eyes, as if the secrets of the universe hid there for him to find.

"I thought you were dead," he said, anguish in his rough tone. "How can you be alive, all these millennia later? You're not a vampire, but you're still exactly the same as the day Atlantis fell and not a day older. How is that even possible?"

"Have you ever heard the tale of Sleeping Beauty?" she asked wryly.

He just looked at her, silent, and for a moment a hint of the shy boy he'd been surfaced in his eyes. But only for a moment. The hard, deadly man he'd become had no patience for whimsy, she suspected.

"They put me in stasis," she explained, arranging the blanket around her shoulders and pulling her knees to her chest. "Maidens intended as brides for future kings of Atlantis. Not just me. There were others, many of them woken long ago, but six of us remained. We've been asleep since Atlantis dove beneath the seas more than eleven thousand years ago."

He released her shoulders and stood up, impatient or disbelieving, and she felt the ache of loss as he walked away from her toward the small fire. He tossed a few pieces of the wood stacked nearby onto the flames and considered his handiwork before turning toward her, still crouched beside the fire.

"That's not possible. What magic could do such a thing? Even Alaric, and the gods know he's more powerful than any sorcerer or witch I've ever met, couldn't do that."

The name distracted her. "You know Alaric?"

"I've worked on the same side as High Prince Conlan and his warriors several times," Daniel said. "Poseidon's high priest often accompanies Conlan and his elite Warriors of Poseidon on missions."

He crossed the room and motioned to the edge of the bed, as if for permission. She nodded, and he resumed his seat, not touching her this time.

"Your Atlanteans have to fight the big, bad vampires, don't you know?" he said, mockery in his voice and raised eyebrow.

"I've heard about the warriors. The temple attendants gossiped enough," she said bitterly. "And I'd prefer not to talk about Conlan. Not now, not ever."

It was his turn to be surprised. "I've always found him to be a decent enough guy."

"He didn't leave *you* imprisoned in a crystal cage for hundreds of years after he learned about you. He didn't plan to wed *you*, either, and then abandon you to remain in that prison after he found a human woman for whom he was willing to abdicate his throne." She shook her head. "Trust me when I say I will never take the man's hand in friendship."

She finally looked up at Daniel and caught her breath. His eyes glowed a fiery red and his face had gone hard and feral. For the first time since she'd found him again, she thought about what becoming a nightwalker truly meant, and her breath caught in her throat.

"Plan. To. Wed. You?" he gritted out between clenched teeth. "You were betrothed to Conlan? After . . ."

"Jealousy? You dare show me jealousy when you abandoned me to be caged and imprisoned for eleven thousand *years*?"

"I didn't know!" he shouted. "I thought you were dead. I woke up and you were gone, and they told me you had died. They took me to deal with the newness of the bloodlust, and by the time I could control it and came back for any scrap of news of you, you and your whole godsdamned continent were *gone*."

A flare of something very like hope flamed in her chest, and she tried to speak but the words wouldn't come. Not until he touched a finger to her cheek and it came back wet did she realize she was crying.

"You thought I was dead? You didn't abandon me?"

The red flames had vanished from his eyes, and they shone a strange, almost silvery black as he stared at her. "I would never have abandoned you. But you were quick enough to leave me."

Frustration robbed her of fluency and she dropped back into her native Atlantean. "How can you think—"

The pain crashed through her again and she cried out, doubling over as the Emperor sent a discordant slice of energy searing through her body and mind. "Someone has it. Make them stop, make them stop," she said, almost sobbing.

Daniel pulled her into his arms. "What is it? Someone has what?"

"The Emperor. They're tampering with the Emperor, and whoever it is will kill all six of us, if we don't find it soon."

# Chapter 5

## Montezuma's Castle National Park, Arizona, inside the castle structure

"Priestess, I'm . . . I'm sorry. My skills aren't up to this. I can't cast a glamour that would cover us both."

Ivy Khetta, high priestess of the Crescent Moon coven, turned away from the view that the Sinagua Indians had enjoyed for several hundred years, until nearly A.D. 1400, when the clan of vampires banished to the desert by their unforgiving goddess, Anubisa, had wiped out the native Americans. These days, none but national park employees and archaeologists were allowed to walk inside the structure that had been hand-built with stone, sweat, and adobe plaster so many centuries ago. She raised a hand to almost touch a spiral design that one of the Sinagua had incised into the plaster wall maybe a thousand years ago, just so she could feel the energy that still pulsed from the long-ago magic and passion of the artist.

She wasn't ready to activate the vortex energy, though. Not just yet.

Ivy was definitely breaking more than a few federal laws just by stepping foot inside the castle, but nobody knew she was here and—in spite of her apprentice's incompetence—

nobody would, except those she couldn't control. She managed—barely—to keep from looking for the vampire and his companions.

Instead, she focused on the young witch. Of course, the fledgling couldn't hide them from the park rangers and crowds of tourists who would soon swarm over the grounds like ants on a coyote's corpse. Ivy was the only witch in the entire state powerful enough to wield such strong magic.

After all, she wasn't a witch at all.

She was a sorceress who specialized in the black. Best that nobody else ever learned that, though, since her particular brand of dark sorcery was punishable by death. Ugly, bloody death that not even a sorceress who could call the black arts would be able to escape. If not death, at the very least she would face eternal imprisonment in dungeons built inside the Rocky Mountains. No, it was better that nobody figured out her secret. At least until she was ready. Nobody would ever treat her like they had her mother.

Best nobody heard about that, either.

"Don't worry about it, ah—"

"Aretha," the witch offered helpfully, nervously smoothing her pale brown hair behind her ears.

Ivy blinked. "Seriously? I thought it was Moon Blossom. Not sure which is worse."

Aretha blushed. "That was what I was trying on for a witch name. My mom's a music fan, so my real name is Aretha. It was almost Madonna. Can you imagine Madonna Moskowitz?"

"Better than Lady Gaga Moskowitz."

Aretha tittered a nervous laugh that echoed while she wandered around. "Did Montezuma really live here? I thought he lived in a gold palace, sacrificing virgins and stuff," the young witch said, looking around in obvious distaste. "This is kind of low-rent for a big-time ruler, right?"

"Are you an idiot?"

"Uh, no. I mean, what do you mean?"

"Montezuma was an Aztec ruler who probably never got this far north in his bloodthirsty life. The idiot settlers who first arrived here in the 1800s named this place Montezuma's Castle, since they apparently had the same mentally deficient history teacher as you did."

"But—" Aretha bit her lip, probably wondering what "deficient" meant, and Ivy thanked the goddess again that she could afford to send Ian to private school.

"Sinagua. Native Americans. You're in a *national park*. Buy a *book*. Get a free brochure. You can read, can't you?" Ivy carefully smoothed the sneer off her face. She didn't want to add wrinkles to her face if at all possible. Magic kept her looking at least ten years younger, but her impatience with stupidity threatened to add it all back. Anyway, she only needed to be patient with this one a little while longer. Surely Nicholas would find her better help after this, and Aretha Moon Blossom Moskowitz could find another hobby.

"I'll get a book, Ivy. I mean, Priestess. I will. I'm sorry."

Ivy tuned out the witch's babbling and raised her hands in the air, opening herself to the elements and letting the biting rush of power flow into and through her. The sun was rising, offering its heat and energy to any who could reach out and grasp it. Ivy's hair crackled with electricity and lifted into the nonexistent breeze to float around her head as she pulled enough power through herself to try again with the gemstone.

First, though, the shield. Brick by unseen, mental brick, she built the wall of silence and cover—the glamour that shielded them from inquiring eyes and unwanted attention. All anyone would see was a shimmer of heat on a sunny Arizona day. Normal, so very normal—and fewer than five small animals had to die to give her all that lovely power. Seemed like a fair enough trade. There were certainly rodents enough out here in the almost-wilderness.

Aretha squeaked with delight as the shimmer of Ivy's power floated around and over them. The view from the opening of the room in which they stood was now like looking through lightly frosted glass, and Ivy knew from experience that she'd succeeded perfectly. No rangers or guests were scheduled to enter the castle structure for any reason today, or so her sources had told her, and it was still well before the park operational hours, in any case.

Time for the main event.

She returned to the spiral design, etched so long ago into the wall, and took a deep breath. She'd found it almost by accident the first time, in spite of the vampire, drawn to the site by the booming waves of energy that had centered here during the last thunderstorm. She loved driving around in storms, attracted by the raw power of nature's fury. Ian had liked to go with her when he was a baby, and the sounds of the storm had made him laugh and then lulled him to sleep. But thirteen-year-old boys rarely wanted to hang out with their mothers, and she wouldn't want him to see this morning's work anyway.

The results, perhaps. When she was so powerful that nobody could ever harm them. Then she would teach him. He was almost old enough to come into his own powers.

"Um, Priestess?" Aretha's hesitant voice jolted Ivy out of her reverie. "That drawing is glowing. Is that supposed to happen?"

"Oh, yes." Ivy carefully curved her hand to curl around the outside of the spiral and then flattened her palm to cover it. Just like last time, when she'd first found it, the heat of the power surge inside the wall felt like it was searing her skin from her hand. She'd wrenched her hand away, only to discover that the heat was magically created and had done her skin no actual harm. The gem had been almost in her grasp, but when she'd pulled her hand away it had disappeared into the wall again.

She wouldn't make the same mistake this time. She clenched her jaw tight against crying out, in case any sound would cause a glitch in the magic. The familiar spinning feeling of vertigo channeled through chaos began to manifest; first in her hand and then rapidly traveling up her arm and through her body in both directions. Her head started to feel wobbly, and her torso tightened as the magic pulsed and swirled, and finally—just when the nausea threatened to force her to release her hold—finally, deep in the stone of the wall, she could hear the resonance of the spell's connection.

The sound echoed through Ivy's bones, and dimly, as if from miles away, she saw Aretha fall to her knees. If the deep toll of a cathedral's bell could echo through a thunderstorm, this would be the sound it created. Deep, profound, and laced with unknowable meaning. Plaster and stone became permeable and then vanished under Ivy's hand, and the rich purple glow of the gem filled the narrow opening.

"Oh, come to Mama," she whispered, unable to help it, as a tingle of delicious anticipation raced through her. If she was correct, she would soon be holding an object of power that nobody had touched in more than a thousand years.

The gem floated through the air toward her, and the sound emanating from it softened to a gentle humming noise, almost as if the stone itself were anticipating reaching her, too. Ivy shivered, finally admitting, if only to herself, that she was slightly afraid. She had no idea what power this stone might contain. Only the vampire's hints of a mystical prophecy from ancient times had guided her decision to return and try again.

Well. That and his threats.

Although the question she'd left unanswered in her greedy desire to obtain the stone still nagged at the back of her mind: how had Nicholas known exactly what gem she'd been talking about?

No time to worry or wonder now, it was so close . . . oh, goddess, it was an amethyst the size of an ostrich egg. Even if it hadn't held such incredible power, the monetary value alone would have made the risk worthwhile. As it was, Ian's future was now secured.

The gem floated closer and closer to Ivy's trembling fingers, and she sent one last prayer to the dark goddess who'd owned her heart since Ivy's first communion with the moon. "Protect me, Lady, and help me to master this new gift I offer to your glory."

The gem stopped its forward motion and shook slightly, almost as if in response to the prayer, but then it soared through the air even faster and slammed into Ivy's waiting hands. She had a moment to wonder at its cool, hard weight before its power smashed through her defenses, through her mental shield, and through any pretense or hope she'd had of being the one in control. Images cascaded through her mind, ancient images and glittering scenes of persons and places so fantastic that Ivy's brain couldn't keep up with the input. She tried to open her fingers to release the gem, to break the connection, but the amethyst clearly had other ideas. Her hands were frozen in place, and she was unable to break her own grip.

The gem's power lashed out at her with a crushing pressure on her mind—either a warning or a punishment—and the last thing she saw before the blackness took her was Aretha Moon Blossom, lying on her back on the dark floor, staring sightlessly up at the ceiling from bleeding eyes.

❧～＿ぉ

Nicholas walked carefully around the dead human on the floor and motioned to one of his blood pride to deal with it. He stood a couple of paces away from the fallen sorceress and stared down at her, listening to the faint, stuttering beat of her heart.

"Are you sure we can't take it away from her?" Smithson asked, greed shining in his beady eyes.

"No. Everything we know about this stone tells us that only the most powerful sorcerers even dare touch it. She has obviously achieved a connection, and it would almost certainly kill both her and whichever unfortunate being tried to take it from her."

"Can we touch her?"

"Only one way to find out."

Vampire looked at human, neither willing to be the first to drop his gaze.

Nicholas finally laughed. "For a human, you're surprisingly unafraid of me."

His temporary ally shrugged. "I'm not just a human. I'm

an investment banker. Some would call me an even worse bloodsucker than you."

Nicholas laughed again. "Ah, such self-awareness in one so young. This alliance may prove to be most entertaining. Are you sure that Ivy Khetta will agree to continue? The young one died, and I doubt she intended that."

The banker, Smithson, smiled. Nicholas had seen just such soulless smiles in the rare demons he'd encountered over the centuries. He managed not to shudder, but just barely.

"She'll have incentive. Trust me," Smithson said.

Smithson pointed at a couple of his thugs, who were hovering far enough away that they hadn't heard the conversation about the possibility of hideous death. "Bring her. Carefully. We have to get out of here before the park personnel show up."

They lifted the sorceress and . . . nothing blew up.

Nobody else died.

Nicholas was faintly disappointed.

# Chapter 6

## A cavern above Dry Creek Basin, northwest of Sedona, Arizona

Daniel watched Serai as she tossed and turned in a restless sleep, her hair tangling around her. He wanted to stroke it back from her face, whisper soothing endearments to ease her, but those were a lover's prerogatives, so he refrained. Also, if he touched her, she might wake up, and she needed to rest. She was exhausted and the sun's pull called to him to sleep, too, but he wasn't willing to close his eyes for a minute. She might disappear again. This dream he was living in which a long-dead love suddenly returned to him at the moment he'd finally decided to face his own death was too surreal to be true. He couldn't trust it yet.

He wasn't sure he trusted her, either.

It was too . . . *something.* Too coincidental, too unexpected, too unreal.

And so, here he was again, back to reality, or the lack thereof. His mind and heart had fought over the problem during the past hour or so while she slept, but he couldn't quite reach a conclusion. Quinn and Jack had been real enough. He didn't know whether to laugh or snarl at the memory of Jack rolling over to show his belly like a submissive kitten being chided by its mother. If Jack had hurt Serai, Daniel would have ripped him to tiny, furry pieces.

Slowly.

But Serai hadn't needed his help. A saber-toothed tiger, of all the impossible things. He'd known she had some magic, back when she was a girl, but this? Again, his mind stuttered at the paradox. Back when she was a girl—no. She'd been a woman then, as she was now. Almost to her twenty-fifth birthday when he'd known her. An important one, in Atlantean culture; the birthday that signaled she was old enough to be courted. To wed.

He'd had plans for that birthday. He'd begun sketches for a piece of jewelry he wanted to craft for her from the most amazing Atlantean metal, orichalcum. Like copper infused with silver, tensile and malleable yet stronger than steel. He'd wanted to design and forge a pendant that captured her beauty and her grace, but nothing had seemed good enough. Never elegant enough.

He'd been a blacksmith's apprentice, after all, not a jeweler's.

She kicked the blanket off again, and he gave in to the impulse and gently pulled her onto his lap. He wanted—no, he *needed*—to hold her in his arms again. To prove to himself that she was real. Her soft warmth belied the notion that she might be a ghost, and he had to fight himself to keep from holding her so tightly she wouldn't be able to breathe. She stirred a little, but didn't wake.

The scent of the ocean surrounded her; more fragile and yet more perfect than any perfume. She smelled of sunlight, salt water, and hope. The hope that he might indeed have a future. One with someone other than his faithful, constant companions over the last millennia: loneliness and despair. The search for redemption alone was never enough to keep a man warm at night, not body or heart or soul.

But Serai—she was everything. If only she could ever forgive him.

If only he could trust her.

If only he could trust reality. He tightened his embrace, as if strength alone could capture moonlight.

Her eyes flew open and she stared up at him, terrified again, as if she remembered nothing, or else far too much. She started to speak, but her body suddenly went into spasm, and she arched up in his arms, her head almost smashing into his chin before he jerked his head back and out of the way. She screamed loud and long, with such a piercing shriek that two of Quinn's guards ran into the room, weapons at the ready.

"It's just a bad dream," he yelled at them. "Stay out."

"Hell of a bad dream," one of them observed.

But they left, and that's all he cared about. As she gasped for breath, he rocked back and forth, making soothing noises, trying to think of what might calm her down or wake her up or whatever it took to make her stop screaming as if she were dying.

The world might not survive the monster he would become if she left him for a second time.

"Daniel?" She looked up at him with those enormous ocean-blue eyes, eyes a man could drown in, and he knew that he was lost. "Why did you leave me? What really happened that day?"

"Shouldn't we talk about more current events? Like what just happened? What or who is the Emperor, and why is it affecting you like this?" He forced himself to release her when she pulled away from him to sit up on the pallet, leaning back against the wall.

She drew in deep breaths, and he tried not to think about what interesting things that did to her breasts under the filmy dress she had on, but hell, he was only a man. Vampire, yes; mage, once; politician, no more; but before and after all of that, he was only a man, and hot damn but she was beautiful.

"The Emperor is a gemstone from Poseidon's trident," she finally said, when her breathing was back under control. "One of the seven that the Atlanteans of my time scattered throughout the world when Atlantis dove beneath the sea."

"Why? And who had the balls to steal jewels from the sea god?"

"There's no need to be crude," she said, and he was intrigued to see the flush that rose in her cheeks, visible even by firelight.

She was blushing. Eleven thousand years old and still an innocent. The lustful images his mind had been playing as he watched her in the firelight washed away in a wave of guilt and shame. She was lost, in trouble, and hurting. She was a maiden, she'd said, and though part of him was primitively, stupidly glad that no man had ever touched her, the weight of the knowledge sobered him. She was a virginal Atlantean princess, and he was a monster. Beauty and the beast never had a happy ending together in real life. He of all beasts knew that.

"Poseidon gave his trident to Atlantis so that we could escape war on the surface," Serai said. "I think it was only supposed to be a temporary measure. But as the years, centuries, and then millennia passed, the secret of where the jewels had been originally hidden—not to mention where they had gone since then—was lost."

Daniel jumped up and walked around again, needing to put distance between them. "What does that have to do with you? I understand on the bigger level, Atlantis needs all the gems to rise, right. But why is the Emperor causing you pain?"

"The Emperor has special powers. Well, all the jewels do, actually. But one of the Emperor's powers is to sustain Atlanteans in stasis, through a connecting gemstone."

Daniel had heard stranger things. He nodded and motioned to her to continue.

Serai shrugged. "I'm not exactly sure of the mechanics of it, if that's what you're asking. Who really understands how magic works? All I know is that the analogy one of the priests used several thousand years ago resonated with me. He compared the Emperor to a great river like the Nile; both sustain life. And, like the Nile overflowing its banks to irrigate Egypt, once a year the Emperor flooded our minds with information, so when we were awakened, we weren't anachronistic, useless women with no knowledge of how the world and Atlantis had changed in our . . . absence."

Daniel realized belatedly that she'd been speaking English as well as she'd spoken ancient Atlantean. "How many languages do you speak?"

"I don't know. All of them?"

His mind flashed back to a movie he'd watched with Ven once on a rare evening the demands on an Atlantean warrior and a vampire leader abated enough for them to escape their responsibilities. "Can you do kung fu?"

"What? What are you talking about?" She stood up and pushed the heavy weight of her hair back from her face, igniting in him a powerful desire to be the one touching her hair. Kissing her sensual lips. Caressing— No.

Stop.

*Virgin.* In trouble. Not taking advantage of her. Not if he ever wanted to live with himself.

"What about kung fu?"

"Nothing. Never mind. Stupid random thought. So why is the jewel hurting you?"

She crossed to the fire and put her hands out to the heat, although it wasn't particularly cold in the cave. Not to him, at least. Maybe to a woman fresh out of thousands of years in a crystal prison, it felt freezing. He had no idea how to deal with this Serai, the woman who had stepped out of a fairy tale, so beautiful and so tempting.

"Sleeping Beauty," he murmured.

She glanced back at him over her shoulder, the fire silhouetting her curves through the thin material of the dress, and his body hardened. Wanting. Needing. Even his fangs were aching, trying to drop down, and he'd had complete control over them for centuries. He realized he was breathing in time with the beat of her heart, and he forced himself to back away as far as he could get. Still, it was a cave. He was maybe a dozen paces from her, a distance he could cross in a split second with vampiric speed.

She could be his, the monster inside him whispered. She

*belonged* to him. He could take her, right now, and never let her get away from him.

"Daniel, I need your help."

He sighed. The four deadliest words in any language, especially when spoken by a damsel in distress. He smiled at the thought of a woman who could become a saber-toothed tiger ever being a damsel in distress, but what the hell. He had his little quirks—the delusion that he could ever be a white knight foremost among them—and he was way past believing he could change.

"You're smiling?" Her voice rose, and he could tell she was annoyed. She'd gotten that little frown on her face, the same patrician, aristocratic expression that had warned her guards all those years ago that they'd better leave her alone for a while or face a highly unpleasant few hours.

"You need my help, and I gladly and most willingly give it, my lady," he said, sweeping his best, if quite rusty, bow. He'd been a blacksmith, not a courtier. "But I need more of the facts. What is the Emperor doing to you, and what do you need my help with?"

"It's connected to me and to the other maidens, who are still in stasis, and somebody is trying to use it. Someone has already tried to channel magic through it, and it nearly killed him . . . no, her," she said thoughtfully. "It felt like female magic. She's gone now, from my awareness, either dead or unconscious, but for a moment we were connected. I could feel the others, too. If this woman, this witch, tries to wield the Emperor again, it could kill us all."

At the thought of Serai's death, the breath left Daniel's body so fast and hard he nearly doubled over, but instead he put his hands on the hilts of the daggers he always wore, even in Washington.

Actually, especially in Washington.

"We need to find it. Now," he said, and his voice rasped as he formed the words.

"I can feel it," she said. "I think I can find it. We should leave now." She started toward the cave entryway, but stumbled before she'd gotten three steps.

"You have to rest first," Daniel said, catching her before she could fall, and steeling himself against the punch of bloodlust. "Sleep. Your body isn't used to so much activity. I don't know how you're walking at all, actually, after such a long period of inactivity. How are your muscles not atrophied?"

"The Emperor and the high priests over the years took care of that. Magic can achieve what science cannot, after all. Think of it. How am I even alive in a world that has changed beyond any possibility of recognition?"

She pulled away from him a little but then surrendered to his unspoken demand, leaning back against his chest and sighing. Daniel realized she was trembling, and he swept her into his arms and carried her back over to the pallet. He arranged the blankets around her again, prepared to wait on the floor near the entryway, blocking anyone from entering, but she stopped him with one slender hand on his arm. He stared down at the curve of her wrist and at her delicate fingers, wondering how something so clearly fragile had the power to stop him in his tracks.

"Please, stay with me?" she whispered. "I'm afraid to fall asleep. I've slept so long and . . . what if I never wake up? Please stay with me and promise me you'll wake me. Promise you won't let me slip away."

He looked up and was trapped. Caught in her gaze, fixed—immovable—by the crystalline hint of tears tangled in her long lashes. "I'll stay. Rest now, and we'll find your Emperor when you wake up."

She didn't close her eyes or relax a single muscle, and he realized she needed to hear the words.

"I promise," he said, and with a long, gentle sigh, she relaxed back onto the blankets, closed her eyes, and almost immediately fell into an exhausted sleep. He sat next to her, fighting his own need for sleep, content to watch her. An hour or so later, a quiet noise alerted him to Quinn's presence in the entryway.

"Is that her? The one you left behind?" Quinn looked

tired; even more tired and thinner than the month before when he'd last seen her.

"Yes. This is Serai," he said quietly, not wanting to wake his sleeping beauty.

"Get some rest, Daniel. I've got some of my top people on lookout. We're safe here."

He raised an eyebrow. "Even from Jack?"

"Even from Jack," she said, smiling a little. "He's still unhappy about the blood bond. We need to talk about that sometime," she added, her smile fading.

"I know."

She turned to leave, and then looked back. "I'm happy for you, Daniel. Don't screw this up."

"But that's what I do best," he whispered when he was sure Quinn could no longer hear him. He finally gave in to the impulse that had been driving him and smoothed a stray curl away from Serai's pale cheek. He thought of Quinn and the unwanted blood bond, and then of Deirdre, dying to protect him.

"I'll kill for you," he vowed to Serai's sleeping form. "I'll die for you. Whatever you need me to do, I'll do to keep you safe. And then I'll leave you, because that's the best gift I could ever give you. My absence."

She curled toward him, into the heat of his body, as if agreeing, and his resolve hardened even as his heart turned to ash inside his chest. He'd already planned to die once this day. Another time was no hardship at all, he swore to himself.

No hardship at all.

# Chapter 7

Quinn entered the main chamber of the cavern, deep in thought but still on her guard, to see that another Atlantean had joined the party. Some days she wished she'd never heard of the so-called lost continent, or at least that it had stayed lost. Hard to forget it, though, when her sister was married to the high prince and would soon be queen. Delicate, sweet Riley, queen of Atlantis. It boggled Quinn's mind. Or it would have, if she hadn't been living in a world gone crazy since the day nearly eleven years ago when vampires and shape-shifters worldwide had announced to the planet that they really did exist and then promptly started taking over, by any means necessary.

The political means were somebody else's problem, not Quinn's. It was the violent means employed by almost all bloodsuckers and the rogue shape-shifters that Quinn concerned herself with these days, and had for the past several years. A girl needed to keep busy, after all. Especially when the girl was leader of the entire North American rebel faction.

Not all of the humans were content to become sheep for the taking.

Her gaze returned to the Atlantean warrior taking up more than his fair share of space in the room, chatting with some of her people. Another ally, although a dangerous and probably unstable one. She could work with that, though. Hell, most of her best friends were dangerous and unstable. By the time she reached him, she was grinning.

"Reisen. Good to see you. How did it go?"

He raised an eyebrow, probably at her uncharacteristic good humor, and then waved at her with the arm that ended in a badly healed, scarred stump just above where his wrist had been before he'd pissed off one of the worst vampires ever to suck blood.

"Only one hand in the grave, so it's a good day," he said, grinning back at her.

It was her turn to be surprised. She didn't think she'd ever seen Reisen smile. He was an Atlantean lord who'd been exiled for daring to touch Poseidon's trident, or steal it, or something awful. Tried to stage a coup, maybe. The details were murky, and none of the Atlantean warriors she'd met had ever felt the need to enlighten her. Reisen himself had come to her and joined the human rebels with a need for vengeance—or maybe redemption—and a damn near suicidal fervor. He'd insisted on taking any mission that had the absolute least chance of success, and somehow he'd made it out of every single one not only alive but successful.

Usually injured, sometimes near death, but always successful. But never, ever smiling.

Until now.

Which, Quinn being Quinn, made her suspicious.

"Why are you smiling? What kind of deep-shit massive trouble have you brought me that could possibly cause you to move your rusty face muscles like that?"

He laughed, and she almost fell over. Laughed? Reisen?

She stalked to the cavern's opening and stared out into the sunlight of the beautiful, clear, Arizona morning, as it reflected off the glorious red rock surrounding them. As always, the sight of this tiny pocket of nature's beauty, unspoiled by death or war or vampires and their evil plots, nearly brought her to her knees in gratitude that there were at least a few of these places left on earth.

"Nope," she said. "No sign of the apocalypse. And yet Reisen just laughed. Is it some horrible bit of magic gone bad?"

Reisen crossed to stand beside her, still smiling. "You smiled, too," he pointed out. "Which is almost as rare. So quit being such a smart ass and tell me who the Atlantean woman is that you're hiding in this cave somewhere. Jack wouldn't let me go seek her out."

She suddenly realized just how very, very wrong and bad this could go. "Reisen," she began slowly, casting around for a way to let him know that the Atlantean woman was with the vampire.

She'd been wrong. The apocalypse *was* on the way. Nothing good could come of this.

"I haven't seen one of my people for almost a year now," Reisen said, looking out at the view, his voice tense with barely suppressed excitement. He clenched and unclenched his hands, probably not even realizing he was doing it. "Did Conlan send her? Is she here to tell me I can go home?"

Quinn turned to her people and gave a hand signal, and they all headed out on patrol, giving her the room so she could talk with Reisen alone. She had no idea where Jack had gone. Probably off pouting somewhere, if tigers could ever be said to pout. Mostly, they just killed and ate whatever annoyed them.

"Reisen, I don't know if Conlan sent her. I didn't get the impression she was a royal emissary, but what do I know about Atlantean politics? All I know is she was in rough shape, and she and Daniel went to get some rest before they make with the explanations."

He whirled around so fast she would have thought he had vampiric speed if she hadn't seen Atlantean warriors in action before.

"Daniel? What in the name of Poseidon's balls is that bloodsucker doing anywhere near an Atlantean woman?" He smashed his fist into the nearest wall so hard that chips of rock shattered and fell to the floor. "I'll kill him. Where are they?"

She held up her hands, palms out, and stepped back so she was standing between the enraged warrior and the entrance to the short corridor that led to the room where Daniel and Serai were resting.

"Unstable and dangerous," she muttered, sighing. "Why am I always right?"

"What are you talking about? Daniel? The vampire is unstable, too? I'll kill him if he touches a hair on her head or a single drop of her blood."

Reisen strode toward Quinn, not even slowing as she moved to block him. In one swift motion, he put his hands on either side of her waist and lifted her up and out of his way. She sighed. She really hated being short.

Luckily, she had other advantages in a fight.

"I'd advise you not to move," she told him in her most pleasant voice, and he froze, hands still on her waist.

Smart man.

"You may notice my knife is pressing into your nuts, big guy. You might want those, in the future. I've noticed most men seem ridiculously fond of theirs," she continued, smiling angelically up at him as she pressed a little harder with the hand holding the switchblade to his family jewels.

The color drained out of his face, and a look of horror replaced the fury in his eyes.

"I'd do what she says," a cheerful voice added. "Have you met One-Nut Mikey? He didn't listen and, well, you can figure out the rest."

Quinn clenched her jaw shut against the laugh that threatened. Trust Mel to back her up and even embellish the story a little. Reisen turned his head slightly, careful not to jostle Quinn, and his eyes widened. Quinn couldn't stop the laugh from escaping that time. Mel had that effect on people.

"Having to teach another little object lesson, Quinn?" Mel sang out, dropping her overstuffed backpack on the cavern floor and stretching her curvy body.

Reisen's eyes widened even farther. Mel stretching was like catnip to men, and apparently Atlantean men were no exception.

"Are you ready to listen to me?" Quinn asked, drawing Reisen's attention back to her and her pointy object lesson–giver.

He nodded. "Fine. Talk fast."

"Ooh, this one is feisty." Mel took off her cap and shook out her short curls, which were blond with blue tips this week. She looked like a maniacal elf princess. The mischievous kind. You'd never guess she was a brilliant computer genius. The cropped shirt and low-rider jeans, combined with the hair and the skull jewelry, certainly wouldn't give her away. "Can I have him?"

Reisen growled, and Quinn rolled her eyes at both of them. "Down, Melody. Be nice to the Atlantean warrior. You two have to go on a mission for me. Together."

Melody, hacker extraordinaire and occasional thief, grinned and blew Reisen a kiss. "Oh, we're going to have so much fun."

"I'm not going anywhere with her," Reisen said. "I need to have a serious conversation with the Atlantean woman. Now."

"I'd like to meet the Atlantean woman, too. This place is better than a soap opera sometimes. Where's Jack?" Mel said, dropping to sit cross-legged on the floor and taking an apple and her laptop out of her backpack. "Speaking of excitement, what is it this time, Quinn? What can I steal for our fearless leader?"

Quinn waited until Mel swallowed the bite of apple, so she didn't need to do any Heimlich maneuvering. "I want you to steal a bank."

〜〜〜〜

Serai stirred, swimming back up through the layers of exhaustion to wakefulness. She felt like she hadn't slept at all, but she had certain needs that were fast becoming urgent. Physical needs she hadn't felt in so long she hadn't even remembered how intense they could be. Her stomach also felt like a gaping, empty hole, and she realized she was hungry. Actually *hungry*.

"I can eat," she said, bolting upright on the hard pallet.

Daniel, who'd apparently been sleeping on the floor next to her, shot up into the air, both hands clutching daggers. His hair was mussed, and after her initial surprise, she wanted to laugh. He looked so funny.

Also gorgeous. *Hot*, even, to use the current slang.

His hair had grown long, past his shoulders, and he kept it tied back with a piece of leather cord. It was still a deep black, but there were a few strands of pure silver mixed in with the silky darkness. His features had matured; all planes and angles. He was now a dangerous, deadly man where once she'd known a boy. The thought sent a thrill of adrenaline through her, and she ducked her head to hide her blush. He must have known many women in all that time; it wasn't as if he'd be interested in an ignorant maiden. A really, really, *really* old maiden.

She didn't have time to worry about it, though, her body reminded her. She needed privacy and certain facilities. Now.

"Daniel, I need some privacy—"

"Have I offended you?" He was at her side in an instant. "Damn it, I don't know how to treat a gentle-bred lady anymore. Not that I ever did. Whatever I—"

Her face would surely catch fire from the heat. "No. I need . . . privacy. Facilities. To . . . wash my face."

"Oh. *Oh*. Of course." He jumped up and held his hand out to her. "Let's find out how they're dealing with that here."

"And then food," she said, brushing her wrinkled skirts down. "Food and drink and things I can taste. Oh, Daniel, after all these years, I want so badly to taste everything."

His jaw clenched and he took a deep breath in through his nose, and then he simply nodded. "Got it," he rasped out. "Taste. Everything. Come on."

She blushed again, not exactly sure why, but her mention of tasting everything had affected him oddly.

One of Quinn's people, a woman with startlingly red

hair, was happy to show Serai out a side passageway into the bright sunshine and to the environmentally friendly way the small camp was dealing with personal needs, and then they met up with Daniel, who'd waited as near to the entrance to the cavern as he could get without facing full daylight.

She'd almost forgotten. He looked so normal. But night-walkers couldn't walk in the sun without facing a hideous death by flames. On that horrible day when invaders had attacked Atlantis, the mage who'd helped her with Daniel had told her that much before he'd disappeared and taken Daniel away from her forever. Or so she'd thought. Here he was again, and she needed every ounce of self-possession to keep from throwing herself at him like the silly girl he must think she was.

She called on the haughty demeanor she'd seen so often in her former life and lifted her chin. "Now we may eat."

His gaze dropped to her neck and she gasped so loudly that he raised an eyebrow.

"Don't worry, I didn't take that as an invitation to suck your delicious blood, sweetheart," he said sardonically. "Let's find you some food and figure out how to find that jewel of yours."

"It's not mine," she pointed out, but he'd already turned his back to her, probably disgusted with her stupidity. Of course he wasn't going to *eat* her. She'd just been alone and asleep, defenseless, really, with him, and he'd never shown any signs of going mad with bloodlust and attacking her.

A small voice in her head wondered why not.

He made a beckoning motion with his hand, and she followed sedately along, drawn as much by the sheer pleasure of watching him walk—oh, the man still had the loveliest backside she'd ever seen, even if it did make her cheeks hot to think it—as by the scent of grilled meat wafting through the cavern.

"Food," she moaned, and suddenly sedate wasn't good enough. She lifted her skirt and all but flew after Daniel, looking for the source of that wonderful aroma. After all, she hadn't eaten in more than eleven thousand years.

Quinn stood in the main entrance to the cave, eyes closed and face lifted to the sun. She was lovely, in a scruffy, too-thin way, and Serai's stomach clenched again, this time at the idea that there was probably much more to Quinn's relationship with Daniel than mere friendship. She'd seen how they were with each other.

Quinn must have heard them, and she turned to smile at Serai. "We have plenty to eat, and you must be hungry," she said, pointing to a long metal table covered with plates and bowls. "Please help yourself."

Serai returned her smile, almost in spite of herself, and queued up in line behind two of the guards she'd seen earlier. They nodded to her but didn't speak, too busy filling up their own plates. She selected a plate and then stopped, stunned at the sight and smell of so much food.

Daniel stepped up next to her and looked at her empty plate. "Not fancy enough for your ladyship?"

She heard the mocking challenge in his tone but was too paralyzed to snap back at him. Instead, she shook her head, and when she spoke, her voice trembled a little.

"I don't know what to try first. I haven't touched actual food in more than eleven millennia, Daniel. I don't . . . I don't even know what I like or don't like anymore. Will my stomach reject food? Do I dare try unfamiliar plants, like that green one? How do they make it transparent like that?"

The hard lines of his face softened, and he almost smiled. "I'm sorry. I didn't think," he said softly. "Of course you haven't. Why don't you do what someone recuperating from an illness does? Try a little of a few different things and see how your system takes it."

He raised one hand and brushed a tear from her cheek, making her feel a fool. She hadn't even known she was crying, and over food, of all the stupid things to finally make her break down. Before she could apologize, or sink into the floor, or do any of a dozen other things she might have done, he poked one long finger at the clear green food.

"And this? Is Jell-O. I'm not sure that it's really food at

all," he said in an overly loud whisper, making her wonder why everyone else started laughing.

She took his advice and chose a few tiny portions of the most recognizable foods. A bit of what clearly came from a game bird or domesticated fowl. Fresh fruit. A sliver of a luscious cake that she probably shouldn't risk, but she couldn't resist the rich, sugary aroma that rose up to tantalize her. She noticed that Daniel piled a plate high with nearly as much food as the human men had taken, which answered the question of whether or not the nightwalkers—vampires, they called them these days—still ate food or subsisted entirely on blood. Her neck tingled at the thought of Daniel biting her. She wasn't sure if the sensation was from revulsion or desire.

He sat on the floor next to the small stool she'd chosen to sit on, crossing his long, elegant legs in front of him and resting his plate on his lap. He glanced at the contents of her plate and grinned up at her.

"Well? What will you try first?"

She bit her lip, wondering the same thing. Of course she should eat the fruit and meat first, that was only proper, but the sweet dessert tempted her so much.

"Go for it," he advised, following her gaze. "One of the few benefits of being all grown up is that you can eat your dessert first."

She laughed and was rewarded by his answering smile. Still, she hesitated until he leaned over, speared a bit of cake on his fork, and held it up to her lips. She was shocked by the intimacy of the gesture; only a courting or wedded couple would feed each other in Atlantis. Or so it had been thousands of years ago.

Daniel's dark eyes held a challenge and something else. Admiration? Desire? A tingle of almost savage glee raced through her, and she leaned forward to allow him to place the cake in her mouth.

*I'm not in Atlantis anymore.*

She closed her lips around the fork and moaned with pure, hedonistic joy at the sugary explosion of taste in her mouth. Oh, by all the gods and goddesses, this was surely the most wonderful pastry she'd ever tasted. She opened her eyes to see that Daniel's had gone dark and wild, and even she, with her limited knowledge of men, knew a moment of very feminine triumph.

He wanted her. In that moment, no matter what else or who else entangled him, he wanted *her*.

"If you make a noise like that again, Serai, I'm not responsible for what I do to you," he murmured, his voice a rasp of steel over velvet, and suddenly parts of her body that had felt nothing for millennia warmed and tingled in an entirely fascinating way.

As he slowly drew the fork back, she parted her lips to release it, and gained another small victory when he inhaled sharply. His face had gone hard and predatory, and she suddenly knew that had they been alone, he would have pounced on her. She wasn't quite sure if she would have fled or pounced right back. Something about the way he was looking at her, as though she herself were a bit of sugary cake that he wanted to taste, made her think pounce.

Definitely pounce.

A wave of warmth started around the vicinity of her toes, heading north, and she enjoyed it far too much.

"I hope you like the chicken," one of the women guards said to her. "That's my mama's special recipe. I'm June, by the way."

Serai tried a bite of chicken and smiled at June, delighted simply to be awake; sitting, eating, and having an actual conversation. If only people knew how wondrous it was to do such ordinary things. "I like it very much. Please thank your mother for me and tell her it is wonderful."

A hint of sadness crossed the woman's face. "Thank you, honey, but Mama is up in heaven with the angels. She got in the way of a vampire."

Daniel stopped eating and rested his fork on his plate, then respectfully nodded his head to June. "I am sorry for your loss."

Serai was impressed with the woman's dignified demeanor. Not a hint of anger toward Daniel showed in her expression or manner.

"I thank you for that, but you should know that I don't blame you for what happened to my mama any more than I blame Jack for what happened to my uncle or, for that matter, blame Quinn for what humans have done wrong in the world," June said with quiet dignity. "There's just no accounting for evil and meanness, and we can't judge a species by a few bad apples."

"You are truly wise, Lady June," Serai said, handing her plate to Daniel and standing up to curtsy to the woman and give honor to those she had lost. "May the oceans of your ancestors bless and protect you and your family."

June wiped tears from her cheeks and enfolded Serai in a huge hug.

"Oh, bless your heart, honey." She patted Serai's back and then let her go before pointing at Daniel. "You take care of this nice girl or you'll be hearing from me, young man."

Daniel nodded gravely, although Serai saw a hint of a smile playing around his lips, probably at being called "young man" by this youngling who'd only lived a handful of decades. "I promise I will."

June bustled off, and Serai resumed her seat and her exploration of the fruit that was so like and yet unlike Atlantean blushberries. She held the large, ripe, red fruit up and raised an eyebrow.

"Strawberry," Daniel said. "How's your stomach doing?"

"So far, so good." She took a bite of the strawberry, almost humming with happiness as the fruit's sweet and tart taste exploded on her tongue. Just for a short while, sitting here and eating what was quite like a picnic back home, she could almost forget the danger she and the others faced. She could almost be an ordinary woman, not a freak conjured by magic and the dictates of an ancient society's breeding program. Right at that moment, she thought she would be perfectly happy to never, ever step foot in Atlantis again.

Naturally, that's when the Atlantean warrior raced into

the cave and, taking in the room at a glance, leapt across the floor toward Daniel, drawing a lethal-looking sword as he came.

"If you hurt her, I will end you, vampire," the warrior shouted.

Faster than thought itself, Daniel was up and off the floor, blocking Serai from the madman. Daniel had drawn his daggers, but she'd seen sword against daggers when Atlantis was attacked, and she never wanted to see it again. Especially not when Daniel was the one with only the daggers.

But before she could even scream, it was over. In midair, Daniel twisted and ducked under the warrior's sword arm and disarmed him, and then slammed his elbow into the man's face on the way down. She'd been right, she saw, staring down at his unconscious face on the floor at her feet. She hadn't mistaken those features. He was clearly and classically an Atlantean warrior, and he'd hit the ground so hard the dust he'd displaced was still settling on and around him.

She looked at his body for the distinguishing mark of the elite Warriors of Poseidon, but he was fully covered, not even his arms bared, and the mark was rarely found on a warrior's hand . . .

She froze, and the scream she'd bottled up earlier found its way out of her throat. She screamed again and pointed, and only when she realized that Quinn was staring at her like she was a lunatic did she stop and manage to speak.

"Why, Daniel? Why did you do it?"

Daniel's dark brows drew together as he looked from her to the fallen warrior. "Why? Did you know him? He's fine. He'll be awake in a few minutes."

She backed away, fighting the waves of dizziness that threatened to claim her. "No," she cried, shaking her head back and forth and pointing at the unmistakable evidence. "No, no, no, no. Why did you have to cut off his hand?"

Impossibly, cruelly, hideously, Daniel began to laugh. "Serai, you don't understand."

Serai didn't want to understand a world where a man she thought she loved laughed at dismembering his foes. Instead, she ran, pushing past a startled-looking Quinn. She ran, escaping all of them, out into the bright sunlight, where neither shadows nor vampires could follow.

# Chapter 8

## Atlantis, the palace gardens

Conlan looked around at his family and wondered how to begin a conversation that would almost certainly explode into a battle, right there in the middle of the flowering bushes and blooming trees. Not exactly a typical battle scene, by any measure. His wife and he didn't exactly see eye to eye on the issue of the maidens in stasis.

Actually, it was more a matter of degree. He wanted to find a way to release them. She wanted to find a way to release them—yesterday.

His brother, by title the King's Vengeance, and by reality the high prince's chief pain in the ass, solved the problem for him.

"So," Ven said, lounging on a marble bench next to the fountain. "This is a cluster, uh," he cast a quick glance at his consort, Erin, a very powerful human witch with little tolerance for profanity, "cluster futz of royal proportions."

Lord Justice, Conlan's other brother, laughed. Technically Justice was Conlan and Ven's half brother, but nobody set store by that. He sat on the ground with his back leaning against his consort, the human archaeologist and object reader Keely. "That's one way to put it. Does anybody know what happened? For example, how Serai got out, where she went, or what in the nine hells is going on?"

Conlan's wife, Riley, high princess of Atlantis and former human social worker, shook her head. The sight of her glorious wealth of red-gold hair flying in the slight breeze reminded Conlan of what they'd been doing with and to each other during one of their infant son's increasingly rare naps, before the crisis in the temple occurred.

Not that this was the time to think of sex. Not even earth-shatteringly good sex. Though Riley's eyes were flashing with so much anger he doubted he'd get to do much more than think about sex for quite a while.

"I told you we needed to release them from that impossibly cruel prison," she said. "I've been trying to get the elders to move their venerable asses on this subject since I first came to this archaic, chauvinistic, sorry excuse for a society."

"You love it here," he said mildly, knowing he was right.

She looked around, her gaze lingering on the flowers and fountains before moving to the delicate crystal-and-marble curves of the palace towers and spires. "Yes, I do. Except for this. Conlan, it's wrong to keep women imprisoned like prized heifers at the county fair for an ancient idea of a breeding program. You know it, I know it, and—"

"Virginsicles," Keely interjected, a dark look on her face. Justice wrapped an arm around her legs and glanced up at her. He never let the stunning redhead get far from him, since her love was the only thing that had ever been able to help him control his dual nature.

Keely almost absently smoothed a strand of Justice's long blue hair off her pants leg and then scowled at Conlan. "I call them the virgin popsicles. Frozen in that damn stasis until they get to be released to be bedded and bred."

"Trust an archaeologist to be blunt," Ven drawled.

Erin lightly smacked Ven on the back of head. "She's right."

"I know she's right. I didn't say she wasn't right, just that she was blunt," Ven said. "Also, ow."

Conlan felt like he was rapidly losing any slight bit of control he'd had over the meeting. He should have called them to the war room. He felt he had at least some semblance of control—or the illusion of it—over his opinionated family members there.

"We've been trying. You know we've been trying," he told them all, but he was looking right at Riley. "The last time the priests and mages were able to release one of the maidens from stasis was when they freed my mother, hundreds of years ago. We have been unable to use the Emperor since then."

"Then how exactly did you expect to marry Serai?" Justice asked, making Conlan want to kick his ass.

Riley's glare turned from hot to glacial in a split second, since, after all, they were talking about the woman who'd been Conlan's intended bride. But he couldn't help or change past history. All he could do was fix the present and do his best to chart the future.

"The priests didn't tell me," he muttered. "The previous temple chief attendant was sure he'd be able to figure out what was wrong, and the high priest before Alaric was afraid to let anybody know there were problems for some asinine reason. We've been working on it since we found out, which was when they were trying to release Serai from stasis for our, ah, for—"

"For your royal wedding," Riley said through clenched teeth.

"Yes. Yes, damn it, yes," he said, frustrated and worried all at once. "We've had our best mages and Alaric himself trying to discover how to free those six women from stasis, and the best they can do is tell me there has been something wrong with the connection to the Emperor. Now, apparently, it's worse."

"And Serai escaped? Or vanished? What exactly happened?" Erin leaned forward. She'd been gone to one of her coven's council meetings on the surface when it happened, and Ven must not have had time to fill her in yet.

"She definitely escaped," Conlan said grimly. "She somehow blasted out of the stasis chamber, knocked out the attendants, then made it to the portal dock and knocked out both of my guards—although how a woman who has been in stasis for thousands of years can take out two of our best guards is beyond me—and fled. Somewhere. The gods themselves only know where."

Erin shrugged. "The answer to part of your problem is easy enough. She has enough magic to take out at least half of all of your warriors in one shot. Maybe more. Maybe all."

Conlan, Justice, and Ven all looked at her in utter shock. "What?"

"Didn't you realize it?" Erin walked over to one of the bushes and leaned down to sniff a cluster of pale pink flowers. She turned back to face them and surveyed their surprised expressions, then shrugged again. "I thought you knew. Just walking by the temple where they slept gave me such a charge of powerful, yet contained, magic that I got a buzz like a champagne drunk."

"Maybe it took a witch or at least someone sensitive to magic to feel it," Keely said. "I've been inside several times, in the course of my studies of everything about Atlantis, and never felt anything like that."

Justice shot up off the ground and grabbed Keely's shoulders, lifting her up and almost off her feet. "Did you touch the stasis pods? That kind of magic could seriously harm you. We would be very distraught if you were to be harmed again."

Ven met Conlan's gaze. When Justice started to speak of himself in the plural, it meant the deadly Nereid half of his soul was rousing to fury, and nobody within reach was safe when that happened. Nobody but Keely, of course.

Keely knew it, too. She put her hands on either side of Justice's face and leaned forward to kiss him. "Put me down, you Neanderthal, or I'll dye your hair pink when you're sleeping. Think how silly you'd look."

Everyone held a breath until Justice grumbled but lowered her feet to the ground and then embraced her tightly. "It's Nereid, not Neanderthal," he muttered.

Keely laughed and hugged him back. Justice released her, but didn't let go of her hand.

"No, I didn't touch the stasis pods. I learned my lesson about objects of magical power with Poseidon's trident." She bit her lip. "Maybe, if it's the only way, I could try—"

"No. We forbid it," Justice roared, and Conlan pulled Riley behind him out of pure reflex. He didn't think Justice would ever harm her, but when the Nereid was out of control, there might be explosions.

"No," Conlan said. "It's too dangerous and probably not useful. The objects tell you something about the past, right? What we need to know is where she went after she escaped."

"I wish you'd quit saying 'escaped,' like she truly was a prisoner," Riley said, folding her arms across her chest. "She *left*. I'd leave, too, if I'd been held hostage against my ovaries for all that time. I'd have done more than just leave a few people unconscious behind me, too."

Conlan very carefully did not smile at his fierce but tenderhearted warrior woman. She would never have hurt innocents, in spite of her tough talk, but he understood her point very well.

"I intend to make an official apology to her and to the remaining five, as soon as I can find Serai and find a way to release the other maidens," he said.

"Oh, I'm sure an apology will help," Riley said, rolling her eyes. "Hey, we're sorry we stole the past eleven thousand years of your life, here's a gold watch. Have a nice day."

"I'd like a gold watch," Ven offered. Erin smacked him in the head again.

"Look, we'll do whatever necessary—give them gold, jewels, houses, whatever they want," Conlan said. "First, we have to find them. And right now? I'm worried that Serai is lost somewhere and hurt. What could she possibly know about surviving on the surface? What if she stepped out of the portal right into the middle of a vampire's lair?"

A cold wind swept through the air, and all six of them looked up to see Poseidon's high priest, Alaric, materialize in one of his dramatic entrances. "It's worse than you realize," Alaric said, as usual not wasting time with small talk. "I've just been to the temple, and the magic that maintains the stasis is in flux. We either figure out how to release those women now, or they may all die."

Ven raised an eyebrow. "How's Quinn?"

"I did not see the rebel leader on this trip to the surface," Alaric said, his eyes glowing bright green with barely restrained power.

Ven snorted. "You mean, you didn't see the woman you're ass-over-priestly-teakettle in love with?"

Erin lifted a hand to smack Ven in the head again, but this time he caught her wrist and kissed her palm.

"Perhaps you should consider your next words carefully, Your Highness," Alaric told Ven. "Should you wish to continue life as one of the palace peacocks, I can make that happen. How is your appetite for birdseed?"

The high priest balanced a sphere of glowing power in his palm, a not-so-veiled threat.

Ven held up his hands in a gesture of surrender. "Dude. Message understood. But you call me Your Highness again, and I'll kick your ass."

Conlan put a hand on Alaric's shoulder. "Stand down, my friend. Ven has chronic mouth-runs-faster-than-his-brain syndrome, as we all know, but none is better in a fight. I doubt he'd serve Atlantis so well as a preening bird."

"About Quinn, though, Alaric," Riley said. "Have you seen my sister recently? She still hasn't met the baby."

"No, I have not. She is entangled with a problem in the southwest United States. Something about bankers funding magic to help the vampires cement their control over the human population."

"A trifecta of bad, bad, and worse," Keely said. "No offense, Erin, but the last thing we need is witches on the side of the vampires."

"That certainly doesn't offend me," Erin said grimly.

"We've been fighting just that in my own coven. The way so many humans hate and fear witches makes the vampire's acceptance very appealing to those who play deadly games with the black, though. An alliance between vampires and sorcerers would be a catastrophe."

"We're not going to let that happen. Not now, not ever," Conlan said. "We are the Warriors of Poseidon, and the vow our predecessors first swore eleven thousand years ago is the same we swear today. We will protect humanity from dark witches and vampires, both. Now, more than ever, we need to find every single jewel lost from Poseidon's trident, so Atlantis can rise to the surface and take her place in the world."

"I'm a little tired of protecting people who *help* the ones trying to conquer them," Alaric said, closing his hand over the energy sphere and squashing it. Sparks flew out between his fingers and fluttered to the ground, burning the grass wherever they fell.

"Not all humans are sheep, Alaric," Erin said, as patiently as if she and Alaric hadn't had the same conversation so many times before. "Wait. Back up a minute. What did you say about Quinn and black magic sorcerers? That's not good. Not good at all. Does she need help?"

Ven's lazy grin disappeared. "Why do you think that putting yourself in danger is the answer to every problem, Erin?"

Erin's mouth fell open as she stared up at Ven. "Seriously? Did you just ask me that, Warrior Man?"

"That's different," he muttered, flushing a dark red.

"No, it isn't," Riley said, standing up. "Does my sister need help? Maybe I should go to her, since she won't come to me."

For the first time since he'd watched, terrified, as she struggled through a difficult birth to bring their son into the world, Conlan felt true panic. Riley in a nest of vampires and black magic practitioners? Over his dead body. But he knew better than to try to forbid it, either as prince or as husband.

"Aidan needs you here, *mi amara*. At least until he is

weaned. Or did you plan to take our son, the heir to the Atlantean throne, into the midst of danger, too?"

Riley glared at him. "Of course I didn't plan that. I just . . . I hate feeling helpless while Quinn is in danger, and now Serai and the other women, too. I need something to do."

"I feel the same way," Erin added.

Keely nodded. "I'm no witch or warrior, but I'm pretty good with planning and a fair hand with a shotgun. Just tell me what I can do to help, and let's get to it. Those women don't have much time, if Alaric is right, and he almost always is."

Alaric bowed to her. "So pleasant to have someone acknowledge reality. Although the qualifier 'almost' was unnecessary."

Justice pulled Keely closer and glared at the high priest. "Don't humor him, Keely. His head will grow larger than the dome covering Atlantis."

"Somebody has to go to Arizona and find out if Quinn needs help," Riley said.

"I will go," Alaric said, in a voice that rang with finality.

Since Conlan had been planning to ask him to do just that, he had no problem with it. "Fine. Before you go, though, is there anything else you can do here to help in the temple?"

Alaric shook his head. "Horace knows the magic of the stasis better than any in the recorded history of the temple. If anyone can keep them stable or find a way to release them, it's him. All my presence and interference is accomplishing is distracting him and making him nervous."

"You? Make someone nervous? Say it isn't so," Ven said.

Alaric glared at Ven, and Conlan ignored them both. "Then go. Find out what Quinn needs," Conlan ordered his high priest, as if Alaric ever took orders anyway. Conlan cast a glance at his wife's pale face before continuing. "Then see if you can convince her to come back here with you for a visit. Tell her that her sister needs her."

Riley's smile was reward enough for any king, and Conlan allowed himself a deep breath as the smallest portion of the weight on his shoulders lifted. International politics, Atlantean magic, the protection of humanity—it was an enormous burden, all of it, but one he would gladly shoulder forever, if only his wife continued to smile at him like that.

Damn. Alaric was right. Marriage was turning him into a girl.

Conlan turned to watch the high priest as he strode off toward the temple, presumably to offer final instructions before he returned to the surface. If Alaric and Quinn ever did manage to work things out, Conlan would laugh his ass off to see Alaric's turn to be humbled by love.

Oh, yeah, he couldn't wait for that. Payback, as the saying went, was a barnacle that bit you in the nuts.

He turned to the rest of them. "Back to the war room, I'm afraid, after we dine. Atlantis must rise, and soon, and now we need to plan for every possible reaction and outcome."

Keely shook her head. "Have you heard the saying 'God laughs when man plans'?"

He nodded ruefully. "I've gone one better. I've *heard* a god laugh when he learned my plans."

Keely's eyes widened, and then she laughed. "I'm never going to get used to this place, am I?"

"We certainly hope you do," Justice said smugly. "We will never let you leave."

This time Keely smacked Justice on the back of the head, and everybody laughed as they headed into the palace to eat. Conlan didn't begrudge them a moment of lightness in a long line of crises. He'd been ruling Atlantis long enough to know that they must take their moments of peace when they could. They never lasted long.

# Chapter 9

### The cavern

Daniel crouched in place, clinging to the ceiling of the cavern, not even bothering to try to appear remotely human. So the rebels feared him. They should fear him. He'd run into the sunlight after Serai, only falling back to the healing darkness of the cave when Jack, of all people, had shoved his burning body out of the sun's deadly reach. Then, his body still smoking, enraged by the pain but most of all by his own helplessness—*yet again*—to help the woman he loved, Daniel had systematically destroyed everything he could get his hands on.

The two men who'd rushed in to try to stop him would regret that act of foolishness for a very long time. Quinn had finally thrown her hands up in disgust and left him to what she'd termed his "childish temper tantrum."

He had a shameful feeling she might have been right, but it didn't matter. Nothing mattered but getting to Serai. He knew she was safe; Jack had followed her and was standing guard near her in tiger form, which probably made Serai feel safer than she would have felt had a man unknown to her offered to do so.

It figured. Daniel had spent his entire life in love with a woman who felt safer with a wild jungle cat than with a person. There was a lesson in there somewhere, but he'd be damned if he could figure out what it was.

He laughed humorlessly and dropped down to land on the floor. He'd be damned anyway. Didn't the religious folk say vampires had no souls? His brief hope that he'd found salvation had been as foolish as it had been short-lived. He'd found a woman who wanted nothing to do with him— who believed him capable of amputating a man's hand in a simple fight.

Well. Of course he was capable of just that, but he wouldn't . . . he didn't . . . at least, not to allies. That would have to be good enough. The only thing keeping him from descending into irretrievable madness was that she'd refused to speak to Reisen, too. Once Quinn had followed Serai and explained about Reisen's hand, Serai had, according to Quinn, shot a withering look at Reisen and demanded by what right he had attacked her companion.

Reisen had pleaded with her to hear his side, but Serai had ignored him as if he didn't exist and asked Quinn for a little peace. Quinn had agreed, Jack had volunteered, Serai had asked for him to resume tiger form, and all of that had happened nearly two hours ago.

The longest two hours of Daniel's life.

Quinn walked back into the cavern and stood, hands on hips, and shot a challenging stare at Daniel. "So? Who's cleaning up this mess? I liked that cake, too."

He looked around the area and realized that bits and pieces of food, drinks, and the table and chairs lay everywhere. One table leg was embedded in the ceiling. He didn't actually remember doing that. He'd always been good at repressing bad memories and making them disappear, but as for the detritus of a destroyed meal, he was as useless as . . . No.

Making things disappear. A long-buried memory of night-walker guild magic surfaced, and he chased it to its source. One of the darker lessons of the guild. When the bloodlust conquered reason, the evidence of murder must be made to disappear.

Humans with wooden stakes had outnumbered the night-walkers then, too.

He closed his eyes and called on powers he hadn't used in a very, very long time. As Serai had reminded him, once he had been a master mage in the Nightwalker Guild. Some little bit of that magic should remain, even though he hadn't used it in thousands of years. What did he need magic for, when ordinary vampire strength had been sufficient?

This, though, was a more delicate task than breaking heads or rescuing humans. He searched for the thin line of silvery power, buried deep in his consciousness, and carefully lifted it with his mind. "*Aidez moi,*" he whispered. *Help me.*

The language spoken didn't matter, but he'd always liked French for magic. He sent the silver ribbon of power out into and around the room, and the debris vanished. Quinn shivered violently when the magic passed over and through her, but said nothing until the task was done.

"Nice," she said dryly. "You can always fall back on a housekeeping job if the vampire politician thing doesn't work out."

"I'm no longer Primator. I quit."

"Why?"

He sliced a hand through the air to cut off the questions. He should have known better. This was Quinn.

"I'm an emotional empath, you know that. Even without the blood bond," she said. "I can feel your pain at not being able to go after her. Why don't you fill the twenty minutes or so until the sun sets by telling me about her?"

"Why?" He sped through the room so fast that she surely couldn't see him. He stopped mere inches from her. "Why do you care?"

She tilted her head and looked up at him. "Because I'm your friend, you idiot. One of the few you have, I'm guessing. So tell me about her. How did you meet?"

He glared at her, which had no effect, and considered

tying her up and gagging her, which wouldn't be worth it. She was right, anyway. His internal clock told him he had twenty-one minutes exactly until it was safe for him to step out of the damned cavern.

"Fine. Let me tell you a fairy tale. This one is called 'The Princess and the Blacksmith,'" he said caustically.

She smiled and dropped down to sit cross-legged on the floor. "Oh, good. I hope it has a happy ending."

"I seriously doubt it. Okay, let's waste both of our time. Once upon a time," he began, "long, long ago . . ."

∽⸻⸺∾

## Eleven thousand years ago, Atlantis

*Our hero, let's call him Daniel, was a young apprentice blacksmith on a life-changing voyage. He'd traveled with his master to the home of the most wondrous metals in the known world—Atlantis. He found magic in the people, the land, and the metal itself. A marvelous metal called orichalcum sparkled in both day and night as if the sun's rays and moonbeams each had poured their light into its very essence. Daniel, who was young and foolish, had believed he could be content for the rest of his life if only he could have the opportunity in his free time, when the day's work was done, to create works of art and maybe even jewelry with such a metal. Similar to copper and silver, orichalcum was rarer and more pure than either and more valuable than both.*

*Of course, that which is rare and valuable is coveted by men, and the value of orichalcum was one of the reasons why so many kings and armies had attacked the Seven Isles more and more frequently as of late, causing all of Atlantis to be in a state of armed defense. But orichalcum wasn't the only reason for the attacks, or even the most crucial. Because when men came to attack and conquer and plunder, they mainly came for another, far more primal and brutal reason. They came to abduct the most sought after prizes of all: Atlantean women for their wives.*

"Women are still thought of as chattel in some places in the world," Quinn interjected bitterly. "Eleven thousand years later, and still the same bullshit."

Daniel aimed a long look at her. "Do you want me to tell this or not?"

She nodded, and he continued.

*When Daniel first met Serai, he understood all of it. She was so beautiful that the gods themselves were rumored to want her. He met her when she came to pick up a piece of jewelry in the shop next to the smithy where he was newly apprenticed. They struck up a friendship, all the more intense for being forbidden. Serai was almost a princess; as the daughter of a powerful, very rich Atlantean lord, who stood high in the ranks of Atlantis's elders, she was destined for a very good match, perhaps even a royal one. Her father would never allow her to become involved with a lowly metalworker apprentice.*

*Daniel's new mentor, the master jeweler and metalworker who owned both the shop and the smithy, was an eccentric man. He only worked in the shop at night since he'd hired a full-time blacksmith for the smithy, and he left Daniel to craft jewelry and run the shop during the day, claiming that he knew an honest man when he saw one and Daniel was just that.*

*The final—and most deadly—attack came before anyone in Atlantis expected it. Daniel was alone with Serai in the shop, her bodyguards across the lane having a mug of ale on a hot summer's day. The armies rode through the capital city so fast that Serai's bodyguards died in the street trying to get to her. Daniel hid Serai in a hiding place underneath the floor of the shop and then tried to fight off the looters who targeted the shop for its treasures. The thieving soldiers of the marauding army stabbed him, struck him in the head, and left him for dead where he fell, lying over the trapdoor to the hiding place, covering it with his body.*

*During the long hours that followed, until day turned to night, Serai was trapped in the dark, unable to move the trapdoor with Daniel's weight on top of it. The worst part? She wasn't alone. When night fell, her suspicions turned to fact: the master jeweler rose from his day sleep. He was a senior mage of the Nightwalker Guild; those who fed on the blood of willing humans. He pushed the trapdoor up, and Serai rushed to Daniel's side.*

*But it was too late. Daniel was so near death that he couldn't hear her; his body icy cold. Only the faint rise and fall of his chest told them that Daniel had any life left in him at all. The Nightwalker mage offered Serai Daniel's final choice: would she allow him to turn Daniel into a vampire, or should they let him die?*

*She chose life for Daniel, and he spent the next several thousand years trying not to hate her for it, since she had escaped into death without him. But by the time she made that fateful choice, the Atlantean armies had beaten back the invaders, and Serai's father's guards burst into the shop and found her. They took her, fighting them all the way, away from the shop, away from Daniel, and away from any future that he and Serai might have hoped for. By the time Daniel was transformed from a nearly dead human into a nightwalker, Atlantis had vanished—destroyed—and all trace of it had sunken beneath the sea, or so everyone had believed.*

~~~⁓~~~

He finished his pathetic tale and looked up, expecting Quinn to mock him for his weakness. What he saw instead shocked him. Quinn, the tough rebel leader who'd challenged monsters and battled horrors that would have made other humans curl up and beg to die, had tears in her eyes.

"Don't," he said harshly. "Don't cry for me. I don't deserve it."

"Maybe I'm crying for both of us," she said quietly. "You know I can never be with Alaric. The best I can hope for is at least I take a bunch of the bad guys with me when I meet my early and violent end."

"A little melodramatic, Quinn."

"A lot true." She shrugged. "You have a chance, though. Go find her. Help her. Be who she needs and save her from all of this. Most of us don't get a second chance, Daniel. Don't waste yours."

An icy wind swept into the cavern, interrupting whatever he'd been about to say, and Daniel threw himself in front of Quinn to protect her from this new danger, but it was only Alaric. Daniel almost laughed, even as the thought entered his mind. *Only* Alaric.

The priest was Quinn's biggest danger of all.

Daniel felt the click inside his being that signaled the setting sun, but he waited to be sure Quinn—his friend—would be okay. "Are you all right with him?"

Alaric made a low sound, deep in his throat, and his eyes glowed a hot green.

"Save it, Priest," Daniel advised. "You don't want to go up against me. Nightwalker Guild. Senior mage. Look it up sometime."

Quinn smiled a little. "Seriously. He's hell on picnic tables. Go ahead, Daniel. I'm fine."

Daniel didn't wait any longer, especially since he knew the priest would give his own life to protect Quinn, and the two of them probably wanted some privacy anyway, to work out their own problems. If there was any possibility they could work them out, Quinn deserved that chance.

Not his business. He launched himself into the air and flew out of the cavern, soaring through the cool dusk sky to where he knew Serai waited. He could *feel* her, and he needed to find her. Now. And make her understand that she could never, ever leave him again until she was safe.

*Then* she could rip his heart out. Not before.

~~~

## Oak Creek Canyon

As the sun finally sank beneath the horizon, Serai wrapped her arms around her knees and prepared to face the music.

Or face the vampire, to be exact. Although she liked the expression "face the music." She'd quite liked "the bee's knees," too, but that one had fallen out of use some time ago. She realized her mind was racing around random irrelevant subjects, but she couldn't help it. She'd spent the past couple of hours trying to contact the Emperor, worrying about what to do next, and feeling like an utter fool over her mistake about Reisen's hand.

One thing was clear: she was done screaming like a foolish girl. It was time to gear up for battle, as her father used to say, although of course he'd spent time as an actual officer in the king's guard, so maybe his meaning had been different. She needed to be strong. What other woman on the planet had so much knowledge of life, after all? Even though she hadn't experienced any of it.

"I can do this," she said firmly, and the sleeping tiger opened one bright green eye and looked at her.

Before she could explain *what* she could do, or even draw her next breath, Daniel was there. Just suddenly there, as if he'd dropped out of the sky, which, on reflection, she realized he had. He pulled her into his arms and held her so tightly she couldn't breathe.

"Never again," he demanded, his voice rough. "Never leave me again. *Never* run into danger when I can't follow you. If something happened to you . . ."

Jack rolled to all four legs and snarled at Daniel, but his heart didn't seem to be in it, since he scratched his ear with one giant paw and then ambled off, probably to find Quinn.

Serai leaned into Daniel, wanting nothing more than to curl up in his arms and hide from the rest of the world and her duty. She pretended, just for a few moments, that they were an ordinary couple who could afford the time to visit a lovely place and hold each other. Play tourist. Grow old together.

He'd never grow old, though, and she might die any minute, if they didn't find the Emperor. She reluctantly pulled away from him.

"I'm sorry. About Reisen. I should have trusted you. I've been stupid, but that's over," she said, squaring her shoulders.

His eyes were perfectly, completely black with some suppressed emotion. Probably disgust. "Never apologize to me. Never. I should have been more careful; I should have—"

"I can feel it," she interrupted, as another wave of pain struck, biting hard. "I can feel the Emperor. We can track it. It's not that far away."

# Chapter 10

Daniel took Serai's hand and headed back to the cave, which also served as the temporary headquarters of Quinn's rebels. There would be supplies. Gear. Whatever he needed to help Serai find that damn stone and be safe. He swept a glance down her curves, now neatly attired in the same nondescript tan pants and white shirt that many of the others wore, and he couldn't help but miss the filmy gown. But even in the plain contemporary clothing, with her glorious hair restrained in a simple braid down her back, she was obviously an Atlantean high-born lady. The way she held her head, the electric charge of restrained magic, even her graceful carriage in spite of the chunky hiking boots that now adorned her feet—nobody would mistake her for anything but aristocracy.

And all he wanted to do was remove every stitch of the new clothing and wrap himself around her until every inch of their skin was touching. Hold her. Explore her curves and learn her body. Teach her the ways of a man and a woman together, and discover for himself what it would be like to be with a woman whom his heart desired, not just his body.

Even her braid tantalized him, as if begging him to release it and spread her hair out on silken sheets. He remembered fantasizing, so long ago, about her wearing nothing to his bed but the necklace he'd designed for her.

A stupid fantasy. The blacksmith and the beauty, indeed. Only in Hollywood's version of fairy tales did a story like that work out.

"Daniel," she murmured. "You're holding my hand a little too tight."

He relaxed his grip, feeling like a fool. Or the beast he'd named himself. She deserved better. Once she was safe and back in Atlantis, he was sure Conlan would find someone for her. Someone far more worthy than a vampire with blood on his hands. It was for the best.

So why did the mere thought of it make him want to kill someone?

"I don't know you anymore," she said. "It's neither excuse nor apology, but I don't know the man you've become, and I don't know what violence you're capable of doing in a moment's anger. I had little contact with nightwalkers— my only experience, in fact, was with the master of your smithy and the fact that he didn't eat me when we were trapped in that hole in the ground."

"I need to hear it. All of it. What happened that day. Why you left me. Why you agreed to this stasis." He stopped and wrapped an arm around her waist and pulled her close to his body in the sweet darkness of newly fallen night. "I know now is not the time, but when this is over and you're safe, I need to hear it. I need to know."

She looked up at him and solemnly nodded. "I know. We have much to tell before we can decide . . . many things. Soon."

Her voice was calm and controlled, but he was a vampire and could hear her heart racing in her chest. Not from fear. He hoped it wasn't fear. Could he dare believe it might be attraction? Even after all these years? Before he could doubt himself, he claimed what he'd wanted to steal from her since the day she first walked into his shop back in Atlantis.

He leaned down and captured her lips with his own, tasting her sweetness. Sinking into her warmth.

And the world shattered.

Heat that surely would melt his flesh from his bones shot through him, and he tightened his arms around her until she could never escape. She kissed him back—at first an innocent brush of her lips and then an ardent and enthusiastic return of his passion. When her tongue hesitantly touched his own, he groaned deep in his throat and was lost. She twined her arms around his neck and tangled her hands in his hair, just as he wanted to do to hers, but he contented himself with wrapping her braid in his fist, another way to hold her, capture her, claim her. She made a tiny sound, a moan or a purr, and his cock hardened to a degree that shamed the rock surrounding them.

He pulled away for an unbearable moment, long enough to tell her, to explain his aggression. "I need you, my beautiful one. By all the gods, I need you."

She blinked, her eyes enormous in her pale face, and tried to talk, but nothing but a whisper of sound emerged from her perfect lips. Not a protest, surely not, anything but that. Acceptance, agreement, acquiescence; he would brook nothing else.

She tried again. "Jack," she managed to say.

Jack. *Jack?* Another man's name was not what he wanted to hear from his woman. A red haze of fury washed over his vision, and he contemplated how much joy he would gain from ripping the tiger to tiny shreds. Or using his skin for a rug.

"Jack," she repeated, but this time she was pointing. "He's calling us, and he's right there."

The meaning behind her words finally sank in, and the berserker rage subsided. She didn't want Jack. Jack was calling them. From right behind Daniel. Serai's hands, he suddenly realized, were still twined in his hair.

His lips curved in a slow, dangerous smile, and she gasped a little. "If ever a kiss were worth waiting eleven thousand years for, that was it, my lady," he murmured in her perfect, shell-like ear. "I will make sure it is not nearly so long a period until the next one."

Even in the dim light from the lanterns, he could see her face flush a hot red, and she pushed against his chest until he let her go.

"You presume too much," she said, but her haughty words were ruined a little by her breathlessness.

"Yep." He took her hand again and headed toward the damn grinning tiger shifter and his lantern. He was almost to the cave when he realized he was whistling.

Life was suddenly looking up.

When they entered the cave, the atmosphere was noticeably chilly, and it had nothing to do with the weather. The positioning of the inhabitants told the whole story in a glance. Alaric leaned against a wall, scowling at Reisen, who stood as far as possible from the priest. Quinn stood, seemingly relaxed, in the center of the space. Only the stress in her eyes and her slightly increased heartbeat told Daniel that she wasn't nearly as calm as she liked to project. A slender, not very tall human woman with blond-and-blue hair and a wicked grin sat on the floor near Quinn, a computer on her lap. She kept shooting glances at Reisen, who pretended not to notice, or perhaps really didn't notice, since he was practically inhaling Serai with his eyes.

But Serai ignored him, her gaze fixed on Alaric, her face becomimg pale and bloodless. "You."

Alaric took a step forward. "Princess. How are you here? What—"

"Stay away from me, or I will hurt you," she said, her voice only trembling a little.

Daniel stepped between them at the same time that Quinn caught Alaric's arm with her hand.

"She must return to Atlantis," the priest said, flinching a little at the contact but not pulling away.

"I will never again listen to an Atlantean who tells me what I must do," Serai said, raising her chin.

Daniel aimed a flat stare at the priest. "Alaric. You'll need to go through me to get to her, so please choose which part of your pretty face you want to get smashed in first."

Quinn glared at Daniel. "That's not really helping. You either, Alaric. Can we discuss what we're here for and then you can have a private meeting about Atlantean issues? I really don't have time for this right now."

She twined her fingers through Alaric's, pulling him back, and the dark look the priest shot at her would have stopped most people in their tracks. Quinn only smiled and shook her head.

"You know better than that," she whispered so softly that Daniel was sure most of the people in the room couldn't hear her. "The only thing about you that scares me is your absence, Alaric."

The priest stood frozen for a long moment and then inclined his head and moved back to his place by the wall. "We *will* have this talk, though, Princess Serai, vampire or no."

"I'm no princess, Alaric, but yes, we will talk. You don't scare me, however, so you can stop trying."

She was lying; Daniel could hear her heartbeat racing. The priest scared her, and Daniel had to fight hard against the rising red tide of fury demanding that he attack Alaric. Neutralize the threat to Serai.

Reisen surprised everyone by stepping into the silence. "I need to talk to you, too, Lady Serai."

"I think not," Daniel said, baring his fangs at the Atlantean, who showed no signs of being intimidated. Maybe once you'd had your hand torn off by a vampire, you didn't much fear the one who'd saved your miserable life.

"Daniel," Reisen said, nodding stiffly.

"Reisen. Long time, no have-to-save-your-ass. Or is that long time, no see? I always get these human sayings confused."

Quinn rolled her eyes. "Really? We're going to do this now?"

"I believe it is an imbalance in the male brain," Serai said regally. "They name it testosterone in this time. In mine, we merely called it stupidity."

Quinn burst out laughing, and even Alaric cracked a smile, which made Daniel almost fall over.

"Either works," Jack said as he entered the cave behind Daniel and Serai. He touched Serai on the arm. "You okay, kitten?"

"Tiger-skin rug. On my floor," Daniel said, but with no heat. He couldn't resent Jack's concern. Beneath all that tiger fur, Jack was a warrior who took his job of protecting others seriously. Daniel inclined his head to Jack in thanks for being with Serai during the afternoon hours when he could not, and Jack punched him in the shoulder.

Serai stared at them both like they were lunatics.

"It's a guy thing," Jack said, shrugging. "He knows now that I'm pissed off about Quinn; I know he's pissed off about you. It's all good."

"Certainly that would make perfect sense, if the world were upside down. However, I choose to ignore rather than debate your logic and simply respond that I am well," Serai said. "Thank you for your assistance today."

Jack grinned. "Tigers love nothing more than a nap in the sun. Throw in a beautiful woman for company, and it's the cherry on the cake."

Daniel narrowed his eyes, but Jack just laughed and walked farther into the cave and leaned against the wall between Reisen and Alaric.

"If we're done posturing, maybe we could get this meeting started so we can move on," Quinn said. "Jack?"

Jack nodded. "Okay, here's what we've found out so far. Banker named Smithson seems to be the head of a massive consortium of investment bankers throughout the world. They're bored with playing with their money, stepping on Third World countries, draining old people's pensions, and the like. They want to dance with the big boys and never worry about trifling little things like banking laws or international monetary regulations."

"Smithson is here?" Quinn asked.

"Right here at Sedona National Bank, which is apparently a front for all kinds of bad and wrong."

The woman with the computer raised her hand.

"Melody, you don't have to raise your hand," Quinn said patiently, as if she'd said it many times before.

"Oh, sure, I'm sitting in on a meeting with the rebel leader, scary tiger man, and possible Area 51 man in black over in the corner," Melody said, indicating Quinn, Jack, and Alaric in turn, before pointing at Daniel. "Plus let's not forget terrifying vampire dude who blows up defenseless chocolate cakes. You think I'm not going to be a little extra polite?"

Serai looked at Daniel. "You destroyed the cake? I loved that cake."

Daniel glared at Melody. "Can we move on?"

Her black-rimmed eyes widened. "Um, sure. We found out that the records of all the consortium dudes are on an encrypted laptop that Smithson keeps in a safe-deposit box in his own bank, because, duh, he, like, runs the place."

Serai tilted her head, clearly fascinated by Melody's outrageous appearance and manner of speaking. "Duh?"

"It's goth chick for 'of course, as you all realize,'" Melody said, grinning. "You're not from around here, are you?"

"You have no idea," Serai said, flashing a genuine smile that made something in Daniel's chest tighten.

Alaric straightened and pinned Serai with a flat gaze. "Yes. About that. You need to go back."

Serai raised her chin. "I think you are the last person to tell me what I *need* to be doing, youngling."

Reisen made a choking sound, and Daniel tried not to laugh. He wondered when the last time was that somebody had dared to defy the high priest of Atlantis—or call him youngling, which, as far as Daniel understood, meant something like "wet behind the ears child."

Alaric stood frozen for a long moment, and then he covered his eyes with one hand and shook his head, muttering to himself. Finally the priest took a deep breath and tried again. "You don't understand. The Emperor is operating incorrectly. You may be in danger."

Serai put her hands on her hips. "Really? I might be in danger? You mean, apart from the bit where the fluctuation in the Emperor's power nearly killed me in the stasis pod, so I had to escape? Or the part where someone is trying to wield the gem's magic and sent me into seizures as I came through the portal? No, wait—maybe the fact that if I can't find the Emperor and retrieve it before whoever has it tries again, the power fluctuations that already almost killed me could kill all of us?"

She was shouting by the time she reached the end, and everyone stared at her in shock.

Finally, Melody raised her hand again. "So, Atlantis has an emperor? That's cool. I always thought Napoleon was the bomb. Who has him? Can I meet him?"

Quinn sighed. "You'd never know she was the smartest hacker ever to turn down an offer from the CIA's elite computer squad, would you?"

Before anybody could respond, June came running in, out of breath and holding her arm, which was bent at an impossible angle. Tears ran freely down the woman's face, but her voice was perfectly steady. "We're under attack, Quinn. Vampires. A lot of them. Three of us are already dead."

Daniel yanked Serai out of range of the entrance and placed her, back to the wall, in the farthest corner from danger, as the others rushed out of the cave.

"Stay here," he commanded.

"You don't get to tell me what to do, either, Nightwalker," she snapped.

"I can't protect you if—"

"I didn't ask you to protect me," she said, cutting him off. Then with a rush of power that smashed through the space between them, in a few short seconds she again shimmered into the shape of a saber-toothed tiger. When he started to speak, she snarled at him and shouldered him out of her way before springing across the floor to follow the others.

Daniel swore steadily in a long-dead language as he raced after her. He was going to slaughter anyone—vampire or otherwise—who dared to get anywhere near her. And when this was over, he was going to throw her over his shoulder, take her somewhere safe, lock her up, and maybe invest in some catnip.

❦

Serai stumbled a little as she bounded across the floor, and hoped Daniel hadn't seen it. If he realized that the loss of connection with the Emperor was making her as weak as she felt, he'd probably spirit her away and bundle her up in a bubble of safety somewhere. Rather exactly like how she'd spent the past eleven thousand years.

She thought not.

The tiger's night vision gave her a clear picture of the area and the dark forms attacking Quinn's group. Jack was already in tiger form himself and launching his body through the night air toward a vampire rushing toward him. They collided with a thud, and seconds later the vampire's head rolled off its body. Serai felt nauseous, exhilarated, and terrified all at once—a far cry from any of the feelings or emotions she'd known in the pod. Daniel snarled something at her about staying down, and then he shot up into the air, daggers extended, and decapitated two more vampires in midair. They immediately began decomposing into an acidic slime that her sensitive tiger nose despised. She backed away from the mess, so it didn't get on her paws, and looked around, stunned at the noise and fury of the battle.

Daniel was a whirlwind of berserker rage, slicing through the attackers like an avenging god. She'd never seen him in battle mode, and she caught her breath at the stark deadliness of his every move. His entire body was an extension of his weapons, and he smashed through a wave of the enemy in a brutal dance of death and destruction.

She shook her massive tiger head and looked around, realizing she'd been spellbound by Daniel for almost long enough that someone could have attacked her from behind. She was lucky; the battle raged on all around her, but none of it approached her yet. Her companions were not so fortunate. Alaric was right in the middle of it, flinging energy spheres from both hands, standing back-to-back with Quinn, who wielded a deadly looking gun in each hand. The rebels were outnumbered, but they apparently didn't think so, or didn't care, because they were steadily evening the odds. Daniel made a joke out of odds anyway. None could stand up to him.

A shout rang out somewhat ahead and to the left of where Serai stood, and she jerked her gaze away from Daniel again.

"*A Mycenae!*" Reisen shouted, pledging his part in the battle to his royal house in Atlantis, as he plunged a sword into one vampire's heart and then withdrew it to remove the fallen foe's head.

Serai snapped out of her mental paralysis at the sight. Daniel was destroying the attackers, Jack was doing the same, even the humans were fighting hard, and Reisen was dispatching enemies with only one hand. While, she, a princess of Poseidon turned into a fearsome beast of old, had four good paws and a mouthful of sharp saberlike teeth, and yet she stood there helplessly, like the foolish girl she'd promised herself she'd no longer be.

She took a moment to find the nearest threat and identified one of the vampires trying to sneak up on Reisen from behind. She roared a challenge and a warning and sprang across the dozen or so paces to where the vampire had frozen, staring stupidly at the oncoming tiger.

Seeing an extinct animal charging him might have thrown him off his game.

She would have laughed if she'd had human vocal cords, but instead she roared again and then swiped one massive claw across the vampire's throat and jumped aside as the fiend's head dropped from its body.

Guess her claws were pretty sharp.

Reisen stared at her in openmouthed disbelief. She tried to smile at him, but when he stepped back a pace, she realized a smile full of teeth like sabers wasn't all that reassuring. She bounded off to find more enemies, instead of worrying about it, and then fell heavily to the ground, mid-bound, when every ounce of her energy and magic suddenly drained completely out of her body and left her nearly unconscious. There was nothing gradual about it; one moment she'd been ferociously killing that vampire and then she was on the ground as if smashed by a giant hand.

She lay on her side, panting, a stupendously large tongue hanging out the side of her mouth, and then the magic sustaining her shape-change vanished and she lay, limp, one helpless Atlantean maiden in the center of a massive battle.

*Out of the stasis pod, into the grave.* Perhaps that would become a new popular expression after she died. At least she'd retained her clothing during the shift and wouldn't die naked. There was something for her memorial service. *Didn't die naked.*

Daniel flew through the air toward her—actually *flew*; her muddled mind told her that if she survived this she had to ask him how he did that—and landed on the ground with one foot on each side of her waist, standing over her prone body.

"If you die, I'm going to haunt you," he growled at her, his fangs fully bared, and then another of the attackers came at him, screaming something about points for killing the Primator. Daniel met the attack with crossed daggers and then he sliced downward, and another head rolled across the ground.

Serai's thoughts tumbled crazily; she realized she was near hysteria when she started to hum "vampire heads are falling down" to the tune of some song buried in her memory about a London bridge, and then when everything went suddenly, eerily quiet, she wondered if she'd lost her hearing or her mind.

Or both.

But then a woman—it sounded like June, maybe, but Serai wasn't sure—screamed, "The tiger is down." Serai had just enough time to be touched that the landwalkers cared about her even though they'd just met her, before

Quinn raced past. A moment later, Quinn started screaming, too, and even Serai's exhausted mind began to realize that it wasn't her they were talking about.

*She* wasn't the tiger who was down.

"Jack!" Quinn screamed, over and over. Just his name, again and again and again.

Then Serai heard Alaric's unmistakable voice. "I'm sorry, Quinn. He's dead."

# Chapter 11

Daniel stared down at the limp, blood-soaked form of the tiger who'd been Quinn's best friend in the world, and a bleak sense of futility washed over him. Why? Why was it always the good guys—the best of them—who paid the highest price? He tightened his hold on Serai, who had insisted on standing on her own two feet when he'd picked her up from the ground. When he'd seen her fall, he'd almost faced death for the second time that day. If he lost her now . . . but no. Better to focus on the immediate reality.

Jack was down, and Quinn was losing her mind over it. He could feel her maddened anguish searing through him because of the blood bond and realized, yet again, that he couldn't help her.

Alaric tried to pull Quinn away from Jack, but she screamed and fought him off.

"No, leave me alone! Wait. You can heal him," she said imploringly, tugging on Alaric's hand. "You healed me before. I've seen you heal lots of people. You can do it. Fix him."

But the priest was shaking his head, a universe of sadness in his somber expression. "He's gone, Quinn. I can heal grievous wounds, it is true, and you know I would do anything for you, but I cannot heal death. Only the gods can do that."

Quinn screamed again, a sound of such utter, hopeless rage that it sent chills snaking down Daniel's spine. Serai shuddered and turned her head to look up at Daniel, and the deep blue of her eyes had spread from her irises to completely cover the white, so that her eyes were entirely blue.

"He's not gone," she said, her voice gone deep with ancient power. "He's almost gone, but a small part of him remains."

Alaric stared at her and raised his hands almost as if to block any attack Serai might try. She made a dismissing motion and ignored him, focused entirely on Quinn and Jack.

"Put me down. There next to Jack," Serai ordered Daniel, and he found himself obeying her without question. The magic resonating in her voice called to him on such a visceral level that it echoed in his bones. He wouldn't have been able to refuse her—looking around, he saw that everyone but Alaric had stepped forward in response to her command, as well.

He helped her to sit on the ground next to Jack, and she gently nudged Quinn to one side and then lay down across the badly damaged tiger, so that her body draped across Jack's.

Quinn grabbed at her. "No! What are you doing? Get off him!"

But Alaric gently pulled Quinn back and held her back by wrapping his arms around her. "Give her a chance, Quinn. The ancients had magic we have long forgotten."

Quinn shook her head back and forth, over and over, but subsided, watching Serai with huge eyes filled with tears that she wouldn't let fall.

She had reason to cry. Gashes so deep that Daniel could see bone in some of them covered every quarter of Jack's body. Serai grasped his fur with both hands and started to hum softly, then turned those blind and darkling eyes to Quinn.

"Part of him lives, but only his animal side is still—barely—on this side of the river of death," she said, so softly it was almost a whisper. "I can call to the tiger that is Jack and help him come back, but his human side is almost certainly lost forever."

Quinn stared at Serai, pain and terror and awe mixed in her expression. "What *are* you?"

"I am Serai of Atlantis, and the Emperor gifted me with ancient magic not seen on this world since before my continent dove beneath the oceans," Serai said in that terrible, beautiful voice of power. "I gift you his choice, as another once gifted me the choice of life or death for one I loved. Shall I let him seek out his ancestors in the afterlife or do you wish him to live, though it be perhaps only a half life?"

Her gaze met Daniel's, and he understood, in a way he never had before, what it had cost her to make that choice for him—both that day and every day of her life since. Now she offered the same painful choice to Quinn, and he could do nothing but stand helplessly by and watch them.

The knife he'd pulled out of his side a little while ago during the battle had hurt far less.

"I choose life," Quinn said, her voice ringing out. "You make him live, do you hear me? No matter what it takes. Make at least part of him live, and I can find the rest of him somehow. Someday. You *make him live.*"

Serai nodded and began singing, first softly and sweetly, and then stronger and more powerfully, as magic threaded through the lyrics and melody of her song. A gentle, glowing, golden light rose from Jack's body and surrounded them, until they shone as if lit from within by miniature suns. Everyone watching them held his or her breath in unison until, seconds or centuries later, a rough coughing noise sounded and Jack's body shuddered fiercely, almost rising completely up off the ground before it fell back down.

Quinn cried out and put her arms around Jack's neck, but the tiger snarled at her and Alaric yanked her back and away, putting his own body between the two of them. Daniel pulled Serai away, too, but she shook her head and he settled for crouching down next to her, between her delicate skin and Jack's powerful jaws.

"Does he know who he is?" Alaric demanded.

Serai shook her head but then nodded. "I think so?" The power had gone from her voice, and all that remained was exhaustion.

"Honestly, I don't know what he knows," she admitted. "Or *who* he knows. If he has reverted fully to tiger and only tiger, he's not safe to be around."

Quinn squared her shoulders but then dropped down to put a hand on Serai's shoulder. "Thank you. No matter what else, you brought him back from death. We'll figure the rest out. I owe him that much."

Alaric called to his own particular brand of Atlantean power, and a silvery blue light soared up from the priest's hands and then spread out to surround the tiger, who snarled weakly and then sat up, shivering in the light. Jack's blood-stained fur was dark and matted, but the gashes were healed.

"I can't tell," Alaric said. "I just don't know. Shape-shifters are too different from Atlanteans, and Poseidon's power recoils from trying to analyze the mind of a tiger."

"Your magic is unbalanced without the soul-meld," Serai said absently, brushing Alaric aside as if he were a troublesome child.

The priest stared at her, his eyes widening. "What do you mean? I am the most powerful—"

"Yes, yes, I've heard it," Serai interrupted. "Most powerful high priest in the history of Atlantis. But it's not true, you know. I've been around for all of them since Atlantis dove beneath the sea. Your power is not even close to that Nereus wielded. At least, before his wife died and he almost drowned the world."

"What—"

Quinn cut him off, and her voice was hoarse with barely repressed pain. "I don't care. I don't care about any of it right now. Not the bankers, or the rebellion, or any damn part of it. I sure as hell don't care about Atlantean ancient history.

I'm leaving, and I'm taking Jack with me. Somewhere he can be safe, until we figure this out. I owe him that. I owe him my life, several times over."

Alaric took her hand in his and nodded. "Of course. I know just the place. I'll take you there now, and I'll never, ever leave your side again."

The shimmer of magic that surrounded Alaric as he said it told Daniel that the priest had just made a vow he wouldn't be able to break without serious consequence. Words had power, and some more than others. Their future would be even more complicated now.

Alaric slashed a hand through the air, and the now-familiar portal began to shimmer in the dark.

"You should come with us, Princess," Alaric said. "We can help you."

"You need *my* help, priest," Serai said, putting a hand on Daniel's arm. "I have protection beyond your knowledge in the presence of the mage beside me."

Daniel didn't deserve her praise. Skills learned as a mage millennia ago were so long gone as to be rusty with disuse. Only good for destroying furniture and cake. He couldn't help, unless . . .

Unless he called to the dying soul of the human—which happened to be a special talent of the Nightwalker Guild. It was better to leave a live body behind than a dead one, according to the rules they'd stuffed in his head. Common decency or morality had nothing to do with guild law, but practicality ruled all.

"I can help, possibly," he said. "Let me try to reach Jack."

"What can you do? Try to blood bond a tiger?" Quinn shook her head. "Go away, Daniel, there's no need for your special skills here."

"I have forgotten more magic than most of your human witches ever possess, Quinn, and one of my talents as senior mage of the Nightwalker Guild was to teach others to call out to the souls of dying mortals," Daniel said. "Let me try. It can't hurt him, not now. Maybe I can help."

Surprisingly, Quinn looked to Serai first, then Alaric. Both of them nodded, Alaric perhaps a little skeptically, but it was still a nod.

"Fine. Try what you can. But then we take him away and let him rest and heal." Quinn moved a few inches to the side, keeping one hand on Jack's fur. The tiger followed her with its eyes but made no move to attack, just sat, shivering, in the center of their small group.

Daniel reached deep inside himself again, for the second time that night, and called for the constructive alter-ego of the destructive force he'd unleashed earlier. The power was too long unused and responded only sluggishly to his call, and at only partial strength of what he dimly remembered from days long, long gone. He'd fought with fists, daggers, and his vampire physical abilities for so long he'd nearly forgotten his magic. Perhaps he didn't deserve a response from power he'd discarded and scorned.

But it did respond. Slowly and painfully, but it finally answered him. He invoked words of power in languages that had existed long before French had dreamed itself into being, and the magic rose to his call, at least enough to fuel one not-so-simple question.

*Jack. Are you there? Jack Shepherd of the tiger pride, have you gone beyond reach of mortal call?*

Daniel waited for what seemed a very long time. Just when he was about to admit defeat, a weak, thready voice that was almost unidentifiable as Jack's answered him.

*I don't know where I am, or if I can come back. I don't know if I want to come back. Leave me be, vampire, or magician, or whatever you are. Leave me to make my own choices. Don't call me again, or I'll leave forever. The choice to die is so very tempting.*

Daniel waited, but the message was complete. Jack had to choose to come back, and nothing they could do would influence him, or so the shape-shifter thought. Daniel, though, knew better. He himself had once rejoined the living for the dream of love of a woman.

Maybe the love Jack felt for Quinn—and hers for him,

though it was not the bond she shared with Alaric—would be enough. It was beyond his reach now. He turned to Quinn.

"I don't know if he'll ever return," he warned her. "All I know is that he's somewhere in there. Deep inside, or maybe even not inside the tiger but very nearby. But he won't come back because we push him. He warned me quite specifically that if we try, he'll choose never to come back."

Quinn narrowed her eyes. "If he thinks he's more stubborn that I am, he's sadly mistaken. Let's go, Alaric. Take us away, and give me time to let this tiger heal and find himself again."

Alaric simply nodded, then took her hand in one of his and made a motion with the other that lifted the tiger on a shimmering pillow of pure energy. The portal, now large enough for a half dozen warriors to enter walking side by side, glowed brightly in the moonlit night. Daniel looked around to see that the piles of decaying vampire remains had all melted into the ground and vanished in the darkness.

Reisen, who'd been standing behind the group around Jack, and whom Daniel hadn't even noticed until then, gazed at the portal with such stark longing on his face that Alaric paused when he saw the warrior.

"Do others here need healing? I forget my duties."

Reisen shook his head. "No, we have only minor injuries in those still alive. You . . . you go to Atlantis?"

"You can return home," Alaric told Reisen. "Your exile was self-imposed. Conlan offered forgiveness and healing."

Reisen took a deep breath, but stayed where he was. "I have one final mission to perform for Quinn."

Melody, her face badly bruised from the fight, looked up at Reisen and put a hand on his arm. "Thank you. For what you did during that fight, too. I'd be dead on the ground if not for you, and the world would be short one majorly terrific hacker."

She tried to smile but failed miserably, and tears ran freely down her face as she turned her gaze to Quinn. "Take care of Jack for me, Boss. I'll be on top of things here."

Quinn nodded, but didn't even glance back. She was already walking ahead of Alaric to the portal, one hand still in Jack's fur.

Alaric turned to Daniel just before he stepped into the glowing oval of light. "Six women and the fate of Atlantis herself depend upon what happens to that gemstone, Daniel. Don't let them down. Since she won't return to Atlantis, I'll send help. A lot of help."

"We don't need help from those who imprison women for thousands of years, failed priest," Serai said, her eyes again perfectly dark, completely blue. The power hadn't left her, then. "If I return now, I lose any chance to retrieve the Emperor. I might be safe, since I'm out of the pod, but I won't trade my life for theirs."

"She stays," Daniel said. "But we'll take whatever help we can get to keep her safe."

Serai glared at him, but he didn't care. He wouldn't risk her life for foolish pride, neither her pride nor his. When she was thinking clearly again, she'd agree. Alaric nodded, and then the unlikely trio moved through the gate: the priest, the rebel leader he loved, and the tiger who might never recover his humanity.

When the light from the portal vanished, swallowing the three, everyone watching exhaled as if they'd all been holding their breath by mutual agreement.

"This sucks beyond all reason," Melody said, her tearstained face at odds with her flippant words. "I'm heading into town for a hotel room and a hot shower. Tomorrow morning is early enough to decide on a plan. Anybody with me?"

"I'm not leaving you until this mission is complete," Reisen said flatly. "Lead on. We must, however, discover who those vampires were, and why they attacked. Are they with the vampire controlling this region? Nicholas? Are they in league with the witches?"

"Or, worse, working for that human banker," Daniel said grimly. "For tonight—what's left of it—we should find shelter and rest."

"Yes," Serai said. "I'd like to experience a hotel before I . . ."

As her voice trailed off, Daniel realized she'd been about to say "before I die."

"Don't even think it," he warned her. "I won't allow it."

She just sighed, exhaustion in every line of her body. "I'm too tired to argue with you, and I need a hot bath. Let's all talk after we rest."

Daniel wondered how they'd get to a hotel, and who would take care of the fallen humans, but this was not the first time the rebels had faced such losses, and they had a system in place. Within the hour, they were ensconced in a hotel in Sedona, and he was systematically drinking his way through every tiny bottle of whiskey in the minibar while he tried not to think about Serai's naked body in the bathtub on the other side of a very flimsy door. He could smell the bath salts she'd poured in the tub. He could smell the soap and the shampoo that was touching her perfect skin and beautiful hair. But a far worse problem than that was becoming more and more evident.

*He could smell her blood.*

He could breathe in the scent of her luscious, life-giving blood, pumping through her veins beneath that perfect and oh-so-fragile skin. He'd channeled so much power, so long unused, and he was growing weak from the drain on his energy. The bloodlust he'd controlled for so many thousands of years was raising its monstrous head to scent its prey.

And Serai smelled like prey.

# Chapter 12

## Sedona

Serai sank farther into the scented water until only her knees and head remained above the clouds of frothy bubbles. The bath salts had a pleasing floral scent, but that of no flower she knew or remembered. It was no Atlantean tub, to be sure. She'd do no swimming or even languid floating with her friends here in this hotel bathroom. After so long without a bath, though, with only magical stasis-maintained cleanliness, this small tub felt fit for a king. Or at least fit for a once-almost-queen. One who wanted nothing more than to scrub the scent of fire and blood and battle from her skin.

The steamy heat sank into her tired muscles, soothing and relaxing them after a day and night of activity that surely had been more strenuous than a normal person's week. Or month. She hadn't even known that she had the ability to shift her shape to that of the ancient tiger, and yet she'd done it not once but twice. The saber-toothed tiger had been her favorite animal to study in the schoolroom. So beautiful and yet fierce and deadly.

Rather like Daniel. An image of him, standing over her and ferociously protecting her from attack, flashed into her mind, and she drew a shaky breath. He was the fiercest warrior she'd ever seen, and every ounce of that rage and power had been focused on saving her.

A tingling sensation swept through her at the thought of him—her vampire warrior and protector—waiting in the next room, with only a door between them. Her nipples stiffened and she blinked to see their pink tips pointing up through the bubbles. She raised her hands to cup her breasts and ran an exploratory thumb over one nipple, gasping at the electric sensation that pinged through her body from that sensitive place to another, even more sensitive place.

How much more exciting would it be if it were Daniel touching her there? She caught her breath at the thought, feeling deliciously naughty and then, suddenly, starkly ashamed. Men and women had just *died*, and she herself had killed one of them. Yes, it had been a vampire who'd been attacking Reisen, bent on killing him. Yes, it had been in battle.

But she'd never even struck anyone in anger, and now she'd killed a man. A vampire, like Daniel. How could she dismiss that so easily? The tears began to run down her face as the horrible inventory unfolded in her mind. Quinn's friend Jack, the man who'd been kind enough to spend part of his day protecting Serai from her own foolishness, was wounded perhaps beyond hope of healing. His humanity might never return. Several more of the rebels—more friends—were also dead or injured.

All of it due to a vampire attack that might even have had something to do with the Emperor and whoever had stolen it. Not to mention the maidens lying helpless in Atlantis, waiting for her to find the Emperor and save them.

And yet—in spite of all of that—here she sat in luxury and peace in her bath, playing at ideas of being a sexual temptress. Shame and exhaustion overwhelmed her, and she dropped her head to her knees and gave in to the sobs that had lain in wait for her since she first stepped foot out of that pod.

So much responsibility on Serai's inexperienced shoulders. Too much, perhaps. If she failed them, her sisters-in-stasis would die—because of *her*. She'd never been responsible for anything more important than choosing a new gown for a ball, and now the fate of the maidens, and maybe even that of Atlantis itself, lay in her hands. The Seven Isles couldn't rise to the surface without all of the jewels from Poseidon's trident.

It was too much. Far too much. She couldn't possibly live up to the task. She pulled a towel from the heated bar near the tub and pressed her face into it, the end trailing in the water, so the sound of her sobs wouldn't reach beyond the bathing room.

When the door crashed open, she knew she'd failed at even that. Moving so fast he was a blur, Daniel crossed to the tub and pulled her up and out of it, cradling her—wet towel, bubbles, and all—on his lap.

"Serai? Are you injured? Should we call for a healer or a doctor?" He stared into her eyes, holding her tightly to his chest, and she felt herself flush so hot her skin must be on fire.

"Daniel! I'm not injured, but I'm . . . I have no . . . I was in the *bath*. This is shockingly inappropriate. Release me immediately and leave the room."

He ignored her completely and instead tightened his embrace and kissed her gently on the forehead. "Then why are you crying as if your heart would break, my beautiful one?"

She shook her head back and forth as the pain rushed up again to choke her, her childish concerns about her nudity forgotten. "The attack. The dead rebels. Jack. My sisters. The Emperor. What if I can't find it, Daniel? My connection to it keeps growing weaker. What if I can never find it and the rest of the maidens die, too?"

"You'll find it. We'll find it together. I swear to you that we will succeed. We'll save those women, and you'll be safe, and you can return to Atlantis and live a long and wonderful life." His voice rasped as he said it, as if he were suppressing some deep emotion. He shifted his position sitting on the edge of the tub, still holding her, and the blood rushed to her cheeks again as she realized she felt a growing hardness under her bottom.

"I'm sorry, Serai, but I am a man," he said ruefully. "Some things are impossible to ignore, and you, naked in my arms, tops the list."

He stood and carefully released her, and then took her wet towel and handed her a dry one, but his searing gaze swept every inch of her body before she got a chance to wrap herself in the soft white cotton.

"A gentleman would have closed his eyes," she informed him rather breathlessly.

"I'm not a gentleman," he said, flashing that wicked smile of his that made her think of dangerous, seductive things. "I'm going to take advantage of every chance I get to see your gorgeous body, especially naked, you can be sure of that."

She blushed again but then frowned. "It's not right. To think of . . . pleasure . . . when such bad things have happened."

He grabbed another towel and started to dry her hair for her. "It's the most normal thing in the world, sweetheart. To affirm life in the face of death. To reach out for a connection to another—it's entirely natural."

He tossed the towel on the floor and put his arms around her, pulling her closer. "Do you know what else is natural? *This* is natural."

He touched his lips to hers, and she stopped breathing, stopped thinking, stopped existing as a rational person as the sensation thrilled through her. He was *kissing* her.

He *wanted* her.

She didn't know why, and she didn't care. She didn't *care*.

She just kissed him back. She threw her arms around his neck and clung, just in case he changed his mind. She wouldn't let go so easily. She kissed him with every bit of the longing she'd built up after so many years of missing him. Wanting him. Dreaming of him.

All of those years of wishing, hoping—she put all that into her kiss, too. All of her enthusiasm, her passion; it had to make up for lack of experience, didn't it?

She hoped. She would—what had he said? Affirm life? Yes. She would affirm life with him. Enthusiastically.

He groaned a little, deep in his throat, and she blushed. Maybe all that enthusiasm was a little too much. She didn't actually know what she was doing, after all. Maybe she was—

"Stop thinking so hard," he said, his lips quirking up at the edges. "Kissing is more about feeling."

"How did you—"

"I could tell. Am I going too fast?"

"No! I mean, no, I just—you have probably kissed so many women, and I don't, well, not that I should have, and what were you doing kissing all those women, anyway?" By the time she got to the end of that convoluted sentence, she was indignant and more than a little jealous.

His eyes flashed with heat and maybe even a little amusement. "There weren't all that many, *mi amara*. But if you want the absolute truth, there has never, ever been anyone who could compare to you."

She clutched the towel closer to her chest and stared up into his eyes. Nothing but absolute sincerity and that exciting glimpse of barely restrained hunger shone back at her.

"My heart has waited for you all of my life. I feel like I'm learning what a kiss is for the very first time, and I want to learn it with you," he said, and she fell.

Fell out of doubt, out of insecurity, out of shyness.

Fell into love.

And knew, without a doubt, that she couldn't let him know. She'd scare him away, with his stupid notions of honor. But she could find a way to show him; that, at least she could do.

*Would* do. Tonight.

He waited, letting her decide, and she framed his face with her hands and pulled his head back down to hers.

"Then maybe we should try it again," she whispered, shyness almost—almost—completely overcome.

He flashed that wicked grin. "I thought you'd never ask."

He kissed her, and time stood still, the stars exploded, and a thousand other lines from a thousand other love songs and poems evolved from data fed to her by the Emperor . . . into truth.

He kissed her, and somehow she was in his arms while he carried her into the bedroom. His eyes glowed like dark stars in the dim room, which was only lit by the light from the bathing room.

"I need you," he said, and his voice was tight with strain as if he somehow hurt because of needing her. She felt a thrill of purely feminine triumph as she tightened her arms around his neck and kissed him in response. She didn't need words, she didn't even *have* the words for what she was feeling—only random thoughts and emotions and feelings whirling around and through her like bolts of electricity or a lightning strike composed of sheer sensation.

He lowered her to the bed and lay down beside her before she could take a breath. The towel had vanished between bath and bed, but he covered her body with his own. He was still fully dressed, and she shivered with the wantonly tactile sensation of his clothing against her skin.

"Are you cold?" He pulled the bed's coverlet up and around them, but she shook her head, laughing a little.

"I feel like I'll never be cold again, if you keep kissing me," she confessed, and she was surprised at the breathless sound of her voice.

He laughed and it was his turn for triumph. His eyes darkened, and she knew, oh, yes, even she in her inexperience knew what he felt.

"There's more, if you'll allow me to touch you," he said.

"I know what making love is." She could feel the heat in her cheeks at her bold declaration, but she didn't want him to think she was completely ignorant.

He kissed her forehead, her nose, her lips, and then her neck. "There's knowing, and then there's *knowing*. May I?"

"Oh! Oh, yes, um, what?"

"May I touch you?"

"Yes, oh, yes," she whispered, and then she lay perfectly still and waited for her world to change.

Daniel thought his brain might explode if she said no, so when she said yes, he didn't hesitate but did what he'd wanted to do since he first saw her again after so long. He touched her.

All over.

He ran his hands down the silken skin of her arms while he kissed her, and then he rolled to his side, pulling her with him, and stroked her back and her hair. And kissed her some more. He couldn't seem to stop kissing her, as if he were drowning and she were the very oxygen he needed to survive. At first she lay still, as if afraid to move, but then she threw her arms around his neck and pulled him even closer. Her kisses were enthusiastic and tentative all at once, as if she was learning the art of kissing.

Which, of course, was exactly what she was doing. He had no idea why the thought of it humbled him at the same time it drove him mad. His cock was so hard the imprint of his zipper would probably be a permanent tattoo if he didn't get out of his pants soon, but he didn't want to scare her by undressing. Not yet.

He took a breath and dared to let his hands drop to the sweet, sweet curve of her hips and ass, and he couldn't help the way his own hips bucked against her when he had both hands wrapped around her lush behind.

"Daniel, it . . . tingles. I never, I don't . . . It feels like I'm empty and hungry for something," she said, her cheeks blushing a hot rosy pink. "I never knew I could feel like this. I want—I want—"

"I want you, too, *mi amara*, but I'm not going to rush you," he said, feeling like a big damn hero. Or a big damn fool. "Not yet. It's too soon, and I don't want to take advantage of the heightened emotions you're feeling right now."

"You want to stop kissing me?" Her voice was barely a whisper, and she peeked up at him from beneath her eyelashes, and he thought this must be the hardest thing he'd ever done. Talk about self-sacrifice.

Nobility.

Cold freaking showers.

"No, I never want to stop kissing you, but I want to hold you, and I want us to sleep," he said, clenching his jaws shut against the *please, please, please, I need to be inside you right now* that he was really thinking.

She squirmed and pushed away from him a little, just far enough for him to see the luscious pink tips of her full, round breasts. He listened to the blood pulsing through her veins, and the monster in him hungered to come out and bite.

He prayed for strength. This was Serai. If he bit her—if he took her blood—then he was nothing more than the beast, and he deserved to die horribly and alone. He deserved for her to shove him away in disgust. He wished she would.

He prayed she didn't.

"I don't want to sleep," she said. "I want you to touch me."

She took his hand and placed it on her breast, and the beast quieted, perhaps in shock at being willingly touched; the man took over. Daniel gave up the idea of complete nobility as a lost cause, because touching her body was a far, far better choice than sinking his fangs into her throat. He could push simple desire to the fore and shove bloodlust to the dark recesses of his soul.

He would. He *must*.

Forcing his fangs to retract, he flipped her onto her back and pounced, taking her breasts in both hands, and finally, oh, by all the glorious wonders, *finally*, he kissed them and then each nipple in turn. When she gasped and clutched his hair, he gave in and licked one peak into his mouth and sucked on it until she was crying out and trembling underneath him, and then he gave no quarter but instead treated the other breast to the same tender care.

He would pleasure her until she came, crying out his name, and then—*then*—he would make her sleep. Surely that was noble enough.

Serai cried out again and was almost rational enough to wonder if anyone could hear her through the walls, but then she didn't care, when Daniel did that wonderful thing with his mouth to her breast and pure liquid fire shot through her body from her nipples to her most private parts. He turned to her other breast and took that nipple into his mouth while he gently pinched the other with his fingers, and she cried out again, wanting something, not knowing what, but *needing*— needing something.

Needing him.

So she told him, since her psychic commands weren't working. "Daniel, I need—I need—"

"I know, *mi amara*," he said, putting his hand between her thighs, right where she needed it, and stroking a finger through the hot wet slickness that had somehow appeared. And then his finger touched her right *there* and she cried out.

It wasn't just heat, it wasn't just passion, it was more, so much more. The man she'd dreamed of for eleven thousand years was kissing her and touching her, and oh, dear Poseidon, she thought she might actually explode from the pleasure and unbearable rightness of it.

"Daniel! That's . . . you . . . oh, *yes, yes, yes*," she said, as he kept rubbing her there in that most sensitive of spots. His finger pushed a little inside her and she gasped, and then his talented fingers, now wet and slippery, applied just the right amount of pressure, and her body shattered into a thousand fractured prisms of light.

He pulled her into his arms and held her tightly, murmuring gentle, meaningless words as she trembled in his arms; just rocking her slightly back and forth, holding her until the tremors shuddering through her body from his touch subsided.

"That was . . . was that . . . was that making love?"

He smiled at her, but his face looked a bit strained. "Yes, but it gets even better than that."

"I'm not sure I would survive better," she admitted, and he laughed.

"You should sleep now," he said, stroking her hair away from her face. "You need to rest. This has been a pretty big day for your first day awake in millennia."

"You have a talent for understatement."

"I've heard that before."

Before she could protest, he tipped her chin up and pressed a brief, gentle kiss on her lips, then captured her gaze with his own.

"You should sleep now," he said again, and a red gleam flared in his pupils.

She knew she should argue with him, but she was just so sleepy, and after all, he was right, they needed to sleep, and— *Oh*.

*Oh, no.*

"You used your nightwalker hypnotic powers on me," she said, fighting against it, but the compulsion was too strong. The last thing she saw was the smile on his beautiful face, and then the room went dark as she sank into sleep.

Daniel smiled at her, even though his body was screaming at him to jump up, take a cold shower, or, better yet, take his cock in his own hand and give himself just a little bit of relief from the screaming pitch of need. He lasted about five minutes lying there, trying to be content to watch her sleep, but—as he'd told her—he was only a man.

He climbed out of bed, hit the shower, and did both.

# Chapter 13

After a few restless hours of not-quite-sleeping and one short trip to the street outside of the hotel bar to relieve a drunken tourist of a pint of blood he'd never miss, Daniel lay again in bed next to Serai, holding a long strand of her silken hair in his fingers and wondering how long he could bear it before he woke her and took her, claiming every inch of her body as his. He wanted her to wake up with his cock sliding into the sweet warmth of her body, and only the knowledge of her innocence stopped him from acting on that desire.

Instead, he gritted his teeth and thought about unappetizing things like turnips, lima beans, and congressional politics. As the first fingers of dawn's light made their way through the tiny gap in the curtains, Daniel heard the measured tread of the footsteps in the hallway. He jumped out of bed, clothed himself, and raced to the door, daggers handy although probably unnecessary. It sounded like Reisen's walk, and Daniel's excellent vampire hearing was generally dead-on about such things.

He pulled open the door to find Reisen standing there with one hand raised to knock. Daniel stepped out on to the green-and-gold patterned carpet of the hallway and gently closed the door.

"She needs to sleep. Yesterday was a strain."

Reisen's eyes widened. "Is that some vampire thing? Gargantuan understatement? A *strain*? She could have died."

"It's even worse than you know," Daniel said grimly. "Is there someplace we can talk?"

"There's a coffee shop in the lobby. Few humans are about at this hour. Melody is waiting there." Reisen paused and then shrugged. "It's against an inner wall, away from any windows. You'll be fine there."

"Not used to worrying about whether a bloodsucker bursts into flames, are you, Atlantean?" Daniel said, grinning.

"It's a first." Reisen waved the stump of his arm in the air. "I figure I owe you one. At least." The warrior's face turned grim, probably remembering that horrible day when an evil vampire named Barrabas had captured and tortured him.

"How about coffee, and we're even?" Daniel hesitated, concerned about what Serai would do if she woke up alone. Whether she'd be afraid. "I'll meet you there," he told Reisen, and then slipped back into the room, wrote a quick note, and put it on the pillow next to Serai. Her face was burrowed in the pillow, so all he could see was the sensual curve of her arm and neck, but it was enough to make him want to climb into the bed with her and finish what he'd started only hours earlier.

"Later. I promise you," he whispered to her sleeping form, before leaving the room in search of the coffee shop.

He easily avoided the patch of morning sunlight streaming in through the lobby windows by ducking around the gift shop to find the coffee shop and Reisen and Melody sitting in welcoming dimness in a back corner. A poster of a smiling skeleton on the wall above Melody's head announced "Welcome to Arizona! At least it's a *dry* heat!" and he wondered, yet again, at the human sense of humor. Three cups sat on the table, and he thanked the fates that he could enjoy a good espresso and wasn't doomed to take in nothing but blood like some comic book version of his kind.

"Good morning," he said.

Melody smiled up at him. Her smile was haunted by a glimmer of sadness, and there were dark circles under her eyes. He clearly wasn't the only one who'd spent a sleepless night. "Thank you for the coffee."

"Hi. You're welcome. Is Serai okay? She was pretty amazing with that tiger shift and then helping Jack like that." Melody's voice broke on Jack's name, and Reisen handed her a napkin. She took it and wiped her face, then leaned against Reisen's arm for a moment before straightening and taking a deep breath. "I'm sorry. Jack was—Jack was good people. I hope he can come back, and that Quinn and Alaric can fix him."

Daniel nodded, wishing he could offer her some words of comfort, but he'd seen shape-shifters lose their humanity before, and he'd never once seen one of them find his way back. The call of the wild was truly that—a *call*—and nature was a cruel mistress who kept her own once they had returned to her.

"What's the plan for today?" Reisen asked, changing the subject as he exchanged a glance of mutual grim understanding with Daniel. The Atlantean had little hope of Jack's return, either.

"We've got a mole," Melody said.

Reisen raised an eyebrow. "What?"

"An inside source at the bank. She can't work openly with us, because she'd lose her job, and she's a single mom with three kids, but she's on our side for sure. Vampires killed her husband, the bastards," she added heatedly. Then she covered her mouth with one hand. "Oh, um, sorry, Daniel. I realize not all vampires are the bad guys."

Daniel shrugged. "I've been a vampire for more than eleven thousand years, Melody, and have seen more evil perpetrated than you could imagine in your worst nightmares. By vampires and by humans; by witches and by shape-shifters. As you well know, one's race or species doesn't determine the depths of the darkness in one's soul."

"Poetically said," Reisen said, narrowing his eyes. "I must ask, though, by what right is one so ancient traveling with a maiden of Atlantis? It is my sworn duty as a Warrior of Poseidon to protect humanity, and yet it is my duty as an Atlantean and a man to protect Serai."

"Did she seem to need to be protected from me?" Daniel asked dryly. "You might be surprised to learn that she is as old as I am. We first met before Atlantis retreated from the world to the bottom of the ocean."

Reisen inhaled sharply. "But . . . she's *that* Serai? Conlan's Serai?"

"Conlan's no longer, not that he ever had claim to her," Daniel growled. "He abandoned her for Quinn's sister."

Melody put a hand on Reisen's arm and Daniel was surprised to see the warrior react to it, visibly calming. Something lay between the two of them, then, or at least the beginning of something. His gaze traveled between the fierce, proud Atlantean warrior and the small, oddly dressed, human woman. An unlikely match, but then what match was not when it came to these Atlanteans? He and Serai? Quinn and Alaric? Even Conlan and Riley, or Ven and Erin, or crazy Justice and Keely? Not to mention cursed Brennan and the lovely Tiernan.

The Atlantean goddess of love was either insane or an evil genius. Perhaps both.

"This is unproductive," he finally said. "Serai and I have a mission to accomplish, or she and others may die." As they drank their coffee, he filled them in on the details of Serai's connection to the Emperor and what had happened to date.

At one point, Melody excused herself to go purchase pastries and more coffee, and Reisen aimed a long, measuring look at Daniel. "I'm not sure sharing all of this with a human was wise."

Daniel glanced at Melody as she stood at the counter, paying for her purchases. "Quinn trusted her, and Quinn's sister is high princess of Atlantis." He shrugged. "Good enough for me. Are you still planning to help her with her plans concerning the bank?"

"I don't know. I made a promise that I would, and yet your mission sounds more urgent." Reisen ran a hand through his hair. "I'm not sure what to do."

"Fulfill your promise and help Melody with the bank," Daniel advised. "I don't believe in coincidences. There might be some reason why the Emperor is being tampered with in the very same place that the head of this banker/vampire consortium is operating."

"That sounds improbable," Reisen said.

"I know, but almost every critical event in this war has ranged from improbable to impossible. We have to keep this consortium from gaining a foothold, or the rebel cause may be doomed."

Melody returned with a bulging bag and a tray with three more coffees, and Daniel took his cup and stood. "I thank you for the coffee, but I must return in case Serai has woken. We'll rest here during the day, and then we're heading out as soon as the sun goes down."

Melody nodded. "What do you need? Do you have money?"

"Yes, and credit cards enough even to make this over-priced place shiver with glee," he said dryly. "One benefit of living forever, I suppose. Do you need money? I know the rebels are chronically underfunded."

Melody tilted her head. "Yes, and since I'm a bona fide computer genius, I happen to have traced a few of our extraordinarily large donations back to a certain vampire primator. Thank you."

"I'm not Primator. I quit," he said tersely. Tired of explaining that one.

"You think somebody else could do that job better?" Reisen demanded. "Poseidon's balls, man, Atlantis needs allies in high places."

"Yes, and everything I do or have ever done should be predicated on what Atlantis needs, of course," Daniel drawled. "Especially since it was Atlantean soldiers who dragged Serai away from me when I lay dying on the ground all those millennia ago. Atlantean mages and priests who decided to imprison her, so she could serve as brood mare to your royal studs in some distant future. Oh, yeah. Whatever Atlantis wants, I'm all over that."

Reisen's eyes flashed emerald fire, and he rose halfway out of his seat before he reconsidered and sat back down heavily. "Well. I'd be a liar or a fool if I tried to pretend that my goals have never collided with those of the powers that be in Atlantis. But the world needs good men to do good things, or it will be overrun with evil before too much longer."

Melody, who'd sat silently watching them during the exchange, her eyes enormous, suddenly glared at Reisen and elbowed him in the side. "Hey! Good men and good *women*, thank you very much. Now maybe we could make with the friendship and figure out our day."

She pointed to Daniel before he could speak. "You. If you're going to be hiking at all, and I bet you are, if they're skulking around trying to hide this gem you talked about, you'll need gear and provisions. I'll get someone to bring it to you."

Daniel inclined his head in thanks.

"You," she said, turning to Reisen, who seemed to be trying hard not to smile as the small human female put them both in their respective places. "I know you want to help Serai. But I need you, too. Can we compromise? You help me today and tonight, and then we'll both find Daniel and Serai and help them. Both objectives met, and Melody doesn't get killed while trying to rob a bank all by herself."

"I will not let anything happen to you," Reisen said, his eyes flashing again.

Daniel thought about the arrogance in the warrior's voice, and a realization came to him. "Is it *Lord* Reisen, by any chance?"

Reisen nodded, though bitterness was evident in the hard

lines of his face. "It was. Reisen of Mycenae. But I thought I knew a better path for Atlantis, and my error cost me everything."

"You attempted a coup, or so I heard," Daniel said.

"Conlan had been gone, prisoner to your evil goddess Anubisa, for seven long years. I thought he was dead, and Atlantis deserved real leadership, not a group of shell-shocked warriors waiting for a dead prince to return," Reisen said, each word falling like a chunk of granite to the table.

"But he was alive," Daniel said, stating the obvious, realizing how much it must have cost the warrior to realize he'd been wrong.

"He was alive," Reisen agreed. "And so a coup became treachery, and I lost a hand in the process. No less than I deserve, or so most of Atlantis thinks."

"Then they suck. I'm sure you did what you thought was best," Melody said hotly. "What else can any of us do, especially in these crazy times? I'm one of the worst cyber criminals in the world, probably, and do you think I ever envisioned a life of crime? No, no, and no. But what I do is crucial to the rebel cause, and a little threat like a life sentence in Alcatraz isn't going to stop me."

"I don't think they use Alcatraz to house prisoners anymore. It's a tourist attraction now," Daniel pointed out, trying to help the obviously distraught woman.

She rolled her eyes. "*So* missing the point, dude. Anyway, we need to go. Like, now. Our meet with the woman from the bank is coming up soon. We'll be in touch as soon as we can."

She dug around in her ever-present backpack for a while and then handed him a small phone. "Untraceable, disposable cell. Not much use in the canyons, of course, but my number is programmed in."

"I can contact Serai on the Atlantean shared mental pathway, if that is possible between us," Reisen said, and Daniel quashed a momentary pang of jealousy at the idea. Of course her fellow Atlanteans would be able to communicate with her in ways that Daniel never could. It was perfectly reasonable.

It was his own problem that "perfectly reasonable" was stabbing him in the gut.

"Good luck to you. I hope your meeting is successful. It would be very helpful to discover who exactly is involved in this scheme."

They stood, and Melody picked up the remaining cup of coffee and the bag of pastries and held them out to Daniel. "Take these for Serai, okay? And tell her . . . tell her I'd like to get to know her. I bet she could use a girlfriend, since hers are all, well, you know what I mean."

"I'm sure she could. Thank you."

Daniel headed back to his hotel room, where Serai hopefully still slept. So many strange alliances and friendships had formed during the course of the rebellion. Life and hope always found a way, and perhaps it had taken one small human with blue-tipped hair and far too much makeup to remind him of that.

It wouldn't be the strangest thing to have happened to him since that fateful day when Atlantis was attacked. Not by a long shot.

✎

Serai woke to an empty room and lay there, disoriented, for a few seconds until it all came back to her. The escape from Atlantis. The danger she was in and the mission she must complete. The battle. Daniel.

*Daniel.*

Her cheeks flamed as she remembered what he'd done to her—what they'd done together. In the very bed in which she now lay. She lifted the sheet and saw that, yes, she was still shamelessly nude, so she could banish any thought that she might have only dreamed the events of the night. Her lips curved into a smile as she remembered the glorious things he'd done to her oh-so-willing body, but then she sat up in a rush, electrified by a sudden thought.

*Was she even still a maiden at all?*

The door opened as if in answer to her unspoken question, and she gasped until she realized it was Daniel, entering quietly and holding a cup and a small paper bag.

"You went for breakfast? Without me?"

He looked up and smiled at her. A little bit smugly, actually, and she blushed again and clutched the sheets to her chest all the more tightly.

"I left a note for you," he said, indicating the pillow next to her with a nod. As he'd said, there was a note, his bold masculine handwriting slanted across the page.

Gone to get coffee and make plans with Reisen. Back soon.—Daniel

She realized it was the first time she'd ever seen his handwriting. "It looks like you. Your writing. Bold and unhesitating."

He crossed the room and handed her the cup, which smelled deliciously of coffee and spice. She took a sip as he sat next to her on the bed.

"I was certainly bold last night," he said, and she choked on the coffee. He grinned at her, that masculine triumph even more strongly written on his face now.

"Am I still a maiden?" She blurted out the question before embarrassment could stop her, and was intrigued to see the hot red flush that climbed up his cheekbones.

"I— What? Yes. Yes, I mean, you're . . . you're still, well, what we did, ah, I mean—"

She helped him out before he strangled on his answer. Oddly enough, his embarrassment helped her past her own. "It's a simple question. Did you, ah, push past any obstruction with your fingers last night?"

He swallowed audibly, almost a gulping sound, and suddenly she wanted to laugh.

"No, I was careful not to, you know, I didn't want to hurt you, only bring you pleasure, and . . . oh, hell, are you sorry?"

Pain creased his face, and she sobered at the idea that she'd caused him to regret any part of the magical moments he'd shared with her.

"No, Daniel. It was a gift, what you gave to me last night. I only wondered if I were still a maiden because it's a burden I so long to be rid of. Without my maidenhood, I lose my value in the game of kings and their need for breeding stock," she said bitterly.

He took the cup out of her hand and placed it gently on the table beside the bed, and then pulled her into his arms. "Oh, sweetheart. It's not like that anymore. Virginity isn't a prized commodity in today's world, at least not in most areas of the world. People are valued for who they are, not for the lack of bedding experience."

She snuggled into his embrace, content to hold and be held by him for a few minutes, before responding. "Can you be sure it is so in Atlantis? And if yes, why didn't they release us long ago?"

"I don't know. I can't speak to how things are in Atlantis, but I have met Riley and I doubt Conlan wanted her for her virginity. She's past the age when women . . . Ah, well, anyway, I doubt it."

She looked up into his face and smiled to see her big, tough warrior vampire mage turning red again. An impish idea took hold of her. "Should we talk about our feelings now?"

The look of horror on his face made her laugh out loud.

"I was kidding, silly man. Some things have not changed in all these years, I see, and some subjects are still better discussed with one's girlfriends."

Daniel shook his head. "You must be feeling better if you're up to torturing me, you little imp."

She tried on what she hoped was a seductive smile, and he bent his head to hers and captured her mouth in a long and deliciously satisfying kiss. She was quite breathless by the time he raised his head, and little tingles raced through her nerve endings.

"Maybe we should talk about this," he said, jumping up to pace across the floor and away from her. He had a slightly panicked expression on his face, and she wondered what she'd done wrong.

Or right.

She experimented by letting the sheet drop, just the barest inch or so, so that more of the upper slopes of her breasts were visible, and Daniel's eyes darkened.

"You're playing dangerous games with me," he said. "We are trapped in this room until the sun goes down, and I can make very sure there is no question at all about your maiden status by that time, if you wish it so."

It was her turn to freeze as she realized she might be playing with fire, and she wasn't quite sure she was ready to face that kind of flame. She pulled the sheet back up.

"I'm not . . . I don't—"

"Not yet?" He smiled but looked disappointed enough to satisfy her pride.

"Perhaps not ever, Mage," she said haughtily, to cover her sudden shyness. "Do not take my acceptance of your advances for granted."

He just laughed. "I wasn't the one draping myself oh-so-prettily in that bedsheet, Princess."

She blushed again and then lifted one shoulder. "Perhaps we should move on. If you will turn your back, I will dress, and we can discuss your meeting with Reisen."

He shook his head and his gaze seared over her. She wouldn't be surprised if he could see right through the sheet. "I don't think so. I told you once already that I wouldn't miss an opportunity to see your beautiful body, and you have no reason to be shy with me. I touched and tasted every inch of that perfect skin last night."

She caught her breath at the memory of his dark head bent against her breasts, and for a crazy moment, she was tempted to toss the sheet aside, walk nude across the floor, and throw her arms around him. He'd be the one unable to catch his breath then.

Before she could decide one way or the other, he sighed. "Okay. I'm no gentleman, but I can pretend to be one for long enough for you to get dressed. We do have a lot to discuss. But move quickly before my instincts win out over this moment of chivalry and I pounce on you."

He turned around and she jumped out of the bed and ran to the bathroom, not stopping until she closed the door behind her.

His deep laughter followed her into the bathroom, and she listened through the door.

"Oh, sweetheart. You do have the most glorious ass I've ever seen."

She looked at herself in the mirror and confirmed that her face was every bit as bright red as she'd feared, but even as the wave of shyness and embarrassment swept over her, she also admitted to a very feminine feeling of satisfaction.

The most glorious bottom he'd ever seen.

Not bad for an eleven-thousand-year-old woman.

# Chapter 14

## Nicholas's mansion, the basement computer rooms and interrogation chamber

Nicholas watched Ivy as she struggled to gather enough courage to touch the amethyst again. The jewel sat on a velvet cushion, inanimate yet somehow serene, as if daring the sorceress to touch it. She wasn't quite up to taking the dare yet.

He smelled the banker's slightly sour stench even before Smithson entered the room. The smell wasn't body odor; the man was clean enough. Nicholas assumed the stink was the smell of soulless evil.

Pot, skillet.

"Do I even want to know why you have a room in your basement with a two-way glass window installed?" Smithson's voice was too cheerful for someone whose plans were falling apart.

Nicholas decided to remind the banker of that. "Do not presume to question me about my actions, human," he hissed, baring his fangs. He was rewarded with the banker's barely visible shudder. Smithson was tough enough for a mortal, but Nicholas had lived for centuries and crushed the spirits of far tougher wannabe predators than this one.

"I'm not questioning you," Smithson said quickly. "I just—"

"The attack at the rebel campground was a complete and utter failure," Nicholas said. "Your intelligence was flawed. Not only were the numbers greater than your men reported, but they had two shape-shifters on their side, both tigers. Not to mention a vampire of their own."

Nicholas's source, one of his blood pride, had actually reported seeing that one of the shifters had been a saber-toothed tiger, but he assumed the vampire had been struck senseless with fear or stupidity. Either way, Nicholas didn't care. He'd sent the sniveling idiot to the true death for his idiocy.

Nicholas didn't like visual reminders of failure, as his subordinates had long since learned. He was a big fan of killing the messenger if the news happened to be bad. Not necessarily a great communication strategy, but eminently satisfying.

"A vampire? I thought you were in charge of all of them in this region," Smithson said. "How could one stand against us? Do you have a traitor in your group?"

In a movement so fast it blurred, Nicholas pinned Smithson to the wall, pressing his arm into the banker's neck. "Do not dare to question me, or I will enjoy draining you of every drop of your blood. There are many humans ready and willing to take your place."

Smithson's face turned the color of an overripe tomato as he struggled to draw a breath. Nicholas finally tired of the game and let him go with a final warning. "Remember that."

Nicholas saw the look of utter hatred that crossed the banker's face, but he laughed. He had far more to worry about than a human's anger.

"She won't try," he said, pointing to Ivy, who still sat huddled on the floor, as far from the gemstone as was possible in the small room. "I think her fear of the gem is outweighing her fear of me, as impossible as that sounds."

"Oh, not for long," Smithson said, retaining a measure of his composure as he rubbed the red marks on his neck.

"If we can't torture them into doing what we want, we can always make life miserable for their families."

The banker walked to the doorway and said something to one of his thugs waiting outside and then returned to Nicholas.

"Watch this."

The door to the room opened, and Ivy flinched and looked up, then cried out and ran across the room. A boy stumbled into the room as if pushed.

"Ian! What—where did you—why are you here?" She pulled him into a fierce hug and burst into tears.

The boy awkwardly patted her back. "Sheesh, Mom, calm down. It's okay. I'm here now, and I'll take care of you."

Nicholas eyed the boy's bruised face and blackened eye, and a slow wave of rage churned through his gut. "What did you do to him?"

"I didn't do anything. Some of my men may have gotten a little carried away." The nasty little banker had the nerve to smile. "I wish I could always do business like this. Threatening their families makes them so much more agreeable."

Almost casually, Nicholson backhanded the banker so hard that the man flew backward and struck the wall before sliding down to the floor.

"We don't make war on children. Remember it," he said.

"Don't ever put your hands on me again, or I'll be sure you never get one word of information about the investors," Smithson shouted. The effect of his belligerence was muted somewhat by the fact he still sat on the floor and cringed when Nicholas turned around.

"If that boy is hurt again, even so much as a minor bruise or cut, I'll *end* you," Nicholas said. "I've survived for centuries without your pathetic excuse for help. You might remember that when you're considering how very fragile humans are."

Smithson struggled to stand up. The man was a worthless pile of excrement, but he was no coward, Nicholas had to give him that.

"You promised to turn me. I want to be a vampire," Smithson said. "Whatever it takes."

"Indeed. Whatever it takes, I promise to drain all the blood from your body." Nicholas let all the feeling and movement vanish slowly from his expression until he stood utterly motionless, like a particularly deadly block of ice.

Smithson shuddered again, but persevered. "And then give me some of yours. Three times. Once is only a blood bond, I know that much."

Ivy pounded on the window, saving Nicholas from the annoyance of a reply.

"You let him go," she screamed. "I'll do anything you want. Just let him go."

Nicholas pressed a button on the panel set into the wall next to the window and leaned forward. "You'll do anything I want, anyway, my beautiful little witch. Now try again with the jewel, and we'll send in food and drink for you and the boy."

Tears gathered in her eyes, but she blinked them back, squaring her shoulders to appear strong for her boy. Nicholas admired that in a mother. His own son's mother had been a sniveling coward, too terrified to even let Nicholas approach his boy. No matter that Nicholas had been forced into this life; he'd not chosen to become vampire.

Ancient history had no place here, however. He banished the unwelcome memories and focused on Ivy. Beautiful and deadly, the witch had dabbled in the black side of her magic often enough to gain the title sorceress and dark powers she had no business wielding. Time enough to put shackles on her later, though. For now he needed every bit of her strength and didn't care overly much where she found it.

"No, Mom, your nose has been bleeding again," Ian said, trying to stop his mother from approaching the amethyst. "You know what the doctor said. Too much magic, and you could get a brain aneurysm, remember? You can't push like this again."

Ivy shook her head. "Ian, you don't understand. I have

to help these . . . men . . . or they'll hurt us." She put a gentle hand on his face and tilted it to the light to better see the bruising, and when she turned back toward the window, her eyes were glowing with a deep purple fire.

"Know this. Whoever hurt my son will pay for it," she said, each word a deadly chip of ice. "If you touch him again, I'll kill you."

Nicholas inclined his head, though she couldn't see it, and touched the panel again. "You have my word your son will be unharmed. The one who bruised him will be punished. We will not release either of you, however, until you achieve our goal. Do you understand?"

It was her turn to nod. She drew in a deep breath and then turned to the amethyst, and three quick steps later she held it in her hands. It did something to her—something he couldn't see but which clearly hurt her, judging by the sound she made and how her face drained of all color. She only tightened her fingers around the gem and closed her eyes, and began murmuring something under her breath, a kind of chant that even Nicholas, with his vampire hearing, couldn't quite make out.

Seconds later, though, a pulse of magic rocked the building, and a weak, pale beam of violet light shot out of the gem, spilling between her fingers and across the room. Its end terminated on the third drawer of the second in a line of filing cabinets.

Precisely spotlighting the single location in the room where he had previously hidden a small cache of gold and jewels.

"Houston, we have liftoff," Nicholas murmured.

Smithson hesitantly moved up next to him at the mirror as the light vanished. Ivy fell to the ground, and her son ran to gather her up. Nicholas stared at the thin stream of blood that trickled from the witch's nose. A brain aneurysm would be most unfortunate at this point in the process.

"We need to find a way to strengthen or reinforce her magic so it doesn't harm her to use the gem," he told Smithson.

The banker blinked rapidly, which had the unpleasant effect of making him look even more like a rodent than he usually did. "You care about what happens to her? I thought she was just a tool."

"I take good care of my tools, as any competent mechanic would. If she dies, she is of no use to us, and we need her for this."

"Are you finally ready to tell me what exactly the plan is?"

Nicholas glanced at the human, considering. So long as he kept Smithson at hand, there was little to no chance of betrayal. Why not, after all? There was no danger here.

"The gem acts as a dowsing rod for other gems and for gold. Any valuable mined from the earth. It might even find oil, for all we know."

Smithson whistled, long and loud. "That's—that's—"

"Exactly."

"How did you find out about this?"

"It was one of your human archaeologists, actually, who recently discovered cave writing that translated into a heretofore unknown legend from the days of the Sinagua Indians. According to these pictographs, the Sinagua hid a great treasure when the vampires first came to the area. Their medicine men warned them that they might not survive as a people, and apparently they wanted to record this story for posterity."

Smithson held up a hand. "Hold up. Your kind is why the Sinagua died out all those years ago? Have you told anybody? All the historians and archaeologists around here would go crazy for that information, and now that vampires are part of society, you can tell them this stuff freely, right? It's not like you can get in trouble for what some unrelated vampires did hundreds of years ago."

Nicholas bared just the slightest hint of fang. "Are you so sure they were unrelated?"

Smithson recoiled a little, but said nothing.

"The vampire goddess Anubisa—Chaos praise her, wherever she may be—long ago laid down a prohibition against sharing our history with mortals. But none of that is your business. All you need to know is that the legend from the pictograph told of a magical gem from the city beneath the waters, and that it could find treasure such as gems and gold and silver, because like called to like."

"The city beneath the waters? Venice?"

Nicholas wished for a moment that he could afford simply to drain the fool now and give his dead body to the members of his blood pride to dispose of. Sadly, necessity made strange crime-committing fellows.

"Atlantis, you idiot."

Smithson started laughing. "So it's a fairy tale. Great. You're basing our hope of funding for the consortium's initial investment on Atlantis? Why not just ask Santa Claus for the money?"

"Atlantis most definitely existed and still does. From what I hear, it's nearly ready to take its place in the world again, if you and your kind don't bomb it back to the deep when it rises. But those are problems for another day. For now, we feed our witch and her son and let them rest, because this evening we're going out to the canyons and caves to see what we can find when fewer prying eyes will be around."

Smithson's expression still said he didn't really believe any of it, but just then Ian, having settled his mother on the bench inside the interrogation room, walked over to the file cabinet and pulled open the drawer which the gem had pointed out just minutes before.

"Holy crap, Mom! There's a freaking fortune in here!"

"Don't say holy crap, Ian," Ivy said tiredly, not even bothering to open her eyes. She'd wiped the blood off her upper lip, Nicholas saw, but she looked pale enough to faint at any moment. Nearly unconscious and clearly in pain, but still mother enough to chastise her son for bad language. As Nicholas watched the lovely witch, he felt something in his chest warm in a way he hadn't felt for more than three hundred years, and he flinched away from the window.

He'd been wrong. There was danger here, after all. He watched her a moment longer and then turned to the banker.

"Bring me the man who hurt that boy. I want to have a word or two with him over breakfast."

He laughed, fangs fully descended, as the banker scurried from the room. Nicholas was in a wonderful mood, and why not? The witch would find the gem, the consortium was on track, and to top it all off, the blood of a man who had hurt a child would taste so much better than scrambled eggs. He glanced through the one-way glass again, his gaze returning to the lovely witch and her son.

Yes. So much better than eggs.

# Chapter 15

### Oak Creek Canyon, just after nightfall

"Are you sure this is right?" Daniel looked around, his night vision excellent, and wondered if Serai's exhaustion was playing tricks upon her connection with the Emperor. She'd fallen back into a deep sleep at the hotel after their conversation about plans, not even waking when Melody's friends brought the gear. Apparently the events of the day and night before and the strain from the Emperor's fluctuations had weakened her far beyond what she'd wanted to admit. He'd spent a restless day trying to sleep, listen for danger, and keep from touching her. Or biting her. Or fucking her.

Or all three at once.

He'd also had three cold showers and a brief period around noon where he feared he was descending into lunacy. Oh, yeah, it had been a hell of a day. And now his fragile, darling, innocent sex kitten of a princess was telling him to shut up.

"Yes, as I said the other five times, Daniel. Please be quiet now, so I can try to sense the Emperor again." She leaned against a tree and looked up into the sky. "Look. It's Draco, curled around the Little Dipper. Was that one of your names?"

"Honey, there's nothing little about my dipper."

She rolled her eyes, but at least he'd made her smile. It lightened the shadows in her eyes, if only for a moment. "No, Draco. Or Drakos."

"How could you know that?"

"Oh the attendants in the temple loved to gossip, and the exploits of Conlan and his warriors were constant fodder. I heard much of their vampire ally Drakos. A vampire who was a friend to the high prince's brother was very gossip-worthy. It never occurred to me that Drakos could be . . ." she finished in a strained voice.

"I've had many names over the years," he said, shrugging the backpack to a more comfortable position. "Something to pass the time. Daniel was not always a name that fit in where I happened to be."

"What are some of the others?"

He breathed deep of the pine-drenched desert night air and caught the slightest scent of sea salt and woman.

*His* woman.

He shook his head. She was his only in his dreams. The beauty never ended up with the beast, despite brief moments of pleasure and the beast's futile wishes.

"Names? Or are you ignoring me on purpose?" she asked teasingly.

"They almost always began with the same letter, for ease of remembering. Drakos, Demetrios. Lately, Devon. Once, for a memorable period, D'Artagnan. Generally back to Daniel whenever possible."

"Because it's your real name."

"Yes, but that's not the reason. I kept coming back to Daniel because it was the name you'd called me," he said softly, but he knew by her indrawn breath that she'd heard him.

"I . . . Wait. Daniel, I can feel it. The Emperor. It's closer than ever before, and it's moving." She started running forward and he caught her arm.

"No. Let's not charge headlong into danger, okay? It's safe to bet that whoever has the gem is not going to want to give it up and is almost certainly not after it for innocent reasons. It has a lot of power, which tends to draw the attention of those who want to accumulate a lot of power. These are rarely the nicest people you might want to meet."

She turned toward him, and he tried not to think about touching the curve of her neck, or the delightful curve where her hip met her waist. Tried not to think about unbraiding her hair and wrapping his hands in fistfuls of those lush curls.

*Tried* not to think about it. Failed miserably, but at least he'd tried.

"Daniel. You're looking at me the way I looked at that chocolate cake," she murmured. "I confess I like it, but now isn't the best time."

He leaned down and stole a single kiss. It would have to tide him over. "You're right, of course. Now tell me about what you feel, and how close you think the Emperor is to where we are now."

"It's north—no, west of here. Where is that?"

"It's the Red Rock Secret Mountain Wilderness area," Daniel said grimly. "Of course they couldn't be at a coffee shop. Well, enough of this. We can't do much with the car Melody's friends brought us, since the direction you're sensing is pure hiking country, but we're certainly not hiking, in spite of these fancy clothes and boots. You're wasting energy you don't need to expend, especially when you're traveling with someone who can fly."

"No!" She backed away from him, violently shaking her head back and forth. "I can't."

"I'll keep you safe. It's just a matter of closing your eyes if you feel dizzy." He knew it was easier to show her, so he swept her into his arms and launched into the air. He made it about ten feet above the ground before she started to scream.

In his ear.

He was so startled he nearly lost his grip on her waist, and she slipped a little and then started screaming even louder. Then her entire body started shaking and spasming in his arms, and he headed back for the ground, fast. When he landed and her feet were firmly on the ground, though, the screaming didn't stop. If anything, it intensified in volume, and she kept shaking so hard he was afraid she was having a seizure.

"Serai, please, tell me what to do. I'm sorry, I didn't know, please help me. Damn it, I don't know what to do here," he said, holding her tightly to try to calm the spasms.

Slowly—ever so slowly—the shaking subsided. She stopped screaming and began sobbing, loud, hoarse sobs that were almost as painful to him as they must be to her. She pulled away from him and sank to the ground, still sobbing as if her heart would break any minute.

"Delia. Oh, no, poor Delia, she was the youngest of us. All that lovely golden hair, oh no, oh no, oh no," she kept repeating, tears streaming down her face.

He crouched down and took her in his arms and patted her back and stroked her hair—anything that might offer her some comfort. He had a sinking suspicion about who Delia might be, and even the monster crouched inside him roared its anguish at the thought. If one of the other maidens had just died, how long might it be until the person wielding the Emperor's powers caused Serai to join her?

Daniel would find this witch and kill her. Take the Emperor back to Atlantis, so Alaric and the rest of them could figure out a way to save Serai and the others. He'd capture Poseidon himself and demand the sea god's help, if need be.

*Whatever it took.*

"Whatever it takes," he said, out loud, as Serai's sobs began to quiet. "We will find the Emperor and rescue your sisters. I swear this to you on my life."

She finally stopped crying and took a deep, shuddering breath before looking up at him. "I felt it, Daniel. I felt her die."

"Delia?"

She nodded. "Yes. She— The Emperor's connection to us stuttered and grew weak, but then a powerful surge of energy speared out through it and the witch who's trying to access its power. She's learning how to use it, Daniel. But I don't think she has any idea that she's hurting people by doing it. She's . . . afraid, I think. And Delia. Oh, Daniel. She never had a chance to live her life at all. It's not fair."

As she cried, curled against his chest like a wounded child, his heart shattered and then re-formed in ice and granite. So the witch who played with the Emperor's magic was afraid, was she? Not *yet* she wasn't. She hadn't known anything like the terror he was going to crash down on her head. When he got his hands on her and anyone else who'd been participating in this deadly game, they'd all be very, very afraid.

They would be afraid, and then they would be dead. He swore it on his ancient oath as a mage of the Nightwalker Guild.

"I can't fly, Daniel. I'm sorry," she whispered, interrupting his silent plans to rip, tear, and maim.

A horrible thought jumped into his mind. "Is that why you had the seizure? Serai, I'm sorry. I thought if you saw how safe it is, you'd—"

"No. No, the seizure was due to the Emperor, but I can't fly. I'm terrified of heights, and I don't know how to calm down. I don't think we have time for me to try to learn how to be unafraid, not now. Maybe later?" She attempted a smile, but her face was far too pale, and her terror was evident in her eyes and the way she bit her lip.

"Don't worry about it. We can find another way. I can walk almost as fast as I can fly. We'll find the Emperor. I promise you."

They took a few minutes to drink some water, and Serai splashed a little on her face, and then they resumed following the path that only she could sense, to wherever the Emperor was now. The hike would have been beautiful in the daytime, Daniel imagined, but imagination was all that he'd known of sunlight for so long—other than those brief moments in Atlantis—that he didn't dwell on it. There was a unique kind of beauty in the dark. The moon's silvery light cast fascinating geometric shadows on the red rock formations for which the areas was famous. He could tell by Serai's pounding heartbeat, though, that she had no attention to spare for scenery.

"Tell me about the fear of heights," he said, mostly to distract both of them from what waited ahead in the night. "I wouldn't have thought there were all that many high places in an undersea city."

She shrugged her slender shoulders. "Not that many. Enough."

He could hear it in her voice: this was no random fear. "Enough?"

"I don't want to talk about it," she said flatly.

"Maybe I need to hear it. What happened?"

"I threw myself off one of the palace towers. I wanted to die."

～～～

Serai sped up her pace, but she might as well not have bothered. Daniel's fingers bit into her shoulders as he swung her around to face him, and his face was strained and harsh in the moonlight; as forbidding as if a stranger faced her. Which, after all, was exactly what he was now, despite what they'd shared in that hotel bedroom. He'd lived thousands of years that she knew nothing about, while she'd waited, trapped in a crystalline cage, bound to millennia of nothingness.

"Why?" His harsh voice echoed in the clear, cool night air. "Why would you do such a thing?"

"Have you never looked into your future and found it so bleak that you decided not to face it?" She shot the question at him but was surprised when he flinched.

"But you were a princess. You had everything to live for—"

"I had nothing. You were gone, and they told me you were dead. After my father's physician *verified* my maidenhood was intact, he told me the *wonderful* news. I was to be put to sleep and locked in a cage for centuries, if not longer, and when I woke up I would get to be queen! Of the Seven Isles! No matter that everyone I'd ever known and loved would be dead and rotted to dust by the time I awoke."

His face hardened, probably at the bitterness in her tone. But what did she care for his feelings? He'd been happy enough to abandon her with no concern for hers.

"I came back for you," he said in a voice like broken glass. "I came back as soon as I was able, and you were gone. No, you went one better than that—you were gone and you'd *taken your entire continent with you*. Atlantis was gone, Serai. Gone forever. Destroyed and all of you dead, or so the Atlanteans remaining on the shore told me. I wanted to die then, too. Tried my damndest to make it happen, but the monster I'd become took over, and all I knew for hundreds of years was the bloodlust."

He bent down to pick up a stone and hurled it through the air so hard it shattered into dust when it struck the nearest rock face. "Bloodlust and despair. Bleak emptiness, for centuries. When I finally met these Atlanteans no more than a year or two ago, it never would have occurred to me to ask about you—a woman who'd lived so many millennia ago. I'm sorry. That was my failure. But had I known you lived, and had I known how to find a city at the bottom of the sea, either then or now, I would have braved the wrath of Poseidon himself to come for you."

She froze, caught by the raw sincerity of his words. It was impossible to do anything but believe him, which meant he hadn't willingly left her.

"You didn't abandon me," she whispered, and he pulled her into his arms in a fierce embrace.

"I would never have left you. But now you have survived imprisonment and stasis, and you deserve to have a life with someone other than an ancient monster." He held her so tightly, almost as if he were saying good-bye, and the surety came to her that he would leave her as soon as they found the Emperor, if she did not take steps to prevent it.

Starting now.

"I will tell you what happened that day, if you like," she said quietly. "If you promise not to leave me again."

He tried to pull away, but she tightened her arms around his waist.

"I promise not to leave you until we have completed this task and you are safe," he finally said, before he broke away and started walking again.

It was her turn to grasp his arm and pull him to a stop. "That's not good enough. You want me. I know you do."

He groaned. "What does that matter? I'm not what you'll want—what you'll need—when you're safe and you've had a chance to think about your future."

"Then promise me that. You won't leave me until I ask you to do so."

He bowed his head and blew out a breath, but finally nodded. "Yes. I will promise that."

She smiled and rose up on her toes to kiss his cheek, and then started on toward the Emperor's faint but steady presence somewhere west of them.

"Though it will probably kill me, when you do ask," he said, so quietly she almost didn't hear him.

She raised her chin and smiled a little. He'd have a very long wait coming if he was waiting for her to ever ask him to leave. Especially after the last time . . .

"Do you want to hear? About what happened that day after you were injured?"

"Yeah. Why not? We have a long walk in front of us, I'm guessing," he said casually, as if it didn't matter one way or the other. But she knew better. She knew she mattered to him.

She was counting on it.

"You, first. What happened after you pushed me down through that trapdoor, to the hiding place underneath the shop?" She paused for a moment to confirm her sense of the Emperor, and then kept walking, not giving Daniel a chance to argue. Still, they walked along in silence for another five or six minutes before he finally spoke.

"I did my best, but I was a foolish boy. The soldiers who attacked were well-armed and no strangers to battle. Or looting and raping and pillaging, for that matter. I probably would have been better to have hidden with you."

"You wanted to protect me," she said, touching his arm.

"You wanted to protect the shop, too, over your sense of loyalty to your absent mentor."

He laughed, but there was no humor in it. "Right. Absent. He was there all the time, all those days I thought he was out buying things for the shop. He was sleeping beneath my feet, hiding from the sun. Sleeping in the dirt like an animal, like he taught me to do."

She shivered at the stark bitterness in his voice. "But I thought he helped you. He was so elegant, the few times I met him, and the jewelry in the shop so exquisite. Where did he find that?"

Daniel shrugged. "I made some of it. The not-as-elegant pieces, although I tried so hard— Well. That's another story. But he purchased some of it, and I did see him fashion some of the more amazing abstract pieces himself. I remember thinking at the time that he had uncommon strength in his hands and fingers, the way he could bend the metals."

She remembered the unusual look of many of the pieces. So very lovely—styled with classic lines and simplicity, instead of the ornate design that had been in fashion then. She'd wanted one for herself, but her father was strict about such purchases, always telling her that one day she'd have a husband to buy things for her.

The wave of anger that swept through her at the memory caught her off guard, as did the sharp loneliness that followed. Though she'd had so many differences with her father and had once hated him for what he'd done to her, he'd still been her father. Now he was gone, along with her mother and brother, her friends, and everyone else she'd ever known. She was alone in a world that had moved on without her, and only Daniel had survived as her single constant from then till now. She slipped her hand in his and squeezed, needing the comfort, and was relieved when his fingers tightened around hers in response.

"One of the soldiers who believed strongly that he deserved a free helping of rings and bracelets stabbed me in the side and smashed the hilt of his sword against my head. That's the last thing I knew," Daniel said. "I suppose I should have been grateful that he didn't use the sharp end and rip out my throat. I knew how to forge a sword but not much of how to use one, at least not in a real fight."

"I think they must have thought you were dead. There was so much blood, Daniel. You had bled so much that I was sure you were dead when we first found you."

His hand tightened around hers with gentle reassurance. "I nearly was."

"Yes, you nearly were," she whispered, her voice trembling. "I hid down there, terrified, until long after the shouts and stamping of the horses had passed. After I'd heard only silence for nearly half an hour, I finally gathered the courage to come back up and find you. But I couldn't move the door. I tried with all my strength and even pushed with a board I found down there in the dirt with me, but to no avail."

"I'd fallen right over top of the trapdoor," Daniel said. "My last-ditch attempt to hide you, I remember. And all I did was cause you more fear and pain." He kicked a tree root.

"No, you can't think like that. You did your best, and you saved my life. Or, at the very least, you saved me from being used as a plaything for those horrible men." She shuddered at the thought of being violated like that. Death wouldn't have been worse—death was final, with no chance of healing. But death might have been easier. Ice ran through her veins at the thought of what she'd escaped.

"You were too valuable for that, *mi amara*," he said gently. "You would have been treated as a precious commodity to become some warlord's wife."

She stumbled over a fallen branch, uncharacteristically clumsy in her shock at his use of the Atlantean term for "my beloved." He'd called her his beloved, and probably didn't even realize it.

She'd never forget it.

But, still, they were talking about the past. "Warlord's *wife*. Prince's wife. King's wife. What does it matter? All of them would have robbed me of my freedom in different ways."

"Would Conlan have forced you to wed him if you said no?" Daniel growled. "I can convince him of the error of that thinking the next time I see him."

"I don't know. I like to think not, especially with the choice he himself made that shattered Atlantean law, but I just don't know. Princes generally choose with politics in mind, not people, or so the Emperor has shown me over the past millennia."

"Back to that day," Daniel prompted. "You finally got out when the mage woke up to help, he told me."

"He terrified me. I was suddenly aware that someone other than me was down there, and I was afraid that one of the soldiers had found his way in, but then I thought it might be a nightwalker. I'd only heard of them—you—vampires," she explained, stumbling over the words. "I didn't know what to think. If his bloodlust was going to mean my horrible death."

"Adrianus had been controlling his bloodlust for centuries by then."

She stopped, closing her eyes and reaching out for the Emperor's unique energy signal again. "I can feel it, closer this time. Daniel, we're nearly there. But, oh, no, not again."

Pain smashed into her as the witch controlling the Emperor channeled power through it once more, and Serai doubled over. "It's stronger this time. I think I'm in trouble. Oh, by the gods, it hurts."

Daniel shocked her by throwing her on the ground, safely cradled in his arms, and covering her body with his own. "We're definitely in trouble. I can hear voices, and they're coming from the trees and sky, and they're moving too fast to be human. This can't be a coincidence. Whoever has the Emperor, they have vampires with them."

# Chapter 16

### Sedona National Bank, inside the vault

Melody grinned at the big hunk of muscled Atlantean roaming restlessly back and forth in the claustrophobic bank vault.

"Does it help? The pacing, I mean. Does it make life better? Make the time pass faster? Cure the common cold?"

Reisen snarled something at her in a language she didn't recognize, but she translated what he said well enough as "impatient man talk." He was clearly the action hero type, not the sensitive-and-prone-to-anxiety type she usually fell for.

*Whoa.*

Even in the privacy of her own mind, thinking "fell for" in context of this man was way, way off base. It was like curling up for a few hot hours of World of Warcraft and finding a gnome and Tauren hot-tubbing in Arathi Basin.

Just not gonna happen. No way.

But man, oh, man, was the guy hot. Seriously hot. Mega hot. All those muscles. Plus those flashing blue eyes and bad boy long black hair combined to make her want to rub up against him and purr.

A lot.

Unfortunately, he'd been the perfect gentleman in the hotel room he'd insisted they share for her protection. She'd been all "right, for my *protection*, heh heh heh," but her flutters of anticipation had turned to stark dismay when he hadn't even tried to touch her once. Not even by "accident." She'd almost thought he was gay, until she'd dropped her towel accidentally-on-purpose and seen the flash of sheer admiration and male lust cross his face. That had been *great* for her ego . . . right up to the point where he'd stalked past her into the bathroom and taken a long and, she suspected, very cold shower.

Alone.

She hadn't quite worked up the courage to join him. A little too brazen ho-bag for her.

Now she sat on the floor of the vault, working her magic on a tough algorithm, trying to get past the encryption on what she figured was some very juicy data, while Reisen paced. And paced. And paced.

"What time is it?"

"Nine o'clock. This is going to take me a while, so you should try to relax."

"What is the value of this data, anyway? Why is it so important?"

"From what Quinn said, it's everything you ever wanted to know about the plans to fund a mega vampire and banker consortium. Their goals are apparently to take over all financial institutions, crush any rebellions, and—so Quinn said—there's even a faction that knows about you guys. They apparently want to convince the world that Atlantis is an evil superpower bent on world domination before you even show up to the party."

"That's ridiculous," he snarled. "Atlantis is and always has been a peaceful nation. In fact, we have served and protected humans for more than eleven thousand years, since the time we first dove beneath the sea. As a sworn Warrior of Poseidon, I know this firsthand to be true. Not that your kind has ever appreciated it. And this latest madness, accepting the vampire race as your equals, when they only look at you as food—that has made many of us believe that you deserve what you get. We don't want to dominate any part of your foolish world. We only wish you'd quit expecting us to fight your battles for you."

"I never expected anything of the sort, big guy," she said mildly, keying in the final codes to break through the encryption sequence. Now it was a matter of time and waiting and hoping there wasn't some kind of self-destruct written into the encryption code, like in a bad movie. She set the laptop on the floor next to her and stretched.

"What's a Warrior of Poseidon, anyway? Some kind of cult of hot guys? Is that what that tattoo on your chest is about?"

He narrowed his eyes. "When did you see that?"

"Um, I might have peeked when you came out of the bathroom in only a towel." She could feel her face turning pink, but what the heck. He'd been totally worth looking at. "What does it mean? Can I see it again?"

He scowled, but pulled his shirt up to show her the tat. She tried not to swallow her tongue as the move revealed his ripped abs and then the broad, muscular chest she'd wanted to get her hands on the night before.

High on the right side of his chest, she saw the tat again.

"This mark was branded on my skin by Poseidon himself when I swore my vow to serve the sea god and protect humanity. The circle represents all the peoples of the world, intersected by the pyramid of knowledge deeded to them by the ancients. The silhouette of Poseidon's trident bisects them both."

He shoved his shirt back down, and a dark flush rose on his cheekbones. She stared at him, fascinated, realizing he felt shy. The big, tough warrior who'd saved her life was shy about taking his shirt off.

The contradiction was kind of adorable, and definitely hot.

"So you swore to protect humans? And you're trying to tell me you're eleven thousand years old?" She rolled her eyes. "I'm guessing, let me think, um, *no*."

"No, I'm not eleven thousand years old, but the first Warriors of Poseidon who originally swore the vow to protect— Oh, hells, are you almost done with that computer?"

She shrugged. "It's working. Could take a while."

"What time is it?"

She glanced at the bottom right of her computer screen. "Nine-fifteen. Fifteen minutes past the last time you asked. Don't you have a watch?"

She could have barbecued chicken in the heat of his glare. Which reminded her that she was hungry. Again. As usual. For more than just food, too, after seeing him in all his muscled glory. But she figured she was out of luck on that one. Scruffy human computer nerds were so not his type, probably.

"I don't wear watches. They don't function properly with Atlantean magic around them. My father—" He stopped talking mid-sentence and glared at her again. "Why am I telling you any of this?"

"Your father?" She rummaged around in her backpack, looking for a granola bar or an apple. Preferably a Snickers. It had nuts. Health food, for sure.

"None of your business, human." He whirled around and started back across the floor.

"Seriously?" She started laughing. She couldn't help it. "*Human?* Are you going to start mumbling 'my Precio-ussssss' next?"

"What are you talking about? I never understand anything that comes out of your mouth," he growled, actually *growled* at her, and she laughed again.

Which seemed to irritate him even more.

"Interesting you mention my mouth, since you can't seem to stop staring at it," she added, taunting him.

He whirled around and flashed across the room so fast she didn't even see him move, and suddenly she was suspended in midair, held up by his big hands on her upper arms. His gorgeous, angry face was inches away from hers, and his eyes were practically glowing a hot, dark blue.

No, wait.

They actually *were* glowing.

Oh, crap.

"I don't want to stare at your mouth," he said, biting off each word. "I don't want to stare at your bizarre hair, or your curvy little body, or the silky way your skin shines even in this hideous light. I didn't want to have to restrain myself from tearing your clothes from you last night while you slept, and plunging into your hot, wet, tight—"

"I get it," she said, gasping. "Got it. Totally. You don't want to want me. Check. You can let me go now."

He lowered her slowly down the length of his body until she was standing on her own two, rather unsteady legs, but he didn't release her arms.

"No," he said, tilting his head. "I don't think I can let you go right now."

He bent his head to hers and she saw it coming, even had time to escape, because he'd relaxed his grip on her arms, but she didn't want to escape. Didn't want to be let go. She put her arms around his neck and grinned up at him.

"This is going to be trouble," she whispered.

"You already are," he said, and then he kissed her, and oh, holy Linux squared but the man could *kiss*. She melted against him shamelessly, every nerve cell in her body dancing a tango—or at least a wild drunken chicken dance—at the feel of his mouth on hers.

Then he put those big hands of his on her butt and lifted her up and into him, against that extremely large, hard erection, and she quit thinking of anything at all except to thank her lucky stars that she'd already disconnected all the cameras in the vault for the entire night.

That decryption was going to take an awfully long time after all.

When her back hit the wall of safe-deposit boxes, and his mouth closed over her breast right through her top, she leaned her head back and moaned as loudly as she wanted. It was a soundproof vault, and nobody was in the bank but them. Nobody was coming, either. Reisen shoved her top and bra out of his way and sucked her nipple into his mouth and she revised that thought.

She fervently hoped at least the two of them would be coming. Soon.

# Chapter 17

### Red Rock Secret Mountain Wilderness area

Daniel finally allowed Serai to stand up when he hadn't heard anything but the sounds of nature for at least fifteen minutes.

"Are they gone?" she whispered, brushing dirt off her hiking clothes. "Also, what was it? More vampires?"

"Yes. I thought a few shifters were with them, at first, but flying shifters would have been birds, silent or chirping or something, not talking. They were vampires, and they were clumsy amateurs. Loud and arrogant, without a clue somebody might have been here to hear them."

"Lucky for us, surely?"

He touched her cheek and smiled at her, trying to shove the knot of fear and rage for her—for what might happen to her if they didn't succeed—deeper in his gut. She didn't need to know he had the slightest doubt.

"Everything is lucky for us. When we're done with this little errand, we'll go to Vegas."

She laughed. "Isn't that in the desert? With the places humans go to shove money in machines and listen to the little bell sounds?"

He shook his head. "I think that was one strange filter the Emperor put your knowledge of the world through."

"Yes, I would agree," she said seriously. "Who is Justin Bieber, and why is his hair poisonous to small girls?"

It was a long time before he could stop laughing hard enough to answer her.

They made good time, considering, and had hiked nearly three miles when she admitted to needing a break. She drank water and ate some bread and nuts from her pack, while he stared at her and tried not to think about how sweet her blood might taste.

It was a very unsatisfying rest break, which only got worse when she pinned him with that sapphire gaze and asked the one question he'd been praying she'd never get around to asking.

"What happened to you after you became a nightwalker? What have you been up to for the past eleven millennia?"

He stood up so fast he knocked over the rock he'd been using for a seat. "We need to get going. Definitely no time to discuss boring details of the past several thousand years."

She put her things away in her backpack and didn't answer him, but he could feel the weight of her disappointment—or disapproval—in her silence.

"It's not a pretty story," he finally said, not looking at her. Not wanting to see her face.

"I don't want pretty. I want the truth. All I've ever wanted. Your history is a part of you, and I love . . . I love to hear about the past," she said, biting her lip.

Daniel felt like the rock he'd been sitting on had just slammed into the side of his head. She loved him? Had she been about to admit to that?

No. Of course not. He was a damned fool to think it.

"Not my past," he said flatly. "Nobody would love to hear about my past."

"Then don't tell me all of it. Just tell me the part that happened right after you became a nightwalker. What happened? Did it hurt? Was the mage training hard?" She slipped her hand in his so naturally that he almost didn't notice it until they'd taken a few steps, and then a wave of warmth and peace swept through him and he tightened his fingers, never wanting to let her go.

They walked in silence for nearly ten minutes, Serai apparently content to wait for his response, while he considered what to say. Finally he shrugged. Let her hear it, then. Let her know firsthand what a monster he was. It would be easier for her to let him go when the time came.

Easier for him to leave *her* to a better fate, as well.

"I became a monster. There was nothing left of the Daniel you knew; he lost himself to the bloodlust and the pain of losing you."

She flinched a little, but tightened her grip on his hand. "I'd heard it was bad at the beginning, for the newly made."

"It's bad enough, as far as I saw from others, but never as bad as I became, or at least that's what they told me. I had lost you forever. I thought you were dead. I had nothing else to live for, so I didn't bother to live. I wanted to die, but the monster's sense of self-preservation was too strong."

He heard her indrawn breath, but ruthlessly continued. She'd wanted to hear it. She could hear it all.

"By the time I was sane enough to think that maybe the story I'd heard was wrong, that maybe you lived, Atlantis was gone. Vanished beneath the sea. After that, I became a monster the like of which the world had never seen. For several years, I raged and rampaged, killing humans and treating them as nothing more than prey for slaughter. I went after the criminals and the rogue soldiers, those who looted and pillaged and raped. I killed them all and drank their blood and I gloried in it."

She stopped walking, but he refused to look at her.

"You were trying to achieve some sort of justice," she said, but he ruthlessly cut her off, before she could get carried away with some false idea of his nobility.

"I was a murderer, after vengeance. Nothing more. Don't try to make me out to be anything heroic. It would be the worst kind of lie," he said roughly.

"So what changed?"

He started walking again, all but dragging her along. "What do you mean?"

"What changed? That's not who you are now, so what changed?"

He flashed back to that moment, that one crystal-clear moment in time. The moment he'd never forget.

"I met a girl who reminded me of you," he confessed, the words almost dragged out of him.

The memory that he could never, ever forget. As if on command, it played again in his head in brilliant, heart-breaking color:

*He'd attacked a small village where a gang of marauders lived, killing and maiming every man in it without regard for anything but the ever-present, voracious bloodlust, when a girl threw herself on his back and started punching him in the head. He threw her off without a thought, but when he turned, he realized that she was only a child. He never, ever killed children. Even in his madness, he'd retained that much of himself.*

*But in a flash of light from the fire, he realized something else: she looked like his Serai. Not exactly, not like a sister or daughter or even a cousin. But there was something in the curve of her cheek and the fall of her hair that arrested him and froze him in place.*

*"How can you do this? Are you a monster?" the girl cried out, but he didn't hear her. He heard her words in Serai's voice, and he was destroyed.*

*He threw all the gold in his pockets at the girl and ran. Ran, and then flew, and never stopped until he found himself deep in the middle of a forest so old and dark and deep that the humans believed it to be cursed. He opened a hole in the ground underneath an ancient tree and threw himself into it, covering himself up and losing himself to the pain.*

*The mage who'd turned him found him and coaxed him back to the surface. Cleaned him up and taught him a few hard truths. Told him he had a choice: study and learn and work to make the world a better place, or become one of the evil, lost ones. The first choice was the harder one.*

*Redemption would not be cheaply bought.*

*Daniel chose redemption. But a thousand years is a very long time, and although the world changed, evil remained the same. Finally his mentor gave in to despair and walked into the sunlight. On that day, Daniel chose a lesser death. He chose to put himself in a state of hibernation for a very, very long time, in hopes that perhaps the world would be different when he awoke. Better.*

*Worth fighting for.*

*He had no idea that he would sleep nine thousand years.*

*When he woke, the world had changed. He traveled all over it, helping where he could, studying and learning the new ways and customs and amazing technology. Unfortunately, people were still dying. But he met an unexpected group of allies: the Atlantean warriors. He didn't bother to ask about Serai, though. Who would know anything about a girl dead for more than eleven thousand years?*

Her quiet voice broke into his reverie. "But before that? You met the girl who looked like me, and then what? You . . . you fell in love?"

"What? No, I didn't fall in love. I managed not to kill her, too, though." He lifted her up and over a fallen tree. "Are we still on the right path?"

She closed her eyes again, for nearly a minute this time, and then nodded. "I'm so tired, though. I can still feel the Emperor, and it's not moving. The witch hasn't done anything with it in a while, as far as I can tell. Maybe they're resting for the night?"

"Maybe. But those were vampires that passed us earlier, and if they are part of a more powerful vampire's blood coven, they won't be sleeping."

She leaned against him briefly, then took a deep breath and started walking again. "Why would a witch be helping a vampire? Why would they want the Emperor, anyway, or even know about it?"

"Who knows? I don't know anything much about Atlantean history, Serai, and anyway, you're not the only one who slept most of the world away. I slept for nine thousand years, hibernating until the horrors I'd seen—the evil I'd done—could fade in my memories."

"Did it work?"

"No," he said, kicking a log so hard that it shattered into kindling. "No, it didn't. But I deserve to live with the memories of what I did. It's my own version of hell."

"Not just bad memories, though," she said, almost whispering. "You remembered me."

"I did. I remembered you." He stopped walking and roughly pulled her to him, needing to feel her in his arms. "I will always remember you, even when you have come to your senses and left me, but I promise you that you will remember me, too."

With a desperation born of passion, he took her mouth with his own. Claimed it—claimed her—though he could never deserve to keep her. Kissed her as if he were a dying man and she the only chance at life.

"Remember this," he said fiercely. "Remember the feel of my mouth on yours, my body against yours, when you find that perfect Atlantean man someday."

She started to protest, but he silenced her with his lips, kissing her so hard and deep that he could almost pretend that she belonged to him and always would. It would have helped him find his way back to sanity if she'd fought him.

Instead she pulled him closer, and he was lost.

Long minutes later, he raised his head, coming back to himself enough to realize they stood unprotected in the middle of the path, and their enemies were closer than was safe. Serai clung to him, her body trembling, and he had never wanted anything as much as he wanted to strip her clothes from her and take her, bury his cock in her warm sweetness, and make her *his*.

His timing sucked.

"I love you," she said.

And the bottom fell out of his world.

He opened his mouth to answer, but nothing came out but a hoarse, choked noise, and then finally he made his stunned brain work and words happened. "Your timing sucks."

Her eyes opened so wide that they were enormous in her pale face, shining like the night stars in the moonlight, and he had just enough time to realize how unbearably hurt she would be by what he'd said before she started laughing.

Serai laughed so hard she doubled over, clutching her stomach, and then she laughed some more, while he grew more and more puzzled. When she finally could breathe again, she rose on tiptoe and kissed his chin.

"Oh, my love. You are still that blacksmith at heart, aren't you? I was afraid you were too elegant and powerful and sophisticated for me, a poor inexperienced maiden, but you are still my Daniel, aren't you?"

He looked away from her, scanning the area, the sky, the trees, the river. Anything to avoid looking at her beautiful, innocent, hopeful face.

"I can never be your Daniel. Forget that boy, that stupid useless blacksmith. What we thought we had was a childish dream, and we're both too old and wise to believe that dreams can come true."

"But, Daniel—"

"No. You deserve better, and I deserve the death I was seeking the day I fell into Atlantis and found you."

All traces of her laughter and even her smile were long gone when he dared glance at her again.

"Oh, Daniel. Older and wiser never has to mean hopeless or in despair." She reached out to him, but he moved away and pointed to the red wall of stone curving away from them about a hundred yards off.

"I know those rocks. There's a hidden cave with a stone structure the Sinagua built around the other side, and it faces onto a small canyon. There are stone stairs leading to spaces with enclosures even deeper in the cave, and we can rest there. The sun will be up soon, and in any event you need to rest."

She shook her head, stubborn as usual, but before she could argue, she cried out and fell to the ground, her body twitching and jerking uncontrollably.

Regretting his harshness, he raced to her and lifted her

off the ground and held her close until the spasms subsided. Why not tell her anything she wanted to hear? If she died from the damn Emperor's magic, at least she'd have been happy for a few short hours. He grimly called himself a thousand kinds of fool until she could speak again.

"She's using it again. The witch. The Emperor is still some distance away, but we're gaining on it. She seems to be learning how to use it. I'm not sure how much more I can take." A bout of coughing interrupted her and she leaned against him until it stopped, but her voice was hoarse when she continued. "Rest. You're right. I need to rest. I can't help any of them if I fall apart before we even find it."

Lifting her into his arms, he strode to the cliff wall and tucked her head against his chest before he climbed the steps carved into the stone face to the cave dwelling. He didn't let her look up until they'd moved back into the cave and away from the opening, so her fear of heights didn't further incapacitate her. He hated to do anything that might scare her, but it wasn't safe on the ground, especially not when the sun rose.

"Rest now, *mi amara*," he said. "We don't dare have a fire, in case the vampires have human thugs working for them who would see it."

She nodded and slumped down against a wall, clearly exhausted beyond the point of arguing or even speaking. He pulled the blankets from his pack and made a bed of sorts for her, then lay down next to her and pulled her into his arms, so her head was pillowed on his shoulder.

"Tell me about that tower," he said quietly, but with an undercurrent of pure steel. He *would* know the truth of this.

She closed her eyes, as if she couldn't bear to look at him while she spoke. "Even the soft ground of the palace gardens is unforgiving if the fall is from a high enough place. I shattered my body."

He inhaled sharply, feeling something inside him shatter, too, at the thought of her pain. "How did you live?"

She shrugged slightly, her eyes still closed. "How does anyone survive anything in Atlantis? When I opened my eyes, sure I was about to die, the healers were running toward me. Soon I was good as new," she said bitterly.

"All but in your mind," he said.

"And my heart. Please, Daniel, let it go. I can't talk about it now."

He kissed her—gentle, brief—and then forced himself to let it go. For her.

"Do you need anything else? Food or water?"

She didn't answer, and he was afraid she was punishing him, but when he tilted his head to look into her eyes, she was sound asleep. Exhaustion and weakness had overcome her, and he needed to keep her safe until darkness came again and they could go on and succeed in their task. Nothing else mattered until then. Nothing.

*But she loves me*, a dark voice whispered deep in the recesses of his heart. *She loves me, and I will never, ever give her up.*

"She deserves better," he said aloud, fully aware that he was talking to himself—out loud—and that was surely step one on the path to madness.

*Mad or no, she loves me, and she is mine.*

The sane part of his mind, he found, had no wish to argue, so he allowed himself to fall into a light doze, now that they were securely hidden from any view from outside.

She loved him. She loved *him*.

But when he slept, he dreamed of purple fire.

# Chapter 18

Daniel woke first, a change in the air pressure alerting him to the coming dusk. He and Serai had slept nearly twelve hours, and each of the times he'd woken to check on her during the day she'd been sleeping deeply, all but unconscious in his arms. He knew the trek was taking its toll on her, but there was no alternative. Her fear of heights wouldn't allow her to fly. If they didn't find the gem— Well.

He would not think of that.

She lay curled against him, and her scent of sunshine and sea surrounded him with its delicate flavor. He wanted to taste her again, and his body hardened painfully at the thought of waking her by undressing her and kissing every inch of exposed skin. She sighed in her sleep and put a hand on his face, as if petting him or telling him to wait just a little while, or so he imagined. He grinned ruefully. Even in the face of impending danger and almost certain death, his blood rushed to his cock at the sight of her. In some ways, he really wasn't much different from that boy she'd known so long ago.

His grin faded as he realized one crucial difference: that

boy would not have been fighting the urge to sink his fangs into her oh-so-tempting neck. The blood thirst was worse than he'd ever known it, and he had a strong feeling that it was more about his feelings for Serai than about the blood itself. He didn't need to feed on blood very often. The blood of the human who had "volunteered" outside the bar would suffice for at least a week more.

No, it wasn't about need. It was all about desire.

Trying to distract himself, he took her hand in his and realized it was icy cold, so he massaged it, trying to provide heat from friction since his own body temperature ran a little cooler than human or Atlantean. He knew she was shaky from the stasis, in spite of the magic. How she could bear up under the pressure and the demands of this quest after eleven thousand years of inactivity was enough to boggle the mind.

"You're an extraordinary woman, Serai of Atlantis," he murmured, and he wasn't even all that surprised when she opened her eyes and looked into his.

"You're quite the bee's knees, yourself," she said, smiling.

He laughed. "I haven't heard that one in a long time. And thank you."

Her brows drew together. "I know. My knowledge of languages is extensive, but my grasp of the correct chronology is rather fluid. I know Rome is long gone, but sometimes I find myself thinking in Latin. The proper speech patterns of England during the Regency period fascinated me, so I might inadvertently drop into those. I find American English a little tiring and flat, if that makes sense, with none of the lyricism of Atlantean, so it's hard for me to maintain conversation it it."

"I never would have been able to guess that," he said, switching to ancient Atlantean. "I think you're amazing. Your brain must be truly a marvel, to keep up with all of those languages."

She shifted, making him all too painfully aware that she still lay in his arms, when his pants seemed to shrink a couple of sizes.

"My strength is up, but my limbs feel weak. Almost as if they weren't connected to my body," she said, also in Atlantean, strain evident in her pale face. "Walking will be difficult this night."

"Let me help." He sat up and pulled her arm into his lap, then began a vigorous massage to get the blood moving and her muscles warmed up. He realized the oddity that he, a vampire, was working to increase Serai's blood circulation without any intent to partake of that blood, but it was far from the oddest thing he'd encountered in the past few days, so he filed it away under "irrelevancies" and continued, moving on to her other arm for a while.

"May I remove your socks?"

She bit her lip, and in the fading glow of what little light reached them this far back in the cave he saw that her cheeks had turned pink yet again.

"You can't possibly be shy at the thought of me seeing your feet after I have seen every inch of you," he said, amused and entranced in equal measure.

"No, but I'm afraid . . . I'm afraid my feet smell bad!"

It took a beat, but then they simultaneously burst into laughter.

"Evil vampires and witches and malfunctioning magical gems, and you're worried about stinky feet?" He shook his head, still grinning. "You really are a princess."

"Maybe, but even a princess can worry about stinky feet," she said haughtily, and he laughed again and then removed her sock before she could protest. He pulled her decidedly non-stinky foot into his lap and began to massage it and her leg.

"You—oh—I—oh. *Oh*," she said, almost moaning by the second or third "oh." "Oh, that feels so good. My poor feet are much abused by my first outing into the world."

He grinned and applied gentle pressure to her calf. "This is not exactly what I had in mind when I thought of you moaning for me."

Serai put her hands over her eyes. "I refuse to let you

embarrass me after the things we did to each other in that hotel."

"Then why are your cheeks so becomingly pink?"

Her eyes flew open. "You can't even see what color my cheeks are, it's dark."

"I have excellent night vision," he informed her, switching to the other leg and beginning the same gentle massage.

"That's not all you have that's excellent," she murmured.

"I heard that."

"A gentleman would be kissing me now," she said.

"I'm not a— Wait. Oh, yeah. I'm definitely a gentleman," he said, releasing her leg and lying back down next to her.

He pulled her into his arms and kissed her, a long, deep, slow kiss that threatened to blow the top of his skull off by the time he was done.

"Definitely a gentleman, but finding it a little hard to breathe right now," he said. "Maybe you should take the lead this time."

~~~

Serai didn't hesitate. She twined her fingers through his silken hair and feathered kisses across those seductive lips of his. She might not have long to live, and she was determined to make the most of every second of it. His scent of woods and musk and man wrapped itself around her and enticed her into kissing his neck and then daring to touch her tongue to the edge of his ear.

He groaned, a long, heartfelt sound, and she jerked back a little, afraid she'd done something wrong, until his arms tightened around her. He pulled her so close that she could feel that intriguing hardness again, pushing up against the juncture of her thighs.

She knew what it meant. He found her desirable. He wanted her. She wanted him, too, oh, by all the gods she wanted him so much, but for some reason she hesitated. Held back. She wanted him. His kisses drove her to the brink of aching, hungry madness, but this was just . . .

"This isn't what I dreamed about," she blurted out.

He took a deep breath and blew it out before answering her, but he didn't move his hands from her back and bottom, holding her in place against him. Part of her wanted to wriggle around and see what happened.

And part of her realized they were lying on a couple of thin blankets on a dirt floor in a cave.

"Dreamed?" He stared at her, and she was pleased to see his eyes were a little unfocused.

"This. Us. Here." She gestured around them, blushing furiously but determined to explain. "I know it's a silly romantic fantasy, but I had not dreamed of giving up my maidenhood in such a place."

He blinked and opened his mouth, then closed it. "I'm a damn fool," he finally said. "I'm so sorry, Princess. Of course you deserve candles and flowers and silk sheets. I got carried away by the feel of finally holding you in my arms. You're just so damn beautiful."

She smiled and kissed his cheek. "I don't need candles or silk sheets, but a little romance and perhaps a little less dirt would not go unappreciated."

"You're amazing," he said, stroking the side of her face. "Even in the middle of all this danger, your sense of humor is still intact. How could I ever think I might deserve you?"

"My father often informed me I was quite obstinate and annoying," she told him. "Perhaps I am exactly who you deserve."

He grinned and rolled up to sit, then stood, pulling her up with him. "I don't know about that. If—"

But she stopped hearing his words after that. He was still speaking, but a voice on a very old and unused mental pathway in her mind came through loud and clear and drowned out any other sound.

*Serai of Atlantis, this is Reisen of Mycenae. I bid you allow me to communicate with you in this manner.*

The response to his formal request came to her unconscious mind before her conscious mind could think of it.

*Accepted and welcome, Reisen of Mycenae. What news of the world?*

*We retrieved what we needed from the bank last night. Melody, ah, the human woman Melody has asked me to meet with certain others with her this evening and then I am free to catch up to you and assist you with your quest.*

She heard the slight oddness in his voice when he mentioned Melody, but it would have been impolite to inquire as to its cause.

*You were successful, then?*

*We were. Now we only need— Wait. There is someone—*

The mental connection between them snapped and then expanded, filled with Reisen's rage.

*They found us. They're outside. Melody—they shot Melody. I have to go. I'll contact you as soon as I can.*

Serai gasped and Daniel was instantly there, wrapping his arm around her shoulders to steady her.

"Are you okay? What's happening? You looked like you went into a trance."

She nodded, distracted, but couldn't focus on what he was saying.

*Reisen, I hope Melody is not badly injured. Be well and safe. Contact me when you can. My best wishes and prayers go with you.*

*And mine with you, Serai. Tell that vampire that if he hurts you, he'll answer to me.*

The connection broke, and she let it go. Reisen had enough to deal with right now. She sent a fervent prayer to Poseidon that Melody would be healed quickly and that they would be safe, and then she realized that Daniel was shaking her.

"Serai? Serai! Answer me," he demanded.

"I'm fine. You can stop shaking me now."

He released her instantly, and then he took a step back and shoved a hand through his hair. "What was that? You were gone. Is that the telepathy thing?"

"Yes. It was Reisen."

A flash of something crossed Daniel's eyes, but he simply nodded, waiting.

"The bank job was a success. They got what they needed, but while we were communicating, Reisen said someone attacked them. Melody got shot."

"Is she okay?"

"I don't know. He didn't know. He was on his way to help her and get them away, I think. He said he'd contact us again when he could." She left out Reisen's threat, figuring what Daniel didn't know couldn't annoy him.

She looked out toward the entrance of the cave, where it was now full dark. "Time to go. I can feel the Emperor, and it's calling me very strongly."

"We're on our own," Daniel said.

Serai held out her arms to the sky and pulled the strength of the Emperor to her, but this time on *her* terms. Its power soared through the air toward her, all but thrumming through her bones. "This is our quest to win or lose. Somehow I feel that very strongly."

He lifted the backpack and slung it over his shoulders again. "Then we really are on our own. Let's find that gem before the witch starts to play with it again."

But it was too late. The witch forced her magic through the Emperor again, and Serai screamed, her skull nearly shattering with the force of the pain from another badly manipulated blast of the gem's power.

When she could breathe again, she gritted her teeth and headed out of the cave. "Now. We need to go find that goddessforsaken witch *now*."

# Chapter 19

Farther into the Red Rock Secret Mountain
Wilderness area, inside an ancient, abandoned
Sinagua Indian structure

"I don't know how to do it!" Ivy realized that screaming at
the man with the gun was probably a bad idea, but blood ran
freely down her lip and chin from her nose, and her skull
felt like it might crack wide open. Whatever this amethyst
was designed to be, a treasure-seeking tool aimed by a kid-
napped witch was not it.

Definitely not it.

This try had been worse than the others, though—far
worse. This time, she'd believed she'd made a connection
with another woman. Another witch, maybe, or at least someone with some kind of magic that happened to resonate with
the gem. The other woman had been in pain, too, and Ivy had
the uncomfortable feeling that she'd been the one to cause it.
She flinched a little as that concern led to another worry; they
still hadn't told her what had happened to Aretha. She didn't
buy the lame story that the apprentice had suddenly decided
to take a vacation to Mexico. The girl had been flighty enough
for something like that, certainly, but something about the
story and the man who'd told it to her didn't quite ring true.

The same man now pointing a gun at her bleeding head.

Ian was frantically digging into his backpack, and he came up with a clean bandanna, which he handed to her.

"Mom, use this and wipe your nose. You have to stop now, this is hurting you too bad," he said, and she would have given anything—done anything—to have spared him the pain and fear showing so plainly on his sunburned face. His bright blue eyes, exactly like his father's, were a little shiny, but her proud boy hadn't given in to the tears. He was worried about being strong for her.

She was worried that Smithson would shoot Ian as quickly and callously as he might swat a gnat. Smithson had an oily, burnt-orange aura that lurched and coiled around him like a sun-drunk rattlesnake, and she had the feeling he was just as deadly.

Which led her back to the gun.

Oddly, however, even though night had fallen with its characteristic desert suddenness, the vampire who she'd thought had been in charge wasn't there. Smithson had dragged her to this new location during the afternoon, after she'd barely gotten five hours of sleep. He'd forced them to eat some nasty beef jerky on the hike from the other cave and given them a little water. She'd felt a dehydration headache looming even before he'd dragged her into this new structure and forced her to use the amethyst again. The vampire wasn't with them, though, and that made her wonder if their criminal partnership was falling apart and, if so, how she could use the knowledge to her advantage.

She put an arm around Ian and wiped her nose with the cloth he'd handed her, and then she looked at Smithson and tried to appear totally unafraid of the gun aimed at her head.

"Where's the vampire?"

His eyes shifted a little, the classic "I'm getting ready to lie to you" indicator, and she wondered why a so-called criminal mastermind wasn't a better liar. Especially since she'd heard he was a banker, too.

Scumbag.

"He's no longer important. I'm in charge now. You can have five minutes, and then I want you to try again." He waved one of his thugs over to give her another bottle of water.

She took the cap off and handed it to Ian first, who took a drink and handed it back. She drank deeply, finishing the bottle, thinking furiously all the while. If he'd killed Nicholas, the odds were against her getting out of this alive. The vampire, at least, had seemed to have a little bit of reluctance to hurt Ian.

If this worm hurt her boy, he was going to die in agony. She was making very sure to retain enough of her magic, protected and shielded from the damage the gem was doing to her, for a last-ditch escape attempt.

Not attempt. A last-ditch escape *success*.

"All right. Stop dawdling," Smithson said, lowering the gun. "You don't need to see this gun to know I'll use it. And I won't even use it on you, because you're too valuable to me, at least for now."

He smiled and glanced at Ian. "I have heard that being shot in the kneecap is very painful. Might mess up a boy's growth forever. What do you think about that, Ms. Witch?"

A red wave of fury pulsed through her brain, and she had to bite hard on her lip to keep from speaking the words to a spell that would maim the bastard. He had too many thugs around the place, with instructions to take her out if she tried anything. She couldn't get to them all before they could hurt Ian, and Smithson knew it.

"I think there is no place in this world or the next that you can hide if you harm my son," she said, slowly and carefully, in order not to scream, cry, or fly into a rage that would get them both shot. "Even if you kill me, my death curse will follow you and your sons and your sons' sons for a thousand years of torment and pain."

Smithson paled and clenched his jaw, but then he raised the gun again, this time pointing it at Ian's head. "Well, then. We both have the same goal, don't we? To get this business over with quickly so you and your son can safely leave this place, and we'll never have to see each other again."

One of the thugs by the door rolled his eyes behind

Smithson's back and grinned at a fellow guard. His meaning was chillingly clear to Ivy. They had instructions to kill her and her son as soon as Smithson escaped. He'd probably paid them enough to make them willing to brave a witch's wrath.

But none of them knew she was more than a witch. She was a sorceress of the black arts, and she would not die alone.

Ian hugged her, and her inner bravado blew away like a tumbleweed in a strong wind. She didn't care about taking them with her; she just wanted to escape with her son. She'd try again.

"Tell me again," she said wearily. "What exactly do you think we'll find here?"

"Rubies." Smithson's voice was dark with greed. "Look at this painting. The chief or medicine man or whatever, bowing to the figure with the staff. Between them, on the floor, is a pile of glowing red stones. Our pet archaeologist thought it must be a cache of rubies."

She caught the past tense. "Thought?"

He grimaced. "He was a little too concerned with preserving our heritage, blah blah whatever. He didn't survive the interview."

"Torture, you mean," Ian said hotly, rising up off the ground. "You're a monster. That vampire was a better man than you, and he sucks blood for a living!"

Ivy grabbed Ian and pulled him back, shielding him from Smithson's gun with her body. "Ian, stop it. He didn't mean it; he's just a boy. Don't hurt him."

But Smithson was laughing. "Sucks blood for a living. That's a good one. Look, I have no time for this and no intention of hurting you or the kid, if you just do your job. Get up off your ass and find those rubies. Then you're done. Simple as that."

Ivy didn't believe a single word out of his lying mouth, but it didn't matter. She had no choice. She hugged Ian again and whispered "stay safe" in his ear, then stood up.

"Give me back the amethyst and point me in the direction you think most likely for those rubies. I'll make it work this time."

Smithson nodded to one of his guards, who held the gem in a cloth-lined wooden box. The man turned a sickly greenish-white, clearly terrified of the scary witch, but he stumbled forward, holding the box as far away from himself as his arms would extend.

She couldn't really blame him for that. The gem had enormous power and would probably fry his eyeballs in their sockets if he touched it with his bare hands. Only she could do that.

Lucky her.

She gently lifted the amethyst, and it immediately began to glow with deep purple light, warming in her hands until it felt almost malleable, and not like stone at all. She glanced at Ian again, hoping beyond hope that what she was about to do wouldn't kill her, but knowing that she would almost certainly die at Smithson's hand if she didn't try it.

She closed her eyes and centered her power in her mind, carefully building it from a flicker to a flame before aiming it at the gem and trying again to combine the resonance of her magic with that of the amethyst. The gem held an old and enormously potent magic, but most of its power was far beyond her reach. This treasure-seeking ability felt like an afterthought to her; almost like a parlor trick tossed off by a master magician simply to amuse the children. She had no idea what the true extent of its power might be, but she had a feeling that even a fraction of it would be enough to burn through her, leaving behind only the smoking husk of her body and mind, if she were foolish or unlucky enough to ever try to access it.

But she didn't need to try this all on her own. The other attempts had felt awkward, straining. This time she would pull out her not-so-secret weapon and open herself to the vortex energy in the area. Traditionalists and so-called practitioners of New Age mumbo-jumbo claimed the vortex energy was limited to Sedona itself, but she knew better. She could access the power for hundreds of miles, especially that from Bell Rock, her totem rock.

She'd just see what the massive power of Bell Rock had to say about one ostrich egg–sized gemstone and its dangers.

Calling silently to the vortex to lend her its strength, she opened her mind to the power of the amethyst, which was now pulsing in her hand like a beating violet heart.

*Lend me your power one last time, please, spirit of this gemstone. My son is held hostage to a greedy man's whims, and I offer you a mother's love and a sorceress's magic as consideration for this request. Help me find the rubies for this monster, before he harms my child.*

An image appeared in her mind; a beautiful dark-haired woman, drawn and pale, who seemed to be staring through space, time, and magic directly at Ivy. The woman fell backward, pierced by a spear of purple light. The image disappeared when the amethyst's magic smashed into Ivy, combining with the energy from the Bell Rock vortex, and levitated her within a column of glowing purple light until her head gently bumped the ceiling. She looked around, and a slim beam of light flashed out from the column around her and illuminated a tiny drawing on the ceiling; a miniature of the design Smithson had pointed out to her below. She lifted a hand to touch it, and a stone panel slid aside—more magic—and a waterfall of sparkling red began to stream out of the hiding space in the ceiling. She tried to move out of the way, but the column of light held her fixed and nearly frozen directly in the path of the falling treasure.

All she could do was shield her head and face with her hands, and try not to cry out when the sharp edges of the stones struck her skin. She could hear Ian shouting something, but the magical light acted as a sound buffer and she couldn't make out the words. She tried to smile reassuringly at him but a falling stone smashed into her cheek, cutting her skin, so she covered her face again, deciding she could reassure him *after* she got out of the path of the rocks.

Long minutes later, the beam of light finally released her. She fell awkwardly to the ground, which was at least two yards beneath where her feet had been hanging, suspended, in the air. She hit the ground hard and crumpled as her ankle twisted underneath her.

This time she cried out. She couldn't help it.

Ian rushed over and helped her up so she could limp, leaning heavily on him, across the floor to sit down near the wall farthest from the enormous pile of rubies. Dozens of small cuts and scrapes from the falling gems ached and bled all over her hands, arms, shoulders, neck, and face.

"I guess whoever hid the gems wanted anybody who found them to pay for it," Ian said bitterly. "It was like one of those Indiana Jones traps."

"Luckily not a rolling boulder," she said, trying to smile. Judging from Ian's reaction, she must have looked ghastly.

"Mom, your nose is bleeding again, plus all these cuts, and your ankle—I have to get you to a doctor."

"If only you were old enough to drive," she murmured, suddenly dizzy and faint. If the exhaustion or the drain of her magical powers didn't get her, the dehydration would. Either way, she would be just as dead, and her son in just as much danger.

Smithson, meanwhile, was ignoring her completely as he all but danced around the pile of rocks. His rubies, then. They must be. Ordinary rocks wouldn't have caused this level of capering glee. She'd seen them anyway, on the way down. Uncut and rough as most of them were, the occasional deep red glow, even in the unusual purple light, had told her all she'd needed to know. There was probably millions of dollars of rubies in that pile—maybe more, she didn't know, she was no gemologist—and surely, *surely* Smithson had to be happy now. His thugs were quickly gathering all the rubies into a dozen or so large duffel bags and, one by one, heading out of the cave.

The slimeball in question smiled at her, rubbing his hands together. "Now, that wasn't all that hard, was it?"

"My mom is bleeding all over, and she hurt her ankle

falling. She could have died! You promised to let us go, so do it now, already," Ian shouted at him.

Smithson paused and pretended to look regretful, but Ivy could see the mad, gleeful joy deep in his soulless eyes. "Oh, I'm so sorry. But your mommy is just too valuable. I'm afraid I still want her, and since I need you to keep her in line, well, it looks like we're all going to take a trip together."

"I will kill you if you hurt my mother," Ian said hotly. He started to say something else, but Ivy shook his arm and gave him her most grim "stop right this instant because I'm your mother and I said so" look.

He subsided, but not for long, judging by the way his lips were pressed together in his "I'm going to explode any second" expression. She'd known this boy since the moment she'd pushed him crying out into the world nearly fourteen years ago, and when her son felt there was injustice in the world, he couldn't keep silent about it, no matter the cost. She'd always loved that about him, but right now it might get them killed.

Still, "I will kill you if you hurt my mother" would have been *fantastic* last words. Ian was so going to score on his next birthday. She might even buy him a car. She laughed out loud, and realized blood loss was making her loopy.

"I want to laugh, too, from the sheer joy of it," Smithson said, flashing his hideous Hollywood-white, over-veneered teeth. "This is miraculous. I do wish Nicholas had turned me, though, before I double-crossed the nasty bastard. Think of all that lovely interest, compounding for centuries."

Ivy blinked. "You're unbelievable. What kind of fool betrays a master vampire?"

Then she blinked again. And yet again. The blood loss must have taken her from dizziness straight to delusion, because she could almost swear she saw a hand sticking out of Smithson's stomach. She decided that it was really a very good time to close her eyes and lie down, before dancing pink elephants appeared, too.

That's when Ian and Smithson both screamed.

She jerked her head up and forced her eyes to open, only to wish that she hadn't.

It *had* been a hand, after all. Nicholas's hand, which had smashed clear through Smithson's abdomen and ripped out much of the man's intestines on its way back out.

"Unbelievable is an apt word. There is much about this scene that I find unbelievable, Ivy Khetta of the Crescent Moon coven," Nicholas said, standing there calmly as if he hadn't just eviscerated a man. "Fortunately for you, I can see that you were coerced into helping this fool who thought he would betray me and get away with it."

Ivy pulled Ian into her arms and hugged him until he stopped screaming, but his thin shoulders shook as he fought back sobs.

"I have been coerced every step of the way, and you're just as guilty as he was," Ivy shot back at the vampire. Pretty brave of her, she figured, considering he stood there with Smithson's guts wrapped around his arm like bracelets. Or else really, really stupid, for the same reason.

She decided to be helpful. "His goons are carrying the rubies off in duffel bags. You can probably still catch them if you leave now."

Unbelievable must have been the word of the day, because—*unbelievably*—he smiled at her. "You have quite a bit of courage, my little witch."

"I'm glad you think so, because I plan to throw up and pass out now," she said, as the light from the lanterns wavered in pretty, pretty patterns in front of her. She tried to hang on, for Ian's sake, but her body and magic had been pushed far beyond the level of her endurance. She clung to Ian and fell forward instead of back, until her head rested on his shoulder. Nicholas said something, and Ian said something else, but the words blurred together in her mind and could have been spoken in Mandarin Chinese for as much as she understood them.

She couldn't leave her son alone with the vampire. She fought so hard to maintain consciousness, she really did, but she had nothing in her reserves, nothing at all, and even when she tried to focus on what they were saying, the last thing she heard didn't make any sense at all, because she was almost certain her son asked Nicholas to turn him into a vampire.

And she thought she heard Nicholas agree.

After that, she didn't hear anything at all.

# Chapter 20

Serai put the cap back on her water bottle and took a deep breath, trying to convince herself, yet again, that she had the strength for this quest. Her legs were as heavy as if sculpted out of marble or orichalcum by a cloddish artist, and each step was harder than the last. The intermittently missing and damaged connection to the Emperor was draining every ounce of her energy, both magical and physical, and she was terrified about what it was doing to the four maidens left in the stasis pods in Atlantis.

Delia was already gone. Helena, Merlina, Brandacea, and Guen remained. Serai's connection to them was weak, and growing weaker every moment, so she wasn't entirely certain that they all still lived.

She hoped they did. If their lives could be sustained by the sheer force of her will, then they did still live.

"What is it?" Daniel asked, soundlessly dropping down next to her after a short flight to scout their area.

"I don't know if I'll ever see that and not be amazed," she said. "That you can fly. How wonderful it must be."

"You can fly as mist, can't you? Or is that only a warrior thing? I've seen Ven and the guys do it. It's pretty spectacular."

She tilted her head, considering. "I think I may still be able to do so. It's simple enough, part of the magic the sea god gifts to his children. I don't know if I could do it now, though, since I'm so tired. And the problem—" She broke off, not wanting to let him see how pathetically weak and cowardly she was about something so minor as a fear of height. Lives depended on her.

He nodded, as if he could read her mind. "The acrophobia still applies. Perhaps, also, your connection with the Emperor won't work when you're in mist form."

She smiled at him, aware that he was giving her a graceful excuse. She was grateful for his kindness, but not willing to spare herself the truth. "I'm afraid, and we both know it, but I think it won't matter. We're very near the Emperor now. We just need to travel a bit farther and—"

The worst pain yet slammed into her with the force of a tsunami. The witch was using the Emperor, and this time she was mixing the gem's power with something else— natural magic from the land around them—oh, *gods*, it hurt it hurt it hurt it *hurt* . . .

She clenched her jaw shut against the scream, but a horrible moaning sound escaped her throat, and Daniel caught her arm.

"Is it the gem again?"

"Yes, it's—"

She couldn't finish the sentence. She couldn't breathe. Her legs wouldn't support her. The Emperor's power drove through her, pulling at her own magic, siphoning off her strength in a flood. She could see the witch's face, and the woman was terrified of something, or someone, but she was being *forced* to channel the Emperor. For an instant, Serai believed she'd made a connection with the witch, but then the power surged again, and she screamed and collapsed into Daniel's arms.

The Emperor ruthlessly took and took, draining everything she had until she knew that it was the end, she would surely die from it, but she didn't even have the strength to tell Daniel that she loved him, it had always been him, it would always be him, before the world exploded in a shimmering cascade of purple light.

~~~~~~~~

Daniel lifted Serai's limp form into his arms and listened for the sound of her breathing, but there was only silence. No breath, no heartbeat, nothing but the sound of finality and death and the end of everything. He roared out his anguish in a single, wordless bellow to the sky, incoherent with rage and loss, but then reason returned for long enough for him to realize it wasn't too late.

He could fix this. She could hate him for the blood bond later, but at least she'd be alive to do so.

He bit viciously into his wrist and then held it over her lips, rubbing his dripping blood into her mouth. At first she was unresponsive, but he gently rubbed her throat to coax a swallowing reflex and after a moment long enough to nearly cost him his sanity, she moved her head a little and then swallowed convulsively. She immediately began coughing and retching, as if the taste of his blood had been so foul she must expel it from her mouth, but he forced her to accept more, enough to ensure she would wake and be restored.

Enough to bond her to him.

Enough to save her life.

If she hated him forever after, it was a small enough price to pay to know that she lived.

She pushed at his arm, and he finally pulled his wrist away from her mouth, now smeared with his blood. He licked his wound to heal it with the anticoagulants in his saliva, and then reached for the water bottle she'd dropped earlier.

"Drink some of this."

She stared up at him, uncomprehending, and so he uncapped the bottle and held it to her lips. This liquid she drank without hesitation, but she sat up, coughing and sputtering, as she choked a little.

"Went down the wrong way, I think," she murmured. "What . . . what happened to me?"

He didn't know how to answer her, so instead he silently tore a strip of fabric from the bottom of his shirt, poured a little water on it, and gently wiped her mouth until no trace of his blood remained.

She caught his wrist again. "Did you . . . did you give me your blood?"

"I did. I won't apologize for it, because it saved your life," he said roughly.

"I didn't ask you to apologize. Thank you."

He sat back a little, stunned at her reaction. He'd expected her to rail at him for his presumption.

"I gave you my blood," he said slowly, making sure she understood his transgression, so she would hate him and not thank him. Clearly, he was the stupidest man on the planet.

"It was the first step of a blood bond. I will be able to feel what you feel and know where you are forever now." He caught her chin in his hand. "Do you get that? I invaded your privacy."

"You saved my life," she shot back at him. "Do you expect me to be angry for that?"

He blinked, realizing that yes, he'd expected just that. "Uh, well—"

She touched his face so gently he almost didn't feel it. "You *saved my life*. The Emperor was draining me, because the witch discovered a way to use the local magic, some kind of vortex magic, in coordination with channeling the gem. I was *dying*."

She kissed him, slowly, gently, and with such tenderness that he thought he might die from it.

"You saved my life, Daniel. I only have one request."

He looked into her eyes, glowing in the moonlight, and realized he would gladly die for this woman. "Anything. *Anything*. You only need ask."

She took a deep breath and put her arms around his neck. "I want you to make love to me. Now."

Serai was astonished at her own boldness, but she'd nearly died. Nearly *died*, after eleven thousand years of living a kind of death, imprisoned in a crystal cage. Nearly died after never having lived. Never having joined with the man she loved.

That ended here and now.

She would gladly give her life, such as it was, to the pursuit of the Emperor. She would find it, retrieve it, and return it to Atlantis. She would save the other maidens. But right now, right here, she wanted something for herself.

She tightened her arms around him and leaned in toward that sinfully seductive mouth of his. "Kiss me," she said against his lips. "Kiss me."

He sat, still as a statue, unmoving in her arms, for so long she was afraid he was thinking of a polite, gentlemanly way to turn her down, although he'd claimed to be no gentleman at all. She was on the edge of losing her nerve when he wrapped his arms around her waist and sprang up, pulling her to her feet so fast she nearly got dizzy again.

"You have no idea how long I've dreamed of hearing you say just that," he said roughly. "You want me to kiss you? To make love to you? Are you sure?"

She didn't have the words to convince him; they'd vanished in her dry throat, victim of nerves and shyness. But she knew another way. She raised slightly trembling fingers to her shirt and unbuttoned the first button, and then the second, and then the third, before daring to glance back up at him. His dark eyes were trained on the pale skin she was revealing, and a muscle in his jaw jumped as he watched her clumsy attempts at seduction.

"That would be a yes?" he said, part question, part command. "If so, be very sure. I want you more than I want to take my next breath, and I will not let you go."

She nodded, then decided that wouldn't suffice. "Yes," she whispered. "Please, yes."

He flashed an almost-feral smile at her and she saw the

tips of his fangs, but rather than scaring her, they excited her. He'd healed her with his blood, but he hadn't tasted hers, and she knew that doing so would be aphrodisiac to a night-walker during lovemaking. His control was too perfect. He held himself back.

She wanted to shatter his control.

She wanted him crazy for her.

She ran her tongue over her lips, tasting a tiny bit of the blood he'd donated to her, and she shivered. Not from cold, but from the thrill of holding this man, being held by him, preparing to fly into the unknown arena of sensuality with Daniel, the one she'd dreamed of for so very long.

He made a deep growling noise, low in his throat, his eyes fixed on her lips as she licked them again, and then he yanked her against him and leaned forward, bending her back a little over one steel-banded arm.

"Now. Need you now," he said, and then he took her mouth with his and showed her just how much he'd been holding back before. She gasped, but he swallowed her gasp, swallowed her breath, took all that she was into himself, claiming every bit of her—even the very oxygen she breathed—as his own.

His hands roamed all over her, stroking her arms and back and bottom before he took the edge of her shirt in one hand and ripped it aside, scattering her remaining buttons, and a couple of them hit the stones on the ground. The sound of buttons clattering on stone seemed to shock him, and he raised his head from hers and looked around, eyes wild and hot.

"Not here. Not in the dirt," he said. "Close your eyes."

Before she could ask or protest or even think, he lifted her and started running, carrying her. She had the sensation of moving too fast to be possible, but within seconds he stopped. She opened her eyes and discovered that he'd brought them to a patch of springy grass underneath a stand of tall trees. She could hear the steady noise of the water rushing down the riverbed nearby.

"I need you," he repeated, and then he bent his head to kiss her again.

His hands were all over her, hungry, frantic, and then he was kissing her neck and down her chest to her breasts, and when his lips closed on one of her nipples, she cried out and clung to his shoulders, hoping he'd never let her go.

"It's so much," she said, moaning a little. "So much sensation, so much *feeling*. I don't know if I can bear it."

He laughed, and the vibrations of his laughter against her sensitive skin made her shiver. He stopped what he was doing, and she felt a pang of loss.

"Are you cold? I can put out our blankets." In an instant, he'd done just that, and he carried her down to lie beside him on the blankets, cushioned by the layer of grass.

"Kiss me," he demanded. "Touch me. I need to feel your hands on me."

She complied, still a little shy, but eager to touch and stroke every part of him. She unbuttoned his shirt, her fingers still trembling, and pressed a kiss to his chest as she revealed each inch of pale, perfect skin. His skin was pure white, like the finest Atlantean porcelain, after so long away from the sun. His lean, muscled chest narrowed down into a perfect abdomen, and she daringly touched his navel with her tongue. He groaned and his big body shuddered underneath her, and when the bulge of his erection grew even larger, she knew for certain that he wanted her as much as she wanted him.

"I want to see you, Daniel. I want to see all of you," she whispered, feeling her face flame at her wanton request.

Before she could say another word, he leapt up and stripped out of his clothes so fast that in seconds he was standing before her, proudly nude, and then he dropped to the blankets next to her and took her back into his arms. She wriggled back a little so she could look her fill at his beautiful body—all lean muscle and perfectly shaped, like the body of a fallen angel come to life. Her gaze went to his manhood and she gasped, feeling her heart plummet in her chest.

"Daniel. There is no way . . . We cannot fit together . . . That is too large."

His eyes widened, and then he started laughing, which embarrassed her even more.

"Do not laugh at me. I'm serious."

"I know you are," he said, still laughing a little, but interspersing the most delicious kisses between chuckles. "You are adorable."

"But—"

He stroked her breasts, still kissing her, and then he stroked her belly, still kissing her, and then he unbuttoned her pants and pushed them down and out of the way, and his clever fingers suddenly were touching her between her thighs.

She caught her breath and then kissed him harder, shivering with a lovely, maddening tingly sensation that spiraled from her lips to her breasts to the exact spot where his fingers were circling around her most sensitive part and . . . oh. *Oh*.

For the second time that night, her consciousness shattered, but this time it was from pure, blissful, pleasure.

Waves of sensation rocked through and over her, centering on Daniel's lips and fingers, and she reveled in the feeling, but she wanted more, somehow, more and *more* and she was sure she knew what that meant, even though she had no idea how the logistics of it all might possibly work out, so she did the bravest thing she could think of doing.

The only thing she could think of doing.

She reached down and took his manhood in her hand.

This time, it was Daniel's turn to gasp.

~~~~~

Daniel closed his eyes when Serai wrapped her slender fingers around his cock, and he wondered if possibly he really had died and gone to heaven when he walked into the sun. Sure, he'd faced danger and been stabbed in the interim, but if all that was just the windup to the big event, and heaven meant kissing Serai, and touching and pleasuring her while she reciprocated, then he'd happily offer to get stabbed every day for the rest of eternity.

She was so unbearably beautiful he almost couldn't stand to look at her; it was like looking into the face of the sun, and—like the sun—her beauty had the power to sear him to ash if he stood too close.

He didn't care. He was already burning, was already on fire; the flames analogy was working really, really well for him, especially if she'd just move her hand a little and, oh, hot damn, she tightened her fingers around his cock and started stroking him, and he thought he just might explode.

"Serai, you can't— If you do that, I'll go off in your hand like a boy. Your touch—I've wanted you for so long, I just, oh, gods, you're killing me here," he said, groaning when she grinned up at him and continued stroking him, even more enthusiastically than before.

She flashed a smile of pure joy, and it stunned him that she could radiate such perfect bliss when they were in so much danger, but then again, if she kept kissing his neck, he'd happily lie here forever.

His fangs dropped down, involuntarily, and a wave of bloodlust slammed into him, reminding him of all that lovely blood rushing through her veins, so close to his mouth, so close to his *teeth*, and that her skin would be so easily pierced.

He wanted to taste her.

He *needed* to taste her.

He did the next best thing. In one vampire-quick motion, he pulled her up and whipped her boots and clothes from her, and then he kissed his way down her perfect body, taking especial care with her lovely breasts, until she was moaning and tossing restlessly in his arms. When she was making little purring noises, he raised his head and looked up at her.

"I'm going to taste you now. It may seem shocking to you, but it's a natural way for lovers to be together, and I have to put my mouth on you or die from wanting you." His voice sounded rough, even to his own ears, but he couldn't help it. He was practically shaking from need and hunger, and if he didn't have her soon he was sure his brain would explode into tiny, vampire-brain pieces.

Her eyes were huge and hot, drowning blue, but she nodded, biting her lip, and he kissed his way down her belly until he reached his goal. He used his fingers to stroke her again, dipping them into her wet heat and then sliding them along her oh-so-sensitive clitoris, grinning fiercely when she cried out.

"Yes. Just like that," he said, and then he put his mouth on her and licked and sucked, holding her thighs down when her hips bucked up and off the blankets. He tested her with one finger, stroking in and out, and then a second, slowly at first, until she got used to the feel of his invasion of her most private place.

Her movements became more frantic, and she clutched his hair and moaned, and he fastened his lips around her clit and sucked hard, and she shattered around him, crying out his name. He gently stroked her while the aftershocks took her, and then he rose over her and fitted his body between her legs.

"I need to be inside you now," he said, giving her a chance to say no, which would probably kill him, but even though he held his breath and held his body as still as he could to let her decide, she didn't say no.

She didn't say yes.

She just smiled and put her hand on his cock again.

"Now would be good," she whispered, still smiling, but he could see that she'd tensed up a little bit.

"It will hurt a bit, just at first, but I promise to go as slowly and gently as you want me to," he warned her.

She tensed up just a little more, but gave him a look of such complete and utter trust that he wanted to slay dragons for her, wanted to protect her and love her for eternity, wanted—more than anything, talk about pressure, her first sex in eleven thousand years—to make the experience perfect for her.

He kissed her again, and slowly, ever so slowly, he entered her until he felt the resistance of her maidenhood. Then he froze, realizing half of him was afraid to hurt her and half of him wanted to thrust into her so far that he became part of her soul.

Talk about performance anxiety.

He was doomed.

∿‿‿∾

Serai opened her eyes when Daniel stopped moving, and when she glanced up at him she realized that he'd closed his eyes. His arm and shoulder muscles were bunched so tightly that his body was shaking, and for a moment she wondered what was wrong.

But then she knew.

Her "I'm no gentleman" gentleman was afraid to hurt her. She took a deep breath and decided to take matters into her own hands, so to speak.

"Daniel, listen to me. If you don't make love to me right now, I'm going to scream really, really loudly, which will bring all the bad guys from miles around racing to find us, and that will ruin everything, and then—"

She couldn't think of what would happen after her "and then," but it didn't matter because Daniel opened his eyes and smiled and then he took her mouth in a hard, branding kiss, and when her body arched up to his of its own accord, he moved forward, driving into her, claiming her in the most primal way.

She made a little sound of distress—he'd been right, it did hurt a little—but he held perfectly still and gave her a chance to adjust to his invasion. When she relaxed and could feel her inner muscles softening to welcome him, he began to move, thrusting gently into her body and then out again, over and over in rhythmic motions as timeless as the waves of the sea striking the shore.

Her own passion rose to meet his, waves of ecstasy beginning to surface again as the feel of his erection, so large inside her, touched places she'd never known she had— nerves and centers of sensation she'd never known existed.

Slowly, and then with growing intensity, she felt her passion for this man, finally in her arms, finally in her body, rise and encircle her with pure, almost magical sensation.

She felt she could face anything and triumph—even if the witch forced power through the Emperor again, she could conquer them both with the power of her love for Daniel and this amazing, miraculous sensation.

"I like affirming life very much," she said breathlessly, and then he plunged deep inside her, deeper than he'd been before, and her entire consciousness, body and soul, jumped, spinning, off the edge of the world.

~~~

Daniel felt the exact moment Serai began to reach her peak, and he increased his pace, building her orgasm as high as he could and then prolonging it, while he captured her cries with his mouth. He kissed her, feeling every tremor and spasm in her body as an exquisite goad to his own pleasure, even while he tried to ensure hers. His cock had never been so sensitive, and he was fighting against release, trying to hold on, but two more thrusts and he was gone, coming and coming inside her, his cock and his brain emptied by sheer, world-shattering pleasure.

He collapsed, but caught himself with his arms, careful not to crush her with his weight but needing to feel all of her body against his own. He pressed kisses against her cheeks, nose, and mouth, murmuring meaningless phrases, until they both stopped shaking.

"You were right," she said seriously. "That was much better."

He laughed, delighted with her. Delighted with himself. Delighted with every damn thing in the universe.

"I'm glad, because that's only the beginning," he said, kissing her again.

She kissed him back but then suddenly stopped and pushed him away, her eyes dark and unfocused.

"Reisen again?" he growled, thinking of all the ways

he'd like to make the damn warrior suffer for interrupting them at such a private time.

"No," she finally said, narrowing her eyes. "Worse. The high prince of Atlantis is on his way here, with his brother."

"Here? Now?" He carefully disengaged from her body and started swearing, cursing viciously in at least three different languages.

"They'll be here in less than half an hour," she said, calmly enough, but he knew her well enough to read the fire in her eyes. "Luckily I have another shirt, with the buttons intact. Time to make use of that river for the bath I've needed all day."

"I know they're your royalty, *mi amara*, but I might have to kick their asses for them," he growled.

She pulled his head back down to hers and kissed him thoroughly and then stood up and headed for the water. "I may help you do it," she said. "I'd enjoy that very much, I think."

Daniel followed her to the river, thinking of the saber-toothed tiger and grinning. "My money's on you."

# Chapter 21

Still warm from Daniel's lovemaking, Serai waited in the moonlight for the man who was to have made her queen of all Atlantis. She'd pictured this moment in her mind so many thousands of times, when she'd been held captive: her first conversation with whichever Atlantean prince would rescue her. Then, when she'd known Conlan was to be hers, she'd tried to listen for news of him during her brief periods of wakefulness each year.

Sleeping Beauty waiting for Prince Get-me-the-hells-out-of-this-glass-coffin.

But now she'd rescued herself. No more waiting. There was no need for the flutter of nerves churning through her stomach.

"Not exactly how I'd hoped to spend the hour after making love to you for the very first time," Daniel said, a rueful grin quirking up one corner of his mouth.

An unexpected glow of warmth and happiness curled up through her, carrying with it a boost to her confidence. She had no need for nerves here. Conlan was the one who should be nervous. She'd show him what it meant to be a princess of the true Atlantis, the Seven Isles when they still rode the seas and Atlantis was a power unmatched in the world.

Or she could always turn back into a tiger and bite him.

"They're coming," Daniel warned, but she had no need for his vampire senses to know this.

She could feel them, High Prince Conlan and his brother Ven, named the King's Vengeance by tradition and right. She lifted her chin, squared her shoulders, and—for only an instant—wished she were wearing one of her rich gowns instead of the drab and masculine hiking clothes. But her gowns were rotted to dust by now, surely. Cloth could not survive the passage of time as well as magically preserved maidens.

"Serai? Are you all right? I can keep them from you if you want me to. Just say the word. Ven is my friend, but I'd be happy to kick his ass for him if you need me to do it."

He glanced at her, his concern clear in his eyes, but he was smiling for her benefit. He rolled up the sleeves on his shirt, and her gaze was drawn to his muscled forearms. The arms that had held her so tenderly.

"I love you, you know," she told him. "Don't respond to that, please. I just wanted you to know it, no matter what happens on this quest."

He opened and shut his mouth a couple of times, but honored her request and didn't speak. Instead, he pulled her close and kissed her with so much fire and passion she was surprised they didn't both burst into flames.

A loud whistle interrupted them, but Daniel didn't release her until a few seconds later. He smiled down at her with that hot, seductive smile of his, the smile that was only for her, and she relaxed even more.

"If you need me, I'm right here, *mi amara*," he said, for her ears only.

She nodded and turned to the Atlanteans, sweeping a perfect court curtsy, as if she did indeed wear a silk and velvet gown. "Greetings, Your Highnesses."

They returned the gesture, bowing deeply. Conlan's eyes were wide, but he didn't say anything. Perhaps this meeting was as awkward for him as it was for her. They were stunning, of course; the Atlantean bloodline bred incredibly gorgeous men, and the royal genes held true in these two. Dark hair, eyes that looked ocean blue in the moonlight, and tall, strong, warrior bodies. But she had no false modesty about her own appearance, so she knew she held her own. She would be no humble maid in awe of the princes during this meeting.

"Oh, boy," said the one who wasn't Conlan, and therefore must be Ven. He swept his keen gaze over her and then looked at Daniel standing next to her, holding her hand. "So, Daniel, is this your version of the princess and the frog? Beauty and the beast? Galadriel and Gimli?"

Daniel stared back at the man she knew to be his friend, nothing but hard challenge plain on the lines and angles of his face. However, she'd seen a tiny flinch at the beauty and the beast reference. Something to pursue later, perhaps. For now she stared down the princes as if they were recalcitrant children who needed a nap.

The thought of naps made her want to yawn, but she held it in. She would not show any weakness, even so tiny as that. Also, using a negotiating technique her father had taught her, she wouldn't be the one to speak first. She waited.

Conlan finally nodded, as if acknowledging that she'd won this round, and bowed again. "Lady Serai, I wish to formally welcome you to Atlantis and ask you to return."

Ah. Bad, bad beginning.

*Bad.*

"I have no need of your welcome to my home, youngling," she said, putting all the haughty arrogance of a princess of ancient Atlantis in her voice and stance. "I walked the fields of our lands when you were not even a wish in your great-great-grandmother's heart, or a drop of seed in your great-great-grandfather's sac."

Ven started laughing. "Oh, are we going to be great

friends or what? Also, please don't call me Highness, Lady Serai. Just Ven."

He crossed to her, extending his hand, and she took it almost without meaning to, because she was so surprised by his reaction. He bowed over her hand, but he was still chuckling. When he straightened, he grinned at Daniel and then lightly punched him on the shoulder.

"You're in big trouble now, aren't you, my friend?"

Daniel pressed his lips together, but she could see the answering grin trying to escape. "I had considered that thought," he said, flashing an amused glance at Serai.

"You presume too much, vampire," Conlan said. An edge of menace turned his words to daggers, meant to wound or warn.

Serai was unimpressed.

Apparently, so was Daniel. "You might want to think again, if you're going to tell me what I may or may not *presume* to do, Atlantean," Daniel said.

Serai thought for a moment and then raised her hands, palms up, and called to small spheres of energy to manifest in each; a clear visual warning that she was not defenseless. She waited until she had the attention of all three of them, after Daniel and Conlan stopped the ridiculous male posturing.

"I need no one, least of all a child of a prince, to tell me what I may do. You lost all right to give advice on my future when you abandoned me to my crystal prison in order to claim your human woman, *Prince* Conlan," she said.

Conlan's eyes widened, and his mouth fell open a little. Not used to anyone speaking up to him, perhaps. Too bad for him.

She inclined her head as another memory surfaced. "My congratulations on your marriage and the birth of your heir. I trust both mother and son are well."

"Yes, they are very well, and Riley is anxious to meet you. If—if that would be acceptable to you," he said stiffly, probably suddenly realizing exactly how awkward that meeting would be.

*Hello, my wife, meet the woman who was meant to be my wife. Let's all have a glass of wine and discuss.*

She smiled at the thought and allowed the energy spheres to vanish.

"Good you have a sense of humor. You're going to need it," Ven said. "But we're on the clock here. Do you want to tell us what happened? How the stasis pod exploded?"

He glanced at Conlan, and they appeared to have a mental conversation. Ven nodded and turned toward Serai, taking her hands. Daniel tensed and stepped closer, but made no other move. She could feel how much he trusted at least the younger prince and, if not trusted, exactly, still respected Conlan.

"We have some very bad news," Ven said, no trace of his smile remaining. "Delia—she died. Some sort of malfunction in the Emperor's power, and—"

She cut him off and pulled her hands from his. "I know. I felt her die. More will die if I don't find the Emperor soon; I know this, too. Is that what you came to tell me? Surely your brother didn't come to apologize to me after all this time."

"I apologized to you, Serai," Conlan said, stepping closer, his gaze searing into her. "You were asleep, of course, but how else was I to do it? We have had our finest minds trying to solve the problem of the stasis pods so that we could release you and the others, but apparently the Emperor has been malfunctioning for quite some time, unknown to us."

"How is that possible? How is possible that the king-to-be of Atlantis can be unaware that the six surviving citizens of Atlantean ancient civilization were in danger of dying horribly, trapped in crystal cages? Trapped for thousands of years beyond what we were originally told; for millennia past what we were promised."

Conlan threw his hands in the air, frustration written all over his face. "How could I know what you were originally promised? All records of the event are lost."

Serai had started pacing, but then she whirled around in shock to face him. "Lost? *Lost?* In an underwater city trapped under its own prison—an all-encompassing dome?

*Where*, pray tell me, O High Prince Conlan, where could those scrolls possibly have gone?"

She turned to Ven and tilted her head, pasting a polite expression of inquiry on her face. "Did giant fish swim by and steal them? Did the people get tired of ordinary food and eat them?"

Ven made a choking kind of noise, and she rolled her eyes and turned back to his brother.

"Did the children of Atlantis decide to use them to wipe their bottoms? Please, Conlan, oh future king, tell me how your lineage managed to *lose the only means to release us.*"

Daniel suddenly shot up off the ground and flew straight up into the air and vanished. Serai stared after him, not understanding why he would leave her at such a time.

Had she sounded like such a shrew that he needed to escape?

Before her mind could circle around that unpleasant idea, he was back, dropping silently out of the sky and landing lightly next to Serai. He put an arm around her shoulders and kissed the top of her head.

"Sorry. Thought I heard something. It was only an animal." He grinned at her. "You were doing so well on your own, I knew you wouldn't mind."

She impulsively rose on her toes and kissed him. "Thank you."

When she turned, Conlan was practically shaking with repressed energy. "You cannot be involved with a vampire," he said. "Poseidon will never allow it."

"Oh, like Atlanteans can never wed a human? Hypocrisy, thy name is Conlan."

Ven wandered off a few paces and sat on a boulder. "She has a point. Also, this isn't a vampire. This is Daniel. Daniel who has saved our lives—who has saved many Atlantean lives—on more than one occasion."

"Daniel is a *vampire*," Conlan pointed out through clenched teeth. "She is a princess of ancient Atlantis, a woman with the pure blood of the ruling elders, fit to one day be queen—"

"If you say anything at all that has to do with breeding stock, I will blast you with energy spheres until you cry for your mother's teat," Serai said sweetly.

"Speaking of blasting, I am standing right here," Daniel said, sounding surprisingly cheerful. "If you want to debate my worthiness to be with Serai, you can talk directly to me."

"You are not a part of this conversation," Conlan growled.

"Actually, he is, since he helped relieve me of the unfortunate burden of my virginity not an hour ago," Serai said, taking a small and perhaps petty joy in telling Conlan about it.

Ven whistled again, but Conlan stumbled back a few paces as if she'd stabbed him. He speared Daniel with a hot glare that would have killed him had it been a dagger.

"I will murder you with my bare hands," Conlan told Daniel, fury all but radiating off his skin. "I will—"

"You will do nothing at all, as you have no right to be angry, or defensive, or hostile over this news," Serai interrupted. "However, it will be interesting to tell High Princess Riley of your reaction."

"I spent centuries thinking my duty would be to protect you," Conlan finally said. "I don't . . . I don't know how to give that up, especially to think of one of our most cherished citizens of ancient times giving herself to a man with no soul."

Daniel made a small noise, as if he'd been struck, but she couldn't look at him. Not yet.

Words never spoken hung heavy in the air between she and Conlan, the maiden-no-longer and the prince who had scorned her. There had never been love, but between them they had hurt pride in gracious plenty.

The realization stabbed at Serai's heart, and she knew she had to let her anger go. At least until they recovered the Emperor and rescued the maidens. "This is unspeakable of us, Conlan," she said softly. "I apologize for the part my wounded pride has played in this conflict. Those women depend on us, and every minute we spend in this foolish debate is perhaps another minute less that they have to survive."

Conlan hesitated, and then he bowed to her, more deeply than he had before. "Of course you're right, and you shame me with your graciousness, Princess."

She shook her head. "Princess no longer, please. Just Serai. Now we have to get moving."

Daniel swung his backpack over one shoulder, but then stopped. "You didn't mention Jack. Is he okay? Did Alaric find a way to help him?"

Conlan glanced at Ven, who shrugged. "Alaric did not return to Atlantis, and certainly not with Jack. We don't even know if Poseidon will allow shape-shifters in Atlantis, so one of our warriors who married a panther shifter has not brought her to visit yet. Why? What happened to Jack?"

Daniel quickly told them what had happened, and Conlan and Ven's faces grew darker with every word.

"We have to find them," Conlan said. "Alaric may be essential to saving the maidens. Horace knows the stasis pods, but only Alaric has the caliber of magic to handle a backlash from the explosion."

"We have to help them," Ven countered, gesturing at Daniel and Serai.

"We will be fine on our own, until you find Alaric and return," Serai said, increasingly anxious to get moving. "Go, find your priest, but be warned he may not willingly leave his consort."

"Jack?" Ven said, looking stunned.

"Quinn is with them," Daniel told him. "Alaric swore a vow never to leave her, and Jack's humanity may be lost— it's complicated. Go. Figure it out and send help when you can. We have to leave now."

"I can stay," Ven offered, but Serai shook her head.

"If you don't know where he is, both of you will need to look for him. Do whatever it takes to find him so he can protect my sisters, in case the witch wielding the Emperor doesn't relinquish it willingly."

"Your sisters?" Conlan's head rocked back. "I didn't know. I'm sorry, Serai—"

She made a dismissive motion with her hands. "Later. I'll explain it all later. Go, now."

Daniel followed her as she started running, as if pulled by a force too powerful to resist, down the bank of the stream and farther toward the northwest.

Conlan raced across the distance separating them and caught Daniel's arm, yanking him to a stop. "This conversation is not over. You cannot hope to have a future with a princess of Atlantis, no matter how great an ally you have been to our people. You don't even have a soul to meld with hers. She deserves better, Daniel."

Daniel twisted his arm in a blindingly fast movement and pinned Conlan's hand behind the prince's back. "Don't ever touch me again, Atlantean. Not if you wish to keep this hand and not end up like your friend Reisen."

He shoved Conlan away and started after Serai again. "And don't worry," he said over his shoulder to the angry prince. "I agree with you. Serai definitely deserves better than me. Right now, though, I'm what she's got, and I would die before I allowed her to be harmed."

❦

Lord Justice, securely hidden behind a stand of trees, slowly released his grip on the hilt of his ever-present sword. Twenty or so paces away, Conlan and Ven were entering the portal, and Daniel and Serai had disappeared into the distance. Conlan had been right; the vampire didn't want them around.

Too bad. Justice would follow them until they found the Emperor, retrieve the gem and the princess, and return to Atlantis with both before Keely had time to miss him.

Whether Daniel liked it or not.

He shot into the air, taking mist form, and followed the unlikely pair farther into the canyons, concentrating on the breathing exercises Keely had taught him that helped him control his Nereid side's unpredictable furies. That a vampire dared to violate a princess of Atlantis was bad enough, but that he'd dare to do so to a maiden only hours out of stasis and clearly so vulnerable was enough to enrage both of the dual natures who maintained a wary peace in Justice's soul.

*We will kill him slowly*, the Nereid half of him announced. A mad glee underscored the words.

*We do not kill our allies*, Justice corrected himself.

*We will at least hurt him. A lot.*

Justice put on a burst of speed, so he could catch up with Daniel and Serai. *Yes*, he agreed. *We will hurt him. A lot.*

# Chapter 22

Daniel caught up with Serai and waited until they'd hiked another twenty minutes or so—long enough for the metaphorical steam to quit coming out of her ears—before he spoke.

"Maybe poking your ex-fiancé with the fact we'd just had sex wasn't the best way to begin the conversation," he said.

"Actually, that was how I ended the conversation," she pointed out, but she ducked her head and hid her face behind her hair for a few paces. His fierce princess was probably blushing again. The thought made him smile.

"He wasn't my fiancé, either, if the term carries some consideration of mutual agreement. More like I'm the woman he ordered off the menu. Anyway, I'm sorry. I didn't mean to put you in a bad position with your friend Ven or with the future king of Atlantis, especially since you are apparently a politician yourself."

"You just said 'politician' in the same tone most people would use for 'cockroach,' so I'm guessing you don't much approve."

She glanced up at him but kept walking. "I don't have the right to approve or disapprove of your life, Daniel. All I know is what politics and politicians did to me. The power of leadership too often becomes tyranny. People are sacrificed to once-noble ideas of the greater good, and the individual rights become lost in all of that planning and scheming. I lost eleven thousand years of my life to it. Don't you think I have the right to be a little bitter?"

He laughed. "I think you have the right to be all kinds of bitter, Serai. I also think you're right that we don't have the time for it now. After this, though? We're going to have a big old wallow."

She started laughing. "With cake? There definitely needs to be cake with our wallowing."

"And beer," he added. "Cake and beer. Fried chicken, maybe."

"You're making me hungry. Do we have more food in that pack of yours?"

He stopped and set the backpack down on a rock and rummaged around and found granola bars and apples. He handed one of each to Serai, along with a bottle of water.

"It's no royal feast, that's for sure," he said. "All we've got for now, though. When this is over, and we're wallowing, I'll take you out to eat at the best restaurant we can find."

"Before or after the beer and cake?" She bit into her apple, and a blissful expression crossed her face, which immediately made him think of what else he could do to cause her to look like that, which made him desperately need another cold shower.

He settled for leaning against the rock, putting the pack on his lap as camouflage, and biting into a granola bar.

"This is delicious," she said. "I missed fruit, perhaps even as much as cake."

"This granola bar is really freaking nasty," he said, spitting it out.

"Try the apple," she advised, taking another bite of her own. "Do you need to drink my blood?"

He was glad he'd already spit out the piece of granola

bar, because otherwise he surely would have choked on it. "Do I *what*?"

She regarded him calmly. "It was a reasonable question, Nightwalker. Do you need to drink my blood? I see no other around to serve as donor, and I don't want my only ally on this quest to be weakened by hunger when we find the Emperor."

"I—you—" He couldn't find the words. Offering her blood to the monster. What next? Baring her neck? Did she have a death wish?

"Or is it thirst?" She tilted her head, still staring at him as if he were a somewhat interesting scientific experiment. "Do you consider the need for blood to be hunger or thirst?"

"I try not to *consider* it at all. The bloodlust is more powerful than either hunger or thirst. And, no, I don't need to drink your blood. Don't ever, ever offer to let me drink your blood again." It took all of his willpower not to shout at her. What the hell was she thinking?

"Fine. It's not like I'm going to offer to let anyone *else* drink my blood," she said, tossing her apple core into the bushes for an animal's breakfast and neatly stowing her empty water bottle in a pocket of the backpack, which was still on his lap, which brought her too close to him for comfort, considering the bizarre conversation they were having.

Far too close for comfort.

The meaning behind her words caught up with him, and he scowled at her. "Damn straight you're never going to let anyone else drink your blood. I'd kill anyone who tried."

He thought he saw a hint of a smile on her perfect lips, but it was gone so quickly he wasn't sure.

"Are you baiting me?" he asked, incredulous. "About drinking your blood?"

"Baiting is such a harsh concept. A little gentle teasing, perhaps," she said, brushing loose tendrils of hair away from her face. "Not about you drinking my blood, but about any others doing so. You seem to be quite possessive about my blood, after all, for someone who claims not to want it."

How had the conversation turned freaking sideways and upside down on him? He'd never been that great with women, and clearly he wasn't getting any better.

"I don't— I'm not— Oh, screw it." He slung the pack over his shoulder, no longer worried about her seeing his erection, since the conversation had been just as effective as that cold shower he'd wanted. "Let's go."

He headed off in the direction they'd been walking before, and her peals of silvery laughter followed him.

They hiked in silence for a while, but it wasn't an uncomfortable silence. He was content simply to be near her, for as long as he could. Until she decided that the beast wasn't who she needed in her life. He was surprised, however, that after thousands of years of silence, she didn't want to talk. He wanted to hear her voice, but he didn't know what to say.

He jumped lightly over a fallen log in the path and held out his hand to help her over. She put her hand in his, and a bolt of electricity shot up his arm from the contact, but he tried to hide his reaction from her. She tightened her fingers on his and her eyes widened, and he suspected she'd noticed. Either that, or she'd had a similar reaction.

He didn't know which to hope for.

"The Emperor isn't moving right now," she said, after she'd crossed the log. She didn't let go of his hand. He decided to take that as a good sign.

"Tell me about what you've been doing recently," she said. "How long have you been awake from the hibernation? How long have you been working with Conlan and Ven? How did you become primator?"

"Be careful what you wish for," he muttered, thinking silence hadn't been so bad, after all.

"What?" She shivered, and he stopped to pull her jacket out of the pack and hand it to her.

"Nothing. It can get pretty cold here at night."

She zipped up her jacket and raised one eyebrow. "That's it? You think talking about the weather can get you out of answering my questions?"

He started walking again. "Are we almost there yet?"

"No. Maybe another couple of hours' walk at this rate. Plenty of time for you to tell me about yourself."

"Fine. I'll talk, but then you have to tell me exactly how you can shift into a saber-toothed tiger."

"Excellent," she said, smiling. She held out her hand and he took it again without thinking, but then he realized he was growing far too accustomed to being with her. Touching her. Holding her.

All the things that would make it worse when she left him.

"I've been roaming the earth for the past thousand years or so," he told her. "When I woke from the hibernation, the lessons I'd learned before had stayed with me. My goals had changed."

"Goals?"

"From vengeance to redemption," he said quietly. Easy words to say; so easy. Far more difficult to put into practice.

"You had so much to redeem?"

"Yes. Far too much. More than I can ever atone for, more than I can ever be forgiven for," he said. "I can't speak of those dark days after Atlantis vanished, Serai. I'm sorry, but I cannot. Not to you, not to *anyone*, but especially not to you. I can't watch your perception of me change, as you realize the monster I became."

She frowned. "You can't think . . . After, then. When you sought redemption. What did you do? The world was a far different place then, even only a thousand years ago. Where were you?"

She stopped and retied the laces of her hiking boot, and he wondered where to begin.

"I was in Europe. Times were bad. Vampires openly captured and killed humans in many places. Fear and superstition, the lack of any consolidated response—it all added up to a very bad time."

"Sounds like 'very bad time' is quite an understatement."

"I've been accused of that a lot lately," he admitted.

"What did you do?"

"What little I could. I decided that, as a vampire, I could go undercover, so to speak, and pretend to be just another vampire looking for a bloody good time. Once I gained entry, I'd . . . change the regime, let's say."

"You'd kill them," she said, glancing up at him and then away.

"Yes. I'd kill them. More murders on my hands," he said harshly.

"More lives saved, I'd say," she retorted. "Do you count that in your tallying up? The lives you have saved by stopping the murders?"

"It's not like I keep a running score in my head, Serai. You don't understand. Saving the lives of a few can never make up for what I did."

She stopped walking but didn't let go of his hand, forcing him to stop, too.

"You saved the lives of far more than a few. Admit it. And I think you *do* keep a running score, only in your twisted perception of yourself, you only remember to count the ones you harmed, not the ones you helped."

He laughed bitterly. "The ones I harmed? You mean, the ones I murdered? The ones I drained dry until there wasn't a drop of their blood left in their bodies? Those?"

A single tear escaped her lashes and ran slowly down her cheek, and he wanted to rip his tongue out of his mouth for shouting at her.

"Don't cry for me, Princess. Don't ever waste your tears on me."

"But it's all my fault," she whispered. "I chose this life for you. I caused you to be a nightwalker, to suffer the bloodlust and the years and years of torment. All my fault. How you must hate me."

She fell to her knees and covered her face with her hands, but he could still hear her sobs, and the hard, blackened shell covering his heart cracked a little bit more.

"No," he said, lifting her into his arms. "Never, ever think that. You gave me the chance to live. To do something worthwhile with my life. It is not your fault that I failed so spectacularly."

She lifted her tearstained face to him. "But you're not failing anymore. You aren't. You're making the world a better place now. You keep saying you're a monster. Even a monster can be redeemed, Daniel. The gods themselves teach us that. Are you so arrogant that the precepts of the gods and their teachings about forgiveness do not apply to you?"

He kissed the tears from her cheeks, one by one. "Forgiveness is a pretty concept, *mi amara*. But some things are too horrible to be forgiven. I have helped to take down some of the worst monsters in history, and still the scales are not balanced. When will I ever be able to do enough? When will I ever be able to live at peace with my past? Never. Only death will give me peace."

"Then you condemn me to live another life without you?" She put her arms around his neck and stared fiercely into his eyes. "Do you think I will allow that? Think again, blacksmith, before you try to defy a princess of Atlantis."

Her soft sniffle diminished the effect of her proud words, but he knew what she was trying to do for him, and his soul warmed with gratitude that she would even make the effort.

"I can never deserve you," he said solemnly.

She flashed a beautiful smile, the tears still glittering on her lashes like miniature stars in the moonlight. "No? Well, you have the next thousand years or so to try, but not a day longer."

"There's more," he warned her, trying to make her understand before he began to believe her foolishness. Before he began to hope. "I am blood-bonded with Quinn. Ven's wife's sister Deirdre died because of me. Everyone I care about dies. You would do well to stay far away from me."

"This blood bond, was it to save Quinn's life, as you did with me?"

"Well, yes, but—"

"And the other. Deirdre," she said, persisting even though he could see the pain in her eyes and hear it in her voice. "Did you love her? How did she die?"

"No. No, I didn't love her. I tried to save her, but she'd lost so many years to torture and despair. She threw herself in front of a death meant for me in order to escape her pain," he admitted.

"I know that other women have been part of your life, but I don't care. I can't be jealous of them or angry with you for any friendship or solace you found when you believed me to be dead. I already lost you once," she whispered. "I will not lose you again. Stop trying to make me leave you."

He cast around in his mind for something—anything—that he could say to convince her, but she wasn't giving him time to think. She was so warm and soft in his arms, and her body against his made him want to take her, over and over again.

She kissed him, and he forgot trying to be rational and stern and noble. Instead, he kissed her back, with everything his soul felt but his mind wouldn't allow him to say.

"Daniel," she whispered, a long time later. "I'm feeling dizzy again."

He grinned. "I have that effect on you."

Her answering smile was faint. "Yes. No. I think—"

Her eyes rolled back in her head, and she slumped against him. He caught her and gently placed her on the grass, hurriedly stuffing the backpack under her head. The damnable Emperor was taking its toll on her, and they were running out of time. She was growing weaker and weaker, and he was helpless to do anything to prevent it.

He leaned over her to reach into the backpack for another bottle of water, and was relieved to discover that her pulse and breathing were both strong. It was temporary, then. A little rest would surely make her better.

He felt the shift in air pressure even before he heard the shout. Somebody was coming in, and coming in fast. He rolled to the side and shot up, daggers in hands, to protect Serai from whatever new danger was attacking, but he was totally and completely unprepared for what he saw.

It was an Atlantean attacking them. A warrior with a long blue braid. A man he knew and had counted as an ally. Just before the sword swung in a deadly arc toward his head, Daniel had time to shout out his attacker's name.

"Justice! What the hell are you doing?"

But then the battle was on, and Daniel saved his breath for the fight because, for some insane reason, Lord Justice of Atlantis was trying to kill him.

# Chapter 23

Upon regaining consciousness, Serai's first thought was that she must be dreaming, because Daniel was battling an Atlantean warrior who was trying his best to kill him. This one had the classic Atlantean looks—tall, dark, and muscled. She might have even thought him handsome, if he weren't wielding an enormous sword against the man she loved.

Daniel deflected a vicious strike with his daggers and launched himself up into the sky, flipping over in midair above the warrior's head and landing gracefully behind him. Daniel's hand shot out and struck the attacker, hard, but with the hilt of his dagger, not the blade.

Why would he do that? She didn't want to distract Daniel, especially against such a deadly fighter, but she needed to know what was going on. She carefully sat up, fighting a wave of dizziness, and waited for a momentary lull.

"Daniel? Who is this, and why is he attacking us?"

Daniel flung himself to the side to avoid another thrust of that wickedly sharp-looking sword, but it sliced through his shirt. "Princess, meet Lord Justice, formerly of Atlantis."

"Formerly? What do you mean by that, vampire?" Justice said, pausing in his attempt to skewer Daniel. "We have not left Atlantis."

"I mean formerly, as in you're going to be dead soon, if you don't stop this right now and tell me why in the nine hells you're attacking me," Daniel growled.

Justice swung his long braid, which looked almost blue in the moonlight, out of his way and took a ready stance with the sword held out and up in front of him. "Perhaps you should have thought of consequences when you attacked a princess of Atlantis. Now you will die for your presumption, and we shall happily be the ones to deliver the true death to you."

Serai pushed herself off the ground to stand up, trying to ignore how shaky she was. If they didn't find the Emperor soon, she was afraid she wouldn't last much longer.

"This is making me very angry, Lord Justice," she said, putting the full force of her position in her voice. "I am getting a little tired of people attacking Daniel. It was bad enough when danger came from our enemies, but first Jack, then Reisen, and now you. All allies, or so you claim, and yet you dare to attempt to harm the one person who is aiding me on my quest to retrieve the Emperor?"

Justice tilted his head and stared at her for a long minute, his eyes narrowed, as if trying to comprehend her meaning. He finally shook his head, dismissing her. "You do not understand, my lady. He was attacking you. Clearly he has used his vampire powers to enthrall you."

Pure, clean, healthy rage burned through Serai, searing the last of her dizziness to ash. "Did you just dismiss me as a silly girl who has fallen for a vampire's tricks?" She made sure to carefully enunciate each word. "You have just insulted the wrong Atlantean, youngling."

Daniel laughed, drawing Justice's attention again. "You're in trouble now, Justice. When she called Alaric and Conlan younglings, she really put them in their place."

Justice turned a shocked expression to Serai. "You did that? How did our brother react?"

Serai raised an eyebrow. "Which one is your brother? Alaric or Conlan? You have a similar look around the eyes as Conlan, but the blue in your hair is pure Nereid. Though of course I have not seen a true Nereid for more than eleven thousand years."

Justice lowered the sword a few inches, relaxing his ready stance a bit. "You have met our kind? Truly? We had known you were one of the ancient ones, but we never thought—"

Faintly, ever so faintly, Serai felt a touch of very old magic sing its way through the space surrounding the three of them. She shot a glance at Daniel and saw that his gaze had gone blank and somewhat unfocused. He was trying to access his nightwalker mage powers, she was sure of it, but he was so out of practice that it probably would take some time.

She would provide a distraction, then.

"Why are you referring to yourself in the plural?" She called to the water magic and formed two apple-sized spheres of water and light, which she casually began to juggle from hand to hand. A bit of fun to distract children, but perhaps it also worked on those who were mentally unstable. A man who referred to himself as "we" would fit in that category.

He watched her with great concentration, a look of joy and fascination on his face. "I have not seen the mummer's balls of waterlight since I was a child," he said. "My mother's sister came to visit me once . . . It is a Nereid magic, I had heard."

Serai noticed Daniel raising his hands, his eyes closed tightly, and knew she had to keep the warrior distracted for just a little while longer.

She tossed one of the spheres toward Justice, who instinctively raised his free hand to catch it, lowering his sword hand even further. He laughed when the sphere splashed and dissolved against his fingers.

"Daniel did not attack me, Lord Justice," she said softly, in a sing-song cadence, riding her own magic on the waves of Daniel's gentle persuasive push, but it was too much, too soon, and Justice's face hardened.

"We saw him. He attacked you, and you fell."

She took a step toward him. "No. I was dizzy from the magical fluctuations of the Emperor. A witch is attempting to use it for her own ends, and the backlash is harming me and the other maidens. Daniel has been protecting me and supporting me as we seek it."

Justice looked doubtful, but she took another step toward him. "Is it not your duty to protect me, as a Warrior of Poseidon?"

"Yes, of course, my lady, but—"

"Then you must allow me to continue my quest, and allow Daniel to help me do so. If I don't find the Emperor, I may die. All of the maidens still in stasis may die."

He hesitated, but then shook his head and raised his sword again, this time in a defensive position, but still aimed at Daniel. "We cannot take the chance that you have been misled by the vampire's magic. We will all wait here for Conlan's return."

"I'm sorry, Justice, but we're out of time, my friend," Daniel said. He sliced one hand through the air, chanting under his breath, and Justice froze in place, as still as one of the statues in the palace atrium, nothing but his eyes moving.

The look in those eyes promised a slow and brutal death to his assailant when the immobilizing magic wore off, however.

"Everything she told you was the truth, Justice, but we just don't have the time to wait. Serai is growing weaker every minute. If we don't find that Emperor soon, it could be very bad."

Daniel raised his hands into the air, and Justice's immobilized body turned sideways and then floated down gently to the grass. The strain from using the magic was plain on Daniel's face, and Serai automatically sent her own magic flowing through the air to support his, not thinking of the cost to her strength.

She staggered a little, and Daniel ran to her and caught her before she fell.

"We must move, now," she whispered. "It's growing worse, Daniel. I don't know how much longer I can go on."

"Can we try to fly again?"

A wave of panic rushed through her at the idea, and she stumbled again as her knees went weak.

Daniel nodded grimly. "I see the answer is no," he said. "We'll hike faster. I'll carry you if I need to."

"Conlan and Ven will find you," Daniel told Justice. "They should be back soon. You can contact them through your telepathy thing, I'm guessing?"

"Yes, he should be able to do so," Serai answered, since Justice obviously could not. "We need to go now, Daniel. Please."

"I'm sorry," Daniel told Justice, and then they set off again, he all but carrying her as they walked toward the resonance of the Emperor's power, shining like a beacon in her mind.

They hiked in silence for perhaps twenty minutes, until they reached an obstruction on the path. She put her arm around Daniel's waist, and he flinched a little.

She pulled her hand back and stared down, uncomprehending, at the dark wetness on her fingers where they'd grasped his waist.

"You're injured? This is blood?" She pulled him around to face her and pushed his shirt away from his skin before he could protest. A slender gash in his side steadily dripped blood, and his shirt and the tops of his pants were drenched.

"How did I not see this?"

He grinned at her, but his face was strained. "It's dark. Tough to see blood in the dark."

A wave of dizziness swept through her again, and she realized she'd been supporting him with her magic, unknowingly, since the battle with Justice. It was weakening her even more, and with that compounded by the Emperor's magical drain, she was barely standing upright. She shut down the flow of her own magic to Daniel, but it was too late. She'd lost too much of her energy during the confrontation with Justice.

"We're in trouble," she said softly. "Serious trouble."

"You might be right," he said, abruptly sitting down, hard, on the rocky ground. "Oh, yeah. We're in trouble."

~~~✣~~~

Daniel stared stupidly at his legs, which wouldn't function anymore. He felt a sudden loss, almost as if—almost as if—

"You. You were pouring magic into my spell back there," he said, feeling like a damn fool for not realizing it before.

"I thought you needed the help," she said wearily, dropping down to sit next to him. "It has been so long since you used your mage powers, and it felt like you needed the support."

He wanted to berate her for weakening herself to help him, but he couldn't say or do anything that might upset her. Not now. Not when they were in so much trouble and might not survive it.

"Thank you," he said instead.

She smiled. "You are very welcome. Now what do we do?"

He dug around in the pack until he found the last bottle of water. "You drink this, and I figure out what we can do until Conlan and Ven get back. Maybe if—"

"Daniel."

"—if we call him. Can't you reach out on that mental calling channel? We can—"

"Daniel," she interrupted again, this time putting a hand over his mouth. "You need to drink, too. I know this much of nightwalkers. Healing a wound is a simple matter if you have blood."

Bleak, black despair swamped his vision, and he couldn't bear to look at her. "I cannot. Please, don't ask me to do this."

She grasped his shoulders, forcing him to see her. "I need you to do it, for me, Daniel. I need you to drink my blood so you can be strong enough to help me."

She took a deep breath, before she continued. "And I need for you to give me some of your blood, too."

He jumped up, wanting to run away. Wanting to kill somebody. He was good at killing.

He was terrible at everything else.

"You don't know what you're asking," he said. "More of my blood? In you? We'd strengthen the blood bond, at the very least. And as for the rest, can you even bear to suffer a nightwalker's bite? I know the venom can be poisonous to your kind."

Ven had told him, on one of their beer-drinking nights. A vampire's bite had nearly killed Brennan once, apparently. Just a single bite.

"I'm immune," Serai said quietly. "Your mentor bit me that day, Daniel. I never wanted you to know, because I knew you'd blame yourself, but it's relevant now."

Daniel roared out his agony to the night skies and then crouched down on the ground next to her. "I am sorry beyond the telling of it," he growled. "If he were still alive, I'd kill him now. Slowly and painfully."

She shook her head. "It's not important. He woke up disoriented from the noise of battle above and released me almost as soon as he bit me. But it was enough for me to learn that I am immune to the nightwalker bite."

"If I were to do this thing, I would truly be the monster you claim I am not," Daniel said, wondering why he was even considering it. But the ache in his side and his rapidly growing weakness gave him reason enough. He'd been avoiding feeding for so long—only taking the least he possibly needed to survive—and now he was paying for it. The wound was deep enough and wide enough that it had drained far too much of his blood.

"If we're not strong enough to succeed in this mission, I will die." She took his hands in hers. "Surely with that on one side of the scales, exchanging blood is not so dire."

"It only sounds bad if you say it fast," Daniel said, mocking himself for the fool he was. He was going to do this horrible, monstrous thing, and use pretty speeches to excuse it.

"We are two halves of this quest; two halves of a whole that was split apart unfairly so many years ago, Daniel. Our destiny is together, not apart. If you can strengthen me and I you, then there is no bad in it."

Serai tilted her face up to his and pressed her lips to his, as if to convince him of the truth of her words. He couldn't let her, but yet . . . what she said had merit.

"I'm not usually so weak," he said, pulling away from her. "Justice scored a hit exactly where that vampire'd stabbed me in the attack the other night. My internal organs were not yet entirely healed from that, I think."

"And you've been abstaining from drinking blood since you found me, haven't you?"

"All but once," he admitted.

Her eyes narrowed. "Was she pretty?"

In spite of the danger of their situation, he laughed a little. "*He* was a large, sunburned tourist with an 'Arizona is for Lovers' T-shirt, and I only took a little."

She tilted her head and moved her braid to one side of her neck, baring the other side to him. It was as sensuous and provocative as if she'd removed her clothing, and his breathing sped up in spite of his resolve not to do this monstrous thing.

"Please, Daniel. Please help me save my sisters," she whispered, and his resolve crumpled into dust like the fragile bones of long-forgotten principles.

His fangs descended, and he clamped a tight control on the bloodlust, which was screaming at him to take her blood, take all of it, take *her*, take *everything*.

"Just a little bit. Just enough to heal this wound."

"And enough to strengthen you for what lies ahead. There are certainly going to be those ready to try to stop us," she said, looking up at him with those incredibly lovely eyes. "I trust you, Daniel. Maybe more than you trust yourself."

"That wouldn't be hard to do." He still only half-believed he was going to do it, but she was right. If they didn't gain a little strength, their mission was doomed, and her death was all but certain.

Or maybe he was lying to himself. It didn't matter,

though. He couldn't fight both Serai and himself. He was going to do this.

He leaned closer and put the tiniest bit of compulsion in his gaze, calling on the nightwalker magic to help him seduce her into enjoying his bite instead of feeling the pain as his teeth punctured her skin.

She sighed as she went under, smiling dreamily up at him. "Oh, Daniel, I want to affirm life with you again right now. Is that normal?"

Her smile blasted through the last of the battle-hardened defenses that he'd built around his heart and he fell, body and soul. He was hers, and she was his. What better way to strengthen that bond?

He kissed her neck, very gently, and then sank his fangs into her skin directly over her pulse. The rush of her blood was like nothing he'd ever tasted or experienced before, and the taste was beyond description. Spicy and exhilarating and delicious; as if a fountain of pure magic were entering his mouth and body. He had to fight against the bloodlust and against his own monstrous instincts to force himself to take only a little; only enough that he could feel his body healing and renewing itself.

He carefully closed the puncture marks on her neck with his tongue, and then he bent his forehead to hers. "Thank you, *mi amara*. You have revived me, my beautiful one."

Her head lolled back against his arm, and his heart jumped in his chest as he realized that even the little blood he'd taken might have been too much for her, in her weakened state.

"'S my turn?" she said, her words slurring. "Feel a l'il drunk."

"Yes, it's your turn. Hang on." He frantically tore the sleeve of his shirt in his haste to get it out of the way and then bit into his wrist. Carefully holding it over her mouth, he lifted her head up so she wouldn't choke.

She hesitated but didn't fight him before she closed her mouth around the tear in his skin and drank. As he watched, he could see the lines of strain on her beautiful face smooth out and disappear. She only drank from him for a very little while—less than half a minute—and the pure sensuality of the experience was enough to drive him nearly mad. He'd shared blood before, but it had never been like this. The headiest aphrodisiac could not compare to the feel of Serai's lips on his skin, and the sight of her throat as she drank. The sensation of his blood being pulled from his skin and into her mouth was enough to sear every nerve ending in his body into a throbbing readiness.

If they ever shared blood while making love, he thought he might die from the sheer pleasure of it.

She leaned her head back, away from his wrist, and he closed the wound with a quick swipe of his tongue. She smiled up at him, and it was the smile of a woman well sated by her man—a smile so sensual and seductive that it took every ounce of his willpower to keep from stripping her clothes from her and plunging into her right there on the ground.

"I feel so very much better," she said, still smiling. "Still a little drunk, but in a good way. I feel like I could run a thousand miles and fight a thousand enemies."

"Drinking vampire blood can have that effect sometimes," he said, returning her smile.

"And the other part? Is it always so . . . sexual?" She bit her lip, as if afraid of the answer.

"No, never," he said firmly. "I have never felt like that when taking blood or sharing my own. Usually it's more like drinking a glass of juice."

She giggled, actually giggled, and he thanked any gods who were listening that this insane plan had worked, but she quickly sobered. "We have to go now, Daniel. I can feel the Emperor more strongly than ever. Its power is building, as if . . . it sounds strange, I know, but almost as if the gemstone is becoming angry at its misuse. Does that make any sense at all?"

"It's the possession of a god, Serai. Anything at all can make sense; the more frightening, the more plausible, I think."

He helped her to stand up, and then, because he could keep from doing so no more than he could keep from breathing, he kissed her, long and deep. The energy from her blood rushed through him, potent and powerful, and he believed he could take on Poseidon himself for that gem.

"Do you hear it?" Serai looked around, an expression of pure awe on her face. "The sounds of the night. They're so clear now. Is that because I drank your blood? Does it always sound so incredibly beautiful to you, as if your dreams themselves were transformed into music?"

"I remember a time, long, long ago, when the enhanced nightwalker senses seemed magical to me," he said. "But never as magical as they do now, with you here to share them with me."

"We can explore the world together, Daniel. After this quest is done, and my sisters safely restored." She twirled around like a giddy girl, laughing and flinging her arms wide. "All over the world, what do you say?"

"As you wish," he said, smiling at the memory of another princess, in a movie Ven had once shown him. "I can be the Dread Pirate Daniel."

She stopped twirling and stared at him, perplexed. "What? A pirate?"

He laughed. "It's a long story, for another time. For now, maybe you should contact Conlan and Ven so they can hurry up and—"

"No! I will not call them, nor answer their call. I don't trust them." She yanked the backpack up off the ground and took off walking so fast she was nearly running.

He raced to catch up with her. "What do you mean?"

"They must have known Lord Justice was planning to attack. Perhaps they even ordered him to do so. I don't trust them. Who knows what secret agenda they have? If my sisters die because of their political maneuvering or whatever reason they sent Justice after us, without telling us, then they will pay for it with every ounce of magic I still possess."

"But we don't know that Justice didn't act on his own. Besides, we need all the help we can get, Serai. I won't risk your life." He knew even as he said it that it was no good. She wasn't listening, but he had to try.

She glared at him, raising her chin in that determined way she had, and he knew he'd been right. "Nor will I risk yours. That sword wound could have killed you, and I blame High Prince Barnacle Dung for it. We go on alone. Now that I'm so much stronger, I can use my magic to mask our trail and my presence, even on the mental pathway, from other Atlanteans." She paused and took his hand. "I feel it, Daniel. I feel that this is the way it's meant to be. Please? I need your help."

He sighed. There they were, those four deadly words again.

"As you wish, Princess. As you wish."

# Chapter 24

As Ivy slept, wrapped in a sleeping bag on an air mattress on the cave floor, Nicholas watched her, reassuring himself that she was well; merely sleeping and not unconscious. Not that he cared about her. No, she was merely a tool, and as he'd said, he kept his tools in good working order.

He forced himself to walk away from her, although there wasn't really anyplace to go. They were holed up in a cave, like animals. Not his first choice of accommodations, especially when he had a perfectly serviceable mansion in Sedona, but he'd been afraid that moving Ivy would harm her further. Overuse of her magic, combined with the shock from seeing him kill Smithson, had pushed her past the limit of what she could endure.

Her son, who had finally succumbed to his own exhaustion, slept in his own sleeping bag next to his mother. Ian had more courage than most adults Nicholas had encountered in his many years. The boy had demanded that Nicholas turn him into a vampire, so that he would be more fully capable of protecting his mother from "scum like you" in the future.

Brave, and a little foolish, like the best of all possible boys. Nicholas allowed himself a moment to mourn his long-dead son and, even more, to mourn the death of their relationship. Lingering on what might have been, though, was never productive. Nicholas lived in the present and dealt with the here and now. He'd always found it a more efficient and useful way to live his life.

He was practical. Pragmatic. Whatever benefited him the most was the course to take. Always.

His gaze involuntarily returned to Ivy, and he scowled. His feelings for this woman were an unwanted complication. A conundrum. She had no value to him beyond her use as a witch who could wield the gem. And yet he found himself wishing he could make her more comfortable.

Get to know her, perhaps. Make her see that he wasn't entirely a murdering bastard.

And then what? Flowers and candlelight?

He pivoted and walked to the entrance of the cave and motioned to one of the vampires in his blood pride. "Find me someone to eat."

"Do you have to do that a lot?" Ian walked up next to him, but not too near. "Eat people?"

"I thought you were asleep," Nicholas snapped. "Go back to bed."

"I can't really sleep when my mom is in danger, and we're hanging out with a bunch of bloodsuckers, no offense, dude." Ian covered a huge yawn with his hand.

"None taken," Nicholas said dryly. "Do you have any sense of self-preservation at all?"

"What, because you could kill me with your little finger or whatever?" Ian shrugged his thin shoulders. "Sure, I'm scared. I'm not stupid. But she's my mom, dude. Wouldn't you do anything—risk anything—for your mom?"

Nicholas glared down at the boy, but realized that, oddly enough, he was willing to continue the conversation. "Yes, I would have done anything for my mother. And don't call me dude."

"Sorry, but I don't exactly know your name," Ian pointed out.

"Nicholas."

Ian stuck out his hand. "I'm Ian Khetta, Mr. Nicholas."

For the first time in centuries, Nicholas found himself shaking hands with a teenage boy. "Just Nicholas. I know who you are, Ian Khetta, son of Ivy Khetta. Do you know your mother is a sorceress of the dark arts?"

Ian recoiled. "That's not true. She'd never do that, not after what happened to her mom. I don't know where you get your information, dude—ah, Mr. Nicholas—but it's dead wrong."

"I'm never wrong, boy," Nicholas informed him, baring his fangs just because he could and because, in some bizarre manner, he felt like he was losing control of the conversation. "Go eat a sandwich or something. Aren't human boys always hungry?"

"Aren't vampires always eating people?"

Nicholas bared his fangs. "Just give me a minute."

Ian's face turned pale under his sunburn and freckles, but he didn't back down, making Nicholas feel a twinge of admiration for the boy.

Which annoyed him.

"Yeah, I get it, you're the big, bad guy here, but I have some information I'd like to trade," Ian said.

"What kind of information?"

"Information that could make you rich," Ian said.

"I'm already rich."

"Richer, then. Look, do you want to hear it or not?"

"In return for this information, which is likely to be useless, what do you want?" Nicholas leaned against the wall of the cave and folded his arms across his chest, waiting for the boy to make his unreasonable demands, so he could laugh in Ian's face.

"I just want my mom to be safe," Ian said, squaring his shoulders. "You can keep me, or drink my blood, or whatever, but you have to promise to let my mom go. She can't channel this much magic, or she's going to get a brain aneurysm and die. Also, like I told you earlier, I want to be a vampire like you, so nobody can ever threaten Mom again."

Nicholas's composure cracked, for just a moment. This child—this boy not even old enough to shave—was offering his own life for his mother's. It had been a very, very long time since Nicholas had seen anything but selfishness from anyone, human or vampire, and his fixed-in-stone worldview took a major hit. It didn't shatter—it didn't even come close to shattering—but the foundations crumbled, just the tiniest bit.

"Ian, I will find a way to keep your mom safe," he said rashly. Stupidly.

"Do you promise?"

He grabbed the boy by the front of his shirt and jerked him up in the air, holding him so high that his feet dangled a good twenty inches off the ground.

"Do not try my patience, boy, or question my word," he hissed, allowing the full force of his power to show in his undoubtedly glowing red eyes. "Give me the information or do not. It matters not a bit to me. I have said I will find a way to keep Ivy Khetta safe, and I always do what I say. Now, go eat something or sleep, or whatever you want to do, but do it quietly, and *do not bother me again.*"

He dropped the boy, but Ian had good reflexes and landed on his feet, knees bent, and then straightened up. The boy's face was glowing a hot red, but he didn't storm off toward his mother, as Nicholas had expected.

"Fair is fair. You said you'd protect my mom, and I said I'd give you information," the boy said. He walked to the center of the cave, directly underneath the hole in the ceiling from which the rubies had poured down, and pointed up.

"Nobody else but me bothered to look up at the ceiling, inside that hole. Everybody was too busy staring at the rubies, or then at what you did to that guy . . ." Ian faltered for a moment, but then he recovered and looked back up at the ceiling. "There's another cave painting in there. Like the one the other guy said was so important to the story of what the deal is with that gem you're making my mom use."

"In the ceiling? Fascinating." Nicholas leapt into the air and rose through the cave until his head was actually inside the hole in the ceiling, which put him close enough to see the painting but unfortunately blocked the light.

He snapped his fingers and pointed to one of his vampires. "Light."

The minion rushed to bring him one of the lanterns and held it up as high as he could reach. Few could fly, as Nicholas could. The ones who could, he had on patrol.

Raising the lantern, Nicholas looked around again and blinked. He blew out a long, slow whistle.

"Boy, you have just earned yourself a reward. I believe this painting contains the secret of the amethyst." He looked down at Ian, who was shifting from foot to foot nervously.

"I am going to be richer than Midas and quite possibly invulnerable. You, my boy, have just earned your ticket to that immortality you asked me for earlier. When you reach twenty-one, if you still desire it, I will turn you vampire."

"Over my dead body," Ivy said. She walked into the space directly below where Nicholas was still floating up by the ceiling and pointed a shaking hand, rimmed in purple fire, at him. "I will kill you now, vampire, before I will let you destroy my son's future."

Nicholas felt a very rare smile stretch its slow and unfamiliar way across his face. "Now, *finally*, things are going to get interesting."

# Chapter 25

Ven searched the canyons and riverbanks as he flew overhead, looking for any sign of a magic amethyst, murdering vampires, or an evil witch and wondering when things had gotten so freaking weird that a warrior from Atlantis felt like he was in the middle of a twisted faery tale.

Or a really bad joke.

*So, a vampire, a witch, and an Atlantean walk into a bar . . .*

Justice's call broke into his mental meanderings with a bang, so powerful and furious that Ven nearly fell out of mist form and slammed into the tree he was soaring past.

*COME NOW COME NOW COME NOW THE VAMPIRE ATTACKED HER AND WE ARE DOWN COME NOW COME NOW.*

He arrowed for the ground, transforming back into his body as he went, and landed lightly next to a shining cloud of mist that instantly turned into his brother.

"What in the nine hells was that?"

Conlan shook his head. "I have no idea. Justice sounds

like he could chew through that sword of his, but the vampire attacked her? What vampire? Surely not Daniel?"

Ven sent a mental message to Justice but only got a zap of weird static in response.

"He's not answering. Either he's down and out, or he's gone so ballistic that the Nereid half of him took over."

"Neither is good," Conlan said grimly. He launched into the air, transforming back into mist mid-jump, and Ven followed his brother's lead, heading up and out to find his other brother, and hoping they weren't too late.

Minutes later, they found Justice, lying immobile on the grass a short distance from the creek bank.

*Trap?* Ven sent to Conlan.

*Could be. Let's go in carefully.*

Justice wasn't sending anything on their mental channel but waves of static and random words like *kill, murder, disembowel.*

Typical, in other words, but not really helpful.

Ven touched down close to Justice while Conlan landed a good twenty paces away. Both of them drew their daggers and scanned the area, but there was no sign of anyone else around.

"What happened to you, big guy?" Ven crouched down next to Justice and felt for a pulse, but it was only reflex. Obviously Justice was alive, if not exactly well. The fury glowing in his spring-green eyes was a bad sign for whoever had done this to him.

"You said vampire. Can you elaborate? Try to calm down enough to think it at me. We can't fix this if we don't know what's going on."

Conlan walked up, still scanning their surroundings but clearly having reached the same conclusion Ven had, that nobody was around.

"Are you getting anything? All I can hear is dire threats of a slow, torturous death for whoever did this to him," Conlan said, grinning.

*NOT FUNNY. WILL KILL HIM. KILL DANIEL.*

The grin faded from Conlan's face, and Ven felt as sucker punched as Conlan looked.

"Daniel? Are you sure? He did this to you? How is that even possible?" he asked Justice.

*NIGHTWALKER MAGE POWERS. KILL HIM.*

Ven rubbed his forehead, which was beginning to pound from the sheer volume of Justice's anger. "Got it, you're going to kill him, but in the meantime, could you hold it down? The only thing you're killing right now is my head."

Justice's lips twitched, and after that his fingers moved slightly.

"It seems to be wearing off already," Conlan said. "Hell of a spell, though. Immobilizing someone with Justice's power takes a lot, and to sustain it from a distance is extremely difficult. If this is really Daniel's work, he's been hiding quite a bit of his capabilities from us."

*He attacked her and drank her blood. He has hypnotized her, too, and she believes he is protecting her. We heard this from her own lips.*

"I can't believe Daniel would compel Serai," Ven said. "Did you see him with her? He had the same puppy-dog eyes you have with Riley."

Conlan glared at him. "I don't want to hear it from you, who acts like a lovesick youngling every time Erin is near."

"Yeah, yeah, whatever. We need to get Justice back to Atlantis. Alaric or one of the priests will be able to fix this," Ven said, and then he remembered. "If Alaric has returned. This week is turning into a damn clusterfuck, isn't it?"

Conlan shot him a look of pure exasperation. "What time in our lives hasn't been? Do high princes get vacations?"

Ven called for the portal, then waited until its shimmering oval began to form before he started laughing. "Sorry, Your Highness. Welcome to your life."

Conlan just shook his head. "I'll take Justice to the healers, and you keep looking for Daniel and Serai. We need to find out what happened, and if she's safe, and I don't trust myself to keep from just tearing his head off when I see him. At least you'll give him a chance to tell his side of this."

Ven suddenly wanted to hit something. "If we're suddenly having to worry about sides—with such a trusted ally and friend as Daniel—then things are getting worse."

*Much worse*, Justice sent. *We are in dire straits, indeed.*

"Dire straits, clusterfuck, apoca-damn-lyptic times. Welcome to the fun house," Ven muttered, as Conlan carried Justice through the portal. "It just keeps getting better and better."

After they'd vanished, he stood perfectly still and sent his senses out into the wind, calling out to the Atlantean princess who might possibly be in thrall to one of his best friends. Better and better.

When she didn't respond, and not even a hint of her presence came to him, he tried to seek out a hint of her trail. The use of Atlantean magic had a unique signature, and he should be able to spot it easily enough.

Should be able to find it quickly.

Should be . . . but couldn't.

Not a single trace.

"Nightwalker mage plus ancient Atlantean princess trumps my magic every time, I'm guessing," he said out loud, to any of the local wildlife who might be interested. "I'm going to need help."

No way could he search the caves and canyons and nooks and crannies of this area by himself in time to find Serai before, oh, next year or so. It was almost dawn, so Daniel would have to head for the darkness. He had time to go for reinforcements. He called the portal again.

"Daniel, I hope you know what you're doing," he told the cool night air, and then he stepped through the portal. Time to go back to Atlantis and regroup.

# Chapter 26

Daniel and Serai hiked steadily, making better progress than they had thus far, until nearly dawn, when he called for a break.

"We'll need to stop soon and find a place to rest." He scanned the area for one of the many caves that would give him sufficient darkness to avoid the deadly rays of the sun.

Serai kept hiking, not even slowing down. "I'm not tired."

"Nor am I, but unless you like your companions slightly flambéed, we need to get out of the sun."

She instantly stopped walking and whirled around. "I'm sorry, Daniel. I wasn't thinking. I just—we're so close, and I can *feel* the Emperor in my brain, pounding and pounding its call, and—"

"I know. I'm sorry I can't help you in the daylight. If you have changed your mind and want to call Conlan and Ven, you know I think it's a good idea."

"No," she said, not even hesitating. "I still don't trust them."

"What about Reisen?"

She shook her head. "I've tried several times to contact

him to see if they're well. If Melody survived. But he won't answer me."

"Or he *can't* answer you," Daniel said grimly. "Neither option is good for us."

She put her hands on his shoulders and looked up at him with nothing but trust in her eyes. "We can do this. We can. We'll rest for the day and find the Emperor tonight."

"If it's still here to be found," he said grimly. "We don't know when they're going to move it, Serai. We need to contact Ven and Conlan, now. Too much—too many lives—depend on us finding that stone for us to wait a single minute longer."

She sighed and moved away from him, saying nothing, but she raised her face to the sky and closed her eyes. A long moment later, she inhaled sharply and opened her eyes.

"There's no response. They're gone."

"That's impossible. They wouldn't have just left, not with the Emperor lost and your life and those other women's lives on the line. Try again."

She did, but then shook her head. This time she looked a little frightened. "They're gone, Daniel. Either dead or gone back to Atlantis, or somewhere else that is far out of my range."

"What is your range?"

She shrugged. "Perhaps a thousand miles, in current measurements? More or less."

"That's pretty impressive. And you're sure? Absolutely sure?"

"Yes. There is nothing. It's different from Reisen; I can feel his presence but he won't answer or has his mental communication pathway shut to all messages, not just mine. But there is no trace of Conlan, Ven, or the Nereid at all."

Daniel put his arms around her and pulled her close, unable to resist comforting her.

"I can call the portal, if you're sure we need them," she murmured, her breath warm against his neck.

He tried very hard to concentrate on facts and the mission at hand, but the reality of her soft warmth against his body was knocking all of his brain cells out of his head as his blood rushed south.

"Portal?" He kissed her cheek, and her nose, and her other cheek, before taking her mouth. Heat rushed through him, a conflagration so intense he almost thought he had been caught in the sun, from her touch and the way she responded to him.

"Sun. Need to get out of the open," he managed, when he could make himself stop kissing her. "Can you call the portal from inside the cave?"

"Of course," she said. "Which cave?"

"There." He pointed to an opening that nature had carved into the face of the rock wall curving away from them on the left, and the rough stone footholds that the Sinagua had added centuries ago to nature's handiwork. "Can you climb that?"

She flashed a wicked grin at him. "Of course. Especially now, with your magical blood inside me."

He didn't have time to think of any coherent response to that before she was racing across the ground and then almost flying up the stairs to the cave. At the top, she turned and looked at him, still standing where she'd left him.

"Coming or not?"

Drops of water splashed on his head, and he turned his face up to the sky, welcoming the first rain they'd had since beginning the quest. Morning showers didn't last long in Sedona this time of year, he'd noticed, and he should take advantage of this one. He flew up to the cave, not bothering with the stairs, and immediately pulled the empty water bottles out of the pack, uncapped them, and set them on the ledge.

"Luckily they have wide mouths. They should fill easily enough," he said. "Thankfully it's finally raining. We were out of water."

Serai looked at him, then up at the sky, and then down at the water bottles. Then she leaned against the wall of the cave and started laughing.

"Are you losing touch with reality?" he asked cautiously. "I know you're exhausted, and this is very difficult, and the burden on you—"

"Daniel. You just told me you're thankful it started raining."

"Yes."

"You just told me, one of Poseidon's own, that you're thankful it started raining, since we were out of water."

He was starting to understand, and feeling like an idiot, when she apparently decided he needed visual illustrations. She waved a hand, and a shimmering silver curtain of pounding rain surrounded them—inside of the cave.

Serai gracefully leaned down to take one of the bottles, held it up to the indoor waterfall, and then, once it was full, handed it to Daniel.

"Taste this."

He drank deeply, and it was the best, purest, sweetest water he'd ever tasted. "Not bad" was all he'd admit, but she laughed at him. Together they filled the rest of the bottles, and then Serai waved her hand once more, and the indoor rain stopped, magically leaving the cave completely dry.

"Water is the one thing—the only thing I can think of, to be candid—that we don't need to worry about," she said, but her smile faded quickly. "I'll call the portal, and we'll find out just what Conlan knew or didn't know about the Nereid's attack."

She raised her hands and softly sang out to call to the portal's magic, but this time the portal didn't respond right away.

"Maybe it doesn't like caves?"

"That has nothing to do with it. I'm so weak, perhaps . . . I'll try again." She called again, but still there was no response, so she tried again.

And again.

And again.

Nothing.

The first pale rays of sun were beginning to glow in the

air outside, lightening the darkness in the cave, so Daniel could see very clearly when the blood drained out of Serai's face.

"It's a test," she whispered. "It's a test, and I have to pass it or we all die."

"Serai, that can't be true. Why would you be forced to face a test when you're fresh out of sacrificing millennia of your life for Atlantis?"

She slowly slid down the wall until she collapsed into a ball on the cave floor. "It doesn't matter what I did before. All that matters is now. The portal—it only ignores a call if assistance is refused."

"No. Ven and the guys said the portal is capricious. Maybe this is some sort of practical joke, and if you try later—"

She shook her head. "You don't understand. I could hear it—hear *her*—in my head. The spirit of the portal. She refused to allow the portal to open. Told me I must face this test alone, with no aid from Atlantis."

He crouched down beside her and took her into his arms. "Never," he said fiercely. "You will never be alone so long as I draw breath. The portal will have to kill me to take you away from me, and let me tell you, I'm very hard to kill, even for a magic doorway."

She smiled, only a little, but it was a smile, and even so much courage was enough to take his breath away.

"I need to kiss you now. I need to be inside you. Now. Please," he said roughly, and he didn't give her time to answer before he claimed her mouth in a kiss that held every ounce of his desperation that she would live, *must* live, no matter what obstacle.

"Yes, Daniel," she said, when he finally allowed her space to breathe. "Yes, I want you, too. I need you, too."

Serai held out her arms, aware in a place deeper than mere consciousness that she'd accepted more than just a kiss. More than just his body into hers. If they made love again, she was in very real danger of reaching the soul-meld with this man, and he would be bound to her for eternity.

Exactly as she hoped. Perhaps not in his plans, however, since he kept telling her she would be better off without him. Was that just a pretty way to say he didn't want to spend very much time with her?

She closed her eyes, refusing even to consider it. She might not live through another day; worry for the future could certainly wait until later. For now, she had this man in her arms, kissing her, ravishing her with his deep, dangerous kisses.

He was hers, for now. She could think about *always* later.

Daniel's strong arms wrapped around her and pulled her up off the floor so quickly that they almost levitated before he realized what he was doing and dropped back down to land on his feet, but she was still held so high and tightly in his arms that her toes didn't touch the ground. He tightened one arm around her waist and used the other to reach up and grasp her braid, twisting it around his hand and pulling her head back so he had free access to her neck.

"Must resist," he growled against her skin, and she felt his tongue touch her neck and then the slight scrape of his teeth, and she froze into perfect stillness as she realized exactly what he was resisting.

"Must not bite you, your blood is so delicious, so sweet and addictive," he murmured, kissing his way up the side of her neck and then gently biting her earlobe as she wiggled in his arms, fighting to get closer, to feel *more*, to bask in the sheer sensation of being in his arms.

Now that she knew what lovemaking truly was, she wanted more and more and more of it.

"I may be a wanton," she admitted, and was surprised when he laughed.

"I really, really hope so," he said fervently, and then he lifted her even higher, so her legs automatically wrapped around his waist, and he walked with her until her back rested against the cave wall. He kissed her again, deeper, darker, until her entire world swirled around her in a haze of sensual delight.

"Thank you, *mi amara*," he whispered, his lips only a breath from her ear. "Thank you for returning to me."

Daniel fought against the competing pulls of desire and bloodlust, both driving him to *take her, take her, take her*. He'd taken her virginity only a short while ago, and she must still be sore from that encounter. He had no right to push her to further sexual activity so soon. But the way she kissed him drove him insane. Her lips were so soft and sweet, and her passion inflamed him and drove him to the edge of madness. His body was so hard and ready, and his cock pushed forward, nudging against her sweet softness like a heat-seeking missile.

He had to laugh at himself for the thought. Now *there* was an analogy that an ancient Atlantean maiden would not appreciate.

"Daniel, why are you smiling? Why aren't you kissing me?" She twined her fingers in his hair and pulled his head back to hers, and the sweet taste of her mouth told him more than her words.

Told him she was *his*.

"Mine, do you hear me? I will never, ever let you go," he told her, desire and need and possession all tangling up to darken his voice. "Don't ever think of that Atlantean man who would be better for you. If he even dares to think about touching you, I'll kill him."

She pulled away a little and laughed up at him. "Daniel. You do realize you're threatening a figment of your own imagination, right? All I have ever wanted is you. You're the one who keeps pushing me off on this paragon of Atlantean manhood who exists only in your own mind."

His fangs descended and he scowled. "Never. Do you hear me? Never. You're mine. Say it."

Her smile faded and she stared into his eyes for a very long time, an eternity, before she finally nodded. "Yes. I'm yours. But you're mine, as well, *mi amaro*. Say it," she demanded, every inch the haughty Atlantean princess he'd once dreamed of in his lonely apprentice's bed.

"Yes. Yours. Always," he growled. "I need to fuck you now."

She gasped, and her eyes darkened, and he hesitated, but she lifted her face to his in acceptance and he wanted to shout and roar his need and possession to the universe. To eternity. Instead, he released her for only long enough to strip out of his clothes and then tear hers from her body, only barely managing to be careful enough not to shred them into pieces in his urgency.

He took her mouth again, so as not to drive his fangs into her skin. He needed all of it. Her body. Her blood. Her surrender. "Now."

"Yes. Now." Serai put her arms around his neck, and he lifted her again, directly onto his erection, slowly but inexorably pushing into her silky wet heat.

"Oh, oh," she cried out, making little noises as he leaned her back against the cave wall, her legs wrapped around him again, but this time nothing between them but the cool dawn air.

"Gods, you're so wet for me, Serai, you're so hot and wet for me. I'm losing my mind here." He thrust farther, farther, until his cock was so far inside her that he couldn't push any deeper. Then he stood still, giving her time to adjust to his invasion, but he couldn't help but bend down to capture one ripe pink nipple with his mouth.

She cried out again, this time his name, and he tightened his grip on her lovely round ass and licked and sucked on her nipples until she was squirming around his cock and driving him completely insane.

"Now, now, now. Move, I need you to move," she said breathlessly, and he raised his head to crush his mouth to hers again. Triumphant and triumphed over.

Serai's entire body was trembling with need. She had never felt so alive, so sensitive, as if every inch of her skin were a nerve center crying out for his touch. For his hands and his mouth and his oh-so-clever tongue.

For his manhood.

"Please. Now," she repeated, and he kissed her again and then finally started moving, thrusting in and out of her in long, slow strokes that put her in danger of exploding. Heat centered between her thighs traveled up the center of her body to her breasts and her lips and her brain, until she thought the world itself must be shattering off its orbit.

He tightened his grip on her bottom and then reached between them and pressed those wonderful fingers of his against that sensitive spot he'd discovered before, and she cried out again, and then he was pressing rhythmically there, pressing and rubbing while he drove inside her, long, hard wonderful strokes, and something was building and building inside her, swirling and spiraling, and tightening every muscle in her body while her nerves screamed for more, for more, for release, and then he thrust into her so hard and so fast, the muscles in his neck straining as he tried to maintain his control, and she realized she didn't want him to hold on to his self-control, not now, not ever, so she tightened her inner muscles around his erection and tilted her head, baring her throat to him.

"Bite me. Take my blood while you take me over the edge."

Daniel stared at her in shock and froze, mid-motion, but she tightened her muscles around his cock again and touched her neck, trailing a finger provocatively down her luscious pale skin, and something inside him broke, his control shattered, and he started fucking her again, so hard and so deep that she would never, ever forget him, never escape him, never ever leave him.

Never.

He sank his fangs into her neck and she screamed, not from pain, he'd made sure not to hurt her, she screamed as she came, shattering around him, convulsing around his cock, over and over until he couldn't help it, he thrust into her one last time and came himself, his seed pumping into her as her blood pumped into his mouth, a circle of want and need and home and forever.

He licked the tiny wounds in her neck closed and rested his forehead against hers, and they stood, locked in place, while they gulped in deep breaths together.

"I think you should put me down, but I'm not sure my legs will work," she said, her voice shaky.

He attempted a smile, but his face wasn't working. All he could do was gasp and try to breathe. He felt as though he'd run a thousand miles in a day, or flown across a continent, and he looked into her eyes while he thought of a way to tell her how much he needed her, but shock rendered him temporarily speechless.

"Your—your eyes," he managed, and then his tongue got tangled as he stared at the tiny blue-green flames in her eyes.

"Yes? What about my eyes? They're bluer than the ocean," she teased.

"They have these little flames in the middle. I know that sounds stupid, but I, they—"

Her eyes widened even farther, until they were enormous in her face. The flames grew even larger, until they were nearly taking over her entire irises.

"The soul-meld? Is it really happening?" Her whisper trailed off, and he realized that he was still holding her up in his arms, against a cave wall, his cock still inside her.

"Maybe we should clean up and talk about your eyes," he began, but she didn't let him finish.

She grabbed his head with both hands and kissed him so fiercely that he had no choice but to kiss her back. His body responded with a vigor that belied the long years of disuse and his cock hardened inside her so fast that he wondered dizzily if mage or Atlantean magic were involved, and then she somehow moved, with him still inside her, lowered her legs and pushed him back until he was lying on his back on the pile of their discarded clothes and she was straddling him.

Gloriously naked, she was beautifully and gloriously naked above him, her ripe round breasts begging him to reach up and take them in his hands, and so he did, while she slowly and sensually rose and lowered herself on his cock. Her eyes were still full of those blue-green flames, but it seemed a distant concern, far less important than rising up off the ground so he could suck on her nipples, until she pushed him back down and arched over him, crying out as she convulsed around him again, and he took charge of the tempo, quickening it, thrusting up into her with the speed and force he needed to reach another climax so soon. She reached down behind her and grabbed his balls and gently squeezed, and he arched up off the ground and poured into her again, harder and more powerfully than before.

That's when the walls of the cave shattered into an explosion of sound and color, and reality shifted as his mind expanded and collapsed and expanded again, and his vision fractured into a prism of sparkling shapes and colors, until he floated gently down to earth in a flash of light, but a different earth, an earth that had vanished thousands of years ago.

*Flash.*

Somehow he stood in Atlantis, and it was still on the surface of the ocean.

Serai stood in front of him, sheathed in silvery light, talking to a man he knew to be her father, but he was long dead, this was impossible.

"Serai," he called out, but even as she ignored him as if he didn't exist, he felt her body warm and pliant against his in another reality.

"I cannot do this thing, Father," she said, tears streaking down her face. "I won't. I must find Daniel. He was wounded, and your guards took me away. I need to find him. I need to help him. I won't be frozen into a box for some future king."

"Daniel is dead," her father said, and Serai collapsed into a faint.

*Flash.*

Serai lying shattered on the ground, bones broken and blood everywhere, resigned to death and screaming a protest against the healers as they converged on her.

*Flash.*

Serai lying down inside a crystal casket, not dead, not even dying, but resigned to spend centuries asleep, alone, as she would always be alone, because the one man she would ever love was gone.

*Flash.*

Centuries of waiting, then millennia, time passing in a constant blur, only one annual semi-wakening to feed information into her mind and reassure her she hadn't crumbled to dust. Every time she woke, his name was the first word on her unmoving lips; his face, the first sight in her unforgiving mind; his love, the only thing in her never-healing heart.

Daniel. Daniel. Daniel.

*Flash.*

The shock of the Emperor's stuttering power. Her escape. Running to the portal, only to find her dream of the past eleven thousand years had become reality. The warmth and love in her disbelieving heart when she saw his face.

*His* face.

*Flash.*

Daniel slowly came back to himself from the waking dream, only to realize that he still held Serai in his arms. She rested against his chest, arm tucked on his shoulder, eyes wide and staring, but unseeing. Whatever had just happened to him seemed to be happening to her.

No.

*No.*

If she saw his history—his bloody and monstrous past—she would never forgive him. Never stay with him.

He shook her and called her name, then resorted to shouting at her, but nothing mattered, nothing worked, so he simply gathered her into his arms and waited, silent as the grave he'd soon be seeking out, for the woman he loved to learn who he truly was and order him out of her life forever.

Serai fell, twirling and twisting, tossed through a typhoon of sound and sensation, through an apocalypse of blood and death, fear and fury. Light flashed all around her, and she woke up in the very same shop where she'd first met Daniel, all those years ago.

*Flash.*

He stood still, staring after a girl who was leaving the shop, and Serai was a tiny bit jealous, until the girl smiled back at him over her shoulder and she realized it was *her*. Herself, eleven thousand years ago, on the very first day she'd met Daniel.

"Hits you like that sometimes," a man standing in the shop said, grinning at Daniel's expression of utter shock. "Been married more than twenty years to a woman who made me feel just like you look right now."

Daniel blinked and opened and closed his mouth a few times. "But—but—"

The man laughed. "Yep. That's what I said. You're done for."

*Flash.*

The fight in the shop, that day the invading army attacked Atlantis. Daniel fighting for his life against looting soldiers, protecting the trapdoor, protecting her. Falling, so much blood.

*Flash.*

Daniel waking, crazed with the bloodlust, calling for her. The old nightwalker telling him she was gone. Atlantis was gone. Gone forever. Daniel screaming her name until he was hoarse, and then falling to the ground, body heaving with great, racking sobs.

*Flash.*

Murder. Vengeance. The flash of recognition in that village; the girl who reminded him of Serai. Hibernation. The quest for redemption. The eventual resignation and despair.

*Flash.*

Walking into the sun, only to look up and see that the sunlight wasn't killing him. The light came from her face. *Her* face. Serai. Love. Desire. Need. In his face. For her.

For *her*.

When she woke from the trance, she gasped and then gulped in great, shuddering breaths, as if she'd been starved of oxygen for hours or days. Daniel held her tightly, so tightly that she wasn't even cold, although they lay on the floor of the cave, still unclothed.

"Well?" His voice was as hoarse as if he'd been screaming. For all she knew, he had. She'd been deaf to him while the soul-meld took her and showed her his life.

"You're leaving me now, aren't you? I understand. I forgive you, and we can just forget all that stuff about 'mine' and 'forever,'" he said, his face so cold and remote that— for a split second—she almost doubted him. Almost.

But she'd seen inside his *soul*. She said the only thing she could. The only possible words to share at such a time.

"Daniel. We have answered the question the elders have asked for millennia," she told him, touching his stern face with her hand. "Nightwalkers *do* have souls. I have just walked in yours, and I want to cry for your pain. Know this, though, my vampire. My love. I will never let you go, and if you mention it again, I may have to hurt you."

Daniel couldn't speak. Couldn't think. Could only *feel*, as a wave of pure warmth and love swept through him. "You've seen my soul? Is that even possible? I'd wondered—I'd feared—"

"You cannot reach the soul-meld with someone who has no soul," she said, smiling, and he realized the blue-green flames in her eyes were still there. "We are bound forever now."

The ancient words came to her, unbidden, mandating her to recite them:

> *"I offer my magic, my heart, and my life to protect*
> *your own.*
> *From now until the last drop of ocean has vanished from*
> *the earth,*
> *You are my soul."*

Shimmering silver threads, clearly visible in the predawn light in the cave, formed and curled around them both, tying them together inescapably. Forever, she'd said.

Daniel couldn't take it all in. It was too much.

"I have a soul?"

"You do," she confirmed. "A badly wounded soul, forced to make so many hard choices, still fighting hard to redeem itself from the dark. And now it, as well as you, belong to me."

"Forever?" he repeated, stupidly.

"Forever."

"Then we will make damn sure that nothing happens to you. I promise you that. Upon my life, upon my oath as a senior mage of the Nightwalker Guild, and upon my love for you, Serai, I swear to you that I will not let you die. We will find that Emperor and save your sisters, this I swear to you."

She smiled and kissed him, and this time the world didn't shatter and the walls didn't fall in and the floor didn't disappear from under him. It was just a kiss, only a kiss.

The kiss that began the rest of his life.

# Chapter 27

## Midday, in a cave only two miles away from Serai and Daniel

Ivy sat on her pallet of blankets in the cave where she'd recently seen a man die horribly, and wondered if she'd brought this all on herself. She hugged her knees and watched her son sleep, knowing that it was futile to waste time on the how and the why of the past. All that mattered was how they'd get out of this situation. A fierce wave of pride and fury swept through her, leaving nothing but icy cold resolve in its wake. Nobody was going to hurt her son.

Nobody.

Dusk was a few hours away, and she needed to figure out her escape plans before the vampire rose from his day sleep.

"I have no intention of hurting him," Nicholas said from behind her, making her jump a little. She hadn't even heard him approach. Damn sneaky vampires. He could have ripped her guts out, too, and she wouldn't have heard it coming.

Although, was that something you'd *want* to hear coming?

"Can you read my mind? If so, I can't imagine you're very flattered right now." She didn't bother to turn around and look at him. He was the last person in the world she wanted to see, now or ever. "Also, shouldn't you be asleep? Evil vampire, and all that?"

"It doesn't take a mind reader to see a mother's protectiveness for her child," he said, surprising her. "Also, I'm old enough to be awake whenever I like. Just because I can't walk in the sun doesn't mean I'm a slave to its passage through the sky."

She smoothed an errant strand of hair from Ian's face, and he stirred but didn't wake up. She filed away the information about the vampire's lack of need for day sleep. Just one more obstacle. She was good at overcoming obstacles.

"If you see my protectiveness, you understand why I would never let you turn him into a vampire."

"I have no intention of turning him into a vampire," he said. "But I thought it was easier to say yes and deal with the topic again when he actually turns twenty-one, in the unlikely event he even remembers asking or still wants it then."

"Kids remember everything. Or at least my kid does. I can't speak to any others. Ian, though, he's special. Always has been. So much like his father."

"Where is the boy's father?" Nicholas's voice had the slightest touch of frost in it, as if he planned to go attack Ian's dad next. He was too late on that one.

"He's dead. He died when Ian was very young. Murdered by vampires. Some of your kind who didn't like the coming out parties, and wanted vampires to be the feared creatures who went bump in the night instead of the neighbor next door who could vote and pay taxes. They killed him and laughed about it. Some of your buddies?" She told the story without any anger. It had been far too long ago for anger. All she had left was cold hatred and the need for revenge.

The need to protect her son, no matter what the cost.

"I am sorry for your loss," Nicholas said, and he was so good—so smooth—that he put actual regret in his voice.

"Don't bother," she said. "You don't need to warm me up or pretend you care about the death of some random human ten years ago. You have me, you have my son. I have to do what you ask, so don't waste both of our time by pretending otherwise."

He stepped forward, into her line of sight, and leaned against the wall, and she was struck again by how incredibly handsome he was, at least when his eyes weren't glowing red or somebody's intestines weren't draped over his arm. So many of them were attractive. Vampires. Beauty disguising evil, or designed to seduce its prey.

A flash of some indefinable emotion crossed his eyes but was gone so fast she'd probably imagined it. Or else he was trying compulsion on her, in which case he was out of luck.

"I was a random human once," he said softly. "As were my wife and son. The memory of my family was not burned out of me by the bloodlust, even in the beginning. I know full well what you would do to protect your son from vampires, because my wife protected my son from me."

She looked up at him, caught in spite of herself by the pain in his voice. Or the illusion of it, she reminded herself. Vampires were masters of illusion. And yet, she knew full well that she was immune to compulsion.

"How did it happen? Why did you choose to become a vampire, then, if you lost your family over it?"

He laughed, but there was no humor in it. "Choose? Did your husband choose to be murdered? There was no choosing involved. I was happy and wealthy, and there were ones who wanted what I had. When I was lost to the bloodlust, they murdered my wife and child, too. Apparently they only wanted my land and fortune, not my family."

"I'm sorry," she said quietly. "I know how you felt."

"No, you don't," he replied, just as quietly. "I had the luxury of killing those who took my family. I doubt you had that."

"No. No, I didn't. Not that I didn't try. Someday, though. Someday they will look up, and it will be me they see, and then they will see nothing forever after." She shoved her hair out of her face and took a deep breath. "On the other hand, I haven't had to mourn for centuries. How long has it been?"

His face changed, and she almost wished she hadn't seen it. The hard lines and angles softened, and he stared at her as if she'd shocked him. He looked almost . . . human.

"No one has ever asked me that, or even spared a thought for my centuries of pain," he said, bowing his head. "Your son is who he is because of you; your soul and spirit. His father would be very proud of him."

She fought the burning sensation of tears, steeling herself with the absurdity of it all. Comforted by kind words from a vampire. Ridiculous. And yet—and yet he had never lifted a hand to harm her, and he'd protected Ian.

No. Foolish. What was she, an idiot with Stockholm Syndrome?

"You've threatened me in order to get me to help you," she said. "Don't pretend I'm here voluntarily, or that you respect me or want us to be buddies."

He raised an eyebrow, and the cold, sneering haughtiness returned to his expression. "I haven't had a buddy in over three hundred years. Why should that change now?"

"Tell me about the painting in the ceiling, then," she said, desperate for a new topic, before she actually started to feel sorry for him. "What did you see? What does it mean?"

"I have no idea. I can guess, but my guesses are pretty wild. I'll need you to confirm that anything I think might be possible, actually is."

"Of course. And if I blow a brain aneurysm trying to channel that damn stone, oh, well, you can always replace me," she said bitterly.

Ian stirred on the cot and opened his eyes, probably because she'd raised her voice, and Nicholas walked away.

"I'm not so sure about that anymore," he said as he left, and she turned to watch him just as he glanced back at her.

The look burning in his eyes terrified her more than anything else that had happened over the past few days. It was *hunger*. She was sure of it.

And she didn't think it had anything to do with her blood.

～～～

Nicholas edged as close to the entrance of the cave as he could get without stepping into the sunlight and bursting into flames. Although flames might be a relief, compared to the confusion churning in his gut. He wanted to rule the vampires of North America. Consolidate his power. Take over the primator position. A little invulnerability to go with his near-immortality wouldn't hurt.

The last thing he needed was to allow a temporary weakness over one lovely witch and her courageous son to interfere with any of his goals. He heard the boy walking across the cave toward him but ignored him.

Unfortunately, teenage boys weren't all that great about being ignored.

"What's the painting about? Did you figure it out after Mom made me take a nap?"

"Are you ever silent when you're awake?"

Ian laughed, and Nicholas caught himself smiling at the sound.

*No, no, no, no, no.*

"Not too often. When I'm eating, mostly."

"So go eat something."

"Did you?" Ian challenged him. "Eat somebody?"

Unfortunately not. He'd had an unexpected change of heart about the terrified human his minions had abducted for him, and he'd compelled her to sleep and then wake up with no memory of the encounter. She was safely home now, unaware of how close she'd come to being lunch.

"Yes," he lied. "Several people. Drained them dry and picked my teeth with their bones."

Ian gasped. Finally. Fear: a sensible reaction.

"Hey! You made that up. Picked your teeth with their bones? Come on. I don't see any bones around here."

"Ian!" Ivy's tone was unmistakable, and Ian scuffed one shoe on the ground.

"Aw, Mom—"

"No. Do you really want to banter with a vampire you saw eviscerate a human being only hours ago?"

The light drained from Ian's eyes, and true fear replaced it. He slowly backed away from Nicholas, who felt a strangely empty feeling in his gut. Almost like loss, although that was ridiculous.

*Ridiculous.*

"Yes, I think I know what the painting means." He pulled out his phone and showed them the picture he'd taken. "I think I know what the gem's name is, too."

"It has a name? Like the Hope Diamond?" Ian stared at the photo, fascination outweighing his momentary fear. Nicholas was inexplicably glad of that.

"I believe it does. Objects of power are often named," Nicholas said. "Do you see how it's glowing with purple light? It must be our stone. See how the people are all bowing to it? And the symbol etched below the stone, I have seen similar symbols before. I believe the gem is called the Ruler, or the King."

"Cool. Also, vampires have smart phones?"

"What did you expect? Carrier pigeons?"

Ivy raised an eyebrow "You get all that from this primitive painting? You're kidding, right? What does that glowing purple skeleton mean, then? The amethyst makes bones dance?"

"Bone Dance would be an excellent name for a rock band," Ian said.

Nicholas and Ivy both looked at him, and his ears turned pink.

"Sorry. Totally random."

"What about the city under the water?" Ivy pointed to the tiny shape in the upper left corner. "What is that?"

"That must be Atlantis."

Ivy started laughing. "Atlantis. Right."

Nicholas shoved the phone in his pocket, caught Ivy around the waist, and soared up to the hole in the ceiling so she could see it herself. This time he brought the lantern with him, although it was much lighter in the cave now since it was midday.

He turned her so her back was to his chest and leaned down to speak close to her ear. "There. Do you see it? A city under the sea, and those shapes you couldn't make out in the tiny photo on the phone are leaping dolphins and possibly the sea god carrying his trident. What else could it be?"

Her heart rate sped up significantly, and he didn't know if it was from fear or something else. Something that was too dangerous to even consider, because if the witch was attracted to him, too, he had a bigger problem than he'd feared.

"I don't know. Maybe. But Atlantis?" she finally said, and her voice shook a little.

"You're a witch, and I'm a vampire," he said, tightening his arm around her waist, just a fraction, just enough to feel the length of her soft, warm, curvy body against his. "Is Atlantis truly so impossible?"

"Yes. No. Whatever. Please put me down," she said, but he could feel that she was trembling, and he had to clamp down with every ounce of self-control he possessed to keep from sinking his teeth into her neck or sinking another part of his body into her elsewhere.

"Mom! What do you see?" Ian's voice had the exact same effect as a blast of cold water. It wasn't exactly good to have wicked thoughts about the boy's mother when he was standing right beneath them.

He floated them back down to the ground and was obscurely pleased to see the flush in Ivy's cheeks when he released her.

"I don't know. It might be about Atlantis. Maybe not. I'm not sure what that means to you, though," she told Nicholas. "What about that dark woman floating in the air above the guy with the trident?"

Nicholas repressed a shudder at the thought of what that dark figure might truly mean. If Anubisa were to claim ownership of the gem, she wouldn't look kindly on any who stole it. And when the goddess of Chaos and Night was unhappy, people and vampires died in horrible ways. None of that was anything he could share with Ivy, however.

"The least that the gem, the King if you will, does is find me enough treasure to gain the power to win the primator job. The most it might do is make me invulnerable to attack. I need for you to explore the full range of its powers."

Ivy narrowed her eyes and clenched her hands into fists at her sides. "I tried, and it nearly killed me. It's not worth my life to try again, unless you let my son go and take him exactly where I tell you."

"I can make a difference," he found himself saying. Telling the truth after so long a time of lies and misdirection. "I can stop the worst abuses that are being perpetrated by so many power-mad vampires out there now. I just need the chance to try. We were better off remaining in the shadows, afraid of discovery and retribution."

"You can't unspill the milk. You can't make people forget vampires exist," Ian said.

"And kidnapping my son? That's not an abuse of power? Or do you believe that the ends justify the means, no matter how horrible, in which case I don't see much difference between you and the ones you want to stop," she said, getting right up in his face.

He lost part of what she said, caught in her golden-brown eyes, and was actually leaning down to kiss her when he caught himself.

"I will have my people take Ian wherever you want him to go, as soon as it turns full dark," he said, stepping back. "If he gives me his word he won't send the cavalry after us."

"More like the army," Ian muttered. "You hurt my mom, and I'm going to go all Call of Duty on your ass."

Ivy's lips quirked up as if she were fighting a smile. "Ian, don't say ass, and don't threaten the scary vampire," she said, and then she blinked. "I just fell down the rabbit hole, didn't I?"

Nicholas wondered if he were getting his first headache in a couple of hundred years. "What is a call of duty in this context, and what rabbit hole?"

Mother and son looked at him in unison, then at each other, and they both burst out into laughter that was tinged with hysteria.

"Humans," Nicholas said, throwing his hands into the air.

"I'm not going anywhere, Mom," Ian said. "I won't promise to be quiet. I'm staying right here with you until we both leave together."

"I need one more thing from you, and then you are free to go," Nicholas said. "But you shouldn't attempt it alone. I have sent for one of your coven to attend and assist you. I don't want you to be harmed."

Ivy shook her head. "No. Absolutely not. You can't put another of my people in danger. I know that your . . . ex-partner lied about Aretha. She wouldn't have just up and left for Aruba without telling me. She's dead, isn't she?"

Nicholas stared at her for a long moment, wanting to spare her the truth but knowing he could not. "Yes, but not at my hand or even his. The power surge from the amethyst that rendered you unconscious killed her."

Ivy stumbled back a step. "It's my fault, then. I killed her."

Ian put his arms around her. "No, Mom. You heard what he said. How could you know what the King stone would do? You're lucky it didn't kill you, too."

"The boy is right," Nicholas said. "If anyone is to blame, it's me for using you and your apprentice like pawns. Yet another bad decision in a long line of them."

"You want me to help you gain even more power, when you admit you make bad decisions right and left? Hurt people? Get them killed?" Ivy patted her son's shoulder and then stepped toward Nicholas. "Why would I possibly do that?"

Nicholas considered mentioning her own use of the dark

arts, but decided against it. After hearing about her husband, he knew why she'd turned to the black. Instead, he told her the simplest truth.

"I am the lesser of many evils, and sometimes that's the best you can do."

# Chapter 28

### Atlantis, the maidens' temple

High Princess Riley, surrounded by the three women she trusted as much as she did her own sister, stared down into the crystal stasis pod, at the dark-haired woman sleeping serenely inside. The story of Sleeping Beauty come to life, right here in front of her. Of course, she was standing in a temple, under a dome, underneath the ocean, in Atlantis, so everyday reality had taken a left turn quite some time ago.

"It's not your fault," Erin said, putting a hand on Riley's arm. "You tried to set them free. Everybody has been working on it."

"Maybe. Maybe I didn't try hard enough," Riley said. "Maybe I didn't really want to meet Serai, the woman my husband was supposed to marry. Hard to measure up to a princess with ancient magic and, oh, yeah, who happens to be the most beautiful woman I've ever seen."

"Yeah, if I were a guy, I'd do her," Keely said.

Riley jerked her head up to stare at the archaeologist in disbelief, only to see that she was grinning.

"Sorry, Riley, but somebody needed to lighten the mood,"

Keely said, unrepentant. "You aren't doing anybody any good feeling sorry for yourself."

"I think you've been spending too much time with Lord Justice. You are losing your sense of tact," Marie, the head of the temple devoted to childbirth, said gently. Marie, the only native Atlantean of the four of them, was a classical beauty like Serai, and wore her dark hair up in its usual intricate braid. "Shouldn't you be with him, after he was caught in that spell?"

"He's fine. Just sleeping off the after-effects and bad mood. Speaking of men, though, how's your kitty cat doing?" Keely replied. "Still smoking hot?"

Marie's mouth fell open, and Erin laughed out loud. Marie was very much in love with the alpha of a panther pride in the southeast United States. Unfortunately, their respective duties didn't allow them very much time together. Riley hoped they could work something out soon. Marie too often looked tired and sad these days.

"Perhaps we could remember why we're here," Riley admonished them. "One of us can surely figure out something. Erin, with your magic and Marie's healing, isn't there something—"

"We have tried, Princess," Marie said. "You know that."

"Tried and tried, and tried some more," Erin added. "My gem-singing magic is growing stronger every day, but the Emperor doesn't respond to it, the maidens don't respond to it—it's useless. *I'm* useless."

Marie chided her. "You are far from useless. Just this morning you saved that woman's baby, and we'd thought he was far too sick to live."

Erin shrugged. "Sometimes I get lucky. So much of this is a wish and a prayer, after all."

"We've all been praying for them," Riley said. "The maidens. Why do we call them that? They have names. Serai is gone. Delia is dead. Merlina, Helena, Brandacea, and Guen remain. We have to save them. We *have to.*"

Keely touched the crystal over Brandacea's face. "She

looks worse," she said grimly. "I don't know how much longer they can take this."

Horace approached them and bowed to Riley. "Princess, I wondered if you will be here for very long. My attendants haven't had any rest or food in quite a while, and—"

"Of course, please send them out. You, too, Horace. And call me Riley, please."

"Thank you, Princess," Horace said, bowing again. "I'll remain here. I've eaten and am rested enough."

She studied his pale face and the dark circles under his eyes. "I doubt it, but I understand. I don't want to leave them, either."

"I wondered—" He broke off and bowed again. It seemed to be a nervous habit.

"Wondered what?" Keely said. "If you have an idea, now would be a great time to quit bowing and tell us."

Horace shot her an unhappy look before turning toward Riley. "I would like to try to release one of them. We are accomplishing nothing by trying to shore up the Emperor's fluctuating magic. Serai clearly survived leaving stasis. What if—"

"What if we could save them by taking them out of the pods? Let's do it," Erin said. Her eyes lit up as she surveyed the four remaining women in their crystal pods. "We have to at least try with one, Riley."

It didn't take Riley long to decide, since she'd been thinking along exactly those lines for a couple of days by then.

"Yes. Yes, let's do it. Who is having the hardest time now?"

Horace turned pale, as he realized that she'd agreed to his idea. "I don't—I shouldn't—"

Keely put her hands on her hips. "Spit it out, Horace. Which one is closest to being lost if we don't rescue her now?"

He gulped and then pointed to Brandacea. "She is so weak; her life force is barely flickering now."

Erin nodded. "It's true. I can feel it, too. If we're going to do this, we should try with her first. She's in the most danger if we do nothing."

"Should we call the high prince?" Horace asked. "This decision is—"

"The decision is mine," Riley said firmly. "Conlan is finally catching a nap after being out all night searching for the Emperor and spending all morning setting up his plans for going back with a contingent of warriors to find Serai, Daniel, and the Emperor."

"What do we do?" Marie asked.

"It's deceptively simple, actually," Horace said. "We just open the lid."

Riley and Erin exchanged a glance. "Why haven't we tried it before, then?"

"We have, Princess. Within minutes, the maiden—it was Delia—was choking for air, almost as if she had lost the ability to breathe. We had to return her to the pod, or she would have died, I'm almost sure of it. She almost did, anyway, but a surge of magic from the Emperor restored her."

"What makes you think now will be different?" Keely shook her head. "We don't even have Alaric here to help, and nobody is a better healer than he is."

"No, but Marie and I together come pretty close," Erin said. "What choice do we have? We try again to release them, or they die anyway, at least Brandacea will. Look at her. She's barely holding on, as it is. Does she have another night, while Conlan and Ven try again to find the Emperor?"

"In addition to that, she may not have time to wait while we figure out how to use the Emperor, even if they can find it immediately," Riley said.

She looked around at each of them in turn: Erin, Marie, Keely, and Horace. "We can do this. It would be criminal not to even try."

"And if we're wrong?" Marie's face was pale. "I am no stranger to death, Riley, but if we do this, and we fail, we will have brought this woman's death upon her."

"Or we can stand here and do nothing, and kill her just as quickly," Erin said. "I know this isn't a democracy, but I vote we try."

"Me, too," Keely said. "I don't want to live with the regret of having stood by and done nothing."

"I am with you, as well, Princess," Horace said.

Riley looked at Marie. "It's up to you, which is fitting, since she's your ancestor. I'll make the final decision—the burden will be on me—but I won't consider it unless we're unanimous."

Marie looked down at Brandacea for a long time, and then she finally nodded. "I can feel her growing weaker every minute. I agree that she will not last the night unless some solution is found. I vote yes, as well."

Riley clasped Marie's hand in one of hers and Erin's in the other, and Erin took Keely's hand, and Keely took Horace's hand. They stood there together, in silence, each of them occupied with his or her own thoughts or prayers, and then Riley looked up.

"Let's do this, and please, God, let us be right."

Horace placed both of his hands, palms down, on the cover of the pod, and he chanted quietly, in what Riley recognized by its cadence must be ancient Atlantean. A shimmering silver light appeared and surrounded the pod and its occupant, until Brandacea's still form glowed as if lit from within.

"Now," Horace said, and four of them lifted the crystal cover from the pod, carried it to the side of the room, and propped it up against the wall while Marie kept watch over Brandacea.

"It's so light," Keely said. "It doesn't seem like the door to a prison should weigh so little."

Horace bristled. "It was never meant to be a prison. They agreed to do this, for the good of Atlantis."

"Seems like somebody should have been more worried about the good of these women," Erin said.

Riley put a hand on Horace's arm. "It's all right. Nobody blames you, Horace. We're just upset and frustrated and more than a little bit scared."

He nodded. "I know, Princess. So am I."

Marie called out, "She looks strange."

Erin pulled a handful of precious gems from a pouch she'd carried tucked into her belt. "Is it okay if I put these in there with her?"

Horace started to answer but stopped and shrugged helplessly. "Honestly, I don't know. Will the resonance of your gems or your singing interfere with the Emperor's magic or will it help? We've never tried this before, so I have no idea."

"You have to try, Erin," Marie said urgently. "She's starting to hyperventilate."

Erin quickly placed the gemstones around Brandacea on the silken pallet, humming as she did so. As soon as she'd arranged the gems to her satisfaction, she began to sing a song of healing and hope. Marie took Brandacea's hands in her own and added her own song. She was no gem singer, but she had vast powers of healing, and Riley hoped Brandacea would respond to the combination of both types of healing magic.

The song filled the chamber, and Horace added his own counterpoint through his chanting, but Riley could see no difference in Brandacea. If anything, her breathing became more labored.

"It's not working," Keely said, grabbing Riley's wrist. "We're making her worse."

"Give it time," Riley said. "They just got started. I've seen Erin and Marie at work with women in childbirth; I've seen how they helped me. We have to give them a chance."

"I'm not sure we have time to give them," Keely whispered. She pointed to Brandacea, who suddenly arched up in the pod, her eyes still closed, gasping for breath.

"It's not working, Riley," Erin said, clutching the side of the pod. "We've got to put the lid back on and get her back into stasis."

Marie cried out. "Now. We're losing her. Put the lid back on, now, now, now!"

Horace shook his head, tears running freely down his face.

"The Emperor isn't helping. Without it, nothing we do will matter. Once the stasis is broken, we can't restore it without the Emperor's magic. We tried before, you understand."

"What about good old CPR?" Keely said. "I'm not as ready as all of you to give up just because the mumbo jumbo doesn't work. Move."

She shouldered them out of the way, bent over the pod, and prepared to administer CPR to Brandacea. "Riley, get over here and be ready to do mouth-to-mouth if she quits breathing."

Brandacea made a horrible groaning noise, arching up again, and then she collapsed back down and the light covering her body vanished. Her face, without the glow of light, was a deadly pale bluish-gray, as if she were a corpse that had died days before.

Riley flinched back for an instant at the sight, before she put the whimsical notion out of her mind and began artificial respiration while Keely began the rhythmic push and release of CPR. Long minutes went by, Riley didn't know how long, until finally she heard Erin shouting at her.

"Riley! Riley, stop. It's been way too long. There's no hope. Riley, you have to stop now."

Riley lifted her head to see that everyone was staring at her. Keely had stopped CPR and every one of them, even Horace, was crying. Numbly, she looked down at Brandacea, only to see that the maiden's eyes were fixed and open, staring at nothing for eternity.

Riley shook her head, back and forth, as if denial would make reality change to suit her. "No. No, no, no. She can't be dead, not because of me. No."

Erin took her arm and tried to pull her away from the pod, but Riley violently shook her off. "No! We have to try again. Try something else. Erin, more diamonds or emeralds or something. Sing louder. Keely, start CPR again. She's not gone, she's—"

"She's gone, *mi amara*," Conlan said from behind her, and suddenly her husband's strong arms wrapped around her, as he tried to pull her away from Brandacea.

Riley fought him with every ounce of her strength. "No! Leave me alone. I can do this, it's my fault, I said to open the lid, take her out of storage. We had to try, but it's my fault. I have to fix it. I have to save her. I have to—"

"You cannot, my love. Some things cannot be fixed." Conlan's face was grim; a forbidding study in grief and despair. The lines around his eyes had deepened, almost overnight, and Riley had a moment of clarity in her own grief as she realized that the job of high prince was killing him. "She's gone. All we can do now is find the Emperor and save the others."

Riley wanted to lean on him and cry, but she forced herself to stand on her own. She had done this. It was her responsibility. Her failure.

"We need to help her. Give her a proper burial," she said, and her voice only wobbled a little. Only a little.

"No, Princess," Horace said gently. "As you see."

She glanced down at the crystal pod, only to see that Brandacea was gone. Vanished completely, as though she'd never been there.

"Without the magic to sustain her, the weight of thousands of years settled on her all at once," Horace said. "She is gone, returned to dust as she would be if she had lived and died so long ago."

Riley walked over to the stasis pod next to Brandacea's and stared down at the golden-haired woman inside. Merlina.

"We won't fail you, Merlina," she promised. "Or Guen or Helena, either. No matter what it takes."

Conlan took her hand. "I swear to you that we will do everything we can."

"I know, because I'll be there with you," Riley said.

Conlan shook his head, but Riley held up a hand to forestall any protest. "Ven said he couldn't find Serai's trail. I'm an empath—*aknasha*—so I can maybe find her emotions even if nothing you can do works. We have to find her and the Emperor, Conlan, and I'm going to help."

A muscle in Conlan's jaw jumped as he clenched it, but he finally nodded. "You may be right. Let's go through now and see if we can pick up her trail, and then I'll return for Ven and the warriors."

He called to the portal and then turned to the rest of the women and Horace. "Please don't take this as your personal failure, Marie, Erin, Keely, Horace. Something had to be done, and you four were very courageous to even try."

"Kind words, Conlan, but meaningless to Brandacea," Marie said, her tearstained face pale and grave. "We all bear responsibility for these deaths."

Erin and Keely nodded, and Riley wanted to scream. "It doesn't matter whose responsibility it was right now, does it? All that matters is that we stop this before anybody else dies. Let's go. Call the portal, Conlan."

He turned to her, his brows drawing together. "I called the portal. It should be right—"

They both looked where he was pointing, at the empty space where the portal's oval shimmer should have been forming.

"There," he continued slowly. "No. Not again. Not now."

He called again, louder. "Portal, heed my call. Answer to the need of the high prince of Atlantis."

The silvery shimmer began to form, and Riley sighed in relief.

A female voice called out from the middle of the ovoid sphere. "Prince, indeed, and yet so ignorant of your heritage, Conlan of Atlantis. Know you not that I heed no call unless I deem it worthy?"

"So my relief was premature," Riley said, putting her hands on her hips. "Could we possibly have one single day without something going wrong? Look, portal, women are *dying*. You pick *now* to do this? Also, I'm arguing with a glorified elevator?"

She could hear the way her voice was rising in near-hysteria, but she didn't seem able to control it. She'd just caused a woman's death, and the damn *doorway* was going to argue with her?

"I have no desire to cause you distress, Princess of Atlantis, but you do not understand our ways," the portal said.

Instead of the oval shape it had always taken before, the light shimmered into the shape of a slender woman, not much taller than Riley. "I was created by the gods themselves to serve as test of whether or not a chosen one was worthy of the task set for him or her. Poseidon bent me to his will when Atlantis sank beneath the sea, and I have long since grown bitter and yet resigned to my role as portal . . . or 'glorified elevator,' as you so succinctly named me."

Riley did something she never would have imagined herself doing. Ever. She apologized to the doorway.

"I'm sorry. I didn't realize— We're very upset, after Brandacea's death—"

"Do not apologize to me, nor will I apologize or give quarter to you," the portal, or woman, or demon from hell, continued.

Riley shot a glance at Erin, to see if the witch had any ideas, but Erin shrugged helplessly.

"My magic can't touch this, Riley. I'm sorry," Erin whispered.

"Wise that you do not try, human witch," the portal said, pointing at Erin. "I enjoy your presence here and would regret destroying you, I think, although regret, like so many emotions, is only a faded echo of what it once was."

Conlan stepped forward, between the portal and Riley, and bowed deeply. "You honor us with your presence and shame us with our lack of knowledge of your existence and purpose, my lady."

The portal actually laughed. Sharp, silvery laughter, like the sound of glass bells, pealed out and Riley shuddered as if a shadow had crossed her grave.

"Such pretty words to go with such a pretty face, Conlan of Atlantis, but you shall not charm me. I will not let you pass until the test set for Serai of Atlantis has been passed or lost."

Riley pushed past Conlan. "Lives depend on finding the Emperor, and whoever you are, however old you are, surely you can't condemn those women to death on a whim?"

The portal's light wavered, and the figure bowed its head.

"Their death is no more my responsibility than yours. The task is set for Serai. She will pass it or not. Just as Alaric of Atlantis will pass or fail his test, and Jack of the nearly lost tiger tribe will face his challenge. The time of the final crisis is near, Conlan of Atlantis, and the gods would have me determine if those who support you in your quest to bring Atlantis to the surface are worthy."

"What? What about Jack? Did you see my sister?" Riley wondered if asking questions of an ancient being made up of light and bad temper was particularly intelligent, but she was past caring.

"Good-bye for now, lords and ladies of Atlantis. I must follow another path, for the tiger has lost one part of his soul and I have found it in my keeping. I will leave you with the magic of the portal while I am away, but it will not come to your call until Serai has accomplished her quest."

"Stop! You can't just leave like that. We need—"

But the portal didn't care what Riley needed, or what any of them needed, because one moment the woman made of light was blathering on with her cryptic BS about the tiger's soul, and the next moment she was gone. She was gone. The shimmering light flicked off like a cheap lightbulb.

Conlan called and called, in every way possible, for the next half hour, until he was hoarse with shouting, commanding, and finally pleading, but it made no difference. The portal didn't return.

Serai and Daniel were on their own.

# Chapter 29

Serai woke up first from the exhausted sleep they'd fallen into after the epiphany of the soul-meld. She still could hardly believe it. Even in her time, to reach such a joining had been a rare occurrence, and for it to happen with a nightwalker—a vampire—was so incredible, so unprecedented, that she was amazed Poseidon himself wasn't swirling up a typhoon here in the middle of desert country to punish her for her transgression.

She curled closer to Daniel, wrapped securely in his strong arms, and opened herself to the magic surrounding them. The vortex magic she'd sensed before was stronger now, due to geography or due to her own willingness to open herself to it, she didn't know. The day was fully on its way now, it must be mid-morning, and Daniel slept soundly, a smile on his face.

He looked peaceful. Content. Descriptive terms she certainly couldn't have applied to him even once since she'd found him again in Atlantis mere days before. The soul-meld and the realization that she would never leave him seemed to have calmed something dark and tortured inside him. She sent a silent prayer of thanks to the gods again that she had found him, and then she turned her senses outward again, seeking the Emperor.

It was there. Still in the same place, she realized, and relief poured through her. Not calling her, though. Almost silent. Faint, as if resting or recharging, if she could apply anthropomorphic terms to what was, essentially, a rock. Such a rock, though. Its power surged once, when she reached out to it, and she briefly connected with the maidens back in Atlantis. The four of them were . . .

The *three* of them. Brandacea was gone. Her life force extinguished. Vanished, as if she'd never lived at all.

Serai cried out as the pain seared through her, and Daniel instantly woke up and scanned the room for danger.

"She's dead, Daniel. Brandacea. Another one of my sisters. She's dead."

She sobbed in his arms for a long time before she could talk or even breathe again. "She's gone," she said, over and over. "I failed again. I was making love when my sister was dying."

"No, *mi amara*. You were healing yourself and me. All of the responsibility for your sisters cannot rest on your slender shoulders. The damn portal is to blame for not allowing you to call for help." He jumped up and reached for his clothes, but she held up a hand to stop him.

"It's still daylight, so we can't go anywhere. We need to eat something and have a shower," she said. "We'll get cleaned up, and then we'll decide what to do next. It will be dark soon, and we're going to find the Emperor tonight, or die trying. I'm not willing to let anything or anyone else get in my way."

He nodded, anger and determination stamped on his face, and held out his hand to help her up. She called to the elements and especially to the water surrounding them, the life-giving water that answered so quickly when Poseidon's children called.

The spray of water danced over them like a shimmering cloak, and this time Daniel wasn't startled, but simply stood, holding his arms out to his sides, under the shower. She watched him for a moment and wondered again how this beautiful, deadly man could truly be hers, but then he opened his eyes and smiled at her and she cast aside her hesitation and stepped into his arms.

"There's soap in the backpack," he said, running his hands down her arms. He kissed her and then retrieved the soap, and they washed themselves and each other, delighting in the joy of touch, even in the face of what they had to endure. Perhaps especially because of that.

"Affirming life," she said solemnly. "It does make sense. We cannot bring Brandacea back by sitting and crying, but only by taking action. We will affirm life by finding the Emperor."

"About that," he said, pushing the waves of dark hair away from his chiseled face. "I have an idea. Are you up for trying something that might be a little dangerous?"

"More dangerous than escaping stasis, casting a spell on the high prince's brother, and falling in love with a vampire?"

His lips quirked up in a grin. "Well, when you put it that way . . ."

She sent the spiraling curve of water through their clothing to clean it, and then reversed the magic to remove every drop of water and dry the clothes and their bodies and hair.

"This is a wonderful bit of magic," Daniel said fervently. "It sounds stupid, in the face of so much tragedy, but I am very happy to clean the sweat and dust off myself."

"Little things mean so much more when you're deprived of them," she said. "For example, I really, *really* need food other than these apples and, what did you call the hateful dry sticks?"

"Granola bars. I agree. Worst food, ever, but very useful at a time like this."

After they'd dressed and partaken of the bars, apples, and water, she was ready to ask again.

"Try what?"

"I think we should pool our magic. Like we did before,

although I didn't know it at the time, when Justice attacked. This time we do it on purpose, and hopefully it will strengthen both of us."

Serai tilted her head and watched as he pulled on his boots, admiring the long, muscled length of his leg even as she considered his words. "Do we need to exchange blood again?"

He dropped his boot and stared at her. "No. Don't even think of it, not ever. If we do a third blood exchange, you could die. Or become a monster. We don't have any idea what happens to an Atlantean turned vampire. Under no circumstances can I ever, ever do a third blood exchange with you."

"Then we need to call on the vortex magic," she said, walking to the front of the cave and into the afternoon sun. "You're going to have to trust me, because I think we'll need to be in the sunlight to do it."

# Chapter 30

### Secret underground base, P-Ops Division,
### Federal Bureau Southwest

Colonel Brig St. Ives had been a full-bird colonel in the U.S. Air Force back in the days before vampires and werewolves and all the other beasties from the especially ugly bedtime stories and campfire tales decided to make his life a living hell. Now he was forced to work with a bunch of jarheads, squids, coasties, and FBI suits in a joint paranormal operations task force, and frankly he'd rather have been doing something more fun—anything more fun—like sitting on a beach drinking beer, or, hey, maybe picking porcupine quills out of his ass with a crowbar.

Had to be more fun than this. He hadn't seen daylight in three days. Missed his wife. Was going to miss the birth of his first grandkid in the next day or so if he didn't get the fuck out of this hole. So when the call came, he was more relieved than anything else.

"Time to go, sir. We've had radio silence from Smithson for seven minutes past his designated check-in time." The fresh-faced lieutenant standing at attention in front of Brig's battered steel desk made him tired.

Had he ever been that young?

Surely not.

"Sir?"

"Seven minutes, Lieutenant? He's a banker, not a marine. Seven minutes just means he spilled his latte on his candy-assed suit, or took a shit and lost track of time. We don't call a go on seven civilian minutes late."

"Sir, yes sir, but you said—"

"At ease, Lieutenant. I know what I said. I also know that we're going to wait until sixteen thirty, and then if we don't hear, we're going to call him, and then and only then will we proceed with Operation Tombstone."

"Sir, yes, sir." The former sailor turned P-Ops flunky saluted sharply and executed a precision turn to leave the office.

Brig just sighed. Operation Tombstone. What the hell these jokers in Washington were thinking, he didn't know. Just because the banker running this scam on the region's head vamp happened to live in the same state as the legendary gunfight, didn't mean it had fuck-all to do with this op. Whatever asswipe had decided the men needed to salute indoors was another paper-pushing moron, too.

But nobody'd asked him. He was just an old pilot, stuck behind a desk, ready to hand off the reins. Ready to meet his grandkid. Ready to make love to his wife again.

He pushed a button on his phone, and the lieutenant's crisp voice sounded through the line. "Sir?"

"Better get them ready to go, son. Just in case."

Never hurt to be prepared.

# Chapter 31

Daniel had taken a step back before he even realized he'd done it. "Sunlight? Serai, you know that the sun and I don't exactly get along."

"Trust me," she repeated, as if saying it again made it more sensible.

"Look, you know I trust you, but telling the flammable vampire to walk into the sun with you might sound romantic, but it's actually a little bit nuts." He leaned down to retrieve his boot and pull it on, and then revised his statement.

"Okay, a lot nuts."

"Nuts means ill-conceived, correct?" She put her hands on her hips, and he steeled himself to get blasted.

"Ill-conceived is a polite way to put it. Crazy, lunatic, bat-shit insane."

Serai narrowed her eyes. "I don't think I appreciate that very much."

"So what you're saying is that soul-meld or no soul-meld, I still have the capacity to royally piss you off?" He grinned at her in spite of the crazy-ass conversation. She was just so damn beautiful. Especially with her freshly dry waves of hair curling down to her hips, instead of trapped in that braid.

She pulled out the bit of cord from her pocket and started to tie her hair back, and he groaned. "Okay, okay. I give in. If you promise to leave your hair loose, I'll take a chance on getting my ass fried."

She blinked and then stuffed the cord back in her pocket. "You are truly mad, aren't you? You don't really trust that I can keep you safe, but you're willing to risk burning to death over how I wear my hair?"

"It's a guy thing."

She rolled her eyes. "Somehow I knew you'd say that."

She stepped back into the shadows and held out her hands. "What if we stand here, just out of reach of the sun, and I call to the vortex energy from here? I'll leave my hair down and you'll feel safe from getting your bottom fried, as you put it."

"Ass," he said, grinning at her like the wild, wicked man he was.

"I beg your pardon?"

"I said getting my ass fried. If I said getting my bottom fried, my guy card would be revoked, probably permanently. Then we could sit around and braid each other's hair."

He strode forward, all long, lean, elegant muscle, a predator in motion, and her mouth dried out a little. She loved him so much, and had for so long, that sometimes she forgot just how deadly he really was.

This was not one of those times.

He held out his hands and clasped hers. "Okay, Princess, you're up. What now?"

She took a deep breath. "Now we call the vortex energy and hope it answers a vampire and an Atlantean."

He nodded, serious now that it mattered, and she realized he'd been trying to help calm her nervousness with his teasing. It had worked, too, she had to admit.

"The vortex energy in this area is deep earth magic. Elemental magic. I learned about the power of the elements as a girl, but have never experienced it directly, at least not nearly as strong as it is here. The magic is so strong, but subtle enough that I almost didn't notice it running counter to the Emperor's pull."

"What do we do?" Daniel leaned forward and kissed her, a quick but firm pressure of his lips on hers, more for reassurance than passion, she suspected.

"We call to the elements, and hope they answer, and then we use the power of the soul-meld to join our magics into a whole much stronger than the individual halves."

"Kind of like us," Daniel said, and she smiled.

"Yes, exactly like us. Here goes. And don't be alarmed, but part of the ritual involves offering my blood."

"I'll offer my blood," he said firmly, and she didn't bother to argue. His blood would serve as well.

Still holding his hands, she moved as far into the sunlight as she could without allowing the deadly rays to fall on Daniel's exposed wrists, and then she raised her face to the sky.

"Element of air, we offer you our breath and ask that you heed our call." She blew out a long, soft breath, and was pleased when Daniel immediately did the same.

"Element of water, we offer our own, and ask that you heed our call." She closed her eyes and thought of the sisters she had lost, and her tears fell freely to the ground.

"Element of fire, we offer you the heat from our bodies, and ask that you heed our call." She shivered as a chill wind wrapped around them, soaking up their body heat and then whisking it away.

Shivering hard, she was barely able to speak the last sentence without her teeth chattering. "Element of earth, we offer you the life force of our own bodies, and ask that you heed our call." She nodded, and Daniel bit his wrist and turned his hand, still holding hers, so that a few drops of blood fell onto the ground.

A profound silence fell, as if even nature herself were holding her breath, and then a spiraling wave of pure golden light danced through the opening of the cave and surrounded them, at first wrapping itself around their bodies in a gentle caress and then clamping on to them like a giant's grip. The world expanded and contracted in time with Serai's pulse, and she closed her eyes, only to see that the vortex had entered her mind.

Daniel was working hard at remaining calm, but the vortex magic was more powerful than anything he'd ever encountered, and it seemed to be trying to swallow them whole. He fought against it as it tried to consume him, tried to swallow his mage powers whole and spit him back out as a hollow shell of a man. Serai's grip on his hands was unbreakable and he didn't know what she'd done or how to save her.

He'd promised to save her, and now he was already failing. No. Not again.

"Not again," he shouted, and her eyes flew open.

She stared at him from eyes gone fully dark blue, again, and he was afraid the magic had already swallowed hers, but her voice, when she spoke, was still her own.

"Daniel, it's fine. Trust me. Open yourself to the magic, and to me. Open yourself to the power of the soul-meld and we will be stronger than even this ancient vortex magic. You have to trust me."

He looked into her incredibly dangerous, insanely beautiful eyes, and he realized he did.

He trusted her.

He'd gladly and willingly step into the sun for her and with her.

"Yes," he said, and he opened his soul to the magic.

It took him down with a knockout punch, funneling into him like a whirlpool of hot, bright, old—so very old—power.

"Daniel, trust me," she said again, and he leaned forward to kiss her, because she was the only thing that had ever made sense in his entire long, hideous, immortal life. He kissed her because he had to kiss her; because kissing her was his only reason for living.

She kissed him back, and the power exploded through

them, between them, roared its way into every dark place in his heart and soul and purified them as it bound them together even more tightly than they had been before. He laughed and she cried and then they both laughed while the power soared through them, amplifying their emotions, intensifying their magics, and expanding their understanding of the universe.

When she finally nodded, he closed his mind to the onslaught, and the vortex energy gracefully surrendered, not a ravaging conqueror after all, but a healer, a magician, a wizard come to play and depart. A lifetime encapsulated into a handful of minutes, and he would never, ever be the same.

He looked at Serai, and her eyes were pure, glowing blue fire.

"Your eyes," they said simultaneously, and she laughed and touched his face with her hand.

"Your eyes are glowing like sea sapphires," she said, awed. "But where did the red go?"

"Yours are glowing, too, *mi amara*, and I am in awe of your beauty."

She kissed him again, and this time the kiss was more than just a kiss, since the magic in each of them resonated, one with the other, and he could feel what she felt, even as the Emperor itself decided to join in the fun and send a bolt of its power driving through Serai.

"The women—your sisters," he said. "I can feel them."

"Yes. Yes!" She tightened her grasp on his hands and concentrated, hard. He could feel her focus, and together they somehow channeled a beam of pure energy across the land, down through the ocean's depths, and into the three maidens waiting in their crystal cases in Atlantis.

Serai cried out, but it was a joyous cry, and she threw her arms around him. "We did it! Did you feel that? We strengthened them! They're better, Daniel, oh, they're stronger now, and we did it. They'll be safe for a little while longer, until we find the Emperor. We *are* better together than apart. There will be no more talk, ever, of us leaving each other or being better off without the other. Agreed?"

He hugged her back and started to answer, but an unexpected sound, a harsh grinding noise, scraped across his eardrums, and instead he held a finger to her lips and listened with his vampire senses on high alert.

It was— It couldn't be. He listened harder, instinctively pushing Serai behind him.

It was the sound of tramping feet and the roar of helicopters. He had a crazy flashback to another invading army, eleven thousand years ago, and then shook his head to clear it of those images.

"It sounds like the army is on its way, and we're still trapped in here by the sun for a little while longer," he told Serai. "This isn't good."

Her face drained of color, but she squared her shoulders and nodded. "It wouldn't be fun if it were easy," she said, and he started laughing.

"Oh, Princess. You are absolutely the right woman for me."

# Chapter 32

Nicholas heard them first, long before Ivy's human ears picked up any disturbance. It was barely dusk, and the apprentice had finally arrived, dragged by his ears all the way, one would think from the way he was sniveling. Ivy had tried to comfort him at first, promising him he wouldn't be hurt, but she'd finally given up in disgust.

Even Ian had rolled his eyes after the first ten minutes or so and told the witch to "man up, dude."

"We're in trouble," Nicholas said. He pointed to the man, Phillips or Phelps or whatever. "Shut up, now, or I'll kill you myself."

Phillips shut up, cramming his fist in his mouth to do it.

Ian shot Nicholas a hard look. "He's a clerk in the New Age shop down by Tuzigoot, not exactly a hard-ass. Scaring him even more isn't going to help."

"Shut up and listen."

Ian, astonishingly enough for a thirteen-year-old boy, actually shut up and listened. Five seconds later, he ran to his mother and took her arm.

"Mom, it's gotta be the army. Holy crap, it really is the army coming to rescue us!"

Ivy and Nicholas shared a grim look over Ian's head. If the army were on its way, the last thing they'd have in mind would be rescuing a witch from a vampire. More likely, they were after the power source of the King stone and would kill all of them to get it. Nicholas had heard rumors that the P-Ops Division was corrupt all the way to the top, and now he might be soon to gain confirmation firsthand.

"Hey, I lied, Phil," Ivy said tiredly. "You're probably going to get hurt."

The man started wailing again, so Nicholas strode across the cave and casually backhanded him to shut him up. Phil's eyes rolled back in his head, and he slumped to the ground.

"That's better. Now maybe I can think." Nicholas walked over to the box that held the gem and stared down at it as if the amethyst itself would give him a clue as to what to do next. They'd been on the verge of trying one final experiment to see if they could learn what the King stone really could do, when the stone had begun glowing on its own, shooting out a beam of light so strong that Nicholas was surprised it hadn't cut straight through the stone cavern wall. Ivy told him that it wasn't just light, either; the stone had been projecting magical energy at a level far more intense than anything she'd seen from it thus far.

"What can we do?" Ivy asked now, holding tight to Ian's arm. "You promised to keep my son safe, vampire, and it's dark enough that you can escape with him in a few minutes. I'll stay here and deal with the army."

"I won't leave you, Mom," Ian protested, and she ignored him as if he'd never even spoken, still staring steadily at Nicholas.

"I won't leave you, either," Nicholas said, leaving her to interpret it as she would. "We'll all get out of here. The members of my blood pride should be here any minute to assist us."

"Why did you send the guy away who brought Phil? He was human. The sunlight wouldn't have bothered him."

"More witnesses I didn't need. Don't worry. We'll be fine."

The voice that shattered the silence, transmitted by some kind of electronic device, carried a weight of authority and command that didn't bode well for their plans.

"This is Colonel Brig St. Ives of the federal P-Ops Division speaking. We have you surrounded, and we have captured your vampire associates, twelve in total. Please come out, sending Mr. Smithson out first, and nobody will get hurt."

An even dozen had been all the members of his blood pride on this mission with him. This could be a slight problem.

"Whoops," Ian said, grinning and almost jumping out of his skin with adrenaline and a sick kind of excitement. "Wonder if they'd accept parts of him? His spleen might be around here somewhere."

Ivy pulled her son closer, her wild eyes fixed on Nicholas as if he were her savior instead of her killer. In spite of everything, he wanted to do just that. Save her. Protect her. Try again later. Forget the damn King stone and everything it might be able to do.

He focused on Ivy so intently that he missed it when Phil, who'd apparently been feigning unconsciousness, made his break, and by the time he realized the man was running out the entrance, it was too late to bother.

"Thank goodness you're here," Phil screamed. "I'm a hostage, I'm here, help me, help me—"

An explosion of gunfire cut off the rest of Phil's plea for help, and Ivy screamed. Nicholas flashed over to the cave entrance and peered out into the gathering dusk, only to see Phil's nearly disintegrated body.

"Interesting interpretation of 'nobody will get hurt,'" Nicholas said. "Maybe we should rethink our options."

Ivy picked up the Emperor and smiled, a wild glee darkening her eyes. "They're wrong if they think nobody will get hurt. They're a danger to my son. I'm going to bring them a world of hurt."

Nicholas bared his fangs and snarled his agreement, and then he smiled. "You, beautiful witch, are my kind of woman."

# Chapter 33

Daniel shot out of the cave like a bat out of the worst of the nine hells the second the sun finally hid behind the horizon. Now that he and Serai were connected by the soul-meld and the vortex magic, he could feel the Emperor almost as intensely as she could.

Which meant he could leave her safely behind while he went after it.

Unfortunately, she had no intention of letting him do anything of the kind. By the time he turned around, she was already down the carved stone side of the cliff and standing on the ground, hands on her hips, staring up at him.

"You can forget that idea right now," she informed him.

"Did the soul-meld give you psychic powers? And if so, can you snoop in everybody's brain or just mine?" He landed next to her and stared her down with his fiercest glare.

Also unfortunately, she wasn't intimidated in the least.

"You know, you're kind of sexy when you scowl like that," she said, flashing a seductive smile, and then blinking innocently when he growled at her.

"Oh, I'm sorry. Was that meant to frighten me into staying here, cowering in the corner like a good little princess?"

He shook his head and gave it up as a lost cause. "I've been around long enough to know defeat when it smacks me in the face. Let's go. We need to find out why the army or P-Ops or who-the-hells-ever is heading in the same direction as the Emperor."

"I have never believed in coincidence," she said, braiding her hair back from her face.

"Neither have I."

She bent to retrieve the backpack and he stopped her. "No need for it now. If we succeed, we can stop back and retrieve it if we need to hike out of here. Do you think you could be up for flying—no pun intended—if we have to do it to escape?"

She frowned but then nodded slowly. "You know, I have your magic inside me now, as well as my own. That should surely sustain me long enough to fly away from danger with the Emperor. And I have no time to harbor childish fears."

"It's not childish, *mi amara*, but I respect your courage," he said. "It's time to go, and we need to go fast."

She threw her arms around him and kissed him, and then the unmistakable sound of a gun being cocked shattered the early evening stillness.

"Going fast shouldn't be a problem, sir," a voice said. "Stand down and be prepared to surrender, or it will go very badly for you."

Daniel cast a quick, reassuring glance at Serai, but he needn't have bothered. She was perfectly calm, smiling out into the velvety blue darkness of twilight.

"We're willing to come with you peacefully," she said. "We'd certainly hate for things to go badly."

Daniel held up his hands in the universal sign for "I surrender," but he started laughing. He just couldn't help it. He was still laughing as the very polite soldier—P-Ops according to the insignia on his black uniform—held a scanner up to Serai and then to him. As soon as he realized Daniel was a vampire, the soldier stepped quickly back and then motioned to one of his underlings to bring the silver strip-cuffs. The silver was on the outside of the hard plastic cuffs so it wouldn't burn him but would keep him restrained and helpless to break free of them.

Or so it would have been, under usual circumstances. He had soul-melded with Serai, and he had tasted her Atlantean blood. Twice. For the first time since he'd been turned, the proximity to silver wasn't hurting him.

Not the slightest bit.

Things weren't going to go badly at all.

～～⌘～～

Serai remained silent while the soldiers took her and Daniel to a large vehicle and politely escorted them inside. But when the men conferred outside the vehicle's closed windows, evidently to gain privacy for their conversation, she took the opportunity to do the same.

"They are far more civilized than I expected," she said. "More like the king's personal guard than invading soldiers. What is this force? What does the lettering 'P-Ops' on their jackets mean?"

"Paranormal Operations. They're a federal police force that deals with all things supernatural. That's why they're so nice to you. They must think you're a plain vanilla human."

She tried on her most seductive smile and glanced at him through her lashes. "Plain vanilla? Really?"

He blew out a long, slow breath and his eyes darkened. "Only you could get me hot when I'm handcuffed in a P-Ops transport. Let's talk about what we do next, instead, maybe, sex kitten."

A thrill of pleasure tingled through her at his reaction, but she quickly stifled it for more urgent matters. "They want to take us to the center of the action, I would anticipate. Agreed?"

"Agreed." He stared out the window at the men, whose

conversation seemed to be wrapping up. The one in charge was heading to the driver's side of the vehicle.

"That's where we want to be, also agreed?"

"Agreed."

"Then this is perfect. Saves wear on our boots." She leaned back in the seat and folded her hands demurely in her lap, the picture of civility, prepared to unleash the full extent of her beautiful court manners on the young soldier.

Gun or no gun, the poor man didn't stand a chance.

# Chapter 34

Daniel watched the scenery fly by at five times the speed he and Serai had been traveling on foot, and tried not to laugh out loud as Serai, sitting up front in the passenger seat, charmed the soldier. He was a young guy, not that it mattered, with short hair, freckles that he probably hated, and ears that stuck out just a little bit. Daniel couldn't imagine there was a straight human male alive, old or young, who could resist Serai when she was being enchanting. She'd already elicited the guy's family details (mom and dad still alive, very proud of their boy Rob), pet's name (Izzy the cat), and favorite hobby (an obscure sport by the unlikely name of cornhole).

"You toss the small bags into holes in the wood, while drinking ale?" Serai tilted her head and smiled encouragingly at Rob, whose head almost visibly swelled.

Daniel would have been a little annoyed by the whole thing if it weren't so damn funny. At least, it was funny until he remembered the day he'd first met Serai, and she'd asked him a similar set of questions, with the exact same smile on her face.

He, too, had been dazed that such a beauty was so interested in him.

Hmmm. He scowled at the driver in the rearview mirror, in spite of the armed guard sitting next to him in the backseat. Rob continued on, blithely ignoring the angry vampire sitting behind him.

Foolish young man. Very foolish.

"Are you from England? Your accent is beautiful," Rob stammered.

"Thank you. I'm from all over Europe," she replied, smiling shyly at him. "Do you enjoy traveling there?"

"I've never been out of the country, except to Mexico—well, and Canada, ma'am," he said, abjectly sorrowful that he'd never been to Europe, just because Serai claimed to be from there.

Damn, but she was good.

"Please, call me Serai," she said, daring to lightly touch his sleeve, just for the briefest of seconds, nothing to alert the guard in the back with Daniel who was actually paying attention to his job instead of to the beautiful woman in the front seat.

The driver actually blushed, if the way the tips of his ears turned red in the lights from the dashboard was any indication, and Daniel had to stifle a groan. If they didn't get there soon, he was going to have to step in and put loverboy out of his misery.

It would be a public service.

The guard next to him said something into his radio and then leaned forward. "The colonel wants us to stop around the next ridge."

"Roger that," the driver said, suddenly snapping to attention. The colonel must be someone with enough authority to make a young soldier remember his duty, even in the presence of his dream girl.

They slowly rounded a corner and pulled to a stop in front of a barrage of lights and a large vehicle like a trailer on wheels. The front door of the trailer slammed open, and an older man stepped out. He was dressed simply in the same black uniform as Rob's, with no special insignia to indicate rank, but the way the two soldiers in the truck snapped to attention told Daniel that this must be the colonel.

Rob jumped out of the truck and saluted. He'd left the door open, so Daniel and Serai could hear everything he said. "Reporting with the prisoners, um, witnesses, as ordered, Colonel St. Ives, sir. One of them is a vampire."

Serai glanced back at Daniel, her eyes full of concern and something else. Something worse. She was fading again; her strength draining out of her as he watched. The soul-meld and the vortex either hadn't been enough, or the Emperor was sucking the magic out of her faster than she could keep up. Either way, this wasn't good.

The colonel walked over to the car, opened the back door, and motioned to Daniel. A hands-on kind of man who didn't stand on ceremony or wait for his minion to do things, then. Daniel admired that, so he didn't immediately rip the man's throat out.

While he stepped out of the car, St. Ives stared at him, his dark eyes assessing. "Why are you here, son?"

"I'm not your son," Daniel said, reasonably enough, he thought.

"No need for rudeness. I'm sure you're probably a few years older than me, in vampire years, but I'm an old country boy with a lot of bad habits. So perhaps you will give me your name and we'll start over, but be warned, I don't have a lot of time."

"Daniel."

St. Ives waited, but Daniel added nothing further.

"That's it? Daniel? Mr. Daniel? Just Daniel? Okay, let me clarify my question. What the fuck are you doing out here in the middle of nowhere with that woman who looks like she needs a doctor, only two short miles from the hiding spot of the worst vampire in the Southwest?"

Daniel took a minute to untangle that question. "My companion is ill, and we'd appreciate if you would escort us to a hospital. We were on our way back from our hike, to do just that, when your soldiers rudely abducted us. You can understand why I don't feel all that friendly or like answering your interrogation. As to the rest, I have no idea what you're talking about."

The colonel eyed him skeptically. "Right. No idea why I would be suspicious of a vampire lurking around, not far from where I found a dozen other vamps hiding in various bushes."

Daniel raised an eyebrow. "That sounds uncomfortable. Was there poison ivy? Vampires can get poison ivy, too, you know."

St. Ives abruptly lost patience with Daniel. "Hold him here," he ordered Rob, and he strode around to the other side of the truck and opened Serai's door.

"Ma'am, I'm going to need to ask you a few questions," he said.

Daniel didn't hear what Serai replied, but it didn't matter, since she stepped out of the car and collapsed into a dead faint in the colonel's arms.

St. Ives cast a long-suffering glance up at the sky. "Son of a bitch. I'm never going to get home, am I?"

# Chapter 35

Serai woke up, groggy and dazed, to find that she was lying on a hard bed in the large mobile vehicle from which the colonel had exited when they arrived. She glanced around from under her lashes, not moving, assessing the situation before giving away that she was awake.

St. Ives was nowhere to be seen, and only two humans were in the vehicle with her, unless there were more hiding in cupboards. She took a moment to send her senses out to explore just such a possibility and found that she'd been right; there were only two of them.

And, for whatever reason, they weren't very concerned about her.

"She okay? Think we should cuff her?" one of them asked, jerking his head in Serai's direction. She quickly lowered her eyelids all the way and feigned unconsciousness.

The other one, a short and oddly square woman, snorted out a braying laugh. "Why bother? What can she do, bat her eyelashes at us?"

Perhaps just a little bit more than that. Serai refrained from glaring at the woman, or at the man when he laughed, and instead she reached inside herself to see if she could find enough power left for a few small tasks.

*Yes*. The magic came quickly to her call. It was less powerful than it had been, and she was exhausted just thinking about wielding it, but it came, blurred in form and shape and resonance. Some residue of her own Atlantean power, mixed with the vortex magic and the Emperor's clarion call, all combined with what she'd gained from Daniel in the soul-meld and strengthened her until she thought she could move on to step two.

Sing the nice soldiers to sleep. She began to hum a little tune, all but under her breath, and by the time the woman finished realizing Serai was awake, both of the soldiers were asleep.

"Lovely trick, if you do say so yourself," Serai said out loud, and then she immediately felt like a fool.

*Find the Emperor now, pat yourself on the back for magic tricks later.*

Okay, on to step three: Find the Emperor. Find Daniel. Save the day.

Actually, that was steps three through five, but she had the feeling that counting steps was very, *very* far down her list of upcoming priorities.

She called to her Atlantean magic and transformed into mist mere seconds before the door opened and Rob the polite driver entered the vehicle. She soared out above and past him so fast that he never noticed the nearly transparent cloud of water vapor as she departed.

*Good-bye, Rob. Good luck with your future. May you have many fat babies.*

The giddiness served as a warning. She was losing strength fast, and she had no time to spare. Her destination was easy enough to find, though. She headed in the direction in which all the soldiers were pointing their guns. She could find Daniel later, if he didn't find her first. She had no worries about Daniel rescuing himself.

For now, the urgent mission was to find the Emperor. And since it was screaming at her, inside her head, reverberating through her skull, that wasn't going to be too hard. She arrowed toward the entrance to yet another cave, which glowed with a powerful, pulsing beam of purple light.

*Another* cave. If she survived this, she would be happy to never, ever set foot in a cave again, no matter how long she lived.

She soared over the heads of the soldiers, marveling at how desperation and magic had overcome her fear of heights, at least while in mist form, and then she entered the cave and shot across the space, through empty air, around the vampire and the human woman and boy, until she reached the Emperor. Its call sounded in her head, in her blood, in her very bones, and she reached out to it, forgetting that it was the sea god's toy, forgetting its enormous and terrifying power, forgetting that its fluctuations had already killed two of her sisters.

None of it mattered—all that was important was the magic, the power, the Emperor's commanding call. Still in mist form, she reached out to touch the Emperor, and it responded by smashing her out of the air and into her physical body, which hit the stone floor of the cave so hard that she actually bounced back up and rebounded.

As she stared up at the ceiling, dazed, the boy's face appeared over her in her line of sight.

"That had to hurt."

She blinked up at him, probably looking like a deranged owl, and then started laughing. She was almost certainly going to die now, but at least she still had a sense of humor.

The woman she'd seen in her vision leaned over her next, hard suspicion in her eyes, and she pulled the boy, clearly her son, back and away from Serai.

"Why are you here and what do you want?"

Serai slowly sat up, making sure her head wouldn't fall off her neck on the way. "I am Serai of Atlantis, and this gem belongs to me."

The vampire bared his fangs at her. "Bold claim for a woman who was just knocked on her ass by the jewel she claims is hers. The King stone doesn't seem to agree."

Serai looked at him, feeling stupid and wishing there were a healer nearby for the pounding headache starting up in her brain. "What? Oh, the Emperor. Where did you get 'King stone'? Although it's certainly close, considering the true name was lost to you landwalkers eleven thousand years ago."

His eyes widened. "Landwalkers? And you flew in here as mist? Are you really Atlantean?"

The boy rolled his eyes, and Serai felt an instant kinship with him.

"Of course not. Do you *see* a mermaid tail?" he asked the adults.

Bizarrely, all three of them stared at her legs. Serai could feel the hysterical laughter bubbling up inside her, and she forced it back down. "No tail, no fins, no gills. No mermaids. Atlanteans are ordinary people, quite like you, except we live underneath the ocean. For now," she amended.

"That's wicked cool," the boy said, dropping down to sit cross-legged beside her. "Can I visit? I would get awesome extra credit for a report on Atlantis. Also, are all the girls as pretty as you? He ducked his head and blushed. "Um, ignore that last part. It was totally random."

"Ian." The woman scolded him. "What have I told you?"

Ian shrugged and grinned, unrepentant, at his mother. "Nothing about hot chicks from Atlantis, that's for sure. I would have remembered."

Serai smiled at him, delighted. "I'm a 'hot chick'? Is that like the bee's knees?"

He stared at her, clearly mystified. "What the heck does that mean? Do bees even have knees? How would you know? Who'd want to get close enough to find out?"

The vampire cleared his throat, although Serai could tell he was fighting not to smile. The entire situation was so impossibly strange and surreal that Serai was almost sure she'd wake up any minute, secure in the crystal pod, having simply been the victim of another stasis dream.

Hot chick, though—she couldn't have made that one up. She held her hand out to the boy, and he chivalrously helped her up, in spite of his mother's not so subtle urgings to stay away from Serai.

"I am Serai of Atlantis," she tried again. "And you are?"

"Ian Khetta. Pleased to meet you," he said, holding out his hand and blushing furiously. "Sorry about the hot chick thing. That's my mom, Ivy Khetta. She's a smoking powerful witch. And he's Mr. Nicholas, a vampire who says he eats people and uses their bones for toothpicks, but we haven't seen that. He did pull a guy's intestines out, but the guy had hit me and hurt my mom, so we weren't too broken up about it."

Serai tilted her head, fascinated by the boy's candor and phrasing, and was trying to think of how to respond to that flow of information when the vampire did so first.

"He hit you? He swore he did not," Nicholas snarled.

Ian rolled his eyes. "Right. Because bad guys never lie to each other. Dude, do you watch TV at all?"

"Don't call me dude," the vampire said, but he grinned at the boy without a hint of fang.

Serai was confused. "So you're not the evil villain the soldiers are here to capture?"

"Depends on how you define evil," Ivy said.

So fast Serai was sure Ivy hadn't seen it, a flash of surprise crossed the vampire's eyes, probably because the witch had defended him.

"You should not have attempted to wield the Emperor, Ivy," Serai said seriously. "It is one of the seven gems of Poseidon's trident, and a mortal should never touch the objects of power that belong to a god. Not if she wishes to live."

"And yet you touched it," Ivy said, folding her arms across her chest, her body language a clear picture of defiance.

"I am linked to the stone; as are the remaining three of my sisters. I must take it back with me to Atlantis to save their lives."

Nicholas stepped into the space between Serai and the Emperor. "I may have something to say about that," he said ominously.

"Say it quickly, then," Ian said. "Because those soldiers are heading right for us, and I think—"

The boy quit speaking mid-sentence and stared down at his shoulder and the knife blade which was suddenly protruding from it. He reached out for Ivy as he stumbled, and the brave young adult presence he'd been projecting crumpled as he fell.

"Mommy?"

Ivy screamed and ran to her son, but Nicholas was there first, catching him as he fell.

Serai raced to the cave entrance, calling to her magic as she ran, and by the time the horrible soldier who would hurt a boy had climbed the rest of the way up the stone steps and into the cave, she carried glowing energy spheres whose heat didn't come close to her fury.

"You would hurt a *child*?" She didn't wait for an answer, especially since the visual evidence—more knives in his hands—was clear for all to see. Instead, she blasted him with both of the spheres, and he fell back, unconscious, to the cave floor.

Nicholas tore past her in a blast of displaced air and before she could say or do anything to stop him, he wrenched the soldier's head from his body and tossed both pieces out of the cave and to the ground below.

"I will have the same again for anybody else who approaches," he roared out into the night.

Before Serai could protest, Nicholas leapt out into the air and was back mere seconds later, carrying a struggling soldier.

"This one is alive," Nicholas shouted. "If you want him to stay that way, keep back."

"You didn't have to kill him," Serai said, staring at the place where the first soldier had fallen.

"He hurt the boy," Nicholas said, and then he punched the new soldier in the side of the head, knocking him out. "An unconscious prisoner is a lot less trouble."

"My son is bleeding to death," Ivy shrieked. "Do something. Get us out of here."

Serai quickly crossed to her side. "Does your power not extend to healing?"

Ivy shook her head, sobbing.

Ian looked up at Serai and tried to grin, but he was pale and it was true the wound was bleeding badly.

"I can repair this injury," Serai said. "I will need to use the Emperor."

"No," Nicholas shouted. "It's mine. I need it."

"It is not yours, and you are a fool to try to claim it," Serai said calmly.

"Nicholas, you can't let Ian die," Ivy said, no longer shouting but with tears streaming down her face. "Not even you could be so cruel."

The vampire stared at the boy, so many different emotions crossing his face that Serai couldn't begin to identify them all.

"Fine," he finally said. "I am a fool. A weak, emotional, irrational fool, but you may take the gem if it allows you to help the boy."

"I will make it allow me to do so," Serai said grimly. She needed Daniel, though. He should have been here by now. She sent her senses out, seeking him, and found him healthy but still detained inside one of the vehicles.

*Daniel, I need you now. Inside the cave. I'm going to attempt to wield the Emperor, and I need your strength. Please come.*

She waited and almost immediately his strength surrounded her in a warm wave of love—and fury.

*Don't you dare touch that stone until I get there, or I will personally tie you down and never let you out of my bed for the next eleven thousand years!*

She almost laughed, in spite of the situation and the danger. Her fierce warrior mage, determined to protect her at all cost. Except this time, it was her turn.

She took a deep breath and centered herself, and then she cupped the Emperor in both hands and raised it into the air. She was prepared for the first punch of power this time, and she opened herself to it instead of fighting it.

"Emperor, answer my call. Heal this boy who does not deserve to be injured in the cross fire of this battle. Heal the women who struggle, caught in stasis beneath the sea, O mighty Emperor, object of power of the sea god."

She realized that she'd spoken the words in ancient Atlantean, but it seemed fitting that she honor the gem with its proper tongue. The Emperor's tremendous power seared through her like a bonfire through kindling and she was afraid, but slowly she adjusted, tuning her own magic to the resonance of the amethyst.

She knelt beside Ian and nodded to his mother. "Please remove the knife now."

Ivy shook her head. "Now? Are you sure? What if you're wrong and removing it causes him to bleed out?"

Ian touched his mother's cheek with the hand on his uninjured side. "No, Mom, she's doing it already. I can feel the pain going away. Please take the knife out before my skin heals around it. That would be so gross!"

Ivy still hesitated, and Nicholas knelt beside her and gently moved her to one side. He took the hilt of the knife in one hand and then stared a challenge at Serai. She nodded, filled with the power of the Emperor.

"Yes, now, Nicholas of the Nightwalker Guild," she said, and she heard the change in her voice. Heard the power of the Emperor taking her over again.

Nicholas looked puzzled and then a little awed, but he slowly removed the knife, and as Serai directed the stream of healing light and magic into the wound, Ian never even flinched. They all watched as the gash in his skin healed completely until nothing but a thin pink scar, barely visible, remained.

"I feel great, Mom," he said bravely, and then his eyelids fluttered shut, and his head fell back against his mother's shoulder. He let out a little hiccupping snore, and the three adults grouped around him looked at one another and laughed.

"I owe you my life, Serai of Atlantis," Ivy said fiercely. "My son is everything to me. Anything in my considerable power to do for you, you only need to ask me. Ever, do you hear me?"

Serai inclined her head, the power of the Emperor calling her further and further away from mortal concerns. "Take your child to safety, that is all I ask," she said, and then she stood and crossed to the entrance to the cave, still holding the Emperor.

"You mustn't stand there, you're a target," Nicholas said, trying to pull her away, but the Emperor slapped out at him and he fell back, dazed from the jolt of electricity that had poured from the amethyst and into his body.

"I think not," Serai whispered. "Not a target, but a prism. Now I will help my sisters."

She called on the Emperor again, this time directing its magic to Atlantis, and rejoiced as she saw in her mind's eye the vision of her sisters waking and rising out of their stasis pods. Guen, Helena, and Merlina, all safe and healthy and whole.

"Thank you, Emperor, and thank you, Poseidon. Thank you for saving my sisters."

The Emperor's power pulsed and glowed in her hands, and then the purple shimmering light began to climb up her arms from her hands, encircling her limbs and sinking into her flesh.

*As you take me, so I take you*, the Emperor told her, and Serai had only a moment to be afraid of what that might mean for her mortal life before the bullet punched into her leg and she fell.

# Chapter 36

Daniel felt the bullet as if it had entered his own body, and he leapt to his feet and roared out his rage to the world, ignoring the three soldiers who were aiming their guns at his head. Both the blood bond and the soul-meld served to tell him how much pain Serai was in, and the fury took him, rolled him under, ground him into shattered bits of madness and despair, until nothing was left of Daniel but a berserker's insanity and a nightwalker mage's terrible power.

"Enough," he roared, and he used his magic to blast through the cuffs and rip the soldiers' guns from them. He blew a man-sized hole in the side of the command trailer and shot through it, bowling over everyone who got in his way, including the colonel himself. He soared through the air, racing through the sky faster than he'd ever flown before, intent on reaching Serai and determined to kill anyone and everyone who had hurt her.

He swept into the cave on a wave of wind and wrath, smashing into the vampire who knelt near Serai.

"I will kill you," Daniel snarled, and the vampire looked

startled for a moment, but then he joined the battle with deadly intent.

They leapt at each other, crashed into the walls and ceiling, and tried their damndest to kill each other. Daniel finally remembered his daggers, the ones that the soldiers hadn't bothered to take, since they were so sure of their pathetic silver cuffs and their pathetic guns, and he drew them in midair.

"Now, you will die for harming my woman," he shouted, but the boy shouted something right back at him, distracting him, and the vampire knocked one of his daggers out of his hand.

"He didn't harm Serai, he was helping her," the boy shouted again, and Daniel glanced at the woman, who was nodding, and he realized that neither the boy nor his mother's heart rate indicated deception.

Terror, but not deception.

"Enough," he called out, just before the other vampire hurled Daniel's own knife at him. Daniel ducked easily, snatched his blade from midair, sheathed both daggers, and then held out his hands, palms facing the other man.

"If you truly tried to help her, I owe you my gratitude, not my anger," he said, struggling to force the berserker rage back down where he could control it. After the fury came the bloodlust, and he could afford neither at this time.

The vampire raised a sardonic eyebrow. "Do you expect me to accept your apology?"

"Didn't offer one," Daniel said, heading for Serai now that he was in control enough to manage the bloodlust, in spite of the delicious smell of the blood pumping from Serai's leg. "What happened?"

The woman raced over to him, then slowed as she approached, clearly nervous about what he might do. To her credit, she didn't let fear stop her from kneeling down next to Serai and pressing a cloth pad over the bleeding wound.

"They shot her. Those damn soldiers. First they threw a knife that stabbed my son, clear through his shoulder. Serai used the King stone—the Emperor—to heal Ian, but then they shot her and we don't know what to do." She turned golden, tear-filled eyes to Daniel. "I want to help her but I'm no healer. I don't know how to use the Emperor like that. Do you?"

Daniel started to reply in the negative, but then he realized that he might, indeed, know how to heal with the stone. He shared Serai's power, didn't he? He stared down at Serai's pale, pale face and knew a moment of pure and utter terror.

"Don't you die on me, you hear me?" He kissed her forehead and then her lips. "Don't you even think about it, because I will follow you into the deepest level of the nine hells and bring you back."

The vampire approached warily. "Ivy, you should tend to your son. He needs you."

Ivy glanced at her son, who was snoring quietly on the floor, and then stubbornly shook her head. "No. She needs me. I promised I'd do anything for her. Anything she ever needed. I'm not going to fulfill that promise by letting her die five minutes later, Nicholas."

Daniel whipped his head around to stare at the vampire. "Nicholas? Regional-head-of-this-area in-league-with-slimeball-vampires Nicholas?"

"I know you, too, Primator," Nicholas said darkly. "Don't be so quick to cast stones."

But Daniel had lost interest. None of it mattered. Nothing but saving Serai. He took a deep breath and reached out to the blazing fire of the purple gemstone that she still held in her hands.

"Do or die," he told them, or told himself.

And then he dared to touch the prized gem of the sea god—a god who hated vampires above all else—in order to save the woman he loved.

# Chapter 37

Brig closed his phone, smelling something fishy even though he was a long damn way from the ocean. First off, Smithson hadn't been quite the upstanding citizen the higher-ups had been touting. Brig was an old hand at working the military communication channels, and he'd gotten the gouge—the unofficial but critically important scoop—on Smithson's background on the call he'd just taken.

Second, there was a kid in that cave. A human kid. A kid that one of St. Ives's men had thrown a knife into. If the vampire hadn't killed the murdering bastard, Brig might have done it himself.

Third, there was the vampire that had just blown through the side of the trailer like a shoulder-launched missile. Brig had interviewed a lot of men and women in his day, and he could sniff out integrity like a bloodhound with a brand-new nose.

That vampire had integrity, and he'd cared about nothing but saving his woman. Not plots or conspiracies or any other damned thing.

The phone rang again.

"You have a go, Colonel St. Ives," a familiar and abrasive voice said in his ear.

"There's a kid in there, sir. A human boy. The vampire's hostage, from what intel could discover. A complete innocent."

With hardly a pause, the voice continued. "Collateral damage. Regrettable, but unavoidable. You have a go."

Brig stood there, staring at the phone for a long time after the line went dead.

"Fuck *that*," he finally said. "Lieutenant? We're moving out."

He had a grandbaby to meet, and he'd be damned if he'd meet him or her with another child's blood on his hands. It was way the hell past time to retire.

He headed out of the trailer, laughing at the man-shaped hole in the wall, and then he stood and watched his men as they loaded up and fell back.

"Good luck, Daniel with one name," he finally said before he went to find his jeep.

# Chapter 38

Serai fell into the magic, the beautiful, terrible purple fire, and she surrendered to the pain. After all, she'd completed her quest. Succeeded at her task. She almost laughed. The portal would come for her, now that she lay dying with no hope of ever returning to Atlantis.

It had been a fair enough exchange. Her life finally held some meaning; some purpose. Instead of living or dying as a useless and unused specimen of breeding stock, she'd escaped and saved her sisters.

It was enough. It had to be enough.

She regretted Daniel, though.

A surge of pain smashed through her, and it took her a minute to realize it wasn't from the Emperor draining her, or the bullet wound, which was healed now anyway, but it was the pain of losing Daniel, after having found him again. She felt as if she could almost hear his voice, calling her name, but then the pain took her again, and he was gone.

There was nothing but the brilliant purple flame.

〜〜

Daniel expected the world to blow up, or at least that *he* would blow up, when he touched the Emperor, but it was another reality entirely. He fell into the purple fire, mind and soul, and was trapped, unable to find a way out. Everywhere he looked, there was nothing but the flame.

"Serai," he called out, over and over and then again. For a lifetime; for an eternity. Lost in the fire, and somewhere in the back of his mind he remembered that he'd left the two of them unprotected against a dangerous enemy.

Not that he particularly cared right at that moment. If she died, he would die with her. One way was as good as another. Or so he thought, right up to the point when he thought he heard her voice.

"Daniel?"

"I'm here." He ran, racing through the never-ending amethyst fire, searching for her voice in some sort of twisted version of the children's game of hide-and-seek. Finally, *finally*, he found her, lying in another crystal case like the one she'd told him about. This one, though, looked exactly like a coffin.

"No," he shouted, and he lifted her limp form out of the coffin and into his arms. He ran as fast and as far as he could, fighting his way through the flames, which now seemed actively to be trying to harm him.

She finally opened her beautiful eyes, but all he saw in them was death. "I'm sorry, Daniel, but I can't fight it, and the Emperor won't release me. It wants to pull me into its prism of power, and I'm not strong enough to escape. Please know that I have always loved you, and I always will."

"No," he told her. "No, no, no, no, *no*."

The beserker rage fought to break free, and he allowed it. Welcomed its red-hot wrath, set it to battle the icy cold purple fire.

The rage won. The anguish conquered. Daniel broke free.

He blinked, stunned, and looked around, only to realize he was still in that damned cave.

"No. She won't die here, trapped in the dark like a rat," he said to Nicholas, who was staring at him with a surprising amount of sympathy. "I'm taking her away from this. Will you cover me from the soldiers?"

"They're gone," the boy said. "They pulled out about fifteen minutes ago. We were just waiting to be sure you were okay."

Daniel shook his head. "We are not. We never will be again. But I thank you for your generosity."

"You abandoned the Primus when you were finally making a difference," Nicholas said. "I am sorry for your loss, but we needed you."

"Then you do it," Daniel told him, utterly indifferent. "Take the job. Make changes. Save the world. I have lived for eleven thousand years and am done with all of it."

Ian's eyes grew wide. "Eleven thousand years? Really? *Duuude.*"

Daniel didn't even have the energy to smile. "I'm taking her to see the sun, one last time. I think she can hold on that long."

Nicholas bowed to him as he rose with Serai in his arms. "I'll do my best," he said.

Daniel didn't bother to respond. He just launched himself into the air, Serai in his arms, and headed for the most beautiful place in the entire area.

He and Serai would meet the sun on the last day of their lives on the very top of Cathedral Rock.

# Chapter 39

### Atlantis, the Temple of the Maidens

Conlan, Riley, Ven, Erin, and the rest of their family and friends stood in a semicircle around the dazed but obviously very healthy women who'd just stepped out of their stasis pods for the first time in eleven thousand years.

"They did it," Riley said, tears streaming down her face. "Daniel and Serai must have found the Emperor and saved everyone."

Before Conlan could respond, the familiar shimmer of the portal formed its oval shape before them, but a very unfamiliar deep male voice sounded from within it.

"I come bearing two secrets for you from the spirit of the portal who inhabited herein before me, Conlan of Atlantis," the voice said. "Do you wish to know how to save the saviors?"

### Cathedral Rock, thirty minutes until dawn

Daniel held Serai's unresponsive body in his arms, rocking her back and forth, wishing he had a voice made for singing. He'd love to be able to sing her to sleep.

To death.

Instead, all he could do was pour out his heart and soul in words that were meaningless and unpoetic.

"I love you" was so insignificant.

He'd waited for her—some part of his heart and soul had waited for her for thousands of years—and now that he'd finally found her again, he would lose her so quickly. His berserker fury had faded, though, as he waited here for the dawn. Rage had no place at his own dying of the light.

Fury was wasted emotion.

All his heart could contain was love, and sorrow, and regret.

A shimmering light began to glow behind him, but it was too soon and in the wrong direction, so he turned to see that the damned capricious portal was opening.

"Too little, too late," he said, laughing or crying. "Go back to the hell you came from, demon."

A dark form stepped out of the portal, silhouetted so that he couldn't see its voice.

"I've been called worse," Ven said, crossing the grass to him. "I hear you've had a rough time."

The prince dropped to the ground to sit next to Daniel and put a hand on his shoulder. "How are you holding up, my friend?"

"You need to stay back," Daniel said dully. "When dawn comes and the flames take us, there is no need for you to be harmed."

"We are unhappy with your decision to die, nightwalker," said another familiar voice. "We owe you an ass-kicking," Lord Justice continued.

Figure after figure walked out of the portal and ranged themselves around Daniel and Serai. Conlan and his wife Riley. Ven's Erin. Justice's Keely. Christophe and a woman Daniel had never met. Brennan and Tiernan, who stopped to put a hand on his shoulder before she moved on. Even Reisen and Melody, who seemed to have recovered from her injury, though she wore a splint on one arm.

"The portal seems to be working again," Daniel observed, too exhausted and anguished to respond to the presence of so many Atlanteans.

"Not exactly," Ven said, still sitting next to him. "It—or rather, *she*—is kind of taking a vacation. But the new portal presence is a little more chatty, and told us a secret or two."

Daniel stared blankly at his friend and wondered why Ven thought he would possibly care about Atlantean secrets.

"First, apparently you really do have a soul."

Daniel just stared at Ven, still not understanding. Maybe answering would make him go away. "I know that. Soul-meld. Can't you leave us alone?"

He pulled Serai closer and rocked back and forth, wishing again that he knew how to sing. Or play the harp. His mind was shattering. His heart had already done so.

But Ven was still talking. "Second, it seems that if you complete a third blood exchange with an Atlantean with whom you've reached the soul-meld, both of your lives will be saved."

Daniel heard the words but couldn't understand their meaning. It was too much. Too hard. Losing Serai . . .

*Twenty minutes until dawn*, his internal clock reminded him.

Losing Serai . . .

But wait. He tried to focus on Ven's mouth, which was still moving. Forming words. Important words.

"What? What did you say?" he demanded.

Ven grasped Daniel's shoulders and shook him a little. "Wake up, my friend. We're running out of time. You need to make a third blood exchange with Serai, and you'll both be saved."

Daniel looked around the circle of people he mostly had dared to think of as friends. "Truly? The third blood bond?"

"Now," Conlan commanded. "For once in your life, listen to me and do it now."

"Please," Tiernan added.

*Fifteen minutes until dawn.*

"If it kills her—" he began, but Ven cut him off.

"As opposed to sitting here, waiting for the sun to turn you both into barbecue? Do it *now*."

When Daniel still hesitated, afraid of turning Serai into the monster he'd once become and feared more than anything he'd become again, Ven drew one of his daggers.

"Forgive me, Daniel," he said, and then he quickly grabbed Serai's hand and drew a line across her palm. Daniel almost didn't realize what Ven had done until he smelled the rich, warm scent of her blood.

"And you," Ven said, and almost blindly Daniel held up his own hand. Ven made the same cut, and Daniel gently placed his hand across Serai's slightly open mouth and lifted her hand to his own. As he drank, too desperate to hope, too terrified to be self-conscious about taking her blood in front of everyone, her lips moved, just a fraction of a movement at first, but then more strongly, as she drank his blood. He felt the pull on his hand and drank more strongly from hers, and the Emperor, lying forgotten between them, suddenly pulsed in a blaze of purple fire.

Serai's body arched up in his arms, and Daniel cried out as the same pain she was feeling—he could sense her pain, as she could feel his—transformed, magically, miraculously, into restorative healing warmth that flooded from the Emperor into both of them, surrounding them, embracing them, giving them life when they'd faced death.

The tsunami of light went on and on, scouring them inside and out, until he fell back, exhausted, on to the grass, still tightly embracing Serai.

"I see we're having a party, and you've decided to invite some friends," Serai said, lifting her head from his chest and looking around. "Perhaps next time, you could wait until I've had a proper bath and arranged my hair."

Daniel stared at her, dumbfounded, and when that sexy, seductive, magnificent smile formed on her lips, he knew he truly had died and gone to the most spectacular of all heavens.

"We're alive?" he asked stupidly.

"We're alive, and I'm really, really hungry," she said, and everyone around them started laughing.

But then the sun rose over the horizon, and the first questing rays of light reached them, and the entire world caught on fire.

# Chapter 40

Serai was staring up at the sky, reveling in the first rays of the sun, when the Emperor caught fire and exploded into a shimmering dome of light. The stone itself was still whole; she could feel it in her hands, but the searing purple flames shooting from it were like the most magnificent fireworks the fire guild had ever created.

It wasn't only the Emperor, though. As she looked around, she realized that the Atlanteans had joined hands and were contributing their own magic to support the dome protecting Daniel from the sun. Protecting her.

Saving them all with love and friendship.

But the Emperor told her a secret of its own, whispering to her through its magical resonance: they didn't need protection.

She and Daniel were now the first two of a new breed of nightwalker; no longer nightwalkers at all. They would be able to walk in the daylight forever more.

"Daniel," she said. "Do you trust me?"

"Always," he said instantly.

"We have to walk into the sun."

Not a flicker of doubt crossed his face. "Yes, except I think we'll fly."

She jumped up, strong and whole and sure, and held out her hand. "Now, please."

He took her into his arms and shot up into the rosy, golden light of the breaking dawn, and together they soared high in the sky, high above the people who loved them and who would wait for them, high above the caves and the darkness and the pain.

The light shimmered on their skin like a caress and they stared at each other in fascinated wonder.

"I have not seen the dawn in eleven thousand years," Daniel said, his beautiful eyes shining in the sun.

"Nor I," Serai replied, laughing and crying and kissing him.

"I want to see every single dawn for the next eleven thousand years, with you," he said, his love and sincerity shining as brightly as the dawn sun itself.

"Well," she said, after some consideration. "I may want to sleep in once in a while."

He shouted out his laughter to the morning skies, and then he kissed her so deeply that they were spinning like a deep-sea whirlpool when the kiss ended. As they floated back down to earth, back down to the top of Cathedral Rock, back down to their friends, Daniel embraced her so tightly she almost couldn't breathe.

"My own Sleeping Beauty is finally awake," he said.

"And my own Prince Charming woke me with his kiss."

As they finally touched back down, still lost in a passionate kiss, they became aware of cheering and applause. When they broke the kiss and looked around, Serai's face flamed red as she realized what a spectacle she'd just made of herself. A proper Atlantean princess would *never* . . .

She cut off the self-criticism, in her father's words, midthought.

"What the heck," she said, looking around at everyone and grinning. "I have it on very good authority that I'm a hot chick."

As if in response to her words, the sky split in two, and a whirling torrent of water and power and silvery light burst into the space above them as a voice like thunder tore through the fabric of the world.

*HOT CHICK, INDEED, DAUGHTER OF MY ANCIENT DAYS. YOU HAVE SERVED ME WELL. I AM PLEASED TO SEE MY AMETHYST AGAIN, AFTER SO MANY THOUSANDS OF YEARS.*

All of the Atlanteans bowed deeply, leaving Daniel, his mouth hanging open like a carp's, staring up at Poseidon. Serai grabbed his hand and pulled him closer to her.

Daniel just blinked. "Is that—are you—"

*I AM POSEIDON, GOD OF THE SEA, AND I SEE THAT YOU DO INDEED HAVE A SOUL, CHOSEN ONE OF MY DAUGHTER.*

"Your daughter? I thought that was just a figure of speech," Daniel muttered, and Serai tried not to laugh.

"It is," she whispered. "Just listen."

*DO YOU AGREE TO CHERISH AND PROTECT MY DAUGHTER FOR NOW AND UNTIL THE END OF THE WATERS OF TIME?*

"Nobody could stop me," Daniel said, finally bowing.

Poseidon's booming laugh split the air like a crack of thunder.

*THEN FEEL THIS, NIGHTWALKER, AND KNOW THAT YOU, TOO, ARE NOW SWORN TO MY SERVICE AS A WARRIOR OF POSEIDON.*

An arrow of water and light sliced through the air and slammed into Daniel, knocking him down, and when he stood, his shirt hung in shreds and the brand of the Warriors of Poseidon had been burned into the top right side of his chest. Serai threw herself into his arms, crying and laughing.

"Now you're mine forever," she told him.

*NOW YOU BOTH ARE MINE FOREVER, TO BE AC-CURATE. BUT ENOUGH OF THIS, I AM WEARY OF THIS HIDEOUS PLACE WITH ITS LACK OF WATER. GIVE MY AMETHYST TO CONLAN. I RETURN TO MY OCEANS*

*AND AWAIT WORD THAT YOU HAVE ALL FOUND THE FINAL GEM MISSING FROM MY TRIDENT.*

As Poseidon disappeared, they could all hear his final words booming through the dawn air.

*HORRIBLE PLACE.*

"But it's a dry heat," Daniel said, and Serai started to laugh, almost collapsing with relief and joy and love.

As Daniel kissed her, right there in front of the departing sea god and everyone else, she heard their laughter, too, and she smiled against his lips. She couldn't think of anything more miraculous than being reborn to the sound of laughter.

"I will love you forever, and never leave you," she said, when Daniel finally let her speak.

"Damn straight," he growled, and she laughed.

"Is that man-speak for *me, too*?"

"You know it."

"Here we go again," Ven called out, still laughing. "This is going to be one wild ride."

Serai held out her hand, carefully cradling the stone, and looked at Conlan and the woman who must be his wife. "I believe this belongs to you."

Conlan reverently took the amethyst and dropped it into a velvet pouch tucked into his belt. "Thank you," he said, bowing deeply. "You may have saved Atlantis."

"You saved your sisters," Riley said, stepping closer and smiling at Serai. "You saved Guen, Helena, and Merlina. They are awake and perfectly healthy, asking a million questions."

"*We* saved them," Serai said, squeezing Daniel's hand.

"And now on to the next step," Conlan said. "We have to find the final jewel from the trident. Poseidon's Pride."

Daniel smiled down at Serai. "I happen to know two people who have plans for a world tour, if you need volunteers."

"This is going to be the best year of my *life*," Serai said blissfully, and then Daniel kissed her again, and by the time she could think or see or even breathe again, the portal again shimmered in the rosy dawn air, and everyone else had disappeared.

She blushed but then pointed to the portal. "Shall I show you Atlantis before we get started?"

He grinned. "Hot bath?"

"And food."

"An actual bed?"

"I don't know, Daniel, I'm kind of developing a fondness for camping," she said to tease him, and he swept her into his arms and headed for the portal, so they could begin the rest of their lives.

Together. Finally, after an eternity, together.

Nothing could ever be better than that.

When the portal deposited them, after its usual swirling, twirling ride, in Atlantis, they were still locked in an embrace that would last them a thousand lifetimes. Serai finally looked around when she heard a discreet throat clearing. Her face flamed a hot red until she realized these were different guards than the ones she'd knocked out with her magic when she'd escaped.

She'd need to make some apologies.

"I hear there is cake, Lady Serai, and that the other maidens are waiting for you on the palace terrace," one of the guards said, a twinkle in his eye.

"I'm very fond of cake," she told Daniel.

"I have very fond ideas of what to do with you and a bowl of cake frosting, and a huge, soft bed," Daniel whispered in her ear, quite wickedly.

She laughed and held his hand as they ran all the way to the palace.

# Chapter 41

**Atlantis, one month later**

Daniel strode through the mansion that the royal family had given to him and Serai, nodding to anyone he passed but not stopping to talk. He held his surprise for Serai in his hands, finally, and wasn't about to let anything deter him from reaching her.

She was sitting in her private garden, of course, among the flowers and in the fresh air. She still couldn't bear to be trapped indoors for long.

"Are we packed? Ready to go find the final gem?"

She glanced up at him, startled at first, and then she smiled with so much love and welcome that he was amazed and humbled all over again that this woman was his. He figured he'd get past that feeling in a few hundred years or so.

"Ready to go as soon as we have a lead," she said, rising to come toward him, her arms held out for a hug.

"Ah, but I can't hug you. My hands are full," he said, teasing. "A present that has waited eleven thousand years to find you."

She tilted her head, still smiling. "I love presents."

"And cake, or so I hear."

She blushed as they both remembered the fascinating uses they'd made of frosting just the night before.

"For you, my lady. My princess. My love," he said, and the power of the emotion surging through him left him unable to say anything else, so he simply held out his hands and presented his gifts.

She lifted the shimmering silver and orichalcum pendant on its delicate chain and gasped. "Oh, Daniel, this is so incredibly lovely. Did you design this yourself?"

"Yes, when I first met you. It took me this long to be able to fashion it for you, but as with everything else about us, time has only enhanced and polished the possibilities we first recognized so long ago," he said, fastening the pendant around her neck.

She turned and threw her arms around him. "I love it. I love you."

He kissed her for so long that he nearly forgot the second gift, hidden in his pocket.

Nearly. But not even her sweet, honeyed kisses could make him forget this.

He stepped back, removed the ring he'd finished crafting only an hour ago from his pocket, and knelt before her.

The tears began to stream down her face before he could even speak.

"Yes, Daniel. Oh, yes, of course I'll marry you," she said, and she threw herself into his arms so exuberantly she knocked them both over.

He laughed and slid the ring on her finger. "Make an honest man out of me, my one true love."

She stared at the ring and its intricate but elegant design and gasped. "It's the most beautiful ring I've ever seen."

"You're the most beautiful woman I've ever seen, inside and out. You will marry me, then?"

She flashed a wicked smile at him. "How could I not? I've seen how good you are with cake."

Daniel rolled over until she was underneath him and he

captured her mouth in a searing kiss. "What do you say we retire to our rooms and affirm life for a while?"

She vanished, transforming into mist for long enough to escape him, and then she was back, standing next to him and grinning. "Race you!"

He caught her before she made it halfway to the house and carried her the rest of the way to the bedroom. On days like this, he still caught himself wondering if he'd made it to heaven after all.

"I love you, Daniel," she said, staring up at him. "Forever."

Forever had never sounded so good.

Turn the page for
a special preview of Alaric's Story
in the Warriors of Poseidon Series

# HEART OF ATLANTIS

by Alyssa Day

Coming soon from Berkley Sensation!

# Chapter 1

## Mount Fuji, Japan

The portal opened and Alaric, high priest of Atlantis, stepped through, followed by a shell-shocked rebel leader and a five-hundred-pound tiger shape-shifter who may have permanently lost his humanity.

"Oh, Alaric," the ancient man who stood waiting for them said, sighing and shaking his head. "You do get into the most fascinating trouble."

"Interesting you should say that, Archelaus," Alaric said. "I need a place to hide for a little while while Quinn tries to help Jack remember that he's not just a tiger."

Quinn barely looked at him, her eyes dull with pain and exhaustion, but she never let go of his hand. It was more physical contact than he'd allowed himself to have with her in a very long time.

Archelaus took them all in with his sharp gaze. The old man, long since retired as mentor to the Atlantean warrior training academy, never missed anything.

"And Atlantis? Are the Seven Isles still in jeopardy?"

"Aren't they always?" Alaric sliced a hand through the

air in dismissal of the topic. "We need a place to rest. Food. A place to hide a tiger."

Archelaus pointed at something behind them. "Who is that?"

Alaric whirled around, shocked to see a Japanese woman step out of the portal.

"Who are you?" he demanded, pushing Quinn behind him. None but Atlanteans could call the portal, and this woman clearly was not one of his people.

She blinked in apparent confusion. "*Konnichiwa*," she began in Japanese, but then she continued in ancient Atlantean as she slowly collapsed until she lay curled up on the ground next to the tiger, who ignored her completely. "I am the spirit of the portal, and I am the woman of this body, who came to Mount Fuji to die."

"We came here to force Jack to live," Quinn said, and then she started laughing, a terrible, almost hysterical laugh. "Lucky we have an Atlantean priest with us, isn't it?"

Alaric stared down at the only woman he'd ever loved and fought the tidal wave of emotion threatening to swamp him. "Yes. I will do what I can for him, as I promised."

Archelaus sighed again. "You have amazingly bad timing, my friend."

"Timing has nothing to do with need," Alaric snapped, finally out of patience with the day, with the situation, with centuries of standing alone as priest to a capricious god.

"Timing has everything to do with danger," the older man returned calmly, as he draped his sweater over the unconscious woman who'd claimed to be what she couldn't possibly be. "Anubisa is back from her sojourn in the land of Chaos, and this time the vampire goddess swears to destroy Atlantis and every member of the Atlantean royal family. You have never been more needed by your people in your entire life, I would imagine."

"I am needed here," Alaric said, staring at Quinn. "Atlantis can burn in the nine hells, for all I care. I have sacrificed enough to Poseidon. My days as high priest are done."

A warrior's mission . . .
A woman's desire . . .
And the unnatural evil
that could destroy them both.

———

FROM *NEW YORK TIMES* BESTSELLING AUTHOR

## ALYSSA DAY

# ATLANTIS BETRAYED

What could Christophe, powerful Warrior of Poseidon, have in common with Fiona Campbell, prim and proper Scottish illustrator of fairy tales by day and notorious jewel thief known as the Scarlet Ninja by night? Answer: The Siren, a legendary Crown Jewel that Fiona has targeted for her next heist. It's said to be worth millions, but to Christophe it's invaluable, for the Siren also happens to be one of the missing jewels from Poseidon's Trident.

But breaking into the Tower of London is a two-person job, so Christophe and Fiona team up to commit the crime of the century. As newfound passions fire their motives—and cloud their judgment—they realize they aren't the only ones after the priceless gem. A dark force is shadowing their every move and threatening to shatter their trust with revenge, betrayal, and a haunting revelation about the past.

**penguin.com**

The fate of Atlantis is on the line—
and the world is at stake . . .

FROM *NEW YORK TIMES* BESTSELLING AUTHOR
## ALYSSA DAY

# ATLANTIS REDEEMED

## The Warriors of Poseidon

Poseidon's warriors have learned that the battle to protect humanity produces unexpected enemies— and alliances. But none can be more unexpected than the bond between a cursed Atlantean warrior and a woman whose sight exposes any lie.

**penguin.com**

# ATLANTIS UNMASKED

**In Alyssa Day's steamy
Warriors of Poseidon series**

Atlantean warrior Alexios and human warrior Grace
are on the hunt to retrieve the legendary jewel called
the Vampire's Bane. Without it, Atlantis cannot as-
cend to the surface and take its place in the world.
But Grace dares to disobey Alexios, defy him, and—
even worse—awaken feelings he'd long believed
buried. When evil threatens and thousands of lives
are on the line, will passion overrule their mission?

The WARRIORS OF POSEIDON
series by *New York Times* bestselling author

# ALYSSA DAY

ATLANTIS RISING

ATLANTIS AWAKENING

ATLANTIS UNLEASHED

ATLANTIS UNMASKED

ATLANTIS REDEEMED

ATLANTIS BETRAYED

VAMPIRE IN ATLANTIS